Dear Reader,

This month we are ~~~~~~~~~~ ~~ ~~~ two brand new **Scarlet** romances b~ ~~~~~~ who hail from both sides of the Atlantic. So many couples choose to get married in spring, but if you're not lucky enough to be going to a wedding this month, our **Scarlet** authors have written novels which feature all the excitement and passion of this romantic time of year.

Claire, the heroine of American author Jan McDaniel's *Dance Until Morning*, is engaged and should be looking forward to a high society wedding – and so she is – until she discovers that money can't buy everything, particularly *not* love! *Lovers Don't Lie* . . . or do they? Jenna, in Chrissie Loveday's latest **Scarlet** romance, is forced to wonder when she meets her first love, Simon, again.

In addition to these two exciting and very special romances from **Scarlet**, we are delighted to announce our first **Scarlet** romance in **Hardback**! In a couple of months time, we shall be offering *you* the chance to own the first one. Keep watching this space, and our end pages, for further news of this exciting new venture for **Scarlet**!

Till next month,

Sally Cooper

SALLY COOPER,
Editor-in-Chief – **Scarlet**

About the Author

Chrissie Loveday was educated in Staffordshire and gained her teaching certificate in Leicester. She taught in secondary schools for many years and worked in Special Education and at Further Education Colleges.

She is currently a part-time lecturer at Cornwall College, working with students who have learning difficulties and physical disabilities.

Chrissie adores travelling – anywhere she can manage to get to! She's already visited much of Britain and Europe, Singapore, Thailand, New Zealand, Australia, Kenya and many other exotic locations.

Her main interests, apart from writing, include people, crafts of all sorts, walking her two dogs and generally living life to the full. She has three sons and two grandchildren.

Other *Scarlet* title available this month:

DANCE UNTIL MORNING – Jan McDaniel

CHRISSIE LOVEDAY

LOVERS DON'T LIE

SCARLET

Enquiries to:
Robinson Publishing Ltd
7 Kensington Church Court
London W8 4SP

First published in the UK by Scarlet, 1998

Copyright © Chrissie Loveday 1998
Cover photography by Colin Thomas

The right of Chrissie Loveday to be identified as author
of this work has been asserted by her in accordance
with the Copyright, Designs and Patents Act 1988.

A copy of the British Library Cataloguing in
Publication data is available from the British Library

ISBN 1–85487–565–5

Printed and bound in the EC

10 9 8 7 6 5 4 3 2 1

CHAPTER 1

'We might as well get married,' Kurt said suddenly.

'What did you say?' asked Jenna incredulously.

'We work well together, enjoy the same things, and I do need you,' Kurt added.

'Oh, come on, Kurt. You're just annoyed that I'm going away. I haven't had a break in ages. Get married? You've got to be joking.' She tried to stifle the giggle she felt rising inside. She would hate to hurt his feelings, but really, Kurt's suggestion was quite outrageous.

'I thought we got on rather well,' Kurt protested, before giving a shrug of acceptance.

'Oh, Kurt. We do. But what can I say? I'm flattered to be asked, but you don't love me. You know you don't. Besides, we *do* work well together, and marriage would rather spoil that, don't you think?'

'OK.' He shrugged. 'Enjoy your holiday,' he added, looking quite unconcerned as he turned back to the work schedules he'd been looking at.

* * *

1

Twenty-four hours later, Jenna sat back in the taxi, thinking about the man who had asked her to marry him. He couldn't possible have been serious, of that she was certain. The previous day they had been standing on the beach, in glamorous sun-baked Nice.

'Glamorous,' she murmured softly. 'Only people who don't have to work there would call it that!'

She churned over the events of the previous evening. She had worked for several years as Kurt Smedley's assistant in his own company, Reality Plus Videos. Never had he shown any sign that he was interested in her as anything more than a colleague. He was bossy and moody – characteristics that probably went with his job – and she knew him only too well. She spent much of her time soothing the bruised egos of the actors doing their commercials. Granted, she knew that he was fond of her, and that their work had made them very close. But his words had to make it the most unromantic proposal imaginable.

She brushed away the strand of hair that had escaped from its usual neat plait. She was tall and slim, with the kind of pale blue eyes that remained totally unfathomable . . . at least that was what Kurt had said.

'You make marriage sound like some sort of an arrangement – a contract, even,' she had told him. 'When I get married it will be because someone loves me with every part of his being, and not because I'm conveniently there to organize his life and host his dinner parties.'

Jenna sighed again. Perhaps she was being unkind,

but she still clung to her romantic ideals, despite her years in the industry. The over-the-top attitudes of most people made her suspicious and unwilling to take most of them seriously. And to think most of her friends envied her job! The exotic foreign locations, working with well-known stars, making the adverts that everyone saw on television . . . undoubtedly it sounded attractive. The reality was very different. Hard work, heat and forever living out of a suitcase removed much of the so-called glamour. But, hard work though it was, she enjoyed the immense variety that made her life interesting. It provided some compensation for a job that encroached, if not completely took over her personal life. She simply had no time to spare for any sort of lasting romantic involvement, despite frequent offers.

The pop video they had just completed had quite exhausted her. The highly pressured few days, working with relative amateurs, had been extremely demanding. She had soothed and cajoled, organized and comforted for four solid days. She felt wearied by the newly popular band, who'd argued endlessly and insisted on effects that were downright naïve at times. Kurt's professionalism and his handling of the technical side of what they termed the 'pop kid culture' held him at the top of the competitive market. His company was always in demand because it got results.

Kurt. She admired his professionalism and she liked him well enough, but she certainly didn't love him. Judging by the calm way he had accepted her refusal, he certainly didn't love her either! He could be good company for much of the time, when work pressures allowed, but he was considerably older than she was and she had simply never thought of him in any romantic way.

'Forget him. Forget it all for a week at least,' she told herself, sitting back comfortably. The taxi whisked her through the narrow lanes towards the isolated Cornish cottage owned by her favourite aunt, Sarah. She was travelling light – just a small bag with the essentials for a totally peaceful few days. It felt like coming home, which truly it was. Jenna's parents had been killed in a car crash many years ago, and her father's younger sister had provided a home for her. Now Jenna had reached the age of twenty-five, and she and Sarah were close, more like sisters than aunt and niece.

'It's just around this bend. You have to drive a bit past the gate to stop safely,' she told the taxi driver.

'Right you are, miss,' he replied, with a wonderful Cornish burr.

Excitedly, she almost ran up the path, longing to see Sarah for what was to be the first time in several months. The cottage was quiet, with no signs of life . . . strange, as her aunt had sounded delighted when Jenna had phoned the previous evening. She walked round to the side of the house and called, but the usual shout of welcome was missing. Where was Sarah's cry?

'*Jenna, darling, great to see you!*' And this would be followed by, '*My goodness, you're looking thinner than ever. Don't you ever eat properly?*' It was the standing joke between the two, and Sarah spent every holiday

4

filling her up with home cooking, wonderful home-made jam and the thick Cornish cream she loved. Tonight there was no welcoming call.

Jenna was disappointed, to say the least, and also slightly concerned. There were no other houses for a mile or so. She peered into the darkening garage and saw Sarah's car. Wherever she had gone, it had not been by car. She looked in through the back window and noticed a little yellow sticker had been fixed to the windowsill.

'Key in usual place', it read.

'Where on earth is "usual" this time?' she asked herself. 'Oh, yes, of course, the watering can in the greenhouse.' They'd had a childhood joke about a watering can being 'the usual place for keeping water'. It was, at least, less obvious than a plant pot near the back door. She let herself into the empty cottage, where she found a longer note, telling her to help herself to supper and saying that Sarah would ring later.

Jenna felt tired and disappointed. Once she had looked around the familiar cottage, touching all the things that meant home to her, she unpacked her few clothes in her usual bedroom. Not even the cat was anywhere to be found. She lifted the lid of the casserole and sniffed appreciatively. Good old Sarah! She slumped in front of the TV, thinking she might catch up with the English news. The phone rang and she rushed to answer it, hoping it was her aunt.

'Hallo? Jenna? Oh, good, you found the key. I'm so sorry not to be there with you, but something's come

5

up. I'm in London and have to stay for a couple of days. I'll be back by the weekend. I'm sorry, you'll have to look after yourself for a while. Did you find supper? There's some wine in the sideboard . . . treat yourself. It will go well with the stew thing. And don't forget to feed Bonza.' All this was said in one breath and Jenna was quite unable to get a word in.

'Sarah . . . hold it,' she managed to say. 'Why are you in London, for heaven's sake?'

'Oh, it's all terribly exciting – and quite secret of course . . . but I know I can trust you. It's all to do with my latest dig. Remember I told you I'd got involved with something new? Well, we've uncovered something . . . something quite special. I needed to pop up to Town to sort out a few things. Library checks – you know the sort of thing. I have meetings tomorrow, possibly going on for a day or two.'

'It all sounds most intriguing,' said Jenna, 'but fancy us missing each other like this. You must have been going one way as I came the other.'

'Well, I did try to phone you this morning, when we decided I really did need to go, but you'd already left. Anyway, Michael's waiting for me now, so I'll have to dash. Sorry again. Oh, I meant to say earlier. There are a couple of sales you may be interested in. I left the local paper out for you. Bye, now, love. Help yourself to everything you want.' With that, she put the phone down, leaving Jenna quite breathless.

'And I thought I had a busy life,' she muttered. 'Looks like I'm in for a couple of quiet days . . . except for Bonza.'

She had seen no sign of the huge cat, named by one of Sarah's Australian students some years ago. 'Real bonza little kitty you've got there,' he'd said, and the cat was instantly named.

Jenna smiled ruefully. She felt a little let down, but then, she had wanted a complete rest. She would find something to do for the next few days, and at least she would be spared from her aunt's constant matchmaking. Sarah was forever introducing her to what she considered were 'eligible' young men. As if she didn't meet enough so-called eligible men through her work! Most of them tried flattering her, using the angle that she should be starring in the videos, rather than assisting with production. That particular line had ceased to have any effect on her. She knew that she would get bored to the back teeth with the everlasting standing around, preening and posing. She preferred action, and the constant pressure of her job excited her.

Sarah never seemed to understand how her niece had managed to reach twenty-five without some strong romantic attachment, though she was herself content to remain unmarried at the great age of forty. Jenna thought again of her aunt's phone call. She wondered who this Michael was that Sarah didn't want to keep waiting. Probably some dusty old professor from the museum. Her aunt had gained a huge reputation in the world of archaeology, both in England and all around the world. Whenever someone needed expert comments for some television documentary, Sarah seemed always to be first choice. But if anyone asked her profession, she

7

modestly described herself as 'someone who potters through old rubble.'

Jenna sat back, resigned to making the most of her unexpected, peaceful few days. She put the dish of casserole in the microwave and opened a bottle of wine. She was on holiday after all, even if she wasn't too keen on drinking alone. She picked up the papers Sarah had left and turned to the page of auctions. She read the advert Sarah had marked and gave a slow smile. Amongst the items listed was everything from a Victorian butcher's block to a stuffed red squirrel – 'in wooden case'. Much more interesting to Jenna was the item, 'small collection of glass paperweights'. She had a passion for beautiful glass objects, and paperweights in particular. The sale was tomorrow. Jenna decided there and then that she would go to the sale and maybe even add to her collection. It was ages since she had been to an auction, let alone bought anything.

The microwave announced with a loud ping that it was dinnertime.

Jenna leapt out of bed early the next morning, delighted to be back in her beloved Cornwall. She drew back the curtains, looking out at the lush green of her surroundings. She felt refreshed by her sleep, but she wished she was about to share a lazy breakfast with her aunt, as she usually did at the start of a holiday. She sat on the doorstep overlooking the pretty garden, sipping her coffee. Bonza the cat turned up and rubbed himself against her legs, purring.

'Hallo, there, cat. You must be hungry.' The cat stared with huge green eyes and miaowed.

The ringing of the telephone broke into her thoughts, but by the time she reached it the caller had rung off. She felt irritated. It might have been Sarah, she thought, and switched on the answering machine, hoping that next time she would leave a message.

'What is it with me? I go away to avoid the phone and then get cross if someone rings off before I can answer.'

Jenna glanced at her watch. A quick shower and she would just make it to the viewing before the sale started. She loved auctions – a passion she had inherited from her father. He had bought her first paperweight for her when she was only six years old. Her mother had been cross with him for buying such a strange gift for the little girl.

'Girls want pretty clothes and dolls, not some great heavy lump of glass,' she had said. But Jenna had instantly fallen in love with it. She was fascinated by the whirling colours and the smooth, cool surface. She had often slept with it held in her hands for months after her parents had been killed, in some strange way deriving comfort from its solidity. Since that early birthday she had added several other paperweights to her collection, often buying them to remember places and events in her life. Antique specimens were often costly and beyond her reach, but just looking was free, she always told herself.

She drove Sarah's car the few miles to Penzance, relishing the glorious May morning. She almost felt glad that she had moved away from Cornwall, as it meant she could return there with renewed pleasure. This way she could never take the beauty of the place for granted. She easily found a parking place and walked up the steep hill to the town and the auctioneers. The room was already filled with crowds of potential purchasers, all hoping to find a bargain. Excited speculation and chatter filled the room as the crowds milled around, peering between shoulders to see the items on offer. Jenna's catalogue showed the glassware low down the list. It would probably be afternoon before they reached it. It looked very good quality, and expensive, and she estimated they would mostly be out of her price range. She found a seat and tried to relax, waiting for the business to begin. What on earth was she doing, sitting in a crowded room on such a glorious day? But it was her own innate passion, a feeling shared with the rest of the collectors as the buzz of excitement grew.

As the early lots came under the hammer she looked around at the other people. It was fun to see what sort of folk were there. Public auctions attracted the widest mixture, from all walks of life, drawn by the common desire to find that elusive bargain. There were country types, a few car boot traders looking for job lots, and various others trying so hard to look casual they could only be dealers. A smartly suited businessman was sitting a couple of rows in front, next to a scruffy-looking woman who looked as if she could scarcely afford a cup of tea.

The man looked interesting. Different from the rest. His suit was obviously expensive, beautifully cut, and with a sheen that probably indicated silk. Although he was seated, she could tell he was tall, and the dark curly hair was immaculately cut. He looked almost slightly familiar she thought, as she found herself staring at him. He turned his head to look at the steward, who was carrying a new lot from the side of the room. He caught her eye, stared at her and gave a half-smile, almost as if he too felt a sense of knowing her. Perhaps he could have been a client of Kurt's video company at some time, or a long-forgotten friend from the past.

The sale progressed, most items reaching the reserve price and others exceeding the guide prices at levels that made the crowd gasp. The smartly dressed man had bought several items – quite large pictures and a bronze statue for which he was the only bidder. He looked pleased with himself. She decided he must be an antiques dealer. When they broke for lunch, the crowd left the room and streamed out into the bright sunlight, seeking some-where to eat. Jenna noticed the man leaving the room and unintentionally found herself following him, though at some distance. If he did think he might know her, he had made no attempt to speak. She went into a pub across the road from the auction room and ordered a glass of wine and a sandwich. As she waited near the bar, the man came in. She saw his reflection in the mirror over the bar and for the first time could see his full face.

It was seeing the eyes that finally convinced her that she knew him. There was surely only one person in the whole world who had eyes of that particular colour. They were a golden honey-brown, with a luminous quality that made them seem as if they were lit from within. Simon Andrews. It had to be Simon Andrews – though a very different-looking man from the scruffy student she remembered. Her mind flashed back over several years to the man who had been her first, her only true love.

She'd been seventeen, and had lived with Sarah for some years. She was home from her boarding school for the summer holidays, to work with her aunt on whatever was the latest project and generally to enjoy Cornwall. Usually her aunt had some students working with her, often camping at the site where they worked and ready for some fun when the day's work was over. This particular summer, Simon had been camping in nearby woods. Whenever they were free, they had gone to the beach to swim and surf and she had fallen hopelessly in love with him. She smiled, remembering how at that time he'd had long hair – a mass of black curls that were scraped back into a ponytail – and he always wore the scruffiest baggy sweaters. Best of all, he rode a huge black motorbike, which was then the love of his life. It had been an extraordinary, sunlit summer, that year . . . a summer she had never forgotten. When September came, she had returned to school for her final year and, foolishly expecting to hear from Simon, had scanned the post every single day. Gradually she had been forced to accept that he had gone back to university and the rest of his life without her.

She came back to the present with a start, as the barman asked for payment. She took her lunch to a table and settled down. Simon – for she was certain it was he – was collecting his own food. He looked across at her and gave another flicker of a smile. He hesitated for a moment, and then sat down at another table. She felt an odd sense of disappointment. She knew that subconsciously she had been hoping he would recognize her and come to sit with her.

Surreptitiously, she studied the man. It must be at least seven or even eight years since she had last seen him. Was that time enough to have effected this total change in his appearance? From scruffy student to obviously affluent businessman? She considered the changes in her own appearance. She had grown up. No longer the gauche schoolgirl of seventeen, she had developed a style of her own. The girl had grown from the still flat-chested tomboy into a curvaceous woman, tall and slender. Perhaps he simply did not recognize her. She remembered how her heart had been broken when that magical summer had ended. He had left without once asking if they could keep in touch. Now, years later, she almost felt again that same, deep rending sadness. In his eyes she'd only been some child he had to be polite to because she was the boss's daughter – or rather, her niece. She had been ready to give him everything but he had pushed her away, ultimately rejecting her with a finality that had taken many, many months to heal.

She finished her sandwich and glanced at her watch. It was almost time for the sale to resume. Simon mirrored her ritual; he pushed the last bit of his sandwich into his mouth, glanced at his watch and rose from his seat. He looked at her again and drew in his breath. With a puzzled frown, he held the door open for her, allowing her to pass in front of him.

'Excuse me, but do I know you from somewhere?' he asked. His voice held the same timbre that she remembered from so long ago. The faintest trace of accent he'd once had was now quite gone. Those amazing eyes held her own for several seconds which seemed to Jenna a positive lifetime.

'Hang on. No, it can't be! You're not Jenna Brown, are you?' The look of shocked amazement on his face was almost laughable.

'Simon. Simon Andrews. I must say, you certainly did scrub up well,' she laughed. The old joke was one of Sarah's favourite sayings. *'He may not look much now, but you should see him when he's all scrubbed up.'* Oddly, he managed little more than a feeble smile at her teasing.

'Are you with Sarah?' he asked, looking around as if the woman was about to materialize through the pavement.

'No. Just down here for a break, at precisely the same time as Sarah has found herself on business in London.'

'So, how are you, Jenna?' he said, sounding polite rather than as if he genuinely wanted to know.

'I'm great, thanks. How about you? Still interested in digging holes in the ground?'

'Occasionally. Only now they're larger holes and I get a digger in to do them. They then get filled with concrete.'

'Not a builder, surely?' She glanced at his expensive suit, which she had decided was definitely silk

14

now that she could see it properly. It was a far cry from the baggy, grubby sweaters of old.

'Hardly,' he said with a sardonic smile. 'Look, I don't want to be rude, but there are several items I hoped to bid for this afternoon. I must get back or I shall miss them. Are you going back?'

'Oh, yes. I intend to bid for something, if it isn't quite out of my range. It's nice to see you again, Simon.'

'And you. Perhaps we could get together for a chat? A drink or something? Remember old times. Are you down here for long?'

'A week, maybe. I haven't really decided yet. I have a few day's leave, but if Sarah is staying in London it seems pointless, really, to stay on by myself.'

'I'll call you. I still have Sarah's number somewhere. Might see you later on, anyhow. But I really must get back. Great seeing you again.' He turned away from her and crossed back into the auctioneers' building.

She followed a little distance behind, her mind preoccupied by her memories. She wondered what he did. Something to do with building? Never, she thought. He simply didn't look the type, despite what he had said about holes in the ground. Antique-dealer didn't quite seem to be his style either. She simply couldn't picture him as some sort of character. But then, when she had known him, years ago, he'd had little thought for anything but archaeology. It was hard to imagine this was even the same person, even if it was seven or eight years on. With a tiny sigh, she left the bright sunshine and went back inside.

Inside the auction room, tension was high as people made their bids. Some turned away as they failed to secure their prize, or smiled as the hammer fell on their successful bid. At last Jenna's paper-weights came up. They were in several lots, divided by their different styles and potential value. She was after a less rare, contemporary set, which she hoped might be within her reach. Bids were high generally, and the first two lots fetched well over a thousand pounds. Excitement filled her as she made her own bid. Two hundred pounds, three hundred, and she was reaching her limit. The temptation to go higher was filling her. Auction fever was taking over her senses. She could afford it, after all. She raised her hand again, suddenly realizing that the price had exceeded not only what she had set as her own limit but what she considered a sensible value. Her bid was capped and she shook her head as the auctioneer glanced at her for a further bid. She breathed a sigh of relief that her good sense had prevailed just in time. It was all too easy to be carried away by auction fever.

'Sold, on my right,' called the auctioneer, banging down his hammer. Jenna felt dejected for a brief moment, and then smiled to herself. It was never satisfying to pay more than market values when collecting – not that she couldn't have afforded it if she'd really wanted the items. Her greatest pleasure came from finding her own particular treasures in some little junk shop, rather than paying a fortune at some trendy auction house. Still, it was always exciting, and one never knew when a bargain might come along.

'No luck, then?' said a voice from behind.

'No,' she replied, not even bothering to turn her head. She knew exactly who was speaking. She caught a whiff of aftershave, not entirely recognizable but a discreet, obviously expensive brand. She smiled. The old Simon had barely managed to shave once a week, but her seventeen-year-old eyes had seen it as a sign of the macho male, primitive and highly attractive. In those days the animal quality of his masculinity had drawn her close to him. Slowly she turned her head. His eyes met hers and she felt the intensity of his gaze drawing her very soul to the surface. There was no doubt about his masculinity, but it was altogether more subtle now. Quite out of character, she felt her cheeks begin to burn. She felt the blood seeming to drain down her body and her heart hammered, making her feel almost light-headed. If he noticed anything, Simon gave no clue.

'I was thinking, as you're staying down here on your own, you might like to have dinner somewhere? I don't have to rush back. What do you say?'

'What now? T-tonight' she managed to stammer. She took a deep breath. The Jenna who behaved like a lovesick teenager had long gone. Nowadays she was well used to smart men who were meticulous in their appearance and who drove smart cars, the more expensive the better. She was certainly used to being asked out to dinner or to clubs. Why was this casual

17

invitation any different? *Pull yourself together*, she instructed herself.

'Why not? It is a little early for dinner, but we could always have a drink somewhere first.'

Jenna swallowed hard. She would have gladly died for an offer like this all those years ago. If her heart hadn't been presently pounding with an excitement she had forgotten could exist, she might, even now, have managed to convince herself that he did not attract her. Trying to gain a grip on herself and reply in the manner of the sophisticated woman of the world that she surely was, she took another deep breath.

'Thanks, Simon. That would be lovely. Do you have anywhere in mind? I'm not really dressed for anywhere terribly smart.'

'I don't know too many places in this area. In my student days, the local pub was my idea of luxury.' He smiled ruefully at the memory. 'In fact, anything that offered more facilities than a tent was my idea of total luxury.'

Jenna relaxed. For the first time she could truly recognize the old smile that made his mouth crinkle up at the corners. Perhaps he hadn't changed completely. She remembered a small hotel nearby, taken over by a friend of her aunt's. It might be nice to support her, and the food was supposed to be excellent.

'There's a little place at Loverne Cove that has recently been taken over by a friend of Sarah's. We could try that, if you don't mind the additional drive. I've got Sarah's little car. In fact, I could

18

even drive you if you like, to save taking two cars. Or are you still riding the Beast?' She was slightly tongue in cheek. The idea of a silk designer suit and a motorbike was highly amusing. His face flickered for a moment as he politely declined her offer to drive. Obviously it didn't satisfy his image, to be driven by a woman in a small car. With fingers that began to burn where they touched her bare arm, he led her up the street to where his own car was parked. Very far removed from the black motorbike of long ago, the low silver-blue sports model seemed to suggest a life-style that breathed luxury and comfort. He helped her in, shutting the door behind her with a smooth, heavy click. The surround-sound CD player came on as the engine started. A Bach choral work filled the car with opulent reverberations, far removed from the funky jazz favoured by the student she remembered.

'Your tastes have changed in more ways than one,' she remarked. He smiled at her.

'I'm not the only one who's changed. You were always a pretty child, but now, words like "beauty" and "glamour" spring to mind. No wonder I didn't recognize you immediately. You too have scrubbed up well!'

'Thank you,' she said, blushing once more. What was going on? She didn't blush. Blushing was not something she did! 'I just grew up. Like you did, I suppose. When did the hair go?' He looked at her blankly. 'The long curls? The ponytail?'

'Good grief. I'd quite forgotten about that. You're

in films, aren't you?' he said, rather obviously changing the subject.

'I'd hardly go that far. I do work for a company that makes films – well, more accurately, videos. We do pop videos, adverts, stuff like that. But I'm only an assistant there. Nothing nearly as glamorous as being "in films". Anyway, how did you know that?'

'I bumped into Sarah one day, at some function or other. She was the guest speaker and we had a drink afterwards. According to her, the whole industry would collapse without you. But then, she always did rate you very highly.' Jenna stared at him once more. There had been a definite flicker of annoyance on his face. What on earth could Sarah have said to him?

They drove as quickly as the narrow lanes would allow. The wild flowers were out in profusion. Masses of pinks and blues bordered every road, neatly finished with an edging of the clean white Cornish wild garlic. The gorse filled the air with its sweet scent, looking like splashes of golden sunlight spilling over the ground.

'Cornish gold. That's what Sarah always calls it,' she murmured.

'We once found Cornish gold. Do you remember?'

'Could I ever forget?' she replied. She closed her eyes and she could picture every moment of that day. She could even feel the scent of that damp earth filling her nostrils, so vivid were her memories . . .

CHAPTER 2

It had been hot that summer. When she wandered down to the site, Simon was working by his tent, totally absorbed in his task. She watched him for a while, seizing the moment to study the young man, whom she was already certain that she loved to distraction. Suddenly he swung round.

'You gave me an awful shock, creeping up like that,' he said.

'Sorry,' replied the seventeen-year-old Jenna, 'but I didn't want to give you away to every tourist in Cornwall.'

'You've obviously been well-tutored. Another budding amateur archaeologist, I presume?'

'I always work with my aunt when I'm home. I don't get so much time now I'm away at school.'

'Of course. Sorry, I'm forgetting my manners. Do you want some coffee?' He didn't sound very gracious about the offer, and she was tempted to tell him not to bother, but her curiosity got the better of her.

'Shall I make it? I think I can just about cope with a camping stove.'

21

Simon's eyes held an amused glint as he stood up. Jenna saw that he had been chipping stony earth from a piece of pottery. Despite the noise, it was very delicate work, and she could at once see that it was something very old.

'It's lovely. Such intricate designs. Where did you find it?'

'It was in the top of what we think is a burial site. We haven't been able to date it precisely as yet, but we think it could be Bronze Age. This is a new piece I found last night. Even Sarah hasn't seen it yet.'

Jenna smiled quietly at his enthusiasm. When he was talking about his greatest love in life, he mellowed. His beautiful eyes shone with pleasure, somehow illuminating his whole face.

'Sorry, I'm boring you,' he said, noticing that she wasn't listening to him.

'I'm sorry. Of course you weren't boring me. It's all very exciting. Are you working alone?'

'Except for your aunt. We discovered this new site a few weeks ago, but only last week we began to realize it possibly has some significance.'

'But what is it? I mean, there's not much to see.'

'We're trying to keep it hidden until we get proper sponsorship by the Society. Until then, this is my home. I'll put the kettle on and then I'll show you some of the discoveries so far.' He poured water into the kettle from a plastic can and set it to boil on a small camping gas cooker. For such a tall man, his movements were graceful, with an economy of effort. Beneath the scruffy exterior, his body was lithe and firm. She adored him.

'The kettle's boiling,' she pointed out after a few moments' study of the man. 'Shall I make the coffee?'

'It's OK. I'll do it.' He crawled inside the tent doorway and came out with two mugs, a jar of coffee and a rather grubby teaspoon. 'I forgot. I haven't been to the village this morning. There isn't any milk. I usually go before breakfast but I missed it today. I wanted to get my new shard cleaned off and I got absorbed in my chipping.'

'It doesn't matter,' laughed Jenna, 'I don't mind black coffee. I can see why you and Sarah get on well. A bit of ancient pottery and you're away. You're both addicts for history, aren't you?'

He laughed, and the tension seemed to disappear.

'Sure about the black coffee? Or shall I go and get milk?'

'Black will do. On the understanding that I'm allowed to see what you've found – I can assure you, your secret is safe with me.'

'It's a deal. If Sarah trusts you, I have no other choice than to trust you. Your coffee, madam.'

Once the ice was broken, they seemed to chat more easily. She extended her long legs to catch the warm sun, a movement not missed by Simon. Seeing his interest, she stretched herself out, cat-like, in front of him. She might only be seventeen, but so what? Plenty of girls were married at seventeen. Why shouldn't she feel this way? She tried to imagine what it would feel like to be kissed by him. He had a lovely smile – a mouth with corners that crinkled. She closed her eyes, and moved her mouth as if she were awaiting his lips to descend on hers.

23

'Is something wrong?' he asked. 'Is it the coffee? You look as if you might be about to throw up.'

Jenna sat up immediately, feeling mortified. Suppose he had guessed what she had been thinking about? So, waiting for his kiss made her look as if she was about to be sick, did it? She would have to practise for many hours in front of her mirror so she could get exactly the right expression. One day, she promised herself, one day he would want to kiss her as much as she wanted him to.

'So, what do you think?' Simon was saying.

'I'm sorry. What did you say?' Gone was the woodland glade and the two young people.

'I said, shall we go straight to the hotel or take a walk first? Wherever were you just then? You looked miles away.'

'In some woodland glade. It was your reminder of Cornish gold. Let's walk down to the cove. We can always park at the hotel and reserve a table first, if you like.'

He nodded his agreement, navigating the twisting lanes with consummate skill, and finally drove into the sloping car park. He stopped near a wall overlooking the steep valley. The sea shimmered in the distance, the brightness dimming only slightly as the sun lowered in the sky. He leaned across her to open the door and she could smell his subtle masculine smell again. Her heart gave another of its involuntary flutters and she lowered her eyes, hoping that she was not about to be covered in an embarrassing blush, yet again.

She swung her legs out of the low car and stood near the wall, gazing down the valley. She turned to see Simon staring at her intently. He had a curious expression on his face, as if he was trying to remember something. In reality, he was trying to reconcile his memory of the girl with the lovely woman standing in front of him. He smiled a smile that lit his entire face and Jenna clutched the wall, feeling a weakness sweep through her body.

'Shall we see about booking that table?' he suggested.

The orange glow of the sky contrasted with the almost navy blue of the sea. The pair stood side by side, gazing at the strong line of the horizon.

'Cornwall has to be one of the most beautiful places in the world,' she breathed.

'I don't spend nearly enough time appreciating it,' he replied. 'I always seem to be rushing around somewhere or other. Today was as close as I've been to a holiday for months. Even that was partly business.'

'What, the sale? An antique dealer, are you?'

He smiled lazily, averting his eyes. 'I do a bit of selling, amongst other things.'

She was intrigued. He seemed unwilling to talk about his work, almost as if he was ashamed of something, and however much she pressed him, he always seemed to avoid direct answers. Curious, she thought.

It was a wonderful evening. They sat on the terrace of the little hotel and ate food which was delicious and quite up to the standard of many of the international hotels Jenna stayed in when she was working away from home. Simon had studied the menu closely and almost gave the impression that his choice was based more on the ideas of the menu than because he liked the food.

'All a bit far from the bacon and eggs fried on a camping stove, isn't it?'

'Life moves on,' he said, with a slight grimace. 'Has Sarah made any new discoveries lately? I'm really out of touch with most things on that front.'

Jenna told him about Sarah's London trip and how excited she was about something or other, but said that, apart from that, she was herself out of touch. She regaled him with tales of her own work, and made him laugh when she talked about the 'pop kid culture'.

'I suppose that means you know all the current stars and you're well up on today's pop scene?' he said with a touch of sarcasm.

'Not really. If anything, it makes me retreat into the older music – the stuff I used to like. In fact, some of the music you introduced me to yourself. I gained lots of street cred when I went back to school that autumn with a collection of jazz funk discs. Most of my friends had never heard of it, or so it seemed.'

'You make me feel about ninety,' he grinned. His mouth still crinkled at the corners and he still attracted her, very much indeed.

When they'd finished their meal, they wandered back to his car. He leaned over the back and gazed at her appraisingly. She blushed once more, a habit she was beginning to get used to. Luckily, it was beginning to get dark now, and she felt marginally less embarrassed about it. How did hormones get to be so uncontrolled? she speculated.

'I've really enjoyed this evening,' he said, in a voice that sounded slightly surprised. 'Can we do it again some time?'

'Me too,' she said carefully. 'I'm only down for a little longer, though. I have to be back in London later on next week. A new job is beginning then.'

'How about tomorrow night? Oh, no. That's no good. I have something on. I'll give you a call when I've got my diary in front of me.'

They exchanged phone numbers and he promised to call her the next day. She pushed the scrap of paper into her handbag and they drove back into Penzance. He pulled up in the road outside the car park and she climbed out. Luckily he didn't drive away immediately, waiting for her to get to her car and to make sure that everything was in order. As she went in, she realized that the barrier was down, nor was there anyone in the booth. Then she saw the sign: 'THIS CAR PARK CLOSES AT 10.00 P.M.'

'Damn,' she cursed. 'Why didn't I think of that?' She turned, and saw to her relief that Simon was still waiting by the kerb. She rushed back to him and broke the news. He grinned.

'What did you expect? This is Cornwall, not London, you know. Get in. I'll drive you home.' There was nothing else for it. She would have to find some way to get into Penzance from the remote cottage and collect the car the next day.

'Are you sure you don't mind? I could get a taxi.

I'm sure *they* don't close at ten!'

Simon wouldn't hear of it. He insisted on driving out to the tiny hamlet and stopped outside the cottage in the lane.

'It's years since I was here. I remember when Sarah invited me to join her summer dig. I thought all my birthdays had come at once. My father was furious. Told me I was wasting my time grubbing about in the ground, that he'd find some gardening for me to do for the vac, if I was so set on digging. But then, he never did understand passion of any sort.' There was a touch of bitterness in his voice.

'Can I offer you some coffee before you drive back?' Jenna offered. He glanced at his watch.

'I have a longish drive, but what the hell? Yes, please.' He followed her up the path and she unlocked the door, warning him to mind his head on the low beams. He grinned ruefully, remembering his earlier encounters with Sarah's cottage. He watched Jenna as she made the coffee, his eyes seeming to take in every detail of her graceful movements, her long legs and almost perfect figure. Her long dark hair was neatly coiled, leaving her beautiful face completely clear.

'And do *you* appear in your videos?' he asked as they sat together on the comfortable sofa. 'I'm sure you must look just as good as any of your star performers.'

'No, I don't. I haven't got the patience to stand around for long enough. I prefer to have things to do all the time. But thanks for the compliment, if that's what it was.' She looked down, suddenly shy of him

28

again. She kept remembering the feelings she had had for him, and sensed that somehow he knew exactly what she had once thought. She tried to convince herself that she was simply coming to terms with first love. Everyone always said it was something you remembered for ever.

She tried to keep the conversation light-hearted, and once again made him laugh with her stories. He seemed to relax at last. He had become quite an intense man, seeming to have lost much of the fun she had once known so well. He hadn't teased her all evening, whereas before he'd always been making some remark or other. Perhaps they had both simply, boringly, grown up.

'I'd better go. Will you be able to organize collecting your car tomorrow? I'm afraid I won't have time to offer to help.'

'I wouldn't expect you to. No problem. I shall get a bus, or even a taxi. If it's a nice day, I might even walk there, along the coastal path.'

'Sounds wonderful,' he said, almost wistfully. 'Thanks again for your company and the coffee.'

'Thank you for dinner. I really enjoyed it.' She stood up and went over to open the door for him. Their fingers brushed and she felt a jolt, an unexpected thrill passing between them like an electric current. How utterly childish she was becoming. Jumping like that just because she accidentally touched someone.

He stared at her and hesitantly took her hand, firmly this time, then drew her close, kissing her softly on the lips. She tasted of honey, of pure

29

sweetness. He looked into her clear blue eyes, wondering exactly what she was thinking. She was no longer the child whom he had liked so much. She was no longer the forbidden girl that Sarah had warned him not to touch. Here was a living, breathing, wonderful woman. She was the embodiment of many lonely nights spent dreaming of his perfect female. Perhaps she was everything he'd been waiting for; subconsciously, he had known the child would return some day, a grown, mature woman.

But he was being ridiculous. He was not free to begin something he could not finish. But her lips were slightly parted, temptingly sweet; her expression was one of fleeting wonderment. A simple dinner out, for old times' sake, was one thing; anything more would be playing with fire and he knew it. He swept his finger gently across her cheek before he drew away.

'I'll be in touch,' he promised, and was gone. Jenna waved him off and shut the door firmly. She hugged herself, delighting in the glow that was sweeping through her body. As she put the safety chain on the door it reminded her once more of her teenage days, when Sarah had admonished her for coming in late after seeing Simon and leaving the chain unfastened.

'Who on earth would break in here?' she'd demanded. 'There's nothing valuable.'

'Well, thanks,' Sarah had exploded. 'There's us, for a start. We're highly valuable. Very precious to each other, if no one else.'

Jenna had taken heed of her warning and from then

on had always kept the chain firmly in place when she was alone in the cottage. Now she leaned against the door, a dreamy smile on her face. Life was such a complicated mixture of feelings. The briefest touch from Simon had sent her heart racing like no one else had ever done. Was he simply the embodiment of the fantasy of first love? Or did he mean so much more to her, now that she had grown up? One thing was for certain: she didn't love Kurt, nor he her. She didn't even need time to think about her answer, as he had insisted she should do following his proposal. He simply didn't see marriage and commitment in the same way as she did. If nothing else, her own reaction to Simon had convinced her that she had made entirely the right decision when she had turned him down.

Kurt's casual acceptance of her refusal proved that he was hardly devastated and probably hadn't meant to be taken seriously in the first place. His only fleeting reference to the whole business had been when he'd left her at the airport. He had asked her to give his proposal some thought while she was on holiday. But he couldn't really expect her to change her mind, could he?

In a gentle haze of pure contentment, she went to bed. As she settled down for the night, she contemplated her plans for the next few days. It would be so good to spend some more time with Simon. That gentle kiss had sent her mind racing, as well as her heart. She had always known he was someone special. Every relationship she had ever had since those student days had been somehow compared to the relationship she imagined she might have had with Simon Andrews. It was ridiculous; she still knew next to nothing about him.

Another glorious morning dawned and Jenna eagerly leapt out of bed. There must be something in the air of Cornwall that made people anxious to start the day, she decided. As it was such good weather, she would walk the several miles into Penzance and retrieve Sarah's car. The coastal path was a wonderful walk, even if it was hard going in places.

She packed some fruit and a drink into a small rucksack, then checked the answering machine was switched on before setting out. There had been no message from Sarah yet, to say when she would return, so the machine needed to be ready to take any calls.

She knew in her heart that it was Simon she was really waiting to hear from. He had promised to call her today and arrange another date. She remembered again those same feelings she'd had when, as a schoolgirl, she'd always been waiting for a letter that never came. She had been so immature in those days: even now, she could almost blush with shame at the thought of the way she had chased him. But that gentle kiss last night had suggested that he did harbour some feelings for her, however small. Her stomach lurched at the mere thought of him and she could almost breathe the scent of him. The raw, animal magnetism might not still be there, but it had been replaced by something much more subtle.

There was a definite spring in her step and she

covered the miles quickly, inspired by the weather, the place and, most of all, the pleasurable thought of seeing Simon again.

The grumpy man in the pay booth at the car park did nothing to dispel her good humour.

'By rights, I should charge you double the rate,' he moaned. 'There's not supposed to be any overnight parking in this park.'

'I didn't believe anyone could possibly close so early,' Jenna countered. He grizzled and grumbled, complaining that he was low on change when she handed him a ten pound note. He continued to moan, saying that he was much too busy on account of the roadworks in the town. He was not impressed when she suggested business should be even better soon, with the summer coming.

'Trouble with summer's the tourists,' he muttered. 'Nothing personal, miss. I sees you're a local from your number plate. Not one of my regulars, though, are you?'

She apologized for the lapse with a grin, and finally got away, realizing that there would always be something wrong for him, whatever she said or did. He was simply one of those sort of people.

She bought some rolls and cheese in the town and stopped in a layby with a spectacular view to eat her simple picnic. She could live here, she decided as she munched. After all, she was rarely in London, as her work took her all over the country and the world. Perhaps she should consider selling her scarcely used London flat and moving down here with Sarah. She suddenly realized she was subconsciously making plans that would bring her nearer to Simon, even though she had no idea where he was actually living. It was obviously somewhere in Cornwall, though throughout the conversation last night never once had he told her exactly where he lived. She seemed to remember that his parents had a home somewhere on the north coast. He had returned there a few times to collect clothes when he was camping. But she had always been too keen on keeping him close to her to enquire where his home was.

When Jenna finally reached the cottage, her first target was the answering machine. The light was flashing and she quickly pressed the play button. She felt a tremor of anticipation, waiting to hear Simon's voice. It was Sarah's voice she heard.

'Hallo, darling. It's all too beastly but I have to stay over till the weekend. I'm so sorry. Hope you can entertain yourself. Something really important has come up. I promise to be with you soon. Lots of love.'

Jenna felt irritated, but mostly it was disappointment. It was ages since she and Sarah had spent time together, and just when she'd made it to Cornwall Sarah had to be in London. She contemplated returning to her flat. At least that way she could have a meal with her aunt, if nothing else. On the other hand, a few more days pottering about here would do her good. Her own next job was in London, so maybe she could see Sarah then, if she was still there. Besides, she was still hoping that Simon would contact her again during this stay in Cornwall.

Trying to decide what to do with her evening, she sat on the doorstep, her favourite childhood place, sipping a coffee. Bonza turned up, the way cats do, and purred as he rubbed against her bare legs. She stroked the soft fur as he arched his back.

'How are you doing, cat?' she said absently. Her mind was still racing. Why had a simple kiss taken on such ridiculous proportions? She'd been kissed very many times. Everyone in her world kissed everyone else, and *'darling'*, *'I love you madly'* and all such trite comments were everyday language for most of them.

For Jenna, it had become a constant source of irritation. She hated the insincerity that everyone showed. She could never believe that anyone ever meant anything, it seemed. She was often all too ready to bite off someone's head when they behaved this way, but she knew it was part of the scene. She enjoyed most of her job far too much to give it up for so trivial a reason. She was certain that if she ever loved anyone enough she would have no difficulty in saying the words. But until then she would never tell anyone, whoever he was, that she loved him.

Once, Simon had said he loved her. Her heart had turned over a million times when she'd heard the words, but she had come to realize that he, too, had meant nothing by them. He had just been excited and thrilled with their discovery.

Simon, the student so passionate about history and archaeology, had made the discovery of his lifetime. Sarah had been away for the day and had left Jenna and Simon to continue to explore the site. The pair had made a discovery that had thrilled them all and made national newspaper headlines everywhere. That day would always remain fresh in her memory . . .

CHAPTER 3

They pushed their way through undergrowth. About twenty yards from the tent, Simon stooped to lift some branches from the ground. Beneath them were several strong, wooden boards, almost completely hidden by leaves. He prised up two or three of them and a large hole was revealed.

'Behold – Chy Sarah,' he said dramatically. 'Cornish for "Sarah's House" . . . that's what we called it.' He gave a grin of pure delight and she smiled back, loving his enthusiasm. 'You can see a long stone over there. It doesn't look like anything special, but when we worked out the markings it suggested to Sarah that there was more to find. We started digging and uncovered what has to be the start of a fogou – a tunnel.'

'It's amazing that no one else found it all these years. I thought every bit of Cornwall had been dug, charted or mined. However did you come across the stone in the first place?'

'Pure accident. We were looking for something else and Sarah noticed some symbols etched on the stone.

37

I hadn't even realized the marks could even be carvings, it was so covered in moss. But that's Sarah's genius for you. She has a nose for it.' As he spoke, his whole face seemed to light up with his enthusiasm, making him look even more devastatingly attractive to the seventeen-year-old Jenna.

They let themselves carefully down into the hole. Jenna noticed it had been shored up with boarding, all round the edges. She never for a moment doubted that it was safe. Her aunt was a stickler about never taking unnecessary risks. Simon handed her a helmet and a large torch, which had been stored in a box at the bottom of the hole. There was rubble lying around what looked like a sort of arch, a carved stone entrance to something.

'This is as far as I'd reached. I've loosened the earth around and now it's just a case of pulling away the fallen rocks.'

Jenna felt a rush of excitement. The enthusiasm of her aunt over the many school holidays she had spent with her had rubbed off, and she too had a sense of wonder. What was on the other side of the rocks? It might be nothing or it could be some treasure.

'Hang on, I've got a small camera in my pocket. It's important to record every step, especially as Sarah isn't here. Will you do the honours? It's got a built-in flash.' Simon handed her the camera and posed near the rocky entrance, not for vanity's sake but to give a sense of perspective to the size of the opening. She took the shot and he started the laborious task of clearing away the remaining earth

38

and stones. Together they heaved until there was a gap large enough to climb through.

'Camera ready,' whispered Simon, shining the torch into the cavity. Jenna took a shot as Simon squeezed through the hole. She followed him, ready to take more pictures.

'Oh, Simon. This is amazing.' They were standing in a place that might have been sealed for centuries. The tunnel itself was surprisingly clear of rubble, and stretched away beyond the torchlight. Simon was silent, rendered totally speechless at the extent of it. His voice trembled slightly when he finally spoke.

'This is more than I ever dreamed possible. I can't believe there could still be undiscovered places like this Jenna, pinch me. I can't believe what I'm seeing.'

Shyly, Jenna put her hand on his bare arm, loving the feel of intimacy it gave. His flesh felt warm and firm, the soft hairs on his arm alien to her inexperienced fingers. They stood together, gazing at a sight possibly unseen by humans for hundreds of years. The torch revealed deep marks on the rocky roof, possibly made by the primitive tools of some ancient worker.

A closeness, a bond was forming between the two of them. They turned and hugged each other in excitement. After several moments, still clutching each other's hands, they crept forward a few more feet. The tunnel was almost Jenna's height, but Simon was forced to keep his head bent low as they progressed, feeling their way carefully and shining the torch on the ground in front of them. A few feet along, a side passage led off and they followed it. About two yards further, it ended in a circular chamber.

'It looks almost like some sort of altar,' breathed Jenna, shining her torch towards a rocky shelf at one side.

'I think this might be the second exit. All these places had a creep hole, with an outlet to the outside – usually up in the roof.' Simon's voice sounded firm and authoritative. 'Flash your light upwards and see if there's anything there.'

There was nothing more than the earth above them, supported by the natural rock formation that had stopped the roof falling in for hundreds of years.

'Nothing to see there.'

'Take a picture, and then we'll go back to the main tunnel and see how far we can get,' Simon suggested.

They walked slowly along for several yards, until they came to a pile of rocks that proved to be an obstacle.

'This is as far as we go for now,' he said. 'We need props and things. It isn't safe to go on anywhere that rocks have fallen. Can you turn round and lead the way back?'

It was chilly in the tunnel, and the air was slightly fetid. They both felt warmer once they had reached the sunlight again. It seemed incredibly bright and clear out in the fresh air.

'I need some time to take stock and decide what we do next,' Simon said, his mind obviously churning around in his excitement. He had a perpetual grin on his face and his eyes were almost flashing with exhilaration.

'Good grief. Can you believe it's nearly three o'clock? No wonder I'm famished,' said Jenna. 'Shall we cook here or go back to the cottage?'

'Here, I think. I can't leave yet.' Simon's response was predictable.

She set to work with the camp stove and cooked the bacon and eggs she had brought to make them some breakfast, many hours ago. Simon chatted excitedly about the find, making and rejecting various plans. Jenna sat quietly smiling. He sounded just like Sarah. He suggested that once the meal was finished they should hide everything away carefully, leaving the site looking just as it was before, and return to the cottage. Jenna could set off and Simon would follow on later, once he was satisfied that everything was as secure as possible. When Sarah returned home, she would decide on the next move.

They ate their meal hungrily. The food tasted good in the open air, and they both began to feel more relaxed after the earlier excitement.

'I suppose I'd better get back now,' Jenna said, almost wistfully.

'Fine,' Simon grunted. He was lying back with his eyes closed and a smile still glued to his face. 'You know, I still can't believe it. I only half hoped there would be something new. So many people have excavated around this area; I'm amazed that it wasn't found before.'

'Perhaps you should hide the entrance again, before half of Cornwall also discovers it.'

'For such a kid, you have a lot of sense.'

She grimaced at his words. A kid? Her? She was almost a woman.

He leapt to his feet and suddenly grabbed Jenna round the waist, swinging her round. He called out, 'I love you, Jenna! I love you.' She burst out laughing and allowed herself to swing with him. They both tumbled to the ground and he put his arms around her slim shoulders and drew her towards him. Suddenly quiet after the excitement, he stared at her. They kissed. Her body surged with the thrill of his closeness. His almost animal scent infused her nostrils and her young body responded to his closeness. She sensed she was on the verge of losing all control but she didn't care; not one bit! After all, half the girls at school claimed they were no longer virgins. They all loved to talk about their many affairs and how sexually experienced they were. She was on the very brink of joining them. Any moment, and she too would know exactly what it all meant.

'Jenna . . . Jenna . . .' Simon murmured in her ear. He pulled away slightly.

'Simon, please don't stop. I want you to make love to me. Right here and now.'

He rolled away from her, thrusting her aside. He looked angry. His eyes smouldered darkly and his generous mouth tightened into a narrow line. He got up angrily and went off towards the tunnel.

'Simon, please. I didn't mean . . .' Her words fell on the air as he disappeared out of sight. 'Blow you,

Simon Andrews. If that's how you feel . . .' She got up angrily and collected her things.

She realized that he must just have been over-excited by his finds. He couldn't possibly have meant what he said about loving her. It was simply the thrill of the discovery, and he had shouted those precious words without any real meaning to them. She felt madly disappointed.

Stamping angrily along the track to her aunt's, Jenna's mind was racing. Foolishly, she had believed Simon really loved her; she'd been ready to give him everything. Yet there he was, showing he was afraid – or maybe he was just a cold-hearted opportunist. Somehow everything had changed. They could not have an easy, friendly relationship any more. Everything had been spoiled. Never again would she take any notice of someone saying they loved her.

As darkness fell, neither Simon nor Sarah returned to the cottage. Jenna sat around, restlessly waiting for something to happen. It hardly seemed worth start-ing anything for dinner, but she felt bored with the inactivity. Should she cook for herself and Sarah, or make enough for Simon as well? Had she ruined everything when she had assumed that Simon wanted to make love? Lovemaking. Was that what it was? More like a childish tussle, a mere roll on the ground . . .

Jenna's brain shot her back to the present. The memories of those childish days faded. How long had she been sitting there, daydreaming? The past had its own uncanny way of insinuating itself into the present. The next day, all those years ago, when

Sarah had gone back to the site and looked at the tunnel, everything had changed. Simon had never come near her again and the final opening of the tunnel had been conducted much more scientifically, with everything being meticulously catalogued. It had lost all the spontaneity of that initial discovery.

Their final shared excitement had been the discovery of a torque, a beautiful golden arm bracelet that must have belonged to someone of high rank in those ancient days. A replica was now kept in a local museum, displayed for everyone to admire. But *she* had been a part of its discovery. Her and Simon. Simon had clamped it onto her arm and taken a photograph of her. The Cornish gold they had mentioned the previous evening.

'I wonder if those old photos are still around?' she muttered. She made up her mind to look for them some time, but now she should see about getting herself something to eat.

The rest of the evening, she was thoroughly lazy. She watched an old black and white TV movie, allowing herself to be captured by the simple old-fashioned sets and excellent story. She enjoyed the relaxation it afforded, for once able to forget about her professional interest in the actual photography and forgiving the occasional lack of continuity in the scenes. In those days they didn't have the benefit of instant photographic shots to check on every detail. There was probably more technical back-up in a twenty-second commercial nowadays than there'd been in an entire black and white movie like this one.

By ten-thirty, Jenna had given up hoping to hear from Simon again. She had stared at the phone several times, as if willing it to ring. The only call of the evening had sent her heart racing, but it had turned out to be a wrong number. Perhaps she should have rung him. It might have seemed a bit pushy, but after all they had been friends way back, and she was only staying in Cornwall for a very short time.

She sensed that Simon was different from any other man she knew. The effect he seemed to provoke in her was proof enough of that. He could never be just another casual man in her life. With a feeling of slight trepidation, she groped in her bag for the bit of paper with his number on it. She dialled the number he had scribbled down for her. A rather formal, businesslike voice answered

'Tregarth Manor, can I help you?'

'Oh, I'm sorry, I must have dialled the wrong number.' She put the phone down quickly and looked again at the scribbled note she had made. 'I'm *sure* I dialled the right number,' she said, and decided to try it again. The same reply came.

'What is the number of Tregarth Manor? I was given this number by a friend. Perhaps I copied it down incorrectly.'

'The number is 01239–405692, madam. Perhaps your friend is a guest? Whom are you calling?'

'I'm trying to contact Simon Andrews?'

'Mr Simon is not available at present – out of reach, I'm afraid. If you give me your name, I will tell him you called when he returns.'

Jenna managed to stammer her name. Why had he been called 'Mr Simon' by this pompous-sounding man?

'It doesn't matter. I'll probably see him soon, anyway.' She put the phone down, her thoughts racing.

In the past, Simon had once spoken of a family home, with a caretaker, but a manor? And whoever heard of a caretaker sounding quite so up-market? She tried to remember what Simon had said. Something about building; something about antiques. No mention of any hotel. Perhaps his mysterious business was a hotel? The man had mentioned guests . . . If it was, why on earth would Simon be so reluctant to talk about it? Very strange. There was nothing wrong with a hotel as a business, especially not in Cornwall. She was puzzled, and even began to feel slightly irritated that he hadn't been honest with her. She would tell him so, when and if she saw him again. The two things she really prized were honesty and sincerity, and he was silly to be so secretive. It all seemed pointless.

Jenna went to bed, but sleep was far away and she felt wide awake. She went downstairs to fetch the phone book and looked up Tregarth Manor in the Yellow Pages: '*Luxury Hotel and Conference Centre. Peaceful, surrounded by lush parkland; sea-views; heated indoor pool; sauna . . .*'

The advert ran on. The place must be worth a fortune! It was certainly many levels away from the tent and the scruffy young archaeologist she had once known. It was on the coast, not far from Tintagel, and probably only around an hour's drive from Sarah's.

Sleep was slow to come, and as she tossed around she began to formulate a plan in her mind. It seemed she had two options: she could return to London and hope to catch Sarah before she left, or, alternatively, she could find out a little more about the man who was currently intriguing her. It was the second option that appealed the most. After all, if she went back to London she would feel obliged to tell Kurt that she was back, and she wasn't ready to return to work just yet. Besides, he might still be thinking about repeating his rather ludicrous proposal, and she really didn't want to hurt his feelings.

The decision seemed to have been made. She would drive to Tregarth Manor in the morning. Simon would certainly not be expecting her, but if he wasn't around she would enjoy looking around Tregarth quite anonymously. If Simon didn't tell her about his home she would have to find out for herself. Perhaps she would have lunch there, just to see what it was like.

It was dull and cloudy the next morning. She ate breakfast in the kitchen instead of on her usual perch on the back doorstep. Jenna felt less enthusiastic about her planned trip to Tintagel. If Simon wanted to see her again, he would ring. If he didn't, why should she go chasing him around Cornwall? She was surely not quite that desperate, yet. She would have to find something else to do today instead. Hadn't Sarah said something about a couple of sales? Maybe she could find another sale to attend? It was a prospect which was not entirely without appeal on a dull day. She searched for the local paper and turned to the auction pages. The phone rang and the answering machine began to whirr.

'Hi, Jenna! It's Simon. Sorry I didn't get back to you yesterday. One pig of a day, I'm afraid, and it was too late by the time I'd finished. If you'd like dinner tonight, give me a call. I'm on the number I gave you until around eleven. Hope to hear from you. Bye.'

For some reason she couldn't explain, Jenna sat listening to the message without even attempting to answer the phone. It was almost as if she was deliberately playing hard to get. She didn't want him thinking she was waiting for him, even though she was. She hadn't behaved this way about a man since she had been, well, seventeen. Odd it happened to be the same man again this time! How childish could she be? She left her breakfast and went to the phone, using the call-back code to save looking up the number. This time, Simon answered.

'Sorry, I didn't get to the phone in time. Thanks for ringing. I'd love to have dinner,' she said breath-lessly.

He had sounded really pleased, she thought, after she had put the phone down. He'd suggested eating at a little place he knew, somewhere on the other side of Truro. It would make it a long drive for him, but he had insisted on collecting her.

'I can't trust you not to park somewhere that might close at some ridiculously early hour,' he had joked.

Her next problem was what to wear. She had

brought very little in the way of clothes with her. There were a few old things she'd left at the cottage, but nothing remotely suitable for a smart restaurant with a special man. Perhaps Sarah had something she might borrow. They were a similar size, except that Jenna was slimmer than her aunt. Maybe if there was something not too close-fitting, it would do. She rummaged through the wardrobe in Sarah's room but could find nothing suitable. She sat on the edge of the bed, thinking hard. Simon was still such a special person to her. She wanted to impress him, to let him know that she too had changed, from a gauche schoolgirl to a sophisticated woman. He might not be quite the man she remembered, but he held the same attraction for her – even more so, with all the additional polish of the man of the world that he had evidently become. There was nothing else for it. She simply had to go out and buy something to wear. After all, they might never meet again, and she wanted to leave him with a good impression at the very least.

Jenna drove the twenty or so miles to Truro, amazed at the way it seemed to have grown even since her last visit there, just a few months earlier. She parked at the edge of the town and wandered round the shops. Most of the well-known high street stores had branches there, but it was in one of the smaller boutiques she found the right dress for the evening ahead. The pale lemon sheath fitted perfectly, showing her slender figure and rounded curves. The colour enhanced her Southern French tan, recently topped up by the Cornish sun. The dress seemed ridiculously cheap, compared with the shops she usually visited in London, and other large cities round the world. She wandered back to the car park past several antique shops, full of what was euphemistically called bric à brac. She glanced round the windows to see if there were any paper-weights. There was a dusty-looking globe down at the corner of one window, and she went in for a closer look. The rather ancient owner fished the weight out of the window and polished it on his grubby apron.

'Lovely piece, this one, my dear. We've been savin' it ready for the right buyer,' he said, with a slightly obsequious smile.

'How much is it?' Jenna asked, ready to do battle if necessary.

'Thirty pounds suit you?' he replied, with a slightly apologetic note in his voice. Jenna smiled. It was undoubtedly worth at least that, even for a relatively modern piece with no particular merit.

'Well,' she said, sounding doubtfully, the usual prelude to a bit of bargaining. It wasn't so much that she expected to get it any cheaper, but it was against every true collector's principles to pay the first price suggested.

'Go on, then. What's it worth to you? I'll come down a bit,' the old man said with a twinkle in his eye. 'Make me an offer I can't refuse.'

'OK. I'll give you the full price,' Jenna decided. 'It's quite a pretty one and it will be a memento of Truro.' The shopkeeper's toothless grin of delight was compensation enough, and she handed over three crisp ten pound notes. He pulled out a grubby, used carrier bag and wrapped the paperweight in it, handing it over cheerfully.

'I'll let you know if I find any more,' he called as she left. She smiled back and he gave her a wave. Funny, she was thinking, how much nicer people are in Cornwall.

Bonza was sitting on the doorstep when she returned, gazing accusingly at her when she opened the door.

'Hi, cat. Missed me?' The huge creature miaowed back as she poured him some milk. 'You're missing Sarah, aren't you? She'll be back soon.' She scratched his neck and he purred, rubbing himself against her. The answering machine was flashing and Jenna pressed the play-back button.

'Out again, I see,' said Sarah's voice. 'Hope that means you're having a good time. Perhaps you've met up with some old friends. Anyhow, I shall be back on Friday night, just for the weekend. Hope you'll still be there. Friday must be tomorrow, isn't it? Oh, dear, I've lost all track of time. I'll call you from Penzance when I get in. Should be around seven, but if you want to go out or anything, I'll get a taxi. Can't wait to see you, darling. Lots of love. Bye for now.'

Jenna smiled happily. She was looking forward to seeing her aunt again and having a good gossip. But before that was the coming evening with Simon. What did she expect? What did she hope for? Was she simply trying to prove to him that she had grown up now? Did she want to make him want her as much as she had once wanted him, or did she truly have

51

deeper feelings for him? She would never forget the way she had felt that day when he had said he loved her. 'I love you, Jenna' he had called out, and her heart had soared. Perhaps it had indeed been simply excitement, the thrill of discovery that had provoked his words, but she had thrilled whenever she thought of it for many long months.

But neither of them had really known what they were doing. No, it was foolish to waste time thinking of the past in this way. They were now two completely different individuals. Why, she had scarcely recognized Simon when they first saw each other again. From the top of his immaculate head to the highly polished soft leather Italian shoes, he was a picture of sartorial elegance. He wore the image with an ease she would never have believed possible after knowing the scruffy student he had once been. Since her schoolgirl crush on him she had been out with a great many men, but few of them had come up to her own high expectations. If they had been great-looking, she had found the personality lacking. If they'd had a great personality, there had usually been something else wrong. Except for David.

She had thought David fitted the picture in every department, to the extent that she'd really believed she loved him – loved him enough to go away for a weekend with him, in Paris. It had seemed like heaven at the time. They had done all the touristy things, stayed in a fabulous hotel, and she'd really believed she would have agreed to marry him, if only he had asked her to. When they'd returned, someone had come to meet them at Heathrow. His wife. David had had a wife. A beautiful wife who was ready and waiting to fly at Jenna, all claws drawn. She had accused her of trying to take her husband away; of seducing him. Jenna had felt humiliated and guilty, even though she hadn't known David was married.

Did all wives always assume it was the other woman who dragged their husbands away? Didn't they realize it was often the husband who initiated the affair? Jenna scowled to herself at the memory. After that whole dreadful business she'd vowed never to love anyone again, not until she was certain that every single thing was right. Everything. She might even go as far as checking – wherever one does check those sort of things – that Mr Right didn't have a *Mrs* Right hidden away. She knew for certain that Kurt didn't have a wife, but then 'everything' was far from right with him as far as she was concerned.

She hung her dress upstairs and took the paper-weight out of its scruffy carrier bag. She washed it in the kitchen sink and dried it carefully. The floral pattern deep inside was bright and clear. She stared at it, wondering about its history. It was obviously late Victorian, but nothing special, she decided. It made a nice addition to her collection and it had really been quite inexpensive. The dealer had obviously known little about the subject. It had probably been bought as part of a job lot. A box of bits and pieces from some house clearance.

Jenna spent the rest of the afternoon lazing around in the pretty garden. She pulled a few weeds here and there, and lay in the sun for a short spell. Although she was already well tanned, and had skin that never burned, she would never risk sunbathing for too long – especially not in Cornwall. Everywhere there were warnings about the dangers of skin cancer. The trouble was, people always admired a tan, saying how well everyone looked when they were a little bronzed.

At six she fed the cat and went to get ready. At least her efforts seemed to be appreciated when Simon arrived. His admiration was obvious from the appraising look he gave her. She knew she looked good, and she felt confident and in control. What more could she want than an evening spent in good company? She thrilled at the memory of the brief kiss they had shared when he left the last time, and secretly speculated about the coming evening. Would he kiss her again? She hoped so! *What a kid I'm being*, she scolded herself.

CHAPTER 4

Simon drove Jenna home to the cottage around eleven-thirty. They had shared an excellent meal and had laughed, joked, and talked about every subject under the sun, or so it seemed. Jenna felt herself relaxing more than she could remember in a long time. She had known Simon was someone very special to her, and now she was beginning to realize just how special. She saw that over the past few years she had somehow subconsciously been comparing every man she had met to this man who had once been the student Simon. Looking at the man of today, she knew that he had matured from that open student into a more complex, very much more interesting person. Obviously many things had changed in his life to make him what he had become.

She was curious about the life he had led between now and the years she had first known him. But he avoided all her direct questions and she could not penetrate any part of his mind that he did not choose to share. If they were to form any sort of relationship in the future, filling all the gaps would make for interesting times. Meanwhile, she recognized that, quite unmistakably, she was falling in love with him all over again. This time, though, it was not a schoolgirl crush but the deeper, adult kind of love that comes with increased years. The very thought filled her with a mixture of joy and apprehension.

'Will you come in for a coffee?' she invited when he stopped the car.

His face tensed, as if he were trying to fight some decision he had made earlier. 'I really ought to get back,' he said, after a pause.

Jenna tried not to show her disappointment and shrugged. 'As you like. Thanks again for a lovely evening. It's been great. I've really enjoyed meeting you again.' She hoped that her unexpected feeling of tearfulness didn't show. The intensity of her disappointment shook her slightly, but she tried to tell herself it was only because she might not see him again for some time. Who could know where she would be next week? The next job was supposed to be in London, but often she could be flying away to anywhere in the world, as new kids zoomed up the pop charts and needed some exotic location for a video.

'Actually, I'll change my mind,' he was saying. She stared at him blankly, wrapped in her thoughts for the moment. 'Coffee? If that's OK? You just offered me some coffee.'

'Yes, of course. Sorry. Come on in.' She felt a renewed thrill of excitement as they walked up the path through the gathering dusk. She was always amazed how it stayed so light at night here. It wasn't the artificial light of the city but a clarity in the air.

'I should think seriously about selling my flat in London and moving down here permanently,' Jenna muttered.

'You'd miss the excitement,' Simon observed. 'You're too used to the bright city lights and dashing off all round the world at a moment's notice.'

'The way I feel at present, I should be glad to know where I shall be the next day. It sometimes drives me mad when I make arrangements which are always broken. This life of mine – well, it isn't as glamorous as it's made out to be,' she added a touch grimly. No wonder she could never form any permanent relationship. Besides never finding the right man, she was forced to break too many dates!

'Most people would be glad of the chance to travel, especially on expenses,' he said with a smile. 'Now, about that coffee?'

Jenna couldn't help but notice that he seemed slightly ill at ease as she sat next to him on the deep sofa while they sipped their coffees. She stared, surprised by the realization. A sophisticated man like him would never look uncomfortable, she thought. Perhaps he simply didn't fancy her. Well, that was easy. She must never let him see how much she cared, then he might not feel obliged to say anything. She couldn't believe that he really didn't like her, not after the special time they had shared together. She got up to collect her new paperweight, using it as an excuse to remove herself from the closeness of him. If he didn't want to be involved in any way, she would try to make it easier for him.

'I may have missed buying the collection at the sale, but I suspect this one may turn out to be a bargain,' she said, holding it out to him.

'It's lovely. I didn't realize you were a serious collector. It's possibly French, isn't it?'

'I don't think so, but I haven't got my reference books here. I suspect it's a fairly common Victorian one, but it's pretty and it was cheap, whatever it turns out to be.' They chatted inconsequentially for a while and finally he rose.

'I really do have to get back. I have a busy morning tomorrow and an early start. I have to go to Exeter on business. Give my regards to Sarah. Tell her I'll give her a call some time and we'll arrange to meet up again. She's one very special lady.'

Jenna smiled. Hesitatingly, Simon leaned towards her and gave her a light kiss on the cheek. His eyes, usually so bright and golden brown, held a slight mistiness, almost a dulling that she could not understand. She reached up to him and kissed his mouth. She felt him stiffen and draw back. She felt foolish, something akin to the day they had hugged each other and kissed at the site of the dig, years ago. She had quite forgotten the promise she had once made to herself.

After the way she had felt that day at Heathrow, when David's wife had assaulted her with such venom, she had vowed never to take the lead with anyone again. Kissing Simon on the mouth had seemed, to her, the natural thing to do. His rejection of her was therefore all the more painful. She gave a feeble smile and turned to open the door. Once more

Simon seemed to hesitate, before he strode out with a slight wave of his hand. He walked quickly up the narrow path and she watched as he closed the gate. Her heart was thumping and those ridiculous tears began to form in her eyes.

How could she have been so stupid? Obviously he had done what he saw as his duty to Sarah's niece, and now he was returning to his ordinary life. Obviously he had never felt about her the way she had felt about him. Perhaps she was, after all, still harbouring the schoolgirl crush that he could never take as being anything more serious.

The memory of her disappointment when she had returned to school after that summer hit her again. She remembered how she had cried herself to sleep more than once when he had failed to write. Stupid, she told herself. It was all stupid. Thank heavens Sarah was coming back tomorrow evening.

At six the next morning, she felt wide awake. It was sunny again and she went out to take a walk before breakfast. Sarah's cottage was about half a mile from the sea, and she wandered down the little lane towards the beach. Her sense of disappointment about Simon's apparent lack of interest clouded her enjoyment of the beautiful day. She tried to reason with herself that she was no worse off now than before she had come to Cornwall.

Before she had met Simon again, she'd thought she had quite got over any feelings she might once have had for him, and in truth she hadn't given him a thought for months – years, even. Just because they had met again, there was no excuse for allowing herself to feel anything more than she would for any other old friend she might have bumped into. She tried every kind of logic she could think of. There had always been something mysterious about Simon. He always seemed to be holding something back. But then, perhaps that was part of his appeal? His mystery? Jenna wondered if it was something to do with his reluctance to talk about his professional life. Was there something he wanted to hide?

She knew so little about him. All she had known as a girl was that he had parents living somewhere in the county. Now, at least she knew it was a hotel. She glanced at her watch. It wasn't yet eight o'clock. If Simon was going out for the day, as he had said, she could still drive over to Tregarth Manor for lunch. No one would know her, and she might find the answers to a few questions. Granted, when Sarah came back she might be able to provide a few of those answers herself, but there was no way that Jenna wanted to give Sarah any grounds to begin speculating about her possible interest in Simon. She would be trying to matchmake in seconds, and Jenna had experienced her aunt's clumsy efforts all too often before.

She made some coffee and toast and sat in her usual place on the step. Bonza came along, as if his built-in radar somehow sensed her presence. She fondled him behind the ears, setting him purring with delight. The green eyes stared.

'What do you think, cat?' she whispered. 'What's the big mystery? Does he like me at all or am

I wasting my time?' The cat purred some more and she smiled. Cats were good. They were self-sufficient, yet comforting when needed. If she ever did return to live in Cornwall, she would get a cat of her own.

She pulled on a pair of loose, silky trousers and a clean shirt. She stuffed swimming things into a bag, and drove Sarah's car out of the garage. As she drove along the sunny lanes she allowed herself to remember Simon's kiss after the first time they went out to dinner and the gentle insistence she had experienced from him. She felt herself grow warm, and the base of her stomach churned deliciously as she remembered exactly how she had felt at that moment. The disappointment that he had failed to repeat it last night still rankled. Had she said or done anything wrong? No, there must be some other reason, and hopefully someone at Tregarth Manor could provide her with some answers. With Simon nicely out of the way, she would be free to make her anonymous inspection of the hotel and its surroundings. Somehow, she simply couldn't, wouldn't accept that he really didn't like her. That first simple kiss had been too sincere, too enjoyable for both of them.

It took well over an hour to drive to the Tregarth Manor Hotel and Conference Centre. It was delightfully situated at the head of a wooded valley, leading down towards the brilliant turquoise sea. Jenna drove through an avenue of birches, the light green leaves making a dappled effect on the car bonnet. The delicacy of the birch trees made an unusual choice for lining a drive like this, instead of the more usual oaks, and there were glimpses of the sea between the silvery trunks. The wide front of the house was built of mellow Cornish stone, with mullioned windows. Wisteria grew over most of the building, neatly trimmed but allowing the gentle curves of its branches to soften the angles. The huge oak door was standing open, welcoming to visitors. She parked and walked round from the side. At the rear of the house were several extensions, built in similar stone to the front but obviously much newer additions. There was a long conservatory down the other side, filled with wrought-iron furniture, and there were elegant palms and flowering plants cascading down the walls. On the other side, a long low barn carried the sign, '*Swimming Pool, Gym and Sauna*.' All round the buildings, green lawns stretched away in the distance It certainly lived up to the advertisement. '*Peaceful, surrounded by lush parkland*' was no exaggeration.

She went into the foyer to reserve a table for lunch. Everywhere smelt of beeswax polish and the old beams and dark, well-polished floorboards gave a wonderful feeling of character to the place. The furniture was antique, and large, beautiful pictures hung on the walls. A huge copper urn was filled with fresh flowers, giving a welcome that was instantaneous in its impact. She picked up a brochure and asked if the pool was open for non-residents. The immaculate receptionist smiled and said that it was not booked today and that Jenna was welcome to avail herself of any of the facilities she cared to use.

She collected her bikini from the car and followed

the signs to the pool. She changed, and plunged into the delightfully warm water. She was a strong swimmer and, although out of practice, swam for several lengths before stopping for breath. One day, she promised herself, she would own a swimming pool, if ever she was rich enough. The sea was OK for splashing about in, but she had loved serious swimming ever since her schooldays. Besides, it was the best form of exercise possible.

When she had finished she sat on one of the many terraces and sipped a cold drink as the sun finished drying her hair. If this was indeed Simon's family home, he was a lucky man. She supposed that his parents must have run the place at one time, when he was at university. Why on earth was he so secretive about it all? In her book it was somewhere to be very proud of. A waiter came to tell her that her table was ready whenever she cared to eat and she smiled her thanks. Somehow she felt more like an honoured guest in a family home than a paying member of the public stopping off for lunch. It was a clever strategy, and, despite her many stays in hotels, she felt this one was delightfully different.

The menu declared itself to be based entirely on local foods, and locally caught fish featured strongly. Fresh vegetables and salads were picked from one of the hotel's own gardens. She chose fresh mullet, served with a dill sauce and green salad. She didn't want anything too heavy, as she would be cooking a meal for Sarah that evening. The panelled dining room was comfortable and had separate bays, cleverly contrived through the use of well-positioned plants, to allow each table to feel secluded without being claustrophobic. There were several other tables occupied, but the soft music permitted conversations to remain private. It was altogether a beautiful room, well planned for the comfort of the guests. She could understand now why Simon had always chosen his food so carefully when they had shared meals. Even when he dined socially he was keeping an eye open for local market forces.

From her vantage point she could see most people as they came into the room. Once seated, they were quite private. Apart from herself, there was only one other woman eating alone. The woman was smartly dressed but had a rather dumpy figure and mousy-coloured hair. The waiters treated her courteously, as they did all the guests, but she seemed to have an indefinable extra air of command about her. Inevitably, Jenna was trying to fit a story to everyone she saw – a habit she had cultivated for her work, when she wanted to get all the details correct for a scene.

She saw this particular woman as possibly the wife of some businessman, left to her own devices whilst the husband was working. The woman glanced at her watch irritably, seeming to be waiting for someone. She ordered a mineral water, which she sipped slowly, making it last for a long time. Eventually her awaited companion arrived. He looked slightly flushed, as if he had been hurrying. He leaned over to plant a casual kiss on the woman's cheek before sitting opposite her. Jenna could see his back and part of the woman. The expression on her own face, had she been able to seen it, was one of shocked amazement. The woman had been waiting for Simon.

From the way she had greeted him theirs was a long-standing relationship, a relationship that showed a familiarity of the most obvious kind. In Jenna's mind there was little doubt that they were a married couple. Their slightly bored air of familiarity was obvious. And the deference shown by the waiters was because *she* was married to the owner of the hotel.

The delicious food remaining on her plate began to taste like sawdust, and she wanted only to leave, to escape from the place. She knew she couldn't possibly get up and walk out without Simon seeing her. Evidently his business had taken less time than he had expected. She didn't want him to think she was spying on him, even if she had to admit that was the truth. She knew she had discovered one thing at least . . . Simon was married. She knew now she must not see him again – ever. Not after her previous experience with David. She must never allow herself to fall into that trap again, even if she did adore the man to distraction. Luckily she had found out the truth in good time, before she had let herself fall any more deeply in love. This time she would not allow herself to start anything that could harm anyone – not least herself. She wondered what he could have told his wife on the two occasions they had dined out together. Some business engagement, she presumed. Thank heavens she hadn't fallen any deeper into the temptation of his attraction and her own feelings. The entire situation would be so much worse now.

After what seemed like a lifetime, Simon and his

wife finished their meal. They left the dining room
together and at last Jenna could stop pretending to
drink her coffee. She paid the waiter at her table,
grasping the opportunity to ask a few questions. She
hoped to give the impression that she was enquiring
about the facilities for business, without actually
saying anything to commit herself. General questions like: How long has the hotel been open? Who
runs it? She got the one answer she was seeking, even
if it was one she might have preferred not to hear.
Simon and Paula Andrews ran the place, he said. And
if that didn't sound like a husband and wife team,
what else could? She knew Simon was an only child
from the time, years ago, when they had been talking
about the problems and joys of being only children.
Paula couldn't possibly be anything other than his
wife.

Jenna left through one of the side doors. No way
could she risk being seen by Simon. She felt very
foolish about all her girlish fantasizing. However
good an actress she might be, she didn't like the
idea of standing around waiting to be introduced to
the woman who was Mrs Simon Andrews. It was
strange, really, that a good – no, devastatingly good-
looking man like Simon should marry such a relatively plain woman. And now she was being catty,
Jenna told herself. The woman obviously had hidden
depths, and everyone knew that looks weren't everything. Perhaps they were even the least important
part of a relationship. She wished she could believe
herself.

She drove away quickly, praying that no one,

especially Simon, should see her. She had come in search of answers and oh, boy, answers she had found! One thing was certain; she would be leaving Cornwall very soon after her weekend with Sarah. They might even be able to travel back to London together. A glance at her watch told her she barely had enough time to call at the supermarket for a few provisions before she cooked dinner for them both.

'Jenna, darling, you made it! Great to see you. How thin you look. Don't you ever eat properly?' Sarah called out, practically before she had opened the door of the train. Penzance Station was filled with people greeting each other with hugs and kisses, demands for luggage to be carried and several screaming children. The passengers looked weary after what had probably been a long journey, and most were obviously glad to be home.

'Great to see you, Sarah. And for the record, I've done little other than eat since I came to Cornwall. I can hardly get into any of my clothes as it is, so don't go trying to fatten me up even more.'

Sarah laughed. She put down her suitcase and hugged her niece.

'Promise,' she laughed. 'Gosh it's good to be back. The only good thing about leaving Cornwall is coming back to see everything looking so fresh. You *are* looking good. No, seriously, I mean it. A bit on the skinny side, but really good. Whatever it is you do, it suits you. Come on, then. Spill the beans. What's been going on? Why are you always out when I phone?'

'You never change, do you? So many questions, I've already forgotten the first six.' Jenna took the biggest suitcase and, laughing together, they strode off along the platform. Sarah continued to bombard her with questions, never waiting for the answers. Jenna left her to ramble on, smiling with happiness at being with her only family once more.

Bonza was delighted to see his mistress again, and rubbed himself in and out of her legs miaowing and purring alternately.

'What is it, boy? Didn't she remember to feed you? Poor little thing. You'll waste away, won't you?'

'That cat is the single most greedy cat I have ever met. Fade away? Just look at the size of him. The media would probably mistake him for the Beast of Bodmin. How come you have this obsession with feeding every creature in sight to the point of self-destruction? Everything, that is, except yourself. Look at you. Skinny as a lath. Now, sit yourself down and have a drink. Dinner's in the oven and won't be long.' Jenna knew her protests were futile, but it was part of life with Sarah. 'Gosh, but it's good to see you. Now, tell me everything about London – and who is this mysterious Michael you spend so much time with?'

'Now who's asking all the questions?' Sarah demanded.

Soon after nine, Sarah was already yawning.

'Must be the journey, and being home, of course. Besides, you've never stopped talking since I got home,' she teased. 'You haven't told me anything about what you've been up to for the last few days. Did you get to any of the sales?'

Jenna filled in the barest details for her aunt, missing out all mention of Simon. She gave a start. After the initial shock of discovery and her drive home, she had managed to push away all thoughts of Simon and his wife. She supposed she must have been carefully avoiding thinking, the sooner to forget the twinges of pain she experienced when she did think about him. She would have to mention him some time, in case he did contact Sarah. He would think it very odd if she hadn't mentioned *anything* about their meetings.

'Oh, yes,' she said, as if she had just remembered it, 'I met Simon at the sale. Remember, Simon Andrews? I met him one holiday, before my last year at school.'

'Could I ever forget? He's scrubbed up well, hasn't he? I didn't recognize him the first time I met him again.' Sarah sounded deliberately light and casual. She stared at Jenna closely. 'And did you find him as gorgeous as ever?'

Jenna reddened slightly. 'I'm not sure I know what you mean,' she said, avoiding eye contact with her aunt.

'Come on, love. I'm not stupid. I know just how much you fell for him that summer. I don't think a single phone call passed when you didn't ask, very casually, of course, "How's Simon?" You were very smitten with the boy.'

Jenna looked away. She hadn't realized Sarah had known, much less understood. Somehow she had never associated Sarah with any men, and had assumed that her aunt was not interested in anything beyond her precious digs and ancient artefacts.

'He took me out to dinner a couple of times. Just for old times' sake, of course. I wouldn't have expected anything more, not now he's a married man.' Jenna gulped slightly. She had forced herself to say the words, however much it hurt, just to make herself get used to the idea.

'Married? Simon? Don't be ridiculous. He's far too busy working to make the hotel a success to ever have time to be married. Tell me something. Did Simon ever try anything with you? You know what I mean. Years ago.'

Jenna stared. What on earth was her aunt getting at? What was she suggesting?

'No,' she said softly, 'though I'd have given anything for him to have succeeded at the time.'

'Jenna!' Sarah said in shocked surprise. 'You were only seventeen years old, for goodness' sakes. Besides, if he had done anything he'd have been out on his ear. I threatened him with a fate worse than death itself if he so much as laid a finger on you. The end of his career, his university course – everything.'

Jenna stared. So that was it. She remembered the look on his face that day when she'd believed they had almost made love. She could recall every detail of the way he had withdrawn into his shell after that, avoiding being alone with her. It all made sense. She'd been forbidden fruit. Poor man, she thought suddenly. There she'd been, flinging everything she had at him, and he'd known that one wrong move would have been the end of all his dreams. Now it was too late. Damn Sarah's protection, she thought. How different things might have been if she hadn't been Sarah's niece.

'Thanks a bunch,' she said miserably. 'He's the only man I've ever really fallen for. Well, except David, I suppose. But we all know what happened there.' Her aunt had been given a strictly edited account of the short affair, the nastier details being completely omitted.

'I'm sorry, love,' Sarah said. 'I thought you were only going through the usual schoolgirl thing. Becoming aware of rampant hormones and all that. But you must understand, I took my responsibilities very seriously.'

'I know. It's all a long time ago. It was still nice to see him again, even if I was a bit too late.'

Sarah stared at her niece, long and hard. She bit her lip. She had simply never thought of Jenna as more than a child in those days, and had believed she was only ever acting for the best. Admittedly, Simon had always seemed different from the rest of her students. She should perhaps have had greater trust in him. Even so, she'd had no idea Simon had married. In fact, the more she thought about it, the more the whole idea seemed impossible. He had kept in touch with her for some years after the dig, and surely he would have told her something as dramatic as that? Perhaps he, too, had experienced deeper feelings for Jenna than a casual student fling.

As far as she knew, he had been forced to abandon

a very promising career in archaeology to run the family estate. She knew few of the details, but a couple of phone calls would surely correct that. Maybe Simon should be invited to dinner the following night, or perhaps she and Jenna could go to the hotel to see him? From all accounts, the place was gaining an excellent reputation. On the other hand, if he did have a wife, it could be an extremely difficult time for Jenna if she really did care.

'I must get off to bed,' Sarah said at last. 'I'm falling asleep where I sit. We'll talk some more tomorrow. Stuff the dishes in the sink. We'll do them at breakfast time. Goodnight, darling. It's awfully good to have you here.'

Despite her day spent travelling, Sarah's mind was too preoccupied to allow for much sleep. She felt responsible for her niece's happiness and desperately hoped that her once well-intentioned interference had not backfired. She carefully made her plans. She would take Jenna for a meal at Simon's place the following evening, and that way at least things would be settled one way or another. If he was indeed married, the sooner Jenna could get him out of her system, the better. If not, then she would be providing the introduction and opportunity for something more, if that was what they both wanted. Simon married, without her knowing? It was impossible. Her mind more settled, Sarah turned over and sank into a deep sleep.

'Put on your glad rags, darling,' Sarah demanded, around five the following evening. 'I'm taking you out for a decent meal. Got to get some weight on that skinny frame of yours.'

Jenna smiled. 'I'm actually quite content with myself the way I am. If it was left to you, I'd probably turn out more like a round barrel.'

'Nonsense. You seem to eat everything in sight and still never put on an ounce. You don't know how lucky you are,' Sarah replied with a touch of envy. 'Shall I shower first, or you?'

By seven, they were driving along the narrow lanes, heading for Tregarth Manor.

'Where are we going?' Jenna asked suspiciously. Only just over twenty-four hours earlier she had herself been driving along this very route.

'Wait and see,' Sarah said with a smile. 'We're going to look up an old friend.'

Jenna's heart sank. As she had suspected, Sarah was blundering into her love-life yet again. She hadn't told her aunt about her own visit to Tregarth, and hesitated, wondering exactly how she should handle the situation. If she said nothing, there was a chance that someone on the staff would recognize her and she would be totally embarrassed. She would look an absolute idiot. Much as she would like to see Simon, she was not prepared for any sort of confrontation in front of a room full of diners.

'Are – are you sure this is a good idea?' she finally managed to stammer. 'I mean, it could be embarrassing for everyone.'

'Nonsense. Simon will be delighted to see us again, and if it turns out that he has made some sort of secret marriage, we can congratulate him suitably and then get on with our own lives. Now, I think we turn off down here.'

Jenna sat back, knowing there was little or nothing she could do. The next few hours could prove to be the most embarrassing of her entire life. Why on earth hadn't she come straight out with the truth? She had already been to spy out the land – and spying was exactly what she *had* been doing the previous day. Her own pride had stopped her from saying anything before, and now it was too late.

'And does Simon know about this coming invasion?' Jenna asked.

'Of course he does. I thought I'd better reserve a table, and then I could invite him to join us. I expect he's a very busy man, and there would be little point coming all this way if he was going to be out.' Sarah was wearing her very worst matchmaking expression; a slight smirk, was how Jenna would describe it. She had seen it too many times over the past three or four years.

With a flourish, Sarah drove into the parking area and flung open the car door impatiently.

'Come on. I'm starving.'

With a feeling of reluctance, Jenna climbed out of the car, her fingers crossed for a change of duty staff. Maybe she would get lucky and no one would recognize her from the previous day . . .

CHAPTER 5

'I'll let Mr Simon know you are here,' the receptionist said. 'Would you like to have a drink in the bar while you look at the menu?'

'Thanks,' Sarah replied, going towards the room the woman was indicating. 'Nice place, isn't it?'

'Lovely. Must have been quite some family home once upon a time. Wonder how long it's been a hotel?' Jenna said.

'I believe Simon is responsible for doing most of it. The family were running at a loss for some years, and apparently almost on the verge of bankruptcy when his father died. There was some hint of scandal at the time, but I never heard what it was all about. Simon had to knuckle down and really get on with the job. Quite turned the place around. His mother disapproved of pretty well all his ideas and moved back to Scotland in disgust, leaving his way clear. There was no end of trouble, I seem to remember, but he'll probably fill us in on the details. Now, what are you going to have to drink? Anything you like. You don't have to think about driving for once.'

Jenna knew that Simon had come into the room before she even saw him. The two women were sitting at a corner table, out of sight of the main door, but she could sense his presence. In fact, she was certain that every woman in the room seemed to be aware of his arrival.

'My, but you've grown up,' Sarah said as he came over. Simon laughed and kissed her on the cheek.

'What? Since the last time we met? Sarah, it's lovely to see you again. It's been far too long. And Jenna.' He leaned over and kissed her on the cheek as well. It seemed that was his standard greeting for every woman he knew.

'Welcome to Tregarth.'

'What a gorgeous place you have here,' Jenna said, hoping no one noticed the trembling mode her voice seemed to have switched into. Damn this man; he could make her behave like a seventeen-year-old whenever they met. She might be glad to feel young again when she was sixty or so, but at this stage of her life it interfered with her current image far too drastically.

'Can I get you something else to drink?' he asked.

'I'm fine, thanks. But do join us. We're delighted you were free this evening, especially as it's a Saturday,' Sarah said.

'I never go out anywhere at weekends, so for once this is a pleasant part of being on duty.' He signalled the bar attendant, who came over with a tall glass filled with an amber liquid, chinking with ice cubes. 'Here's to old friendships,' he said, raising the glass. Again, Jenna found herself studying the man, almost as intently as she had done at their previous meetings. Tonight he was wearing a cream shirt of fine lawn, impeccably laundered. His light brown suit was beautifully cut and hugged his slim body without a crease or wrinkle in sight. The patterned silk tie had bands of a deep honey colour, exactly matching those extraordinary eyes. No wonder every female head turned when he came into a room. He was devastatingly good-looking, and the aura of power that surrounded him seemed to slice through the very air.

Her body suddenly began to ache in a way that seemed all too familiar. She found herself longing to touch him – his hand, his hair, it didn't matter. It seemed that schoolgirl crushes didn't end with leaving school! What a pity, a terrible pity, that he was already married to someone else. She cursed the fate that had caused the delay in reuniting them, until it was too late.

'So, what's it to be?' Simon asked, picking up the menu.

A couple of hours later, the trio were sitting with coffee and brandies in huge balloon glasses, in the conservatory. They were surrounded by the exotic plants and the sea view was rapidly fading into darkness; the new moon shone, a silver crescent in the deepest blue sky. Simon and Sarah had done most of the talking. Jenna was left in peace, to wallow in her thoughts and longings, listening to the two swapping tales of university days. She noticed a bronze statue in the corner of the room, half hidden by luxuriant foliage.

77

'Oh, it's lovely,' she said out loud. The others turned to see what she looking at. 'Isn't that the one you bought at the sale the other day?'

Simon laughed.

'I knew it was perfect for that corner as soon as I saw it. Lucky no one else wanted it.'

'I thought you were some sort of dealer after our first meeting. I see now you were buying things for the hotel. It certainly helps to give a marvellous atmosphere to the place.'

'I may have been forced to give up scrabbling in the ground for my bits of history, but I guess I shall always be fascinated by lovely things, whatever their age.' He was looking at her with mild amusement in his eyes, obviously placing a double meaning on his words. 'I do deal occasionally, however. I use the whole place as a sort of showroom. You'd be amazed how many times people offer me ridiculous prices for things they see in the hotel. I seem to have the knack of displaying what they want to buy, and seeing it in these surroundings make them think they're buying the family heirlooms. Makes them feel a part of it. We get letters from all over the world, actually thanking us for making them part with thousands of pounds. Hence my visits to local sales whenever I can get away.'

Undoubtably, he was a shrewd businessman.

'And do you manage the place single-handed?' she asked innocently.

'Pretty well. I have excellent staff.'

Jenna hesitated. If he had intended to say anything

more, he had changed his mind. She asked the question that had been burning the entire evening.

'No wife to help you?' she said, her voice strong enough to hide the tremor that was building inside her.

'Haven't had time to go in search of a wife,' he said, looking her straight in the eye. How very much she wanted to believe him, but she couldn't challenge his reply, not without admitting she had been here before to spy on him. But whatever he said, or rather, didn't say, she knew about Paula. She had got away without being recognized so far. The one waiter who might have known her from the previous day was attending to another table and had merely smiled at her. She was an attractive woman and men often smiled at her. No one had noticed anything out of the ordinary at all.

'I still don't know how you've managed to stay single all this time.' Sarah was laughing. 'If I was ten years younger, I'd certainly put in a bid.'

'I might just accept,' Simon replied fondly. 'How about you, Jenna? No men in your life?'

'Never have time,' she said.

'I can't believe that. Showbiz people are always in love with someone.'

She choked slightly. 'Showbiz? Me? You have to be joking. From what I know of my own little part of that world, I'd have nothing to do with any of them. Not even my boss, and I shall never believe his proposal was serious.' The other two stared at her. She cursed her own stupidity. She should never have mentioned Kurt.

'What's this? Come on. Spill the beans,' Sarah ordered, her eyes wide.

'N-nothing. Really,' Jenna stammered. 'Oh, it was just Kurt. He asked me to marry him the night before I came down here.'

'Marry him? Oh, Jenna, darling. Why on earth didn't you tell me?' Sarah demanded.

'And will you marry him?' Simon asked grimly, his eyes flashing with almost perfectly disguised anger.

''Course not. He isn't in love with me or I with him. It was a spur-of-the-moment thing. If I thought he'd meant it, well . . .' Her voice tailed off.

'My, my, who ever would have thought it?' Simon was saying with a mocking note in his voice. 'Our little Jenna marrying the boss of a film company.'

'"Little Jenna", as you put it, is doing nothing of the sort. I've told you, it was nothing serious, nothing more than a suggestion out of convenience. I don't love him. In fact I doubt if I shall ever marry anyone. It's all too much trouble. Besides, how does anyone ever know they've found the right person? Someone you can stay with for ever?' Her icy blue eyes were flashing dangerously.

'For ever and ever, amen. Certainly it's a long time,' Simon said, an irritating smirk beginning to curl his mouth. Jenna coloured.

'I don't see marriage as a laughing matter. I think love should be real, deep, sincere. I can't bear the *"Darlings, I love you all"* image. Especially not from someone like Kurt. I don't think I'd ever be able to trust him, for a start.' She was becoming heated, and felt herself forced to talk about something she was not ready for.

'I think perhaps it's time we left,' Sarah suggested tactfully. She yawned. Besides, she was picking up tensions in the air that might be best left right now, before anything was said that could ruin their friendship. But she was not yet quite ready to give up her self-imposed task. She had decided to do her best to get the young pair together, whatever it took. 'Perhaps you'd like to come over to our humble abode for dinner one night? Before Jenna goes back to her high life.'

'I don't know when I shall be going back,' Jenna began to hedge.

'Well, you're certainly not going tomorrow, are you? Come over tomorrow, Simon, if you're free,' Sarah said firmly.

'He said he had to be here at weekends. Tomorrow is still the weekend, isn't it?' Jenna protested.

'I'd love to come. Thank you, Sarah. My assistant manager can take over. She owes me a few evenings off.'

'Good. That's settled. We'll see you about eight? OK?' Sarah stood up.

'I'll look forward to it,' Simon said, giving her a hug. 'And tonight's meal is on the house,' he added.

'Don't be silly. It was my treat,' Sarah protested. 'However are you going to make a success of the place if you give away wonderful meals like this?'

'Trouble with you is that you always have to argue. You never change. Now go home. I'll see you tomorrow.' Simon propelled them to the door, an arm round each of their shoulders. 'My goodness. Two such beautiful ladies, I should be paying for your company, let alone buying a simple meal.'

'Nothing simple about that meal,' Jenna said, her smile hopefully covering her real emotional turmoil. 'It was all delicious. Thank you very much.'

He walked them to the car and waved as they drove away. He disappeared into the darkness. When he went back into the reception area, he noticed the woman standing on the stairs. She was watching him, an expression of almost intense hatred in her eyes. She came down and stood before him.

'I suppose I'm not good enough to be introduced to your posh friends.' Paula Andrews glared at him.

'Come on, Paula. You know that's nothing to do with it. You'd have been bored with them. They're very old friends from my archaeology days.'

'The young one doesn't look much like an archaeologist. Far too glamorous. Just watch it, Simon. Don't try to fool me around. I've seen you before with beautiful women. Wasps round a honey pot. She's after you; I can tell. Why else would she be here for two days running?'

'I don't know what you're talking about. This was her first visit.'

'Was it, indeed? Shows how little you know.' She turned and went back upstairs.

Simon sighed deeply. He wasn't sure how long he could go on with this woman dominating so much of his life. But he knew he had made a promise he could never break. The situation always got to him. For heaven's sake, he was a hugely successful business-man. His father might have died in near poverty, but now, seven years on, he, Simon Andrews, was sitting on a fortune. If he could manage a considerable portfolio of stocks and shares, in addition to building up a successful business like this hotel, surely he should not have to put up with a sour, embittered woman like Paula? His mouth tightened. One day he had to find a way out, but for now there was still work waiting to be done.

Throughout their journey home, Sarah was relent-lessly pumping Jenna for information.

'Let it drop, Sarah, please,' Jenna begged. 'I don't want to marry Kurt. I don't love him.'

'And Simon? Don't you love him either?'

'No. Yes. I don't know. It doesn't make any difference now, does it?'

'But he said he wasn't married. I believe him.'

'Fine. I don't. I'd like to but, well, I just don't think I can believe him. He changed the subject much too quickly. If you noticed, he didn't say he wasn't married, just that he had no time to search for a wife.' Jenna felt weary. Her emotions had been jangling all evening. Sarah's playful matchmaking was becoming more than a little tedious, as well as uncomfortable.

The two spent a lazy Sunday morning, companion-ably sipping coffee and reading the papers. The subject of last night's conversation was not men-tioned. Sarah's well-stocked freezer would provide

83

the makings of dinner for their guest and there was little to do until later.

Stretching out in the sun, Jenna tried to relax. If Sarah insisted on forcing her and Simon together, she would have to come to terms with her emotions and try to think of him as merely another friend. She must have dozed in the warm sun, and awoke to see Sarah coming out of the house with a suitcase. She sat up hurriedly.

'What on earth are you doing?' she demanded.

'Got a phone call. I have to get back to London. Meetings tomorrow. I am sorry but you'll have to entertain Simon on your own.' Jenna gaped at her aunt.

'Why so suddenly?' she asked. 'Surely you could have waited till tomorrow morning? I could have travelled with you. Perhaps I still could? What time's the train?'

'Haven't you forgotten our dinner guest?'

'Ring him. Tell him not to come. Tell him we'll see him some other time. I don't know, use your imagination.'

'Jenna, For heaven's sake. You were planning to stay another week, or so I thought.'

'What's the point? I came to spend time with you and you insist on going away to London all the time. You never used to be like this. You never used to drag yourself further than Truro, and only then when really pressed.'

'And now you're sounding like a spoiled brat who always wants her own way. What is the matter with you? Is there something you haven't told me about?

It isn't this Kurt chap, is it? He hasn't been pestering you, has he?'

'Of course not. I'm disappointed. You've only been here five minutes and you're off again. I might ask you a few questions. What's keeping you in London all the time? What's the sudden interest there?'

Sarah looked away. She was obviously hesitant about something she wanted to tell her niece. She took a deep breath.

'Nothing much. I'm writing another book and need to research a few things. It seems that while I've been in Town, a few people have got to know and offered me some lectures. I decided to say yes for once. Besides, it does me good to exchange ideas.'

'And is there someone to exchange them with? Someone special?' Was it Jenna's imagination, or was Sarah blushing just a little?

'Look, I really do have to go. I've ordered a taxi and it'll be here soon.'

'But what about Simon . . .?' Her voice tailed off as her aunt went back inside, out of earshot. Damn. She must have been doing it on purpose. Perhaps this was what she had planned all along. Well, she wasn't going to stand for it. She would phone and cancel him and she, too, would get out of Cornwall.

Sarah came back into the room, carrying a briefcase.

Simon's out for the afternoon, if you're thinking of phoning him. I tried. To apologize in advance for my rapid departure. The butler said he was out for the rest of the day and was also dining out. That must mean he's doing something before coming here.'

'I doubt he even *has* a butler,' Jenna snapped. 'You've set this whole thing up, haven't you? You wanted us to be thrown together.'

'Don't be so dramatic. As Hamlet said, "*The lady doth protest too much, methinks!*" I shall begin to think you really do feel something for the man. Damn, there's the taxi. Look, love, enjoy yourself. I trust you to know the right thing to do. I'll call you tomorrow and we'll catch up in London, very soon.'

Jenna waved her aunt off and walked slowly back into the pretty garden. How on earth did Sarah manage to keep it looking so good if she was never here? How on earth could she get out of spending yet another evening with Simon? It was a terrible *Catch Twenty-two* situation. His very presence set her emotions churning and she knew that he could set her on fire with the slightest gesture. It seemed there was no way to avoid the evening ahead, so she would have to make the best of it. As long as she didn't allow herself to feel anything. She must try to stay light-hearted and be entertaining. Surely she could get through it without making an idiot of herself?

She went into the kitchen to see what Sarah had taken out of the freezer for dinner. There was a lasagne and a bowl of salad, ready in the fridge, with a bottle of home-made dressing waiting to be poured on. A delicious looking soufflé sat in another dish, decorated with cream and nuts. There was even a bottle of sparkling wine chilling. Whenever could Sarah have done all this? she wondered. It was all just a bit too ready – instant dinner for two and not three. Jenna was certain this was a deliberate ploy on her aunt's part. Probably she had always intended to return to London this afternoon, even before she had invited Simon. Besides, she had heard no phone ringing or packing being done. Nothing. Perhaps she hadn't even tried to put Simon off.

She glanced at her watch. There might be time to stop him, or at least to let him know that they would be spending an evening alone, with only her to entertain him. It was too bad of Sarah to play her ridiculous matchmaker games. She began to dial the number but she put the phone down before it rang. What if Simon was telling the truth? Perhaps this Paula woman she had seen was a relation of some sort? She supposed it was possible that she was a cousin or something, and shared the same name. For a brief moment or two she allowed her imagination to run riot. If Simon were unmarried and free, would he actually feel anything for her? She would never know because the fact was there: he was already married and that was it. Game, set and match.

She showered and changed into a long cotton skirt, covered in poppies and meadow flowers. A simple red silky-knit top completed her casual outfit. She brushed her dark hair until it shone, leaving it hanging loose. Blow trying to look sophisticated for once, she thought. She sat outside in the garden, on one of Sarah's mushroom-shaped granite stones which were dotted around. The light breeze ruffled her hair but the sun was still warm. Lost in her thoughts, she failed to hear Simon's car pulling up in the lane outside. Quietly, he came into the garden.

'You look like a very exotic bouquet of flowers, sitting there,' he said softly.

'Simon. I didn't hear you come. Look, I'm afraid Sarah's gone. She had to leave for London. She claims it was unexpected, but somehow I find it hard to believe her. I am sorry.'

'Would you prefer me to leave?'

'Up to you. She left everything ready for dinner, but if you would rather not stay on your own – without Sarah, I mean – I shall quite understand.'

'I should love to stay. Oh, I bought this for you. I hope you like it. I was visiting an antiques fair and saw it on one of the stalls.' He handed her a package, heavy for its size. She pulled off the paper and stared. A millefiore paperweight, obviously old and very beautiful, lay in her cupped hands.

'It's quite exquisite,' she breathed. 'I just love these tiny flowers. They almost remind of Sarah's wonderful borders. Masses of colours jumbled together. But it must have cost a fortune. It looks very old, almost one of the earliest designs. Thank you, Simon, but I really couldn't accept it. It's much too valuable for a casual gift.'

'I told you, it was a bargain. Besides, I'd like you to have it. You're a very special friend and I had hoped you might still feel something for me. Even after all these years.'

'You know that's not possible,' Jenna said, her voice shaking slightly. She felt heat rising, colouring her cheeks in the now familiar way.

'But I thought you said that this Kurt, or whatever his name is, meant nothing to you? I suppose I just assumed there was no one else.'

'Not as far as I'm concerned, but surely you can't say the same. What about your wife?'

Simon's jaw dropped visibly. 'My what?'

'Your wife. Paula, isn't it?' Too late, she realized that she was not supposed to know anything about that particular lady.

'And what makes you think she is my wife, for heaven's sake?'

She blushed and looked away from his gaze.

'Hang on. Paula said she'd seen you before. Why on earth didn't you mention you had already visited Tregarth?'

'I was going to, but the chance sort of slipped away and by then it was too late.'

'But why on earth did you go there in the first place?'

'Curiosity. I wanted to see where you lived, find out more about you. I guess my schoolgirl crush took a long time to get over. Seeing you again reminded me of all those old feelings. Someone mentioned your wife. I . . . saw you together. I suppose I didn't want to embarrass you. And now I apologize for landing you here again, on false pretences of a dinner with Sarah. She did say she'd tried to phone to let you know she was leaving but she couldn't get through to you. I guess being in charge of your own empire is time-consuming, and you have to make yourself unavailable some of the time.'

Simon's expression was inscrutable. He listened

silently to her speech, without any sign of a smile. He remained silent until he could see she was about to burst out again. He took a breath and she waited.

'Of course I should have wanted to come anyway. If Sarah had really wanted to get in touch, she would have done. I have been out all afternoon – the antiques fair I mentioned? – so perhaps she did plan to set us up. I suggest we make the most of it and enjoy dinner together. Sarah was always a wonderful cook. I never knew how she managed to produce such amazing meals in zero time. As I said earlier, you're a special friend of mine whom I hoped would have some feelings still. Schoolgirl crush, was it? Who can say what a crush might turn into?'

'Simon, what does it matter how I feel? Paula's very existence prevents us from being anything more than friends. Now, if you would still like to stay for dinner, I suggest I go and organize it. Will you have a drink? Sarah left some wine in the fridge. Perhaps you'd open it?'

She went into the house to sort out the food and lay the table. Simon followed her and sat watching her movements as she worked. Her once coltish beauty had turned into a mature loveliness. He wanted to touch her, to hold her, the way he had once been forbidden from doing. He poured her a glass of wine and smiled as he handed it to her. She felt her heart pounding, her body growing warm with the closeness of the man. He was not safe to be so near. She knew she would find him impossible to resist if she allowed herself to come any closer. She gave a light laugh, hoping it sounded just that – light, with not a sign of the nervousness she was feeling.

'Relax, darling,' Simon said softly. 'Whatever you think, I am still Simon Andrews, the man who helped you find that golden torque and the amazing site that half of the country have been to visit. If only you knew how much I wanted you then. You may have been just a school-kid, but you were a very sexy one.'

'You couldn't have cared that much. If you'd really wanted me, why didn't you keep in touch? I thought I'd made my feelings fairly obvious.'

'Tell me about it! I neither said nor did anything because Sarah would have kicked me off the project and then I'd have lost my place at uni. If I'd so much as laid a finger on you – well, you can imagine! She can be a very fierce lady where you are concerned. Very protective, is our Sarah.'

'Oh, yes? And so this same protective Sarah organizes an evening leaving us alone together, in the same house, in one of the remotest spots in Cornwall? That really does sound highly likely.' The first clap of thunder began, right on cue. If she had been organizing sound effects for a video, the crash couldn't have been better timed.

'I thought it had been a bit oppressive today,' Simon remarked.

Jenna glared. Sarah seemed totally unable to keep her nose out of her niece's affairs. First she threatened everyone to keep off, and next minute she decided to organize dates for her.

'Yes. Well, Sarah obviously doesn't know anything

91

about the person I have become. I won't have an affair with a married man. Never again.'

'So you have had affairs, then?' Simon asked. His smile was almost cynical, though the crinkle at the corner of his wonderfully sensuous mouth had not changed at all. The golden honey-coloured eyes were dancing with laughter, as if lit from within, the way she loved.

She ignored him, busying herself with tossing the salad and checking the oven. There was a flash of lightning quickly followed by a huge crash of thunder.

'Damn,' Simon said suddenly, getting up from the stool he had perched on. 'I left my car roof open. I'd better close it before the whole thing is flooded.' He rushed out, cursing as he went. Jenna gave a cynical smile. Even the mighty Mr Andrews could a be a victim, it seemed. He returned a few seconds later, his pale denim shirt spotted with rain. He carried a holdall, the sort used to carry sports gear. It had the obligatory designer label, of course, she noted.

'Didn't want to leave this outside. Even with a locked car, there are opportunist thieves around. Especially when the weather turns sour.'

'I'd hardly think too many opportunists would be out here tonight. It's miles from anywhere.'

'I picked up a couple of other items this afternoon,' Simon said, ignoring her remarks. He pulled out a tiny portrait of a woman. Her long hair was piled on top of her head with dark tendrils hanging round a beautiful face. 'She reminded me of you,' he said with a smile.

'A long-lost great aunt, I expect,' Jenna replied with a grin, flattered by his comments despite herself.

He dumped the bag on the floor and picked up the wine bottle.

'Like a refill?'

She nodded. 'The food should be ready soon.'

Simon delved into his bag again and produced a bottle of Italian red wine.

'Should have opened this earlier to breathe. It'll go well with pasta. One of my favourites. Sarah always used to make it for me, and from the smell, I guessed right.'

'I'm not sure we ought to have another bottle,' Jenna remarked. 'You do have to drive home afterwards.' Simon made no comment but gave a slight shrug of the shoulders. Jenna stared, wondering what he was thinking.

She served the meal.

The tension she was feeling gradually lifted as they ate, undoubtedly aided by the wine. The thunder had subsided and now they could hear the rain hurling itself at the windows in the way that only a Cornish storm can do. It had got dark much earlier than usual.

'Sounds a bit wild out there,' Simon remarked. 'Let's hope it stops before I have to leave.'

Jenna stared at him. Why was it that every single thing he said seemed to suggest some double meaning? Perhaps it was just her imagination working overtime.

'Coffee?' she suggested when they had emptied all the dishes.

'That was wonderful,' Simon said, folding his napkin. 'And, yes, please, I'd love some coffee.'

'If you'd like to go through to the lounge, I'll put it on.'

He stood up, his head almost reaching the low ceiling.

'Mind the beam,' she warned. 'This place was built for smaller people than you.'

He smiled ruefully. 'There's more than one bit of my blood decorating this cottage, I can tell you. And in those days I hadn't even finished growing.' He left her and she heard him switch on the stereo. She smiled when she heard one of her old discs playing. She was immediately transported back to an evening when Simon had made her listen over and over as he'd described the intricacies of the funky music.

'Just listen to that technique,' he had said. 'Wait for the bass to come in . . . one, two, three.' And he'd beat the air before him in time to the music, his long dark curls flying around his head in a whirl. Whatever he was now, that young student she had once known had made a major impact on her life. She still had to be very careful not to allow herself to fall in love with him all over again, if it wasn't already too late.

'Or did I ever stop loving him?' she was forced to whisper. She picked up the coffee pot and two cups and went into the lounge.

CHAPTER 6

Simon was lying back on the big sofa. He had kicked off his shoes and his eyes were closed. He had switched on the low table lamps so the room was bathed in soft light. Jenna stared at him but he made no movement. She put the tray down and sat beside him, pouring the coffee.

'Listen, wait for the bass to come in,' he murmured. 'One, two, three . . .' He leapt up and played his air guitar just the way she had been recalling only minutes before. She laughed delightedly.

'Doesn't quite tally with the new image,' she remarked.

'It's so good to be here,' he said, joining in with her laughter. He pulled her to her feet again. He drew her close and began to dance to the slower beat now coming from the stereo. He held her close and she heard him draw in his breath. 'Jenna, Jenna. My lovely Jenna. Lord, how I've waited to do this.' He pressed his lips to hers, feeling the warm response. He held her tightly in his arms and it seemed the kiss lasted for ever. She felt herself floating in his heat and she was kissing him back, opening her lips slightly to allow his tongue to penetrate the soft folds of her mouth. She felt as if she was sinking into warm fluid, her bones melting until there was a danger that they would no longer support her. He drew away, holding her still in his arms.

'Well?' he asked. 'How's that schoolgirl crush feeling now?'

'Simon . . . Oh, Simon, I don't know what to say. I want you but I can't. Paula is . . . well, she's . . .'

'Hush, my darling. This is us. Us, and nothing to do with Paula or anyone else. I want you, Jenna. I want to make love to you all night, all day. For ever.' Jenna felt herself sinking once more, her own desire burning through her very bones. She was drowning in her love but she shouldn't. She knew she shouldn't, mustn't. No more married men, ever, she had promised herself. But at least this time she was not being conned, she told herself. At least this time she did know he was married.

Just as she was fighting what seemed to have become the greatest battle of her life, the whole house was suddenly plunged into darkness.

'Wow,' Simon exclaimed. 'How did you do that?' They both began to laugh, relieving the tension that had been growing.

'Must be the storm. The power was always going off at one time.'

'And I thought it was me! One thing's for certain: I'm not going to leave you alone in the dark. I'll give Tregarth a call to let them know I won't be back tonight.' He picked up the phone and dropped it back, cursing. 'The lines must be down. I'll use my mobile, if I can find my way back into the kitchen.'

'There's a candle here. Wait a sec.' Jenna groped her way through the inky blackness to the mantelpiece. She found the holder and some matches lying beside it, always ready for such an emergency. The light flickered and Simon took it, leading the way into the kitchen. He pulled the holdall open and groped among the things for his phone. He pressed a single button and spoke briefly.

'Fine,' he said as he shut it off. 'All sorted.'

'And do you always carry that thing?' she asked.

''Course I do. Can't afford to be out of reach at any time, in case of emergency.'

'So presumably they can always get you, wherever you are?'

'Naturally. But why all the interest?'

'Oh, I would have thought news of a cancelled dinner date would have reached you. Or wasn't that important enough for them to contact you?'

'Ah,' he said, smiling in the candlelight. 'Yes. I confess it all. Guilty. I did know Sarah wasn't going to be here, but she assured me that you would still be expecting me. Sorry. But I think that makes us even, doesn't it? You didn't tell me you had visited Tregarth and I didn't tell you about the mobile phone.'

Jenna shrugged. He had a point.

'Now, where were we?' He pulled her close again and began to renew his assault of her willing mouth. One hand pressed on the small of her back, drawing her close to his body. She felt the muscular chest against her breasts, crushing them to him. His hands slipped down, encasing her buttocks and pulling their bodies closer. Her body closer to his body. She felt his hardness through his jeans, pushing against her own centre of desire. He moved his mouth and she gasped. She felt herself panting, and her own excitement seemed to be matched only by his own. His other hand moved to caress her rounded breasts, feeling their taut nipples and sending waves of desire coursing through her body. She felt herself growing weak, as if without his support her body would simply melt to the floor.

'Jenna, Jenna.' he whispered. 'Come to bed with me, please.'

She hesitated. Her conscience was screaming, no, no, no. Her body was screaming slightly louder, yes, yes, yes. She had wanted this for as long as she could remember. The young student she had fallen in love with years ago had turned into the most exciting, the most devastating man she had ever met. No one else she had ever kissed had made her feel this way.

His thumbs were gently weaving circles of heat around her swollen nipples, constantly renewing the waves of desire that swept through her. He leaned down and brushed their raised centres with his lips. His hands pushed under the soft silk of her top and slid over her hot body to feel the lacy fabric of her bra. With an adept hand, he loosened the fastening at the back and the other hand caressed her scorching flesh. She gasped as she felt the contact, her mouth desperately seeking his once more. He pulled her even closer, until she felt his heart pounding against her own breast. His insistent tongue probed deeper and she was responding. Whatever her conscience might be trying to tell her was completely drowned by her desires, her needs. An image of Paula insinuated itself unwelcomely into her mind and she released her breath, pulling away as she did.

'Don't push me away. You can't stop now,' Simon whispered huskily. His eyes were glowing with an intensity that was ready to burn through her into the very depths of her being. She had never wanted anyone so much, never felt this all-consuming passion that threatened to destroy her.

'But Paula . . . your wife. I mustn't, Simon.'

'For Pete's sake, Jenna. She means nothing to me. She's only a part of my life because of some ridiculous promise I made, years ago. I can't be expected to live with one mistake for the rest of my life. And I promise you, she is not, nor will ever be my wife. Oh, Jenna. I'd forgotten how much I cared for you, how much I'd had to push you away from my thoughts when you were just a kid. When I first saw you again in Penzance last week, my first thought was that you had turned into some wonderful dream, the epitome of everything I'd always wanted. Please share your love with me. Don't push me away.'

It was the longest moment of her life. She fought with her conscience, her heart telling her that if she lost this moment she might never have another chance. Was Paula really his wife or could she truly believe what he was telling her? She looked into his eyes, knowing this very action was probably enough to seal her fate. The truth seemed to shine out of them. She held her breath before answering him. Her gentle kiss on his lips told him what he wanted to know. His mouth hardened in response and he pulled her body back to his.

'If you don't take me upstairs to your room, I promise I shall ravish you in an uncontrolled frenzy right here. Bonza may never recover from the experience.'

'What's it got to with Bonza?' She grinned, taking his hand and pulling him towards the stairs. She desperately wanted to believe everything that he said. She wanted him with all her being, and his assurances had satisfied her, at least for the present. She finally believed him. She held the flickering candle and carried it up the stairs. His wide, generous mouth held a grin of pure delight, and his anticipation of joys to come was apparent from the way he cleared the stairs behind her. Feeling suddenly shy, she opened her door, glancing back over her shoulder as if she needed to be certain that he was really following her.

The thunder had moved away but there were still distant crashes rumbling around the hills. The house remained in darkness, except for the single candle.

'You look even more lovely by candlelight,' whispered Simon. He leaned over to reach her hand and pressed it firmly to his lips. He gently took her first finger and sucked it gently into his mouth. Jenna felt powerful waves of desire rushing through her body. How could a simple gesture on a fingertip have such a profound effect? He smiled again, releasing her hand, and touched her swollen breasts. The nipples immediately responded again and became firm and erect. He pushed up her top and kissed the bare flesh as it appeared. She helped him to remove the garment, pulling away the loosened bra at the same time. He gasped at the sight of her generous breasts, released from their covering.

'Each part of you is more beautiful, more desirable than the last,' he managed to whisper, his voice thick with his own longing. She smiled gently, and shyly pulled at the buttons of his shirt. The dark curls of his chest were slightly damp from the oppressive heat that accompanied the thunder. It seemed somehow deeply intimate to feel his body heat this way. It enhanced his own unique smell, making him even more desirable to her as she ran her fingers through the soft curls. His hands wandered freely over the top part of her body until she could bear it no longer.

The exquisite torture of wanting had to be satisfied.

Tentatively, she pushed his hand down to her waist, helping him to remove the skirt and wanting him to touch those parts of her that were still screaming out for satisfaction. He smiled again, loving the freedom of spirit that allowed him to see so clearly what she wanted from him. He suddenly stood up, leaving her bereft. She gasped, for a moment thinking that he was about to leave her after all. Her eyes clouded. Had she made a fool of herself yet again? But he was simply unfastening his own jeans. They fell away, leaving him clad only in a pair of black silk boxer shorts. Her own flimsy pants barely covered her dark triangle of hair and he sank back onto the bed, his hands stroking, ever stroking her burning flesh. She ran her own hands over his smooth back, down to his boxers, and slipped her fingers inside. She sighed in pure delight as she felt him respond with a groan.

'Simon, dear Simon,' she murmured. 'How much I want you.'

'Slowly, darling. There can only ever be one first time. Make it last. Make it special.' She stiffened. Desperately she wished this was her own first time. But David had spoilt that. She felt a shiver run through her. She hated the possibility that she could disappoint this man whom she had loved since for-ever, it seemed.

'What is it?' he asked, sitting up a little as her tension reached him.

'I'm so sorry, Simon,' was all she could whisper. The tears filled her eyes, choking her throat.

'What is it? You can't stop now. I beg you. Don't turn me away now. Tell me what's wrong. Have I done something to hurt you?'

'It's just that . . .' She sobbed, unable to speak further.

'You can't tease me like this,' he said, suddenly sounding angry. 'You're surely not still thinking about Paula. I don't love her, I tell you. How could I?'

'It wasn't that. Though I am still a bit . . . well, you know.'

'I don't know. For heaven's sake, woman, what is the matter with you? I love you dammit, and you made me think you felt the same way. Is it this Kurt? Or is there someone else? Come on. You owe it to me.

At least tell me if I've done something wrong.' His hand raked his hair as if somehow he might discover an answer.

'You've done nothing wrong. It's me. When you said it was the first time, well, something inside me snapped. You see, it . . . well, it isn't the first time.' Her voice trailed away into a whisper. She couldn't bear to look into his eyes, feeling that in some stupid way she had betrayed him. But she had never really expected to meet him again, let alone find herself in this particular situation.

'Darling Jenna,' he breathed in relief. 'I didn't really expect it was your first time. But this is *our* first time. That was all I meant. Come here, you silly, adorable girl. I'm surprised there isn't a whole string of men beating at your door. Ready to haul me off. You are one very beautiful woman. Now, come here and let me prove it to you.'

Very gently, he pulled her close, and began the delicate process of arousing her once more, so slowly that she almost wanted to beg him to touch her, to enter her. He remained unmoved, and teased her with his fingers until she felt great waves of heat rushing through every part of her. She felt her hips beginning to move in a frantic motion, beating time with the rushes that drove her body towards its inevitable climax. And all the time Simon was touching and fondling, sucking her and gently squeezing whichever part of her he happened to be near. She felt she could die with pleasure, but only if he would move inside her soon, very soon, before she felt she would explode without him.

103

She put her hand on his hardness and gently guided it to the place she most wanted it to be. He gave a deep, shuddering sigh and began to thrust, harder, harder, until they were matching each other's movements with a compelling rhythm that sent them to dizzying heights. Finally the waves crashed on the shore and they both floated into a warm haze of satisfaction and contentment. They lay together, neither of them ready to move or willing to break the spell.

'Wow,' Simon said finally, as he rolled off her. The narrowness of her single bed meant that he almost fell onto the floor, but Jenna grabbed him, laughing.

'You're probably used to something a little larger than my small bed, but when you live in a cottage with rooms of this size, double beds are something of a luxury!'

'Any bed with you in it is something of a luxury. I hope I was up to standard?' he said, only partly in jest.

'That was simply mind-blowingly wonderful,' Jenna replied. 'And before you say any more, I'm not all that experienced.'

'I don't want to know,' he said calmly. 'Whatever your past, it's what you are today that's important. Your past has made you what you are. There's no point being jealous of it. Though I must say I might certainly regret lost opportunities.'

Jenna looked at him, at his body still glistening damply after all their exertions. 'I know what you mean,' she sighed. 'I think I've been trying to find someone who was just like you ever since that time when I was seventeen. No one came anywhere close.'

'I could do with a shower, if you don't mind,' Simon said, as the candle finally spluttered and went out.

'Have to be a cold one, if there's still no power. And be careful you don't slip, groping round an unfamiliar place in the dark.'

'Then you'll have to come with me to make sure I don't slip,' he said, gently drawing her to him again. 'I intend to make love to you all night . . . well, at least until we fall asleep with exhaustion. Jenna responded with a hug of pure delight. It sounded as if she had finally reached her own particular heaven. 'But first, that shower?' he added.

'I shall volunteer to go down and find another candle,' Jenna announced firmly. 'You can go and start cooling yourself off, ready for the next time. Won't be a minute,' she laughed, leaping out of bed and out through the door. She tried the light switch but there was still no power. In the kitchen, she groped in a cupboard and found a pack of candles. She lit one and turned to go back upstairs . . . to Simon and the joys of loving him and experiencing his beautiful body.

His mobile phone started to bleep and she picked it up from the kitchen unit where he had left it. She carried it upstairs, still bleeping away madly.

'Someone wants you,' she called through the sound of the shower. Evidently he had decided to start without her or the candle's illumination.

'Get it for me,' he called back. She pressed the button and spoke. A woman's voice replied.

'Who the hell are you? I'm calling Simon Andrews' private number.'

'He's unable to come to the phone at present. Can I give him a message?'

'I bet you're that cow from Penzance who's been pestering him.'

Jenna gulped. Pestering him? Cow, was she? No one, but no one was going to call her names without getting the sharp edge of her tongue. She'd suffered enough with David's wife haranguing her a couple of years ago.

'Now look here –' she began.

'You listen to me, you evil bitch. Simon is mine. Do you hear me? Marriage-wrecker! You just keep your claws off him. Nobody is going to drag him away from under my nose, least of all some bimbo like you. I hope you've got that clear. Don't think I haven't seen you snooping around here, making eyes at him. You can tell him Paula Andrews called. Paula *Andrews*! Got that?'

Before Jenna could even draw breath to reply, the phone was snapped off. She folded it thoughtfully, her expression grim. She gave a sudden, slightly hysterical chuckle, a relief from the ear-bashing she had just endured. She was standing in Sarah's cottage without a stitch of clothing on, with a candle flickering its gentle light, listening to Simon's wife, or whatever she was, giving her hell about spending time with her husband. And to think they had just made the most wonderful love ever. Even thinking about it made her feel weak. But the truth began to insinuate itself into her mind. The woman had accused her of being a marriage-wrecker. If Paula wasn't his wife, why was she so possessive about him? He said he had made a promise once in his life. He said it had been a mistake. Perhaps that mistake was part of his marriage vows. They were a promise, weren't they? A whole string of promises, she told herself, thinking of the words of the marriage ceremony.

Simon had duped her. He'd wanted sex with her and she'd fallen for his lies. All the time, much as she had enjoyed the experience, she had sensed that there was something wrong. But what next? He would be out of the shower in a few moments. What on earth was she going to say to him? She gave a shiver. Her whole body felt chilled to the bone, despite the heat and closeness of the evening. She reached round her bedroom door and found her wrap. She pulled it on, anxious to cover herself before Simon emerged from the bathroom. She heard the shower turned off and a crash followed by a curse.

'Did you find another candle?' he called out. 'If so, will you please bring it in here? I'm in danger of damaging myself irrevocably.' She pushed the door open, allowing the light to fall on Simon's dripping body. She felt weak at the very sight of him. His muscles had certainly filled out from the rather skinny student she remembered. His hips were slim and the once skinny legs had become well-shaped and muscular. He certainly kept himself in very good condition. There wasn't an ounce of spare flesh on his entire body.

'Finished the inspection?' he asked with a huge

grin. 'I hope my lady likes what she sees. Why don't you come over here and see if it feels the way you expected?'

She stared at him, feeling the blush creep across her cheeks. She so desperately wanted to do as he suggested, but she knew she must never again go near him. The very sight of his slim body, its muscles so firm and taut, made her feel almost dizzy with desire.

'You'd better dress and get out of here,' she said, as calmly as her screaming emotions would allow. Her tears, a mixture of anger and deepest hurt, were in danger of exploding at any moment. But she refused to allow herself to let him see her true feelings. During their lovemaking – if it could be graced with the name of love rather than sheer lust – she had probably given far too much away. She cursed herself for allowing her deepest feelings to be so exposed. Where had all her carefully rehearsed good intentions gone?

She became aware that Simon was staring at her.

'What is it? Who was on the phone? Come on, Jenna. Speak to me. What's wrong?'

'It was Paula. She wants you home.' She didn't trust herself to say more.

'The interfering . . . What did she say to you?' His eyes flashed with anger and his mouth had become a taut line.

'It doesn't matter,' Jenna replied, suddenly feeling overcome with weariness. 'Just get out of here.'

Simon rubbed the towel over his damp body, dropped it on the floor and came over to where she was standing before him. He reached out a hand to touch her cheek. She drew back as if scalded.

'Keep away from me. I don't want you touching me. Never again.'

'But, Jenna . . .'

'I mean it, Simon. I've decided that I'm going back to London tomorrow. I don't want to see you again, ever. I've been hurt enough already.'

She had mixed emotions when he brushed past her and pulled his clothes on roughly. His tight jeans clung to his damp body, making it difficult to get them on properly. She resisted the urge to help him, knowing that if she allowed herself too close she might fall again into his arms. She wanted him to go; she wanted him to stay, to tell her everything was all right. But she knew better. However he felt about Paula, however much he regretted their relationship, she had first claim on him and no way was Jenna going to be branded a marriage-wrecker.

Simon looked up as he fastened his shoes, as if he was about to say something, but she turned away. The rain was lashing at the windows once more, hammering its persistent beat and matching the pounding of Jenna's breaking heart.

'Foul night to have to drive,' remarked Simon.

'I'm sure you'll cope,' she retorted.

'Oh, yes, I'm sure I will. It's something I've grown used to over the years. Simon always copes. Right, well, I'll be on my way. I suppose it sounds corny to say thank you for a wonderful evening.'

'Thank Sarah. She prepared the dinner.'

'That wasn't what I meant and you know it. Still, if

109

that's how you feel.' He got up from the bed and came towards her. She shied away.

'Don't worry. I won't touch you, but you're standing in my way. If I have to leave, the doorway is much the quickest route.' His face was grim and his powerful jaw was clamped in rigid anger. Jenna drew back, feeling slightly foolish. He stormed down the narrow staircase and groped his way through to the kitchen to collect his bag. Jenna followed him down the stairs, candle still flickering in her hand. She pulled the door open. The fury of the storm lashed into the tiny hallway, soaking her in seconds. Her flimsy wrap clung to her, showing every sensuous curve of her body. Simon drew breath to speak, but thought better of it and went out into the darkness.

Jenna shut the door behind him and leaned against the solid wood. She was still shivering with the shock of all that had happened, the cold, wet wrap only adding to her discomfort. The candle had blown out when she had opened the door and now everywhere was totally, insistently black. She heard his car roar off and a great screech of tyres as he rounded the bend. Whatever she was feeling about him at this moment, she prayed that he didn't have an accident. She had sent him out herself. He had been drinking – probably far too much wine to drive – and the weather was particularly foul that night. He was also in a raging temper, everything fusing together to provide a lethal combination. A driver looking for an accident.

Whatever he had done or said, she knew that she

loved him in spite of everything, and she didn't want him to be hurt. She had rejected him for his own sake, and Paula's. But she would never forget Simon had lied to her. Perhaps she should call him on his mobile and try to reassure him that she would tell no one what had happened, that she would never again allow herself to be in a position to harm his marriage or his business in any way. But she had no idea of the number of his mobile, so that idea was out. Besides, surely she was only trying to find excuses to speak to him again? She had told him she didn't want to see or hear from him, so it would be a foolish, transparent gesture. She must do as she had suggested – never see him again. It was already too late for some things, and she had knowingly placed herself in a position to be hurt and to cause hurt even more.

She gradually became aware that she was clutching something in her hand. She stared at the object. Of all the idiots, she chastised herself. She was still holding his wretched phone. She had been so fraught with shock at the time that she had failed to hand it back to him. Now she would have to post it back to him. Perhaps he was so well-off he wouldn't even notice it was missing. She tried to console herself with the thought, but she knew that she was being ridiculous. Pulling herself together, she went back upstairs and into the bathroom. The room was suddenly bathed in light as the power came back on. At least she could now have a hot shower and warm herself up.

She scrubbed at herself until her flesh shone red, as

111

if she were trying to remove all traces of Simon from her body. Once she had some dry clothes on and a hot drink inside her, she would soon be feeling better.

The kitchen looked like a battle zone, with dirty dishes everywhere. Jenna scraped the bits of food into the bin and ran a bowl full of soapy water. She quickly washed up and cleaned the surfaces. If she was indeed returning to London next day, she had a great deal to do. She went upstairs and dragged the sheets off her bed and picked up the wet towels from the bathroom. She stuffed them into the washing machine, knowing it was probably too much for one load. But she wanted everything that reminded her of Simon, his smell, his body – everything – to be removed from the house. She was kidding herself if she thought she would ever forget this particular evening but removing the physical evidence was a start.

She decided to sleep on the sofa rather than refresh the all too recent memories of her own bed. She pulled an old travel rug over her and tried to sleep. She was in a light doze, her mind still buzzing round, when she heard a grinding noise from the kitchen. She hauled herself off the sofa and went to investigate. She was met by a stream of water pouring from the washing machine.

'Hell,' she cursed. Her own impatience had broken the machine. In a fury, she switched the machine off and collected a bucket and mop. 'Damn, damn, damn,' she fumed. 'Serves me right for being such a simple idiot.'

Tomorrow she would get back to a more civilized

existence. If she could totally immerse herself in her work, she would soon forget all about this temporary blip. Who could tell? Perhaps she should, after all, reconsider Kurt's offer. Perhaps it wasn't such a totally bad idea to marry the boss.

CHAPTER 7

Monday morning brought brilliant sunshine that
made everywhere become instantly hot. The paths
were soon steaming themselves dry after the previous night's unrelenting storm, though many of
the plants were flattened, beaten down by the
lashing of the rain. There was an air of destruction
and desolation around the normally immaculate
garden. Added to the mess inside the cottage,
following the washing machine disaster, Jenna realized that in fairness to Sarah she certainly couldn't
walk away from the place without making some
effort to restore it.

She telephoned an electrical repair man, who
promised to come and look at the washer some time
during the day. She set to work to empty out and
rinse the mass of wet washing. It was hard work, but
it served to take her mind off the other worries
churning round her mind. She hung the dripping
sheets and towels over the washing line, hoping the
hot sun would be enough to dry them. She mopped
ineffectively at the floor, noticing that some of the

floor tiles were already loosening. It was becoming more and more of a nightmare every moment.

Then Simon's mobile phone began to bleep. It was lying on the kitchen dresser and she stared at it in horror. There was surely only one person who would be calling? It had to be Simon himself. He must have realized he had left it behind. After a few moments, it stopped and she picked it up. Didn't these things have an answering service? She pressed a button and waited.

'Please enter your identification code,' said the impersonal recorded voice. She could not follow that instruction. She would simply have to package it up and return it to him. The main telephone rang and she heard the short message he left.

'I left my mobile. Be grateful if you could drop it back to me. Thanks.' The machine switched off.

'Don't waste time, will you? Come straight to the point, why don't you?' she snapped to the machine. Still, what more could she expect? There was simply nothing else that either of them could have said.

She tidied up the rest of the house and picked up the forgotten paperweight. It was certainly very beautiful. She felt certain it was a very special one, possibly even a French one. It could even be a Clichy or a Baccarat. But they could never be picked up at some antiques fair. They were much too rare. It was slightly battered, almost bruised-looking. That suggested it was probably quite old – a utilitarian object from the days when people had abused them as insignificant trifles. It had even been known for them to use them to hammer the odd nail or tack into chairs, no one ever realizing how valuable they might become one day. It was a pity, but she must send it back to Simon along with the telephone. Under the circumstances, she could not possibly accept such a potentially valuable gift from this man.

As Bonza rubbed himself against her bare legs, she leant down to fondle the huge cat. 'Oh, Bonza,' she said out loud. 'Life is just too difficult. Why is it the men you like most are always spoken for? Cats have much simpler lives. If they like something, they just take it and then walk away afterwards.' The solemn green eyes stared back. He stretched himself and walked away, his tail held high as he elegantly stepped across the still steaming lawn. Jenna sighed and went back into the house, to continue cleaning up the mess from the leaking washer.

It was the following day before she was able to leave the cottage and return to London. She sat on the train as the countryside flashed by. The long journey would give her time to adjust her mind to what lay ahead. She had bundled the paperweight and Simon's phone into her suitcase, unable to find suitable packing materials at Sarah's cottage. She could post them from London just as easily. Once that was done, she would have no further need to have anything more to do with Simon. She was unlikely to have any reason to go anywhere near Cornwall in the foreseeable future, especially if Sarah was to spend more time in London. She refused to allow Simon Andrews to make any difference to her life. After all, she loved her job, usually managed to have lots of fun and she had plenty of friends to spend time with. She could very nearly be convinced by her own words.

Jenna's flat felt empty and unwelcoming as she pushed the door open. Apart from her brief overnight visit before travelling to Cornwall, she had been away for several weeks. As she still had a couple or more days before her leave ended, she would have time for a bit of domesticity. She would give the place a thorough clean, maybe even plan to do some redecorating. If she kept busy, she tried to convince herself, she would soon forget all about Simon Andrews and get on with the rest of her life. She picked up the mail from the mat and glanced at the pile of envelopes. Mostly they were circulars, the odd bill and a couple of handwritten envelopes. Her answering machine was flashing and she pressed the play button, listening to the messages as she put the kettle on to make some much needed coffee. Amongst calls from various friends there were no less than two from Kurt. The second one sounded urgent.

'Saturday evening. Seven o'clock. Need you to call soonest. Job's come up and you're essential. Everyone else is stupid or deaf.'

She smiled at his dramatics. He should have been an actor himself. She made her coffee and sat down to open her post, to read as she drank. One of the handwritten letters was from an old schoolfriend and the other was from Kurt himself.

Dear Jenna,
I know you thought my proposal was some-

117

*thing of a joke . . . perhaps I wasn't entirely
serious at the time. But I do ask you to think
carefully. I believe love could grow from the
respect we share for each other. I have thought
about you constantly while you've been away.
You have the ability to make my life run
smoothly, to provide the companionship I
need, and I've missed you.*

Call me when you return.

My love, Kurt.

Jenna was completely flabbergasted. This was
Kurt in a seriously romantic mood, far different
from the usual Kurt who faced the public in a haze
of bluster and moodiness. She felt unexpectedly
touched by his words. How many women had he
really known well? She knew of one long-term
relationship he was supposed to have had, but more
recently she had come to realize what a very lonely
man he was. This was probably as close as he came to
a love letter, but it fell far short of her own idea of
how a man might ask her to marry him. What had
he said? '*You have the ability to make my life run
smoothly.*' That, actually, said it all. Love was only
ever a secondary consideration.

She thought of him and pictured his older man sort
of good looks. There was nothing wrong with him at
all. Many of the people he worked with would have
done almost anything for the sort of attention he was
offering to her. Then the image of Simon flashed
through her mind. Kurt did not compare favourably,
but then, if Simon wasn't even in the starting frame,

she shouldn't be spending her time thinking about him. It was so difficult not to think of him, though. He had rocketed back into her life after what she recognized had been many years spent dreaming about him. He had proved to be everything she had longed for and more. Kurt and Simon. Simon and Kurt. It was no contest. But, for now, all of her romantic thoughts needed to be pushed to one side. She had a job to do and her boss needed her talents. That was all Kurt would ever be, could ever be – her boss. She dialled his number.

'Hallo, Kurt? I'm back in London. I got your message. What's the job?'

'Jenna, great. Look, hop into a taxi and get round to my place, will you? I've set up a meeting for this evening at six. We'll have time to go through a few details first.'

'But Kurt, I've only just got back,' she protested. 'And my holiday still –'

'Great. Good job you're back early. See you in a few minutes.'

'But Kurt –' she complained, too late, as she realized that he had put the phone down. Where was his romantic side now? He was all work and professionalism. How could that be any basis for a marriage and possibly a family? And she did want a family one day, when she had truly found the right man. She had a vision of what a child of Simon's would look like. The same honey-gold eyes and dark hair. A miniature version of Simon as a boy, probably very skinny, and with long, black curly hair, just like his father. She sighed and went to have a shower.

This was her life now, constantly at Kurt's beck and call . . . or as often as she allowed. She didn't even have time to call Sarah to let her know she was back. But then, it might be sensible to wait and see exactly whereabouts in the world this new job was about to take them.

'Great to see you back,' Kurt said. 'Come in and meet the others.' He ushered her through the large hall and into his extremely modern, stylish lounge. Two men in dark suits and the inevitable silk ties rose as she entered the room. A smart younger woman sat with a clipboard. She smiled at Jenna and nodded as they were introduced.

'Greg Rawlings and Colin Johnson – and Sylvia, isn't it? These gentleman are from Hudson International, Jenna. They've asked us to make a management film for them. We've managed to get Alistair Dodds to agree to play the lead role. Gentlemen, this is my right hand, Jenna Brown.'

She smiled and shook hands with everyone. She was glad she had changed from her travel-stained clothes into one of her smarter casual outfits.

'Right, let's get down to business.' Kurt directed questions at his clients, wasting no time. Being the thorough professional he was, he seemed to be asking for every possible answer they were likely to need, about the business and all aspects of the film.

Ever the professional herself, Jenna listened carefully, making a few notes but relying largely on her excellent memory for detail. It sounded as if the project might be fun. The film would be slightly longer than their usual stuff, a real chance to develop something. Alistair Dodds was also some coup. Most females in the country had been in love with him since his last TV series. The dashing good looks and all-action image, even though he was believed to be in his forties, were enough to turn anyone's head. She would be working with him herself for several days. If that didn't help her through this difficult patch, then nothing would.

'Right. I think that's everything,' Kurt said, after a couple of hours. 'Perhaps I can take everyone to dinner?' The two men smiled their acceptance but Sylvia asked to be excused.

'I have to get back, I'm afraid. But thanks for inviting me.' She seemed a tense young woman Jenna thought. Pity. It might have been nice to have another female on the team. She often needed an ally.

'Phone Jay's for me, will you, darling?' Kurt asked Jenna. 'Looks like it's a table for four. Half an hour.' Jenna obediently made the call and then, leaving the men to chat, showed Sylvia out.

'I don't know how on earth I'm going to cope with getting away, even for a few days while the filming takes place. My mother will never manage alone. She's unwell. Can't be left. But if I refuse to go, I might lose my job,' confided Sylvia.

'Can't you get back at nights?' asked Jenna.

'What, all the way from Cornwall? I don't think so, somehow.'

'Cornwall?' squeaked Jenna, shocked. 'What's Cornwall got to do with anything?'

'The film's being shot there. But of course. You haven't seen the script yet. It's all analogous to the sea and its various moods. Quite clever, actually.'

'I see.' Jenna spoke absent-mindedly. 'I just came back from Cornwall today. Seems I shouldn't have bothered.'

'Sorry, but I must go now,' Sylvia said. 'I look forward to seeing you again soon. Once I can sort my mother out, of course.'

'Perhaps she could come too. Have a holiday while you work.'

'If only,' smiled Sylvia. 'But I simply couldn't afford it. Besides, the unfamiliar surroundings wouldn't do much for her condition.'

Jenna felt suddenly sorry for the girl. What a burden she must have to carry. She returned to the lounge, where the men were standing waiting. Kurt was in an expansive mood, refilling wine glasses almost before anyone had time to empty them.

'You'll be delighted with our work, I'm sure. Jenna, here, is an absolute wonder – memory like a computer. Anything you want to know, check with her. She always has the answers.'

One of the men came over to chat to her. He was obviously in a mood to flirt and she made her usual cool responses . . . putting him off in the nicest possible way. She was becoming quite expert at fending off unwelcome attentions.

Kurt was smiling indulgently, almost like a proud father showing off his daughter's talents, Jenna realized with a start. And he thought they could have a basis for a marriage? Who was he trying to kid?

They walked round the corner to the restaurant, a favourite of Kurt's, not least because of its closeness to his apartment. It meant he could always drink and walk home without any problems.

'So, where are we shooting this epic?' Jenna asked conversationally.

'Great little hotel in Cornwall. It's exactly what we want. They sent out brochures recently – to every company in the country, from what I can make out. Very go-ahead sort of place. Loads of facilities,' Kurt replied.

'One of our guys went there for a holiday at the end of last year,' Greg said. 'He was very impressed and suggested it would be just right for the sort of thing we are planning.'

'And the script-writer knows the area well, so it all fell into place,' Kurt concluded. 'The brochure was so good, I was able to see right away that it was exactly what we wanted. Don't even need to make preliminary visits. The stills are quite good enough.'

'Seems like it's all settled, then,' Jenna said miserably. She had made her escape from her beloved Cornwall so that she could stop thinking about the man who had come back into her life, but to no avail, it now seemed.

'We'll be travelling down tomorrow morning to get everything finalized. The shooting schedule starts in about a week. Jenna can sort out the interior shots with the hotel people and suggest some locations we might use. It's your home territory, isn't it, Jenna?'

Jenna felt herself growing cold. It could never, not possibly, be the one place she had decided never to

123

visit again. Not Tregarth Manor, surely? That would be stretching coincidence just too far.

'Depends where it is.'

'Place near Tintagel. Shades of King Arthur and all that. Do you know it, Jenna?' asked the man who had been flirting with her, the one called Greg.

'Slightly. I had my home further west. I know a few places near there,' she added miserably. It was so impossible, but of all the places in the world they might have chosen she just knew it was Tregarth. Brochures to every company in the country were exactly Simon's style. No wonder the place was proving such a success.

'Let's eat. Come on everyone,' Kurt ordered. He was loving every minute of his role as chief of the company. He ushered them into the restaurant and ordered champagne. He could afford it. The contract would be worth many thousands of pounds, even allowing for costs.

They ate well, with good food and wine flowing freely.

'Will you be going to Cornwall for the filming?' Jenna asked the two representatives for the company.

'Unfortunately not. We may sneak a flying visit, but time is always short. If we make it, you must show us round, seeing that you know the area.'

Jenna smiled. 'You haven't told me the name of the place yet. It's a surprisingly large county, and there are hundreds of hotels.'

'Tregarth Manor, it's called' Kurt said cheerfully. But inside she had already known. There was no obvious way out of it, not that she could see. This

124

would really give Paula something to crow about.

She gave a shiver as she pictured what might lie ahead. She was possibly about to face the worst weeks of her life. She clung to the forlorn hope that she had somehow made a mistake. She had misunderstood. But a heavy feeling was settling at the pit of her stomach. She felt utterly exhausted, but then, she had been travelling most of the day and she had slept little the last couple of nights. She could scarcely believe it was only the night before last that everything had happened . . . the storm, Simon, Paula's phone call. She did allow herself a tiny secret smile as she remembered the pleasures of loving Simon's beautiful body. It made her feel hot deep inside, simply thinking of it. Then reality once more sent a cold shiver through her. The venomous words of Paula had ruined everything.

How could Simon have lied to her? Had she really been gullible enough to fall for his words? Naturally, any married man would deny his marriage under those circumstances. Men did that sort of thing to get what they wanted. If they were known to be married, they'd say their wives didn't understand them. If no one knew they could pretend they were still single. Even the practice of calling them 'Mr' managed to hide their marital status. Unlike women. They had to be 'Miss' or 'Mrs'. Attempts to use 'Ms' seemed to have backfired as people got another wrong impression.

She tried to push the teeming thoughts from her mind and make herself concentrate on her food. Seated next to Greg, she became aware that his thigh was pressing close to hers. His hand touched her knee and she turned to look at him.

'Have you dropped your napkin?' she asked, seemingly in all innocence.

He looked uncomfortable for a moment.

'I must have done,' he replied with a grin, and delved under the table. He ran his hand the length of her calf as he sat up again, with a supercilious smirk on his face.

'Perhaps you'd like a lift home? I can drop you off on my way,' Greg suggested.

'I'd hate to take you out of your way. Your wife will probably be worried if you're late.'

'My wife is very understanding. She's only too pleased to have the unlimited budget I provide, so she knows she can't complain if I have to work late.'

Jenna was beginning to dislike his self-satisfied smirk.

'Then you are indeed a fortunate man. I find that so many men complain their wives don't understand them at all.' She gave a sweet smile and folded her napkin. 'Now, if you will excuse me, gentlemen, I have a busy day ahead. Besides, I have to unpack from today's journey and start again for tomorrow's, and all without finishing my leave.' She threw a glance at Kurt, making sure he was aware of her discomfort.

'I'll pick you up at nine-thirty,' Kurt said. 'We can talk on the way. I'll have a driver so we can work undisturbed. Goodnight, darling. Get a taxi home. Can't have such a valuable commodity as you walking the streets at this time of night.'

'It would be no trouble to drive you,' Greg said again, half rising from his seat.

'I shall be fine, thanks,' Jenna insisted. Apart from wanting to get away from him, he had drunk far too much to be driving anyone. 'Goodnight, everyone.' As quickly as she could, she left the restaurant and prayed she would get a taxi quickly.

What a terrible mess she had got herself into. She would be seeing Simon and Paula together, every day for possibly three whole weeks or more. She would have Kurt with her the whole time, and possibly the awful Greg as well. The one potentially bright spot amidst all this was Alistair Dodds. He was attractive enough to have most of the female population swooning at his feet, even if he was the wrong side of forty. He might be fun to be with, or, as often happened with successful stars, he could turn out to be sleaze of the month.

Wearily, she turned her key and began to unpack her bag. She stuffed her dirty clothes into the washer and set her alarm for six. If Kurt thought they could work on the long journey all the way down to Cornwall, he'd be lucky! She was so tired she doubted she would stay awake for much more than a few minutes. But somehow she had to find a way of coping for the next few weeks.

Despite the turmoil in her mind, Jenna slept heavily. She awoke feeling slightly hungover, though it was through tiredness rather than excess alcohol. She hauled herself out of bed and did a few quick exercises – the routine she had been neglecting lately. She showered, and dressed in comfortable clothes for travelling. She took the washing out of the machine, mentally thanking Sarah again for the gift of the washer-drier a couple of Christmases ago. She was also glad of modern fabrics that survived with little or no ironing.

Though it was almost June, she packed several warm outfits, knowing well the vagaries of the British weather, especially in Cornwall. She would need masses of different clothes for the inevitable socializing, as well as more practical stuff for work. She would also try to get plenty of swimming in, not only for the exercise but also to occupy her as much as possible. That way she was unlikely to spend quite so much time avoiding meetings with Simon or the dreaded Paula. It wasn't going to be easy for them, having her staying at their hotel.

At nine-thirty sharp, her doorbell rang. It was Larry, one of the company drivers.

'Morning, Jenna,' he breezed. Obviously he had managed an earlier night than she had. 'Kurt asked me to collect you first. Seems he had rather a heavy evening.'

Just another problem to add to my list, thought Jenna. The prospect of a grumpy boss for a five-hour journey or more did not appeal much.

'Hope you've got a good supply of Alka-Seltzer on board,' she said cheerfully. 'We could be making more stops than usual. OK. Let's get this show on the road.'

Larry picked up the larger of her two cases and stowed them in the boot. She locked the door and briefly wondered, once more, why she bothered to keep her flat in London at all.

'Cornwall, here we come,' she muttered.

The large car ate up the miles, and with Kurt sleeping off his hangover Jenna was able to relax a little herself. But however desperately she tried to push her mind into working mode, an image of Simon always crept into her mind. Did he realize she would be a part of the company booking? Of course he couldn't know. He would surely have mentioned it if he *had* known. The usual practice was a block booking for so many rooms and facilities, all in the company name. No way could Simon know she would be among this group. Only when they actually registered as individuals would her name appear on any lists.

They stopped for lunch in Exeter and Kurt outlined the plans for the next few days. It looked like being fairly hectic. It was just as well, she thought grimly.

'Now then, my dear,' Kurt said when they were once more back on the road. 'Have you given any more thought to my little idea? I did write to you when you were away. I did miss you.'

Jenna stared at him blankly for a moment. His casual tone made it sound exactly like some work-related subject. He smiled and nodded. 'You know what I mean.' Jenna gave a start of realization. This was so typical of the man. 'Kurt, I don't know what to say. You don't love me, for a start.'

'So what is this love you keep talking about? I see the most important thing in any partnership is to get on with each other. You're a lovely young woman . . .

129

which is an added bonus as far as I am concerned.'

Jenna laughed. 'Thanks for the compliment, but I still say you don't love me at all. I'm an efficient deputy for you and I'm good at organizing you. You don't have the first idea of what I'm really like – as a person, I mean. We only ever meet when we're working. Even our social encounters are purely for work.'

'Have dinner with me tonight. A personal dinner, nothing to do with work.'

Jenna's heart sank. This was going to be difficult. She did expect to have some work to do this evening, and she was already desperately tired. Besides, Simon would probably want to talk to her, to set out the way they would have to cope with things. She didn't want to be fully booked up the moment she arrived. There was a great need to clear some air before this project began in earnest.

'We'll find time to talk,' she promised him. 'But, Kurt, please don't keep pushing me all the time. Take some time to get to know me the person, not just your assistant.'

'I thought we could spend some time chatting through the locations,' Kurt said, snapping back into his working mode. 'We'll discuss it over dinner this evening, once we've had some time to look around.'

It was hopeless, Jenna realized. One way or another, Kurt was determined to keep her fully occupied. Perhaps it was just as well. At least Simon would realize that it was nothing to do with her, this sudden arrival at his hotel. The coincidence would take some believing, and she guessed that dear Paula would most certainly capitalize on the situation.

'Nice scenery,' Kurt said conversationally as they drove deeper into the heart of Cornwall. They were nearing their destination and were able to glimpse the sea every now and then.

'Excuse me,' Larry said, turning round as he slowed down. 'Do you actually know where this place is? I have an idea there's probably a short-cut, and if you do know it, we could save ourselves some time.'

'I'm not sure from this direction. Whenever I've been, it was from the west.'

'Do you mean you've actually stayed here?' Kurt said incredulously.

'Not stayed, but I have eaten here a couple of times.'

'Why on earth didn't you tell me? I could probably have saved hours of planning. You'll be able to tell me whether the various locations are suitable.'

'You'll be able to see for yourself soon enough,' Jenna said, a trifle tetchily. 'I suggest you take the next left, Larry. It isn't far now.'

Soon the gates at the end of the drive came into view. The avenue of birches rustled their leaves in the afternoon sunlight.

'Not bad,' Kurt allowed as the car swept to a halt, spraying gravel as the wheels came to a standstill. 'Get the luggage, Larry. We'll get this show on the road – or off it, perhaps I should say.'

Jenna smiled feebly. Her heart was thumping madly, as if it was trying to make a burst for independence from her very ribcage. Kurt pushed the door open and walked into the hall and reception area. The woman behind the desk was all smiles.

'Welcome to you, sir. We're delighted to meet you and hope you will enjoy your stay.'

The smile froze as Paula's eyes met Jenna's.

'You!' she breathed, a hint of a snarl in her voice.

'Good – good afternoon,' Jenna managed to stammer, hoping desperately that there would not be a scene. To her credit, Paula managed to remain calm and went about the business of registration forms.

'And exactly who is to have bar credit, sir?' she asked. 'I mean, who will be allowed to sign for drinks etcetera?

'Just myself and Jenna, here. The rest of my people will be down next week. They'll get meals and rooms on the company, but I certainly don't trust them with a blank chequebook.'

'Very well. If you would both put your usual signatures on this form, we can arrange it as you wish.'

It seemed that Kurt hadn't noticed anything at all of the tension between the two women, thought Jenna. Paula was really going to hate having to be polite to her, having to wait on her and treat her with the respect needed for a client. Perhaps it might not be as bad as she was expecting after all.

'Mr Simon asked me to notify him of your arrival,' Paula continued, speaking to Kurt and studiously avoiding eye contact with Jenna. 'He wanted to invite you to dine with him to give you both the opportunity to discuss your exact requirements.'

'Great. We'll meet in the bar around seven, shall we, Jenna?'

'I think Mr Simon was intending to meet with just yourself, sir. He asked for a table for two.' She had a smirk on her face as she spoke, but Jenna had no intention of showing any discomfort.

'I need an early night anyhow,' she said, as cheerfully as she could. 'I might have something sent up to my room.' It would actually be an enormous relief, she thought. And it would give Kurt and Simon a chance to get to know each other without having her in the way.

'Won't hear of it,' Kurt was blustering. 'Jenna is my right-hand man. Can't do anything without her help. Make it a table for three and we're in business. And no arguments from you, madam,' he added, nodding towards his assistant.

This promised to be working up towards being one of the worst evenings of her life.

CHAPTER 8

'Nice place you've got here Simon,' Kurt was saying expansively as Jenna joined the two men in the bar. After she had finished unpacking, she had spent half an hour pushing herself up and down the swimming pool. The sheer physical effort had fully occupied her mind and she felt surprisingly refreshed, in spite of her earlier tiredness.

Simon had his back to her, but even the sight of his dark suit and neatly styled hair was enough to set her heart pounding. He was perched on a stool at the bar and turned as Kurt smiled at her.

'Simon, I'd like to introduce my assistant. Jenna Brown, meet Simon Andrews. Lucky chap is the owner of this place.'

The look of blank amazement crossing the handsome features almost made Jenna want to laugh. Paula had obviously not told him that she was among the film company who had booked this stay. She was about to say they didn't need any introduction when Simon spoke first.

'Miss Brown. What a pleasure it is to meet you. I

do hope your stay will be a pleasant one – and a successful one, of course. We've been hoping to expand and diversify, so your company doing the filming is particularly welcome. Do you know the area at all?'

So that was the way he wanted to play it. Very well, she would go along with his game. Whatever his reason was, he was pretending they didn't know each other.

'My home isn't far away. I have dined here a couple of times. But this time, of course, it's business.' Superb, she thought, watching him at work. He had taken her hand as politely as he would any guest. The slight delay in releasing it had taken but a moment, and passed quite unnoticed by anyone other than herself. It had just been sufficient to set her heart pounding yet again. She caught a brief scent of his aftershave, a smell she could never forget. Perhaps if they were to pretend they didn't know each other, it could make things easier. For a brief second she could imagine the pleasure of meeting him for the first time, of putting the clock back to the time before they had met again, only a brief week ago. How very different it might have been now. His eyes danced with suppressed laughter, as if he had some secret joke he was enjoying.

'Right. I expect you're tired after your journey. I suggest we have an early dinner and we can begin to organize everything you need tomorrow. I am at your disposal, Kurt. Anything I can do to help, just ask. We're very excited about the whole project.'

Gradually, helped by the wine, Jenna was able to

relax, and even began to enjoy the meal. Simon was being thoroughly charming to both of them, and Kurt seemed to be lapping up the attention. The food and wine were delicious, and, best of all, there was no sign of Paula throughout the whole evening. Maybe, just maybe, it was going to be all right, after all.

They were reaching the coffee stage when a waiter came and discreetly spoke to Simon. A slight flicker of annoyance crossed his face before he politely excused himself.

'Please forgive me, but I'm needed elsewhere. Unless there is anything else? Well, then, I'll say goodnight to you and see you tomorrow.' He rose and smiled as he left them. Jenna watched him until he was out of sight.

'Nice bloke, isn't he? I should think he'll make a real go of this place. He's got the right attitude to his guests, though I do think I might have to watch out for you. I noticed him staring at you several times this evening. Good-looking chap too. Perhaps we might find him some little part in the film. It sounds as if he had to work hard for all this. I say, have you seen that sideboard over there? I'd swear it was a real antique.'

'You're probably right. The place is stuffed with them. Look, Kurt, I'm nearly falling asleep where I sit. Do you mind if I get off to bed now?'

'How about a brandy or something? A nightcap? We could go upstairs to my room. I'm only next door to you. Then, if you really want to retreat to your own room . . . Well, haven't we talked about getting to know each other better? Isn't this a heaven-sent opportunity?'

'For heaven's sake, Kurt. I've told you, there really isn't any future in this. I'm sorry, I'm truly exhausted. I desperately need an early night. No nightcap; no getting to know anyone. OK? You've never given me any problems before when we've been away. Please don't start now.'

He gave a shrug and rose as she left the table.

'Goodnight darling,' he said loudly, catching her hand and trying to pull her close to him. She brushed cheeks with him, desperate to get away before anyone else noticed his clumsy gesture. As she turned to the stairs she saw Paula, standing with a smile on her face. She pursed her lips together, giving Jenna a knowing nod of the head as she passed. Obviously she had seen Kurt's peck on the cheek and was about to capitalize on it. Doubtless she'd soon go running to Simon with news of such scandalous behaviour. At this particular moment, she simply didn't care.

She was just sinking into the first wave of sleep when someone knocked gently at her door. For a moment she wondered where she was, but, quickly realizing the whole mess was far from being some dream, she sat up.

'Who's there?' she called out.

'It's me, Kurt. Just wondered if everything was all right.'

'I'm asleep,' she called back. 'See you tomorrow.' There was a pause, and after a few minutes she heard the sound of a door clicking shut. Thank goodness, was her last waking thought.

Feeling thoroughly refreshed, Jenna rose early the next morning. She slipped a towelling robe over her bikini. A swim before the day got going in earnest seemed like a good idea. The pool was still and clear, the blue water immaculate and undisturbed. She left the robe on a chair before diving into the refreshing water. Her slender body cut through the water cleanly and she was soon swimming strongly, length after length, until she began to feel breathless. She floated on her back, her long hair streaming like fronds of seaweed on the sea's surface. She stared up at the glass panels in the roof of the old converted barn. The sky was a perfect blue. It was going to be a hot day. She hoped Kurt's plans included a little outdoor work, like looking for some outdoor locations.

'I didn't expect to find a mermaid in my swimming pool,' said an unmistakable voice from the end of the barn. Jenna gave a start. She had been fully occupied by her thoughts and had been quite unaware of anyone else coming into the room. She stood up and smiled at Simon, aware of a sudden trembling that was spreading through her whole body.

'Good morning. Mr Andrews, isn't it?' she said, with just a hint of sarcasm.

'Miss Brown, I believe.'

'Why on earth didn't you admit we're old friends?' she asked.

'I don't know. I suppose I thought it might be easier for you this way.'

'I don't know why. It seems to add even more problems to the whole silly business.'

'You're right of course. I suggest we have breakfast together and talk it through. We really can't go on like this, Jenna. We do have to work together for the next few weeks, after all.' His voice held a note of urgency. She stared at him. Even in a pair of jogging pants and a tee-shirt he looked incredibly sexy. Lucky Paula. He threw off his clothes to reveal a pair of tight swimming trunks and dived into the water. His powerful arms cleaved the water and his long body moved past Jenna with a speed that would easily outrun her own. He swam back to her, scarcely even breathing faster than usual. He certainly kept himself fit.

'You beat me to it this morning. I usually get here long before anyone else is even stirring. It was a nice surprise.'

'I have to do something to counteract all this rich hotel food. I like to work out or swim at least once a day,' she said, hoping she wasn't showing the ridiculous trembling her body seemed to adopt whenever she got close to this man.

'Very commendable. Now, about this breakfast?'

'I have to meet my boss, but thanks for the offer,' she replied.

'Ah, the highly esteemed Kurt. Yes, of course. Did you give him the answer he wanted?'

'I don't know what you mean.'

'I thought you said he'd proposed to you?'

'Oh, that. Of course not,' she snapped. 'I don't love him.'

'But you do have adjoining rooms. He demanded it especially. Very convenient. But then I suppose you don't need to love someone to . . . well, I'm sure you know what I mean.'

'Oh, for goodness' sake. Don't be so stupid! He always *does* have a room next to mine when we're away on location. We do have work to do, you know. Things to discuss. He doesn't want to have to spend hours wandering round looking for me.'

'I'm sure he doesn't. What does it matter anyhow? Why should I care who you go to bed with? It's nothing to do with me, as you made perfectly clear.' He turned and swam away, moving swiftly through the water with barely any splashing. She watched him for a moment, then swam one more length herself before climbing out of the pool. She had a quick shower and wrapped herself in the towelling robe once more.

'I'll try not to disturb you again. Perhaps I'd better come in even earlier tomorrow,' she called as she left. Simon made no response but continued his endless lengths across the pool until she had left.

'Damn,' he muttered. 'Why should I care so much? She's just another guest, after all.' He wondered exactly who he was trying to convince.

Kurt was predictably expansive at breakfast. He was looking forward to the day's work and ordered a huge cooked breakfast.

'Come on, Jenna. Get something sustaining inside you. You could do with putting on a bit of weight.'

'You're beginning to sound like my aunt,' she protested, helping herself to a large bowl of stewed fruit.

'That won't keep you going all day,' he said. 'I doubt we'll have time to stop for lunch. Besides, there probably won't *be* anywhere to stop once we're away from the hotel.'

Jenna laughed. 'Honestly, Kurt. Where do you think we are? This is Cornwall, land of holidays. There are beach cafés, restaurants, fish and chip shops in places you wouldn't believe. The one thing holidaymakers always need is masses of food.'

'That's as may be, but I think we should order a packed lunch just to be sure. Organize it, will you? Larry will be driving us, so make sure there's plenty. Oh, and we might as well have a decent bottle or two. Something cold.'

Jenna finished her fruit, ate a piece of toast and left Kurt to his plate of bacon, eggs and heaven alone knew what else. That man was destined for an early heart attack, Jenna told herself. She went to Reception to order the packed meal.

'I'm sorry, madam, but orders are normally taken the previous day. We can provide you with something, of course, but it will take a little time, I'm afraid.' Jenna recognized the voice of the man she had spoken to on the telephone.

'We need to leave by ten,' she said. 'I'd appreciate it if you could have it ready by then.' The man glanced at his watch doubtfully, before speaking.

'Chef is still busy with breakfasts, but I'm sure we can arrange something. Leave it with me.'

'Is there a problem?' asked a voice behind her. Would she ever be able to move anywhere without Simon appearing at her heels?

'I don't think so,' she replied with a sweet smile. 'Everything seems to be under control. And I will try to order in good time on the next occasion,' she added to the man she always thought of as the butler.

'Thank you, madam. It would be appreciated. Now, if you will excuse me, I shall take your order to Chef.'

'Make certain everything is the very best,' Simon instructed. 'We have to make sure things are perfect for Miss Brown and her . . . companion.' His wonderful eyes flashed with light and he gave her a smile which seemed to turn her stomach right over. If only he meant it sincerely, and that smile was an expression of something . . . she knew she would be in seventh heaven.

But always Paula was looming in the background, and, however much their relationship might have deteriorated, she had laid her claim on Simon. If Jenna was foolish enough to allow her own feelings to gain the upper hand, she would be guilty of the worst sort of behaviour . . . the sort of behaviour she would despise in anyone. The trouble was, she thought, he was just her sort of man. Funny, attractive personality, good-looking, and, though she didn't rate it as especially important, he was obviously very rich. The latter was really indicative of the part of him that made him succeed. It was his tenacity, his ability to make things work that attracted her, and doubtless hundreds of other women too. Paula must really have some hold over him to keep him the way she did. Being thoroughly catty, Jenna just didn't think she seemed to be his type. But then, one never knew what went on behind the closed doors of any marriage.

'Off somewhere nice today?' Simon asked, sounding like the perfect hotelier.

'Working, as usual,' she replied with a wry grin. 'Checking on suitable sites for the film. It's surprisingly hard work,' she added defensively.

'I'm sure it is. The picnic should help, especially if you take a couple of bottles of wine. Champagne, is it to be?'

'Are you going to snipe the entire time we're staying? If so, I might just try to get transferred to somewhere else.'

'Snipe? Me? I wouldn't be bothered. I was merely ensuring you have exactly what you want. Now, if you'll excuse me, I have work to do.'

'Simon . . . I . . . Oh, never mind.' She turned back to the dining room and sat down with Kurt. She poured another coffee and smiled brightly at her boss.

'So, have you decided exactly what we're looking for, today?'

'It's certainly a beautiful county,' Kurt proclaimed later that afternoon. They had driven many miles and looked at a large number of possible sites. Jenna had been busy recording them on an instant camera and video, each place carefully noted and a few details written in the log so they could easily return to set up the various shots. The cameramen had the final say over the technical points, but Kurt knew what he wanted as far as the actual settings were concerned.

'It will be a case of finding the right weather

conditions. It looks set fair for some time, so we might have some waiting around to do for the storm scenes.'

'Ironic, isn't it? Most people coming to visit Cornwall complain if there's any bad weather, and here you are, demanding storms.' Jenna had enjoyed the day, visiting places that were new to her as well as some old favourites. 'It always amazes me how there are still new places to discover even when I've been living here for half my life.'

'I'm surprised you haven't run into Simon before now,' Kurt said, gazing intently at Jenna for some clue as to her tension whenever she met Simon. He had known her for a long time and believed he could usually pick up on her moods. She drew in her breath. Was this the moment to tell him?

'Are we ready to go back now, sir?' Larry interrupted. 'Only, some of the technicians will be here this evening and I thought you'd want to be around when they arrive.'

'Quite right,' said Kurt. 'Thanks for reminding me. OK, Jenna. You got all you need? Shall we make for home?'

The rest of the crew turned up before dinner. They were staying in one of the many converted outbuildings, where Simon offered self-catering facilities for families who preferred it to living in the hotel itself. Besides, they did tend to get a bit rowdy at times, and, being such a close-knit group, might cause complaints from other guests at the hotel. The camera crew, sound engineers and Kurt went into one of their huddles after dinner. They pored over

144

the shots Jenna had taken and discussed the technicalities. The actors wouldn't be arriving until the following week, so they would be able to get everything organized well before then.

Jenna wandered away from the group, out into the lovely grounds of the hotel. They seemed to stretch away for miles and the warm evening made her feel relaxed. She wandered among the rosebeds and further away, into the wild garden. She loved the wild flowers that grew everywhere. It reminded her of the cliffs near to Sarah's cottage, where each season brought its own special colours to the land.

'You managed to find my favourite place, I see.' Simon again. He was sitting peacefully on a bench, partially hidden by tumbling rambler roses just coming into bloom. His book lay on his lap, unopened. 'If I didn't know better, I'd believe you were deliberately following me,' he said cheerfully.

'Likewise. Wherever I go, you seem to find me.'

'Perhaps it's simply that we share so many tastes. Why don't you sit down for a few minutes? Or perhaps your boss expects you to be working absolutely every hour of the day.'

Jenna glared and sat down beside him. She knew she was playing with fire, just by allowing herself to get this close to the man, but he had goaded her. She deliberately took several deep breaths, as if trying to clear her head.

'This is silly, Jenna. We simply must talk. We have to clear the air.'

'Fine by me. Carry on. What did you want to talk about?' she asked.

'We have to get things cleared up between us. When we made love, I wanted to tell you how very special you were . . . are. Very special. In fact, I wanted –'

'Please, Simon. It's no good. You know it isn't. I couldn't help coming here, to this particular hotel. Believe me, if I could have got out of it I would. It was the very last place in the entire world I would have chosen to visit. If you weren't so keen to send out your brochures . . . But you've seen what Kurt's like. "Enthusiastic" falls well below my description of him. Once he's got an idea, he worries at it until it succeeds.'

'And does that include you?'

'I don't understand,' she said, genuinely puzzled.

'Will he keep on worrying at you, until you give in?'

'That's only a phase he's going through. I'm certain he'll get over it.'

'I doubt it,' Simon said a touch grimly. 'He looks pretty determined to me. Do you actually realize how hard it is for me to sit by and watch what he's doing to you?'

'I don't see what it's got to do with you. You have no rights over me.'

'But Jenna . . . Damn you, woman! Perhaps this will give you some idea of why I feel it has something to do with me.' He leaned over and pulled her close. Angrily, he clamped his arms around her waist and drew her even closer. His lips were demanding, fierce and hungry. They pressed against her own in what could only be described as a frenzy.

She tried to push him away, but powerful arms held her fast. She tried to avoid the contact of his generous mouth, but she was not strong enough either to escape or to refuse his advances. The insistent pressure on her mouth grew, and before she could gain any sort of control over herself she was melting against him. She parted her lips to allow his tongue inside her mouth, and groaned gently as she felt all her desires rush to fill every inch of her body. He pulled her down to the ground with him. The springy turf was soft beneath them and they rolled, as if playing some game. But this was no game. He was in deadly earnest. He wanted this woman, and as far as he could tell she seemed to feel the same way.

'Simon, we can't. Not here,' she managed to whisper when she caught her breath.

'Where, then? Your room?'

'It could hardly be yours, could it?' she said harshly, her desire completely taking over from all common sense.

He touched her breasts gently, sending quivers through her body. He gave a slight groan. 'You are so lovely, Jenna. So very lovely.' He leaned to kiss her again, very gently this time, as if knowing his every wish would soon be granted. 'Go up to your room. I'll follow you in a few minutes. Please. Go on, darling.'

She held out her hands for him to pull her to her feet. As she stood, he pulled her close and kissed her again. She felt as if she were drowning in some warm, enchanted sea and, almost dizzy with desire, she wandered into the house and up the stairs. She knew

147

she was wrong to be feeling this way. She knew she was going to hate herself in the morning, but she also felt quite powerless to resist. She was a grown woman after all. Perhaps she was destined to love other women's husbands. How very shocked Sarah would have been if she knew what her niece was about to do. 'Adultery' was a most unpleasant word, but surely this could have nothing to do with the real, true love she was experiencing. In her own dreamy world, she seemed to float along the corridor. Her key card in her hand, she slotted it in to open her door.

'There you are. I missed you after dinner,' said Kurt, almost rolling along the corridor wall that stretched between their rooms. 'I've brought some brandy with me. I thought we could discuss a few things for tomorrow.'

'I'm sorry. It – it isn't a good time. Not now,' she stammered. She felt herself blushing, her longing for Simon making her feel slightly detached from this world.

'How will we ever get to really know each other if you never allow me to get close?' he demanded.

'Kurt, I keep trying to tell you. I don't love you. It isn't a good idea to mix work and pleasure. This certainly isn't my idea of pleasure. Please. Go to bed or go back to join the others in the bar, if you think you can cope with still more to drink.' If he didn't disappear quickly, Simon would be here and find Kurt in her room.

'But Jenna. Lovely Jenna. I love you.' His voice was slurred from excess alcohol. He leaned over her and tried to put his arms round her. 'Come on. Give me a kiss.' He pulled her face towards his. She smelt the brandy on his breath and was immediately revolted.

'You're drunk, Kurt. Go to bed and get room service to send up some coffee.'

'I'll go to bed, all right. You get me some coffee. I'll wait here for you.' To her total consternation, he pushed past her and flopped onto her bed, lying back on her pillow. What could she do now? He was much too heavy to move and he had practically passed out. She could hardly get someone to come and carry him out. What on earth would they think? Perhaps when Simon came he would help? She stood in a quandary, wondering what her next move should be. All thoughts of love and desire had completely disappeared as she looked at this man lying on her bed. She went over to him and tried to rouse him.

'Kurt. Come on. Wake up. Please get up. You can't stay here.' She tried to pull on his arms but he was by now gently snoring and quite dead to the world. She might try getting some coffee into him, but it was probably more than that she'd need if she was going to manage to get him out of her room. She lifted the phone and asked for a pot black coffee. Seconds later, there was a knock at her door.

'Come in. It's open,' she called, renewing her efforts to rouse her boss. He stirred sleepily and flung an arm round her neck. She tried to haul him up but collapsed on top of him, pulled down with the almost dead weight of the man. He laughed and started muttering something indistinctly. Curse the man, what did he think he playing at? Her arms and legs flailing, she became aware of someone standing behind her.

'Put it on the table, will you? I could do with some help here.' By the time she had managed to free her head, Kurt was muttering again.

'Darling Jenna. Come back to bed. You're a very sexy lady, do you know that?'

She finally wriggled free and stood up. A grim-faced Simon was standing watching the scene.

'Simon! I'm sorry but Kurt's drunk. He came into my room – I couldn't stop him – and collapsed onto my bed.'

'I'd hate to interrupt anything,' he said coldly. 'Ring down to Reception if you need help, but I'm sure you'll cope.'

'But, Simon . . . it isn't what you think.'

'You couldn't begin to know what I think. Paula mentioned the extremely close relationship you seemed to enjoy with your so-called boss. I didn't want to believe her. I thought she was simply gossiping. But I see now she was probably right. I'm sorry I bothered you. Whatever you seem to think about me, at least I don't carry on like you seem to be doing. And after all Sarah's great efforts to keep you so pure and innocent. Goodnight, Jenna. I'm sorry to have interrupted you like that. Most embarrassing for you.' He turned to leave as another knock came on the door.

'Black coffee, sir, madam.' The waiter came into the room and placed the tray on the side table. 'Do you need another cup?' he asked, noting there were three occupants of the room.

'I'm just leaving, thank you,' Simon said, his lips tightly clamped. No sign now of the loving man Jenna had spent time with in the garden, only minutes before. He turned and left the room, saying nothing more. Jenna watched him leave, helpless to say or do anything to stop him. Her heart pounding, she flung a silent curse at the man lying on her bed.

CHAPTER 9

'Will there be anything else, madam?' the waiter asked.

'Do you think you could help me get Mr Smedley back to his room? I'm afraid he's had rather too much to drink.' The waiter had a definite smirk, Jenna thought as they both hauled the man to his feet.

'I think perhaps sir might take some coffee now,' the waiter suggested, when Kurt was finally back on his feet. They struggled to support him, one on each side.

'Let's get him into his own room before we try anything else. I don't want him collapsing in here again,' she said, struggling to keep the man upright. How on earth had she ever come to allow him to push through her door? He hadn't seemed quite so drunk at that point. The two of them struggled to make Kurt move towards the door and out into the corridor. Jenna prayed there would be no one around to witness the spectacle. Fortunately, for once, the corridor was empty. Kurt's door was firmly locked. Jenna felt in his trouser pocket for his room card. He gave a grunt of pleasure as he felt her hand in his pocket.

'See? I said we should get to know each other better,' he mumbled, his words slurred and indistinct. 'Can't leave me alone, these women,' he added. The waiter smiled patiently. He was used to dealing with people who drank too much. It was all just part of the job, really.

'Thank heavens,' she muttered, drawing the card from his pocket and swiping it through the slot. The door opened and they manhandled him towards the bed.

'Shall I get the coffee, madam?' asked the waiter.

'Thanks. Perhaps you could get him to drink some. I have a call to make.'

'Certainly, madam. Perhaps I might use the phone to inform the desk where I am? They'll be wondering why I'm away for so long. Leave it with me, then.' Gratefully, Jenna nodded her thanks and left the room. If Kurt had the granddaddy of a hangover in the morning, then he deserved it and she didn't care a damn. What was so much worse was what Simon thought. She had to speak to him again, and as soon as possible. She dialled Reception and asked to speak to the manager.

'Mr Simon has retired, madam,' said the butler-person who was on Reception. 'Is there anything I can do to help?'

'It's personal, thanks. Is it possible to speak to Mr Simon on his private line?'

'Who's calling?' he asked.

'Tell him it's Jenna.'

'Room seventeen, isn't it?'

'Correct?'

'I'll call you back if he is able to speak to you, madam.'

She hung up and paced up and down the room as she waited. The chances of him even listening were pretty remote, but she felt it was at least worth a try. After ten minutes, she gave up. She went into the shower and stripped off her clothes. To think, less than an hour ago, she had been contemplating making love to a married man and now here she was, alone as usual, and once more feeling in a state of turmoil deep inside. She was about to step under the spray when she heard the phone ring. She leapt across the room and snatched up the receiver.

'Simon . . .?'

'It's Paula Andrews. Was there something you needed?'

'I wanted to speak to Simon, please. It is important.'

'He's asleep. Unless it's a matter of life or death, I am not prepared to wake him. He's extremely tired.'

'Sorry to have bothered you. Let him sleep,' Jenna said, feeling thoroughly miserable. She replaced the receiver, wishing she could be equally relaxed – enough to let her sleep soundly. The thought of Paula sitting in his room, watching him as he slept, made her feel extremely jealous. She could imagine his long dark lashes resting on his cheeks and the sound of his steady breathing. If Paula could possibly have known Jenna's thoughts at this precise moment, she doubted very much that she would have sounded even remotely polite.

She lay on top of her bed, tossing from side to side. The awfulness of what she had been preparing to do . . . make love to Simon, right here in his own home, with his wife nearby, suddenly hit her. The enormity of her own desires shocked her more than she could have realized. She felt very ashamed and hated herself, even despised herself. Why did it have to be so very wrong to love someone so much, even if he was married? Everyone did it nowadays. The divorce rate was never higher than now. She even allowed herself to dream a little, but deep inside she knew she was in the wrong, however much her desire for Simon was driving her. But he was wrong as well. It was he who had begun this particular evening's fracas. Now there was nothing she could do or say to console herself. It was an undeniable fact; she still knew that she loved him deeply.

She tossed and turned for most of the night and finally gave up at five-thirty. She rose and put on her swimming things. A stint in the pool might clear her head. She wondered if Kurt would be up bright and early this morning. Somehow she doubted it, though he had surprised her many times in the past. He seemed to have an enormous capacity for alcohol, to the extent that she sometimes wondered if he had a serious drink problem that needed attention. But, however close she was, she could hardly be the one to tell him to seek treatment.

The air in the barn was still chilly. The pool was

rippling gently on the surface, as the circulating pump stirred the waters. She shed her robe and dived in. She drove herself hard again, quickly powering her way through several lengths of the pool as if she were hoping to wash away the sense of self-loathing that she was experiencing this morning. What was she doing chasing a married man? She was still young, attractive and healthy. She knew she was intelligent enough for many men to find her interesting. The world was full of unmarried men, so why was she wasting her time this way, chasing the married ones?

She heard the door click shut and began to swim again, as fast as she could, up and down, up and down, as if she were trying to escape from something or someone. She felt her heart pounding and stopped, looking to see who had come into the pool area. The room was deserted. Whoever had come in must have had second thoughts and left. It would have to be Simon at this hour. No one else would be swimming this early. Obviously he couldn't bear the thought of being alone with her any more. Fine, she tried to tell herself. It would all make life so much easier if they avoided each other.

Jenna climbed out of the pool and wrapped herself in her robe. The towelling mules supplied by the hotel dried her feet as she walked back to her room. She felt in her pocket for her key. 'Good grief,' she said aloud. 'I haven't even managed to being that with me.' She went down to Reception and rang the bell. In shirtsleeves, Simon came out from the back.

'Yes? Oh, it's you. Is there a problem?'

'Just one of many. I seem to have locked myself out of my room. Do you have the spare key?'

He stared at her. He looked momentarily angry.

'If you're trying one of your little games . . .'

'Don't be ridiculous. I don't play games,' she said, with an icy calmness she didn't feel inside. It would have to be Simon on duty, of course. 'I went for a swim and forgot to take my key card. Please would you open my door and let me in, before I freeze to death in my wet swimming things?'

Simon picked up a battered master key card from behind the desk and silently walked across Reception to the stairs. Equally silent, Jenna followed him. They walked along the corridor and he swiped the card through the lock mechanism. The door clicked open.

'Simon, I must talk to you –' Jenna began.

'I don't think there's anything else to say.' He turned away from her and she put a restraining arm on his sleeve. She could feel his warm flesh through the thin short sleeves and she drew away again sharply as if she had been stung. He swung round.

'Look here. You've made it quite plain what sort of woman you are. Paula may be very far from my idea of what I'd want in a wife, but at least so far she has always remained loyal to the one man she has known. In the biblical sense, I mean.'

Jenna fell back against the doorway. Finally he was admitting that he and Paula were married. Just as she had always known they must be. She felt angry,

157

madly angry. He was still managing to put all the blame on her.

'I don't know why you seem to be blaming me for everything. You were the one who stopped me in the garden last night. You were the one who started making love to me.'

'I suppose you didn't respond to me either?' he snapped. 'Refresh my memory. Were you objecting? If so I missed it.'

'This is getting us nowhere. We'll talk when you feel a little more inclined to listen,' Jenna suggested. Her lack of sleep and physical exertions were taking their toll. She felt emotionally and physically drained. Her face was pale and she felt that if she didn't lie down for a few moments she might fall down. 'I'll doubtless see you later.'

Simon turned and walked away. She looked up to see Kurt, still dressed in his clothes from yesterday, watching them.

'You're a quick worker,' he said. 'Only met him a couple of days ago and already entertaining him in your room. Very nice.' She didn't even bother to reply. Let him think whatever he liked. She turned and went into her room, firmly shutting the door behind her.

She lay on her bed and drifted into a light sleep. She woke around nine-thirty and showered and dressed. She had missed breakfast, but then she knew she couldn't have managed to swallow solid food. There was, however, still a day's work ahead, which she had to face. The crew were going out to take a few preliminary shots – film they could use later when the final editing took place. With luck, she would manage to spend most of her day with them rather than be alone with Kurt for long, difficult periods.

She went down into the foyer and looked around for everyone. One of the company vans was parked outside. She joined Terry and the others and soon the light-hearted chatter began, relieving her own tension and allowing them all to get on with the job. Fortunately, Kurt seemed to be keeping well out of the way. She knew she would have found ordinary conversation with him very difficult. It wasn't every day you had to turn the boss out of your bed, she thought angrily. Perhaps he wouldn't even remember it this morning. Pity it had managed to ruin her own love life, but then, was it really such a pity? Perhaps it had saved them all from another series of dramas if a far more hurtful situation had been allowed to develop.

The crew were a fun crowd to be with. There was constant banter and joking between shots. They all knew each other extremely well and the camaraderie managed to relieve most of Jenna's rather gloomy feelings which had lingered on after the disturbances of the night. She was made to stand in for the various actors as they lined up possible shots – a reasonable amount of preliminary work on a project like this one meant that they saved considerable time and money later – and they teased her, joked with her and even flirted with her. Her quick wit kept them guessing for much of the time. Only when they teased her about her devoted boss did she lose her cool for a moment.

159

'I don't want to talk about Kurt,' she snapped. The men glanced at each other and pulled wry faces but they let the subject drop. It was inevitable that a pretty young assistant would have to take this sort of teasing, but she was not in the mood today.

When they finished work early, Jenna decided it was time for a rest. She had various schedules to sort out and would need to spend time working during the latter part of the evening. Normally she would have done something energetic, a swim or a workout, but for now she felt so drained of all energy that she needed to catch up on some sleep. The reception area was quiet. The woman on duty smiled as Jenna came in and exchanged some pleasantry with her. As Jenna turned towards the stairs, she noticed a child sitting on the floor in one corner. He was engrossed in playing with some toy cars, driving them along the lines of pattern in the carpet. Jenna smiled.

'Nice to see a little boy who can enjoy playing so quietly,' she remarked to the receptionist.

'He's a very good boy, aren't you, Tom?'

The child looked up. He had a mass of jet-black curls framing a face that looked all too familiar. She had only ever seen those deep, honey-coloured eyes on one other person. The boy was an exact replica of Simon. The smile froze on her lips. The presence of a son, aged around seven or eight years, she would estimate, made everything very different. Despite that other occasion at Sarah's cottage, a wave of relief flushed her body. Thanks heavens she had not followed her baser instincts and gone to bed with Simon last night, after all. She would have been feeling even more wretched now if she had. If the boy was seven or eight, he must have been conceived that very summer she had been falling in love with Simon. No wonder he had never written to her, not with all this going on around him. What a total idiot she had been, both then and now. How on earth could Simon have even looked twice at the kid she'd been? Not when he'd had Paula waiting at home, and pregnant to boot.

'Do you like my car?' Tom asked, holding out a silver-blue sports car exactly like Simon's.

'I think it's a lovely car,' she managed to squeak. The child was quite adorable, and she marvelled that she had never seen him before, either on her previous visits or during this stay.

'Come on now, Tom. You'd better clear up and go back upstairs. Your mummy should be back by now, and you know she doesn't like you playing in the hotel areas.'

'Do you like swimming?' the child asked Jenna.

Recovering herself, she replied, 'Oh, yes. You have a lovely pool here. Do you go into it sometimes?'

'Only very sometimes, 'cos there's usually some guests in it. I'm not allowed to go then. I can swim a whole width without armbands,' he announced proudly.

'That's very good.' Jenna smiled, totally captivated by the little boy. He was exactly what she would have expected of a child of Simon's. She felt an odd pang of sadness that she would never be able to get to know him. She also felt a new sense of finality to end all her dreams. There could be no question of Simon

161

divorcing Paula, not when a child of this age was involved. She knew the loneliness of being an only child without one or more parents. However much Sarah had replaced her own parents, there were times when she couldn't help wondering what her own life would have been like, if they had lived.

'I'd better go now, Tom. I have some work to do. Perhaps I shall see you again.'

'Why have you got some work to do if you're on holidays?'

'We're making a film here.'

'Like on television? Are you in it? Can I be in it?' His voice was filled with excitement at the thought. What a pity one couldn't put some of this enthusiasm into storage and feed it back when children became bored adolescents, Jenna thought.

'We shall have to see. Perhaps we can organize something one day, if your mummy and daddy agree.' She forced the words out, making herself try to get rid of the awful feelings she was holding inside. She felt as if another part of her had died suddenly. She had to accept that the wonderful love she had been feeling for Simon was quickly withering and had to be pruned right off the plant, before the disease spread out of control.

'Tom, please get your things together and go upstairs now. Miss Brown is tired,' the receptionist said.

'I'll see you again,' said Jenna, leaving the boy and going up the stairs.

She flung the windows open when she reached her room. It was in one of the newer extensions, but the furnishings and style of the rooms was similar throughout the hotel. It was all very solid-looking, with dark oak floorboards and furniture. There were light rugs scattered across the floors and chintz fabrics used for curtains and bedcovers. Everywhere there was a sense of extremely good taste and comfort.

The weather felt warm and humid. She stripped off her clothes and showered before lying on the bed to rest. How on earth was she going to cope for the next few days? If only she could leave now and get away somewhere on her own for a spell. She could save herself having to avoid Simon, Kurt and Paula. But that was impossible. She had a job to do, and her professionalism could not allow personal feelings to get in the way. Eventually she drifted into a dream-filled sleep that swirled her through a whole range of difficult situations that all blurred together.

When she finally awoke, it was almost seven o'clock. She dressed for dinner in the plainest frock she could find in her wardrobe. No jewellery, no added colourful scarf, and she wore no make-up. Somehow she felt that if she didn't look her best she might get away without any further complications. The last thing she felt like this evening was Kurt flirting or pursuing his wish to get to know her better.

The bar was deserted when she went down before dinner. She hadn't seen anything of Kurt since the early-morning encounter in the corridor, when, presumably, he had believed Simon was leaving her room after being there all night. If only, was the thought that popped into her mind . . . until she remembered Tom.

She ordered a wine and soda. She might just need to keep a clear head this evening, she thought. When no one else had arrived by eight o'clock, Jenna decided she might as well dine alone. The boys had probably gone in search of somewhere a bit more lively. The local pub might be more to their taste. Normally she would have joined them, but she didn't feel like being part of a noisy group, not this evening.

She picked at a light meal and went up to her room without seeing anyone she knew. She pulled out her papers and worked steadily through her schedules, making endless notes at the side of the script. It was a relatively long film for their company, who were more used to adverts and pop videos. It was, on the other hand, short compared to a TV film. The script was witty and amusing, featuring the Alistair Dodds character on a voyage of discovery through the management of a company. Crashing waves represented the trials he faced, with calm seas and tiny waves lapping the shore for the progression scenes. It would be tricky to get the sea in all its moods, especially at this time of year.

She remembered the fateful thunderstorm at Sarah's cottage, the night that Simon had made love to her. She felt herself colouring with the memory of the excitement and thrills of joy they had shared. She had never realized before then what pleasure sexual fulfilment could bring. Making love to David had been as nothing compared to the joys of Simon's

164

body. With a jolt she remembered what had brought the magic to an end. 'Marriage-wrecker', that was what she had said. That fateful call from Paula on Simon's own mobile phone. The very same phone that was still sitting in her drawer. She pulled it out, knowing she should have returned it to its owner days ago. Could she leave it at Reception? Perhaps she could wrap it up in something and return it without anyone wondering why she was in possession of it in the first place. How utterly stupid she was. And there was also the matter of the paperweight. She pushed her clothes aside and retrieved it from the cupboard, where she had dumped it the first night here. It was totally beautiful, and, whatever he said, it certainly couldn't have been something he had picked up cheaply at some antiques fair. Apart from any other considerations, it brought back too many memories.

Her bedside telephone rang, bringing her back to reality.

'Jenna? Are you all right?' Kurt's voice asked. 'Only I haven't seen you all day. I think I might have made a fool of myself last night. No hard feelings, I hope? I hadn't realized you and Simon had become an item. How does his wife take to that? One of these modern marriages, eh?'

'Kurt,' Jenna interrupted, 'I'm fine. There is nothing going on with Simon, or anyone else, and, yes, you made a fool of yourself last night, and, no, I don't hold any hard feelings. I am also working just now, so if there's nothing else, I shall get back to it.'

'Goodnight, Jenna,' he said, and mercifully he put the phone down.

'I might as well get ready for bed,' Jenna muttered. There was little point in sitting staring at the wall. At least she could try to sleep.

The pool was a wonderful asset, she decided the next morning as she completed her morning lengths. She knew she glowed with health and looked good, even if she didn't feel it. Back in her own room – she had remembered her key card today, to avoid any possibility of repeating yesterday's unpleasantness with Simon – she carefully shampooed her hair to wash out any traces of chlorine. A quick blow dry, and she made her usual working-style plait, ready for a busy day.

She had managed to spend a whole twenty-four hours without running into Simon. Hopefully she would be able to spend most of her time here working hard and avoiding encounters with the man she loved but whom she knew she could never have.

She saw no more of the child, and was almost beginning to think he might have been a figment of an overworked imagination. If she hadn't noticed a toy car left under one of the seats in Reception, she might easily have believed she had dreamed the whole encounter. After all, the child looked so exactly the way she had imagined a child of Simon's would look, she might have dreamt she had seen him.

Over the weekend, she saw Simon at a distance, going out in his car. She had bundled the mobile phone and the paperweight into a rough parcel, scribbled a brief note of explanation and left it at

166

Reception. The rather distant man she called the butler had been on duty, and not a flicker of emotion or curiosity had crossed the impassive face. He'd taken the parcel and put it under the desk, promising to hand it directly to 'Mr Simon' at the first opportunity.

Late on Sunday afternoon, Alistair Dodds himself had arrived, complete with a small entourage of dresser, make-up artist and a couple of the other actors playing the supporting roles. The representatives from Hudson International, the company funding the film, were also coming for a few days to watch the early stages. Kurt had arranged a dinner party for them all for that evening. He and Jenna would host the gathering, and then the crew would meet everyone tomorrow morning, when they hoped to begin shooting in earnest.

Jenna was intrigued to meet the great man. She had heard conflicting reports about him and read much of what had been written about his private life, mainly in the more sensational tabloids. According to one he was bisexual, and had a veritable string of both men and women among his conquests; another said he had married several times and had a huge number of children, and yet another claimed he was the perfect family man, loyal father and devoted husband. That largely covered all the options, Jenna thought. She would make her own judgements once she had met him.

Alistair Dodds was, ostensibly at least, a fairly quiet sort of man. His on-screen persona was an act, a face he showed to the public. She immediately dismissed most of the press reports she had read as pure sensationalism. She sat next to him at dinner and had the opportunity to watch him and talk to him relatively privately. If she hadn't known better, she would have thought him a very innocuous character, who could easily pass unnoticed in a crowd. He was attractive in many ways, though not really her type. She liked him, she decided, which was just as well, considering how closely she would be working with him for the next few days. He chatted comfortably with everyone and made them feel at ease. It made a change from the pop kid culture characters they so often spent time with.

Greg and the other Hudson's man were both there, while Sylvia, the girl with mother problems, would be joining them the next day. Jenna looked forward to having another woman with them. It was not that she ever consciously distinguished between males and females working together, but sometimes the almost exclusively male company left her wishing for someone else to share girl-talk with occasionally.

As the wine flowed freely, the tension they had all been feeling earlier lightened and there was a lot of laughter. Other guests tried to look surreptitiously to see who the celebrity could be. Jenna gave a secret smile to herself as she saw them wondering and questioning each other as to whether this unobtrusive man could really be the television star. One of them bravely came over and asked if he really was Alistair Dodds, presenting a hotel napkin for his autograph when he acknowledged his identity. He was so gracious about the intrusion, and very polite. Jenna once more thought about some of the pop music folk, who could make themselves very unpleasant at times.

The party was breaking up – at a reasonable hour, to allow for the early start the next morning – when Simon came in and glanced round the room. Jenna tried to keep her cool and smiled politely, hoping that no one else would notice her blushes or hear the pounding that had begun to assault her heart yet again. He was wearing one of his many dark business suits this evening, with a pale blue silk shirt and matching tie. The clever eyes swept the table, assessing the people he most needed to speak to. He pulled a chair over, having nodded to Kurt, and sat between Jenna and Alistair. He apologized for not welcoming the star personally on his arrival, made the usual noises about Alistair just asking for anything he needed, and the two men chatted comfortably for several minutes.

Jenna watched the consummate professional at work and admired his skills in making everyone seem special. She was totally caught in the spell of the man and felt ridiculously proud of him. He had accomplished so much in his own world.

'Jenna,' he said, nodding at her as he left the table. He spoke to everyone in turn, but to each person it seemed as if they were the only one present at the time.

'Nice chap,' Alistair said as Simon left the room. 'Should think he'll make quite a success of this place.'

'He's very good at his job,' Jenna said carefully, watching Kurt to see if he had noticed anything. 'I think, if everyone will excuse me, I shall turn in now. Busy day tomorrow.' They all nodded and called their goodnights as she left the room. Kurt rose and followed her out.

'I should appreciate a little more discretion from you, Jenna. Now we have Alistair and the others with us, there will probably be a number of the press getting wind of it. I don't want any derogatory reports made about your own particular goings-on, especially with any married men, if you understand my drift.'

'I can't think what you're referring to. And if we weren't in the middle of the hotel foyer, I should take great delight in slapping you across the face, as hard as I could manage it,' she said softly so no one else could hear. She smiled sweetly as she spoke. 'How dare you speak to me like that? After your own quite disgusting display the other night, I should think you are the last one to comment.' Her eyes flashed icy blue, the chilling depths enhanced by the anger that threatened to overtake her if she stayed with the man for a moment longer. She turned away angrily.

'Jenna,' he said softly. 'Jenna, I didn't mean anything. It was the thought of you spending time with that . . . that jumped-up hotel-keeper. Perhaps I was just jealous. But seriously, do be careful. You know how the press can be with anyone remotely famous. You only have to read recent headlines to know that more than one of the cheaper papers are quite capable of making something up if they can't get at or don't like the real truth.'

Jenna relaxed, her anger dying as quickly as it came. It was just Kurt being Kurt. Protective, jealous, demanding Kurt. He was a complex man whom she now knew she could never marry under any circumstances.

'Goodnight, Kurt. See you in the morning.' She went upstairs to her room and checked through the next day's schedules. She would have to get duplicates for everyone before work started. She should perhaps take them down to Reception now, so that there would be plenty of time to get them copied. Inevitably, it was Simon who was working in the office. He glanced up as she knocked on the door.

'Sorry to bother you. There are some papers I need copied for tomorrow. About ten of each should do it, please. Do you want me to sign for them?'

'There'll be the usual form to sign attached to the envelope when you collect them. Thanks for returning the phone, by the way. I'd hoped you'd remembered to bring it.'

He obviously didn't intend making any further comment about the paperweight, so she turned to leave. She hated this icy politeness. In fact, she was a little surprised at his complete detachment concerning the whole business. How could he be so calm and unemotional after the loving they had shared? Perhaps she truly was one of many women in his life. Even in his shirtsleeves, working at an office desk, he was magnificent. There was an air of control about everything he did. Perhaps self-control was his secret. She sighed gently as she left. She desperately wanted him to call after her, to say something – anything – but he remained silent. It was so hard to be in love with a man who was forbidden to her.

CHAPTER 10

Alistair proved to be a positive joy to work with. Thoroughly professional when he was working, his talents as an actor and comedian were ever-present. He listened to directions and performed exactly as requested. He patiently stood around for retakes without a complaint, never once using his star status to gain favours. By the end of the first day's filming everyone was delighted. Kurt was expansive and generous with his praise – most unusual for him, especially so early on in an assignment.

'Makes some of our pop kids look the amateurs they really are,' Kurt muttered to Jenna after one particularly difficult scene was finally wrapped up.

He and Jenna spent a couple of hours working during the evening, organizing their plans for the rest of the week. They planned to do all the exterior shots as soon as they possibly could, while the good weather held. The interiors would follow later, as there was bad weather forecast for later in the week.

'Let's hope we get some really good storms in the

can. It will make for a much better film if we don't have to splice in too much from the library shots.'

'Knowing Cornwall, storms one can usually rely on; sunshine – well, that is quite another matter. I can always go and stir up the swimming pool if you get desperate.'

'Actually, I heard Alistair saying he'd like to swim. You go in a bit, don't you?'

Jenna nodded. 'Most mornings.'

'I'd like you to go with him. Make him feel important – you know the sort of thing.'

'I should think he's well able to look after himself, and to decide if he wants to swim.'

'Jenna, please do as I say. He'll be flattered to have a beautiful woman dancing attendance on him.'

Jenna shrugged. 'Anything to keep the boss happy,' she breezed.

'Just make sure it really is *anything*,' Kurt said cryptically.

'You know, if I didn't know you better, I might think you were making immoral suggestions.' And this from the man who had earlier objected to her spending time with Simon because it made him jealous.

'I can't think what you're talking about. Look, we need to have dinner with everyone again tonight. Greg and Colin are leaving tomorrow, but that little woman is staying on for the rest of the week. Sandra or Shirley or something.'

'I think you mean Sylvia. Good. I like her. She'll be able to help out with some of my workload. Checking stuff, letters and all. Can't say I'll be sorry to see the back of the two men, however. Greg has hands all over his arms.'

'He *is* a client, Jenna.'

'I don't care what he is. I refuse to be groped by him. That is not in my job description.'

'You are here to do whatever I tell you, Jenna. And keep anyone happy I tell you to.'

'Good Lord! And you think I could marry you? I don't think you have a clue. Now, if you'll excuse me, I have to get ready for dinner.' The man was quite impossible. What did he think she was?

Once again Jenna found herself sitting next to Alistair, but this time she was opposite to Sylvia. The woman seemed shy, and slightly ill at ease.

'I hardly ever go out socially these days,' she whispered confidingly. 'My mother, you know.'

'Did you get someone to look after her?' Jenna asked.

'The company have paid for her to go into respite care, but she wasn't happy about it. Thought she was off to the seaside with me, just because I'd mentioned Cornwall.'

'Let's hope you manage to enjoy yourself while you're away.'

'I shall certainly try,' Sylvia whispered. 'But it is work really. I have masses of notes for you or Kurt, or whoever needs them. My boss at Hudson's seem to think every "t" needs crossing and I'm the only one who's capable of doing anything. Though I do intend to try and have some fun. Make the most of the opportunity.' She smiled almost conspiratorially. 'By the way, who's that man by the door? He is 'just gorgeous.' Jenna turned her head to look.

'Simon Andrews. He owns the hotel. Very anxious to be sure we have everything we need for the film. He's built this whole place up from nothing and seems to be really going places.'

'I expect he's been snapped up by some gorgeous woman. He doesn't look the type to be on his own for long.'

'Married and has a child,' Jenna told her. She was proud of herself. The way she talked about it all, she sounded just like any another uninvolved guest, gossiping about the place they were staying in.

'Wow. Just my luck.' The other woman giggled. It seemed as if she was unexpectedly beginning to enjoy herself thoroughly.

'How do you cope with Greg the Grope?' Jenna asked with a grin. She was feeling relieved at his imminent departure and enjoying the company of another woman to chat to. Sylvia was giggling in a quite unrestrained way now. She put it down to the unaccustomed wine she had drunk.

'You've been neglecting me,' Alistair accused Jenna a few moments later. 'I hear you're a great one for swimming?'

'Every morning if possible,' she replied with a grin. 'Six to seven, or thereabouts.'

'Good heavens, woman. Where do you get the energy? What time are you going tomorrow? I'll join you.'

The others laughed and immediately started placing bets as to the likelihood of Alistair making it to the pool.

'Not only will I be there by, say, half-past six, I shall challenge you to a race. Fifty quid says I'll beat you, Jenna. You on?'

'I shall be taking my swim whether you're there or not. I usually do around thirty lengths.'

Alistair cringed slightly.

'I can't remember the last time I went swimming,' Sylvia said in a small voice. 'I wish I'd brought some things with me now. I simply never thought.'

'You can borrow one of my bikinis if you like,' Jenna offered. 'I've brought lots.' If there were a few people swimming together, Alistair was hardly likely to make things difficult.

'Looks like it's a communal activity, then,' Alistair said, sounding marginally disappointed.

'Let's wait and see who turns up,' Jenna laughed. She was used to people making such plans – until it came to the point of actually getting up from their beds.

'Right, an early night for us all. The new fitness regime starts here,' Alistair announced. The party began to disperse, leaving a hard core of stalwarts, including Kurt and a couple of the crew who had joined them in the bar. Hesitantly, Sylvia asked if she could really borrow one of Jenna's bikinis, and shyly went up to the room with her.

'Isn't this a wonderful hotel?' she said. 'And the setting too. I don't think I've ever seen anywhere quite so lovely as Cornwall. As for Simon, he is just gorgeous. Don't you think so? I could really fancy him.'

Jenna smiled. Fancy him? And how!

The two sat on the bed and chatted for a while. Sylvia's mother had developed some form of dementia and was extremely difficult to cope with. The poor woman had demanded to stay at home and Sylvia had wanted to do her best for her. It was obviously very tough, though, keeping a job and caring for her mother. It had already lasted for three years and could go on indefinitely. Physically, the old lady was very strong.

'I don't know how you cope,' Jenna said. 'I thought it was bad enough when my parents died, but at least it was sudden and not a long-drawn-out business.

'You're very blunt,' Sylvia said.

'Gosh, I'm sorry. I didn't mean anything . . . Look, perhaps you'd like a drink, or some coffee or something?' She felt she must try and make it up to the girl.

'No thanks. Forget it. Just lend me your bikini, if you think it will fit. You are somewhat better endowed round the top than I am. Hopefully I'll see you in the morning.'

At six prompt Jenna went to the pool and began swimming her usual morning lengths, all alone until about six-thirty. Then Alistair joined her, and was quickly outpaced by Jenna.

'Wow, you can certainly move,' he said admiringly. 'You have a lovely body,' he added. He came close to her and put his hand out to touch her bare shoulder. 'Muscles too,' he whispered. 'I love a muscular woman.'

Jenna stared at the man. He suddenly seemed much older to her. Somehow the bare flesh exposed by his swimming trunks looked flabby and distinctly unattractive. He had a look on his face that Jenna recognized as potential desire. In fact, his wet face was pushing closer to hers, and she knew it was tactics time.

'What's your strongest stroke?' she asked suddenly. 'Let's race.'

'Breast-stroke, of course. Come here, Jenna.'

She darted away from him and, trying to sound as if she was happy, called, 'Come on. There were bets made on who would win.'

'I always win, one way or another,' he said. 'One kiss if you beat me and two if I win.'

Some bet, thought Jenna. 'I thought fifty pounds was mentioned somewhere?'

'That was before I saw you at work. I stand no chance whatsoever against you. The bet's off! You also have a few years on me. Just a few, of course. No, I like the idea of a kiss as a prize.'

'You'll have to catch me first,' she called as she sped off down the pool. She was spared further embarrassment by the opportune arrival of Sylvia, wearing a white bikini of Jenna's. She looked good, Jenna realized. Free of the severe hairstyle and glasses, she was actually a very attractive woman. Shyly she slipped into the water and began to swim a gentle breast-stroke. Alistair was watching her, his attention momentarily taken away from Jenna. They swam companionably side by side, until they decided it was breakfast time.

'I trust you're looking after Alistair properly?' Kurt asked her later, during the morning.

'I think so,' she replied frostily. 'As well as I look after all our clients.' His glare obviously meant that he had more to say later.

They worked on, moving from one beach to another, stopping for short breaks and food from one of their larger vans. Used to making very short videos, they wasted little time and kept everyone busy for the entire day.

'I'm quite exhausted,' Alistair said during the afternoon. 'Your boss is regular slave-driver. Does he always squeeze every last drop of blood from his artists?'

'Come on, where's your stamina?' Kurt shouted through his megaphone. 'Scene twenty-five next, please. Come on, everyone.'

'I simply don't think I can face getting wet for one single minute longer,' protested the star. 'Get a stand-in for me. I'll shoot the wretched scene when I've had a rest.' With that, he turned and went into the caravan they were using as a dressing room and shut the door firmly behind him.

'Take five everyone,' called Kurt. 'Jenna, for God's sake sort out that jumped-up little man again. I can't quit now. There's bad weather forecast. We must get this lot finished today.'

With a sigh, Jenna went over to the caravan. She was forever having to sort out Kurt's messes when his temper got the better of him. She hoped Alistair hadn't heard the comment about a 'jumped-up little man'. Five minutes later, after a lot of quick talking,

Jenna led a slightly pale-faced Alistair back onto the set. He did truly look quite exhausted.

'One half-hour more and that's it. That's my lot,' Alistair said firmly. 'Your assistant can be very persuasive, Kurt. But half an hour and I'm out of here. OK?'

'Sure thing,' Kurt agreed. 'Thanks, Jenna.'

Jenna shrugged and turned away. She had other things to do and wanted to get away from both men before she, too, lost her temper.

A few minutes later everyone had to stop work anyway as the rain began. They drove back to the hotel and sat in the conservatory for afternoon tea, immaculately served and quite a change from their usual, hastily grabbed mugs of something hot from the nearest van.

'This is all very civilized,' Alistair said.

'We do try,' Kurt answered with a slight bow. 'I was pleased with today, you know, despite the rain. One more day on the beaches and we should be home and dry. We'll go down below tomorrow and try for some dramatic shots of the castle, before you appear at the top as King Arthur himself.'

'As long as I'm not expected to scale those damned cliffs,' Alistair replied. 'Have we got a stuntman coming for that?'

'No. We'll fake it. No worries. You start the climb and then we film you from the top, as if you've just arrived.'

'As long as I don't look an idiot – well, in the literal sense. I suppose we don't have any climbers in our midst?' he asked, looking round hopefully.

'I've done a bit in my dark past,' Jenna admitted. 'Though usually down holes rather than up cliffs.'

'Tell us more. What a very surprising young lady you are,' Alistair smiled.

'My aunt is an archaeologist. I used to go on digs with her when I was a kid.'

'She once found a gold armband, or something,' Kurt added. 'Photographs in the press and everything. It's in some local museum or other, isn't it?'

Jenna nodded, realizing she would much rather not talk about it any more. Having pretended she didn't know Simon, it would make her look as if she had something to hide, if the association was discovered at this stage.

'Fascinating,' Alistair said. 'I'd love to see it. Is it somewhere local?'

'Not really. It's miles from here. Near Penzance.'

'Let's go there now. It's still early. Come on, Jenna. Take me to see your discovery.'

'But I thought you felt exhausted?'

'Only for work. This sounds like pleasure to me,' Alistair insisted.

'I'd really rather not go. I have a lot of work to do.'

However much she protested, Kurt would hear none of it. He insisted that Larry would drive the two of them while he did the next day's planning on his own. With a shrug, Jenna gave in. The last thing in the world she wanted at that moment was to drive to the other end of the county, especially in the company of this particular man.

'The museum will probably be closed by the time we get there,' Jenna suggested.

Kurt shook his head.

'Perhaps Sylvia would like to come too?' she said hopefully.

'I want her to do a report for Hudson's on our progress,' Kurt insisted. 'Enjoy yourself, you two. Don't hurry back. You might like to have dinner somewhere.'

'Any other orders?' Jenna asked sarcastically.

'Keep him happy,' Kurt demanded, with a knowing nod of his head. Jenna glared. Whatever did he think she was?

In the big car, they covered the miles quickly, arriving at the museum just a quarter of an hour before closing. Jenna led her companion to the exhibit and waited while he read the article.

'Simon Andrews? Where have I heard that name before?'

Jenna avoided his eyes and pointed at the replica of the famous torque. The original was far too valuable to leave on display in a local museum. 'It's lovely isn't it?'

But Alistair was not listening. He was staring at another press cutting. One that had a photograph of both herself and Simon. 'Cut the hair and smarten him up a bit. That is, undoubtedly, the famous Simon of hotelier fame; I'd swear it. Well, Miss Jenna Brown. What do you have to say to that?'

'Yes. You're right. We've known each other for years.'

'But why pretend you didn't know him? Kurt seems to think you've only just met.'

'For some reason Simon wanted it that way. I can't

explain his reasons.' Jenna felt herself shaking inside. Looking at the display had made her feel almost uncomfortable, a little sad and very nostalgic. So many happy memories, all soured by people growing up. Young people can never wait to be adults, yet, once they are, they spend for ever reminiscing about when they were young. That thought alone was enough to make her feel old.

'Can we go now, please?' Jenna asked, before her mood deepened further.

'I want to see the site. See the actual place where you made the discovery.'

'It will be closed now. It's open daily through the summer, though. You'll have to make a special visit some other time if you really are interested.'

'I have the distinct feeling there's something you're hiding here. Spill the beans, come on. We'll have dinner somewhere and you can tell me all about it.'

Suddenly Jenna felt safe with this man. He was, after all, a very nice person. Perhaps her first instincts had been right after all. The suggestive remarks he had made in the pool that morning had been just a form of bluster. Probably even an attempt to recapture his own youth.

'OK. Dinner would be nice.'

'This is your home patch. You suggest somewhere.'

'It was difficult to think of anywhere she liked and one that didn't have memories.

'There's always the fish restaurant in Padstow. The one that everyone talks about. It's on the way back. Well, almost. We might get in without booking if we're early enough.'

'Suits me. To Padstow, then, Larry,' he commanded.

They chatted easily in the back of the car, the conversation light and undemanding. They drove down to the quay of the little fishing town and managed to find somewhere to park.

'Are you joining us, Larry?' Jenna asked out of politeness.

'Thanks, but I'll find somewhere a little more to my taste,' he smiled. 'I'll take a look around the town, I think.'

Jenna and Alistair went into the light and airy restaurant, already quite crowded for so early in the evening. The receptionist looked up.

'Do you have a reservation?' she enquired.

'I'm afraid not, but as we're only passing through, I hoped you might fit us in somewhere. Just the two of us.' Alistair was using his renowned charm to great advantage.

'Excuse me asking, but aren't you . . .?'

'Hush, my dear. I'm definitely incognito this evening. I've even got the dark glasses to prove it.'

'Just a moment and I'll see what we can do. Please take a seat and I'll get someone to bring you a drink.'

'It's smaller than I expected, but extremely nice,' Alistair commented. 'Now, what will you have to drink?'

The meal was quite perfect, complemented by a light, crisp white Burgundy. The food was simple, but the fresh fish, and perfect cooking and blending of the ingredients made it a memorable occasion. When they reached the coffee stage, Alistair leaned back in his seat expansively.

'Now, spill the beans. What's the big mystery? About you and Simon Andrews?'

'No mystery, really. For some reason he decided that we should pretend we were meeting for the first time. I expect he didn't want any complications with his wife and son. We had a . . . a sort of fling, I suppose. I didn't know he was married.' Suddenly she found herself pouring everything out, including her own anger at being duped.

'And when I saw his son playing in Reception one day, I could hardly believe it. Can you imagine anyone who would actually try to sleep with one of the guests when his wife and son were only a few doors away?'

'Perhaps he was trying to keep his guests happy,' Alistair suggested.

'Come on. What sort of man would do a thing like that?'

'Your dear boss obviously expects you will, for a start. He's as good as told me to ask for whatever I want, and I think that included you.'

'He's a swine, then. I can't believe him sometimes. Do you know, he asked me to marry him? I can hardly believe it. I've worked with him for years and he still thinks he can use me this way. I've never given him cause, I assure you. Sorry, perhaps that sounds very disloyal.'

'You're still in love with this Simon, aren't you?'

'I don't know what you mean.'

'I mean, you fell in love with him when you discovered your antiquities, and when you met him again you fell in love for a second time. I assume that was when you discovered he was married.'

'You're quite perceptive, aren't you? Considering you've only just met me.'

'For an actor, you mean? People are a bit of a hobby of mine.'

Jenna sat silently for a few moments. If a relative stranger could see the way things were, who else might have guessed about her private thoughts and longings?

'And does he feel anything for you?' asked Alistair.

'He said he did, but I suspect that was the usual chat-up stuff.'

'And is he good in bed?'

'I beg your pardon?' Jenna exploded. 'There are limits to the things I talk about, you know. I don't discuss my private affairs with anyone, thank you very much.'

'Oh, so you do have affairs? Sorry,' he added, sensing she was about to explode again, 'none of my business.'

'I think it's time we were leaving,' Jenna said, feeling the evening should be brought to an end as quickly as possible. She signalled the waiter for the bill and fished in her bag for a credit card.

'This is on me. I insist.' Alistair took the bill from the waiter and signed the credit card slip. 'Think how disappointed that receptionist would have been not to have my autograph. Especially after finding us a table without a booking.'

'Thank you. Food *and* counselling. Can't be bad,' Jenna commented wryly as they left the restaurant. She had overcome her earlier resentment at his questioning. Was Simon good in bed? he had asked. From her very limited experience, Simon Andrews had to be the very best possible.

'My guess is that you love the guy because he is, or was, the best in bed,' Alistair said lightly. 'I would also surmise that perhaps there haven't been too many for you to compare him with. Am I right? OK, I know, it has nothing to do with me. But take my advice: don't waste all of your life waiting for something that never comes. There are plenty of other men around. You could be surprised.' Jenna gasped, yet again surprised by the man's perception. He had summed up her very thoughts just as she was thinking them.

'And you're included among the "plenty of other men", I suppose?'

'You have doubtless heard of my reputation?'

'But you're not like that in real life. Why, anyone who didn't recognize you would see you as a perfectly ordinary man, polite, kind and understanding. I'm sorry, I hope you don't think I'm being rude.' He grinned and took her arm, marching her along the tiny streets of the little fishing port.

'I take it as a compliment. Your secrets are safe with me. But I might demand that you put the bit about understanding in writing, just for my second wife to read. She thinks I'm the pits as far as decent human feelings go. Now if you want to hear someone's opinion of what *I* am like in bed, you should ask her. Or on the other hand . . . you could do worse than try for yourself.'

He ducked as she took a friendly swipe at him.

The hotel seemed deserted when they returned around ten-thirty. The bar was empty and the dining room seemed to have closed. Jenna and Alistair went straight to their rooms, but not before he placed a gentle peck on her cheek, almost paternal in its simplicity, she thought. She sensed she might have gained an ally.

Jenna's escort from the previous evening joined her in the pool before anyone else was stirring the following morning. He said he was determined to get himself into better shape. He made no comment about her revelations regarding Simon but he had formed a plan, hoping to bring everything out into the open. Young people could go on and on wishing for something and never having the confidence to ask for it, he believed. He wanted to help this girl, who seemed to have had a bit of a raw deal.

If Jenna had got even at a hint of his plan, he knew she would have rocketed into orbit with horror. As it was, they swam peacefully up and down, up and down, neither of them driving themselves too hard. She heard the door open and caught a glimpse of Simon. Alistair gave a secret grin of delight. His little plan was going to begin to work sooner than he had expected, but that was all to the good.

'You've quite exhausted me, Jenna,' he said loudly. 'Especially after last night's little outing as

189

well. I simply don't know where you get all your energy.' He hauled himself out of the pool and blew a kiss at her as he left the barn. She stood watching his retreat, open-mouthed.

Simon dived in and powered along in his strong free-style stroke. He stopped briefly as he passed Jenna.

'Glad you're enjoying yourself,' he said coldly. 'It obviously doesn't take you long to get over your so-called love affairs.'

'I don't even begin to know what you're suggesting. You obviously have the mind of a sewer rat. Love affairs? I'll leave you in peace to enjoy your swim. I'd hate you to feel contaminated by another person sharing your pool.' She swam to the side and hauled herself out, rushing to find her robe and get as far away as possible from this man.

'A word of advice, Jenna,' he called after her. 'If you're going to spend your life in and out of men's beds, I suggest you do something about taking precautions. You could end up with something nasty. Especially if you sleep with people like Alistair Dodds. You must be aware of his reputation.'

She gaped at him once more before turning and marching out of the room in a blaze of anger. How dared he? Who did he think he was? The cheek of the man. She thought of Alistair's parting comments. Of course. It was obvious. That was what Simon had been referring to. He had the impression that she and the TV star had been sharing more than just a meal last night. How stupid could she be?

Alistair's comment had been deliberately provocative and Simon had been quick to take the bait. Well, thanks a bunch, Mr Dodds, she thought. What an idiot she was. She would most certainly be having words with him later.

CHAPTER 11

Jenna joined the rest of the group at breakfast, taking a bowl of her favourite stewed fruit and yogurt. Kurt was tucking in to his usual fry-up, talking nineteen to the dozen as he did so and waving an eggy fork in the air as he spoke. The others were listening politely as he went through the day's plans. Alistair was eating a slice of toast, ostentatiously taking a low-fat spread.

'Jenna has finally convinced me that I need to get fitter,' he was saying. 'After a wonderful evening she was still full of energy and I was quite exhausted. I may not be in the first flush of youth any more, but I shall have to take steps to keep up with the lovely Miss Brown.'

Kurt gave a knowing smirk and grinned at Jenna approvingly. He, too, must have picked up on the innuendo pouring from Alistair's mouth. She felt herself growing cold inside. At this rate she would have not a shred of reputation left; at least not the sort of reputation she really wanted to have.

'Can I see you before we start work this morning, Alistair?' she said, getting up from the table. She felt renewed anger surging through her veins. What was the man playing at? She thought they had developed some sort of rapport the previous evening. She had even thought of him as an ally. But now this. She stood in Reception, drumming her fingers together, waiting for the man to appear. At last he strolled from the dining room and almost walked past her.

'What the hell are you trying to do? Making dubious comments like that? What on earth Simon thought of you, I just don't know. And then to tell everyone at breakfast that I had worn you out! What the heck do you expect they made of that? I thought you were my friend. I trusted you. You've let me down badly. I take back everything I said about you being understanding and anything else nice. You're obviously a devious swine. The press were right – *and* your second wife.'

'Have you quite finished?' he asked. 'I thought it might help if Simon was jealous. If he thought you were involved with a TV star and all, I thought he would realize what he was losing.'

'Don't you know anything? You've probably totally ruined my reputation and driven him even further away. He now thinks I go to bed with anyone and everyone. He even suggested I should use some protection if I'm in and out of so many different men's beds. Thanks a bunch, Alistair. If you have any more bright ideas, keep them to yourself.'

'But, Jenna . . .' he called out as she stormed up the stairs. He turned and noticed Simon standing, grim-faced, in the office behind the reception desk. The door was open and he must have heard much if not all of the argument. Alistair gave a shrug.

'Women, eh? Can't live with them or without them.'

'Perhaps a little more discretion, sir? Even in a remote place like this there is always someone hanging around after titbits of gossip. Especially concerning a celebrity like yourself.' If Simon really cared, he allowed no expression flicker across his handsome face.

'She's a lovely girl, isn't she?' persisted the actor.

'Very attractive,' agreed Simon, his face a mask of indifference. But his eyes held a different expression, one of unfathomable hurt.

'Known her a long time, haven't you?'

'Is that what she told you?'

'Oh, I guess I wormed it out of her. You don't do any of your archaeology stuff now, I take it? No, you couldn't possibly, not with all of this to take care of. I suppose if you have time for anything now it's antiques, judging by your stock here.'

'I do have that hobby,' agreed Simon. 'Now, if you will excuse me, sir, if there's nothing else? I have work to do.' He turned back into the office and Alistair went to collect his things for the day ahead. He had probably blown it for the pair, but of one thing he was certain: the look of pure pain in Simon's eyes told him that the man still cared for Jenna. But he would always be a man in control, whatever the outcome.

The storm broke around midday. The crew were down on a remote beach and everyone was soaked through by the time they got back to the vehicles.

'Damned place,' grumbled Alistair. 'Nowhere civilized even to park a car.'

'At least you didn't have to carry all the heavy gear back up the cliff,' someone commented.

'We should have a helicopter standing by,' someone else suggested.

'You're lucky the budget stretches to a push-bike, mate,' said one of the lighting technicians. 'You should try climbing up some of those mountains in the Andes, with a bunch of kids who think they're God's gift to music – especially with a full camera kit and extra lighting gear. Not to mention a totally unbelievable amount of sound stuff.'

They all laughed as they watched the rain streaming down over the windows.

'I guess we might as well get back and do a few interiors. This rain looks set for the day.'

'The week, more like,' grumbled Alistair. 'What do you think, Jenna? You're the local girl after all. Know the area like the back of your hand – underground included.'

Luckily, Jenna thought, everyone was far too busy to take up his comments.

The days gradually passed as the film took shape. Some of the extras went away and finally there were only the crew, Sylvia from the sponsors and Alistair himself left. Kurt was content to think that 'his girl' was keeping the star happy, and had left her to get on with it for most of the time. Simon had kept very much in the background, allowing them free rein to

195

do their job. He was always available when needed, but fortunately Jenna had mostly been able to avoid him. She believed she was coming to terms with his situation, and once or twice she had even managed to look straight at him without so much as a blush colouring her cheeks. Once this dreadful week was over, she might never have to see him again. Although that prospect made her want to weep, she knew it was sensible, and probably the only way she was ever likely to get over him completely.

At last, the final day arrived. There was a degree of tension amongst everyone connected with the film, knowing this was their last chance to get the remaining shots. Once they had left the area it would be very expensive to get people back. The bad weather had allowed them to take reels of footage of moody storms, including an inshore lifeboat dinghy bouncing over high waves on its way along the coast. It would make the perfect background for some of the commentary. Alistair would come into the studio for voice-overs, once they were back in Town.

During one of the breaks, Alistair came over to speak to Jenna.

'I'd like to keep in touch when we're back in London.'

She had more or less forgiven him his crude attempts to make Simon jealous and he had behaved impeccably ever since.

'I suppose,' she said doubtfully. 'But I'm not really sure what I shall be doing, where I'll be going after this. I never did finish my holiday.'

'You could always take a holiday with me,' he

offered. She made no comment, but glared at him suspiciously. Sometimes she couldn't be sure whether he was joking or not.

'What are you two love-birds plotting behind my back?' asked Kurt, creeping up on the pair.

'Love-birds?' echoed Jenna.

'I'm just trying to persuade her to come away with me to somewhere exotic.'

'What could be more exotic than Cornwall in a storm?' laughed Jenna.

'Indeed,' said another voice from behind. 'Jenna is excellent in storms, aren't you, Jenna? Especially thunderstorms.' Simon stood on the fringe of the group, a fixed smile on his face. 'Excuse me for interrupting, but there's a call for you, Miss Brown. Your aunt needs to speak to you urgently. You can take the call at Reception.'

Puzzled, she went to speak to Sarah.

'Sarah? Is everything all right? How are you?'

'I'm fine, darling. Just wanted to touch base, see how you are. I had to say it was urgent or no one would have bothered to seek you out. I'm still stuck here in London, and likely to be here for ages yet. When are you coming back? We can meet up soon perhaps?'

Jenna listened to her aunt leaping from one question to the next, as always. Finally, when she did manage to get a word in, they arranged to meet early the following week and do some catching up. It was almost at the end of the call before Sarah asked about Simon.

'He certainly sounded rather strange for him. Sort

197

of tenser than usual. Is everything all right between you?'

'Sarah, once and for all, there is nothing between us. He has Paula and Tom. I don't suppose you knew about Tom, did you? Yes, Simon has a seven-year-old son, the spitting image of him. Imagine a miniature version of Simon – the eyes, the hair, long and skinny, even at this age. He's quite adorable . . . So forget about pushing me and Simon together. Forget it.' She put the phone down and, feeling desperately unhappy, tried to pull herself together and fix her public face firmly back in place.

'I'm glad you've seen sense,' said Paula, moving into Jenna's view from the office. She had obviously overheard much if not all of her phone call. 'Simon has commitments and he is trying to take them seriously. He can do without someone like you trying to entice him from his duties and wreck his chances of making a successful marriage.'

'Entice him? Me? You've got to be joking. But you needn't worry. I shall be leaving in the morning, and with any luck I won't be troubling you ever again.'

'You're right. Tom is the absolute image of his father, isn't he? But when did you see the child? I always try to keep him safely out of the way of guests. It isn't good for him to mingle with so many diverse people. He might get a totally false impression of what the world is like.'

'He . . . he was in Reception one day when I came in. He's a lovely little boy. You must be very proud of him.'

'He's certainly a great asset,' Paula said, her face remaining unsmiling.

Jenna went back into the room they were using. An 'asset', Paula had said. That was a rather strange word to use about a child. She shrugged and tried to get her mind focused on her work. Simon was still talking heatedly to Alistair and Kurt. They looked angry, as if they were arguing. She hesitated. Should she join them, and possibly become embroiled in an argument, or leave them to sort themselves out?

'Damned cheek, that's what I call it.' Alistair said angrily, and stamped away from the other two men. Kurt shrugged and held up his hands in a gesture of defeat. Simon swung round, and with a stare at Jenna walked away.

'What was all that about?' Jenna asked Kurt.

'I don't know who he thinks he is. He just came out with a load of insinuations about all of us, you included, and immoral behaviour. Said the other guests and some of the staff had complained. How narrow-minded can you get? Cheeky sod. Anyone would think he was your father or uncle or something. Said I should make sure you looked after yourself better and that if I wanted to "hire you out", I should treat you with more care. Most unprofessional for someone in his position. And I thought he wanted this business to succeed.'

He followed Alistair, also stamping his feet as he went. Jenna went white and felt herself flooding with anger. What right had Simon to say all those awful things about her? It seemed totally out of character for him, as well as being quite unbelievably unprofessional. He was obviously remembering every single encounter they'd had over the past weeks. Alistair must be right; he was jealous. Who would have thought it? But that made no difference to his situation. He was still on the unavailable list.

She considered brazening it out with Simon, but the thought of encountering him and Paula at the same time was more than she could bear. She knew she would say things that she would regret later if she allowed herself to speak while she was in this emotional state. She would, however, challenge him if she *did* meet him on his own before she left. If nothing else, she would hate her last encounter with this man to be one of anger, leaving him thinking so badly of her for ever. Besides, Sarah would come back to the area at some stage, and it might well cause endless problems for her. This was certainly not her aunt's battle.

'I seem to have made rather a mess of things, haven't I?' Alistair said when Jenna joined him. 'Sorry, love. I was truly only trying to help. Simon obviously cares very deeply about you, by the way. Accused me of using you and making unfair demands on you. Kurt tried to set him right and was virtually accused of acting as a pimp. Never heard the like. I tell you, I shall be glad to get back to London and the relative security of dodgy headlines.'

Jenna couldn't help but smile. Her anger was not directed at this man. And her frustration was not really anything to do with Kurt. Whatever Simon thought about her morals, he was the only one who had any real cause for guilt. After tomorrow, it would all be over, once and for all.

'Right,' she said brightly, despite her desperately aching heart, 'what else is to be done?'

The final dinner that evening was a lively affair. Everyone who remained had been invited, including Simon, who provided several bottles of champagne. He was obviously trying to recover face after his unforgivable outburst earlier. It was his form of apology.

Jenna had managed to place herself at the opposite end of the table from Simon, between two of the technicians and facing Sylvia. The girl had positively blossomed during her time away from home and the demands of her sick mother. Her reddish hair was loose and fell in natural waves round her shoulders. The deep turquoise sun-dress, a purchase from a local shop, suited her perfectly. Even Kurt was remembering her name now, Jenna noted with pleasure. In fact, she realized, Kurt was paying a great deal of attention to Sylvia. Jenna sensed her inbuilt alarm bells ringing, and wondered if she ought to warn the girl about him. How could she, though, without sounding like a spiteful, jealous rival? Sylvia was definitely old enough to look after herself, she tried to comfort herself.

She noticed a disturbance along the table. Alistair had decided that dinner should become a moveable feast, or at least that the diners should all start moving. He was so unsubtle, she thought, assuming he was trying to sit next to her. The wretched man reorganized the entire seating plan for the next course – not for her to be seated next to him, but to Simon. She tried to glare at Alistair, but he refused even to cast a glance in her direction.

'So, here we are again,' Simon whispered softly, through slightly gritted teeth.

'Perhaps you shouldn't get too close. You never know what you might catch.'

'Jenna, Jenna . . . I'm worried about you. I suppose I feel responsible for what you seem to have become. I apologize for my behaviour this afternoon. I don't know what came over me but it was quite unforgivable. You have so many talents . . . quite enough not to need to go selling yourself. I'd hate to see you turning into a cheap tramp.'

Jenna exploded, all the pent-up emotions of the past weeks finally released. He had gone too far. She almost shouted as she spoke.

'Listen, everyone, Simon thinks I'm a cheap tramp. It isn't true though, is it? Kurt will tell you. Alistair will tell you. One thing I am not is cheap. I am *very* expensive. Too expensive even for you, Mr Simon Andrews.' She flung down her napkin and ran out of the room. There was a deathly silence which lasted for several minutes.

'Have some more champagne,' Kurt said loudly. 'Come on, everyone, the night is young.'

'But the fizz had gone out of the party and conversation was stilted and forced. Kurt struggled to keep things going until he finally gave up and invited Sylvia to join him in his room for a nightcap. Jenna heard their laughter, well into the night, as she lay sleepless on her bed. If she had intended to warn

Sylvia it was too late. She hoped the girl wouldn't be hurt, but now it was up to Sylvia herself.

Jenna had cried herself out. Simon had knocked on her door and called out her name a couple of times but she'd refused to answer. The bedside phone had rung several times, but she'd ignored that too, guessing it was probably Alistair. If only she'd had her own transport she would have left that evening, but she had far too much luggage to manage alone. Besides, the hotel was too remote to reach any station and catch a train at this time of night.

As it seemed there would be nothing to drag her back to Town in the immediate future, she planned to go and stay on her own at the cottage for at least a couple of days. She had cut her leave short anyhow, so a couple of days plus the weekend would make it a worthwhile break. It would give her time to lick her wounds. She would phone Sarah to explain that her return was being delayed, once she arrived at the cottage. She would tell no one where she was apart from her aunt.

She decided against a swim the next morning, fearing she might have too many early encounters. She had a quick breakfast, well before anyone else had begun to shake off their champagne hangovers. With luck, she could get Larry to take her to the nearest station, or maybe he might to drive her all the way back to the cottage if he had time.

She finally discounted this idea, as it might give the game away about her hiding place. She needed peace and solitude. Kurt could deal with all the immediate chores for once, and she could check everything later, when she eventually returned to work.

By ten o'clock she had reached Penzance station. There was the usual row of taxis waiting and her luggage was piled into the boot of one. They drove through the quiet lanes and the peace of her beloved home county once more began to calm her jangling nerves. The driver helped her to carry the mound of luggage to the door and he drove away, leaving her to greet the delighted Bonza. She must call Mrs Kernow, the lady who came in to feed him when Sarah was away, and tell her that she was home. Home. She could forget about everything for a few days and then, refreshed, she could return to London and begin all over again.

CHAPTER 12

The cottage was quiet and peaceful and exactly what Jenna needed after the exertion and traumas of the past weeks. She unpacked and shoved grubby clothes into the washer. She phoned Mrs Kernow to relieve her from cat-feeding duties, then drove Sarah's car to the village to buy milk and bread and a few necessities. These ordinary, mundane activities were what she needed to help her return to an ordinary life. Film-making was a crazy world. There were no such things as normal working hours on a project like this or any other. You worked when light and weather were right and snatched meals when possible. At least staying in larger hotels meant that dinner was usually a safe bet in the evenings, whatever hour the day's work was finished.

Sarah had not been back to the cottage since Jenna herself had rushed away, following that night with Simon. The memory insinuated itself into her mind and stayed, despite her attempts to block it out. She allowed herself a few moments to wallow in it. She felt the familiar warm glow suffuse her body and even lay on her bed, touching herself on those same magical places that he had visited, bringing her to life with such devastating effect. She rolled over, angry with herself.

Since she had first met Simon he had brought her nothing but heartache, endless days of longing. The actual contact between them had really been so very little. A few weeks of working together as youngsters on a dig; a couple of meals out; one night – correction, one *evening* of passion; several difficult encounters over the past weeks and that was it. She was allowing herself to sink into such despair following no more than a handful of encounters with a married man. Well, it was time to call a halt. Life was for living. She would only pass this way once and she had wasted quite enough time on Mr Simon Andrews. What was it Alistair had said? Simon cared deeply? Good. If he was right, then it was Simon's turn to suffer. He had presumably got himself into his particular situation; it was up to him to live with it. She had done nothing wrong, apart from the small exception of loving Simon.

Jenna dozed for most of the afternoon and awoke feeling heavy, and with a headache which lasted well into the evening. She stretched and yawned and went downstairs to find something in the freezer for dinner. She felt quite weak and realized she had eaten nothing more than her fruit at breakfast. If Sarah had been here, she would have accused her niece of fading away.

Sarah. Jenna really needed to talk to her beloved aunt. She dialled the number Sarah had given to her.

Evidently she had moved out of the London hotel and was now staying in a friend's house. Most unusually for her, she had said very little about this particular friend.

'Michael James,' said an unfamiliar voice.

'Good evening. Jenna Brown, here. Is it possible to speak to my . . . to Sarah Brown?'

'Of course. One moment please.'

'Jenna, darling. You're home. Do you want to come over? I'm sure Michael won't mind. He's longing to meet you. How are you? When did you get back?'

'Sarah, just listen for a moment. I'm at the cottage. I didn't come back to London. I just needed a bit of a break.'

'Is everything all right, Jenna? You sound dreadful. You sounded awful when I spoke to you the other day too. I've been worried about you. I called the flat several times today but only ever got your answering machine. I was planning to call round there in the morning, to check up on you.'

'I'm just feeling a bit down. It's been very hectic for the last few weeks and I need a break, that's all.'

'If I know you, my girl, you need to talk to someone. Oh, Lord. I'm really tied up here for the next couple of days. I'll try to sort something out. Maybe I could get down for the weekend.' She covered the handset and was obviously talking to the mysterious Michael. She took her hand away and continued. 'I think I could get away in a couple of days. Will you be all right until then? You sound so depressed, darling. Not a bit like you.'

'I shall be coming back to London after the weekend, so don't bother. I can see you in London almost as soon as you could get here. Thanks, Sarah. I just needed to talk a little, and now I need some peace and quiet. And Bonza's company, of course.'

'If you're sure. Keep in touch and make sure you eat properly. Empty the freezer if necessary, but please feed yourself. OK? I shall call you again, very soon.'

Jenna agreed, for the sake of peace rather than intending to follow the advice. She warmed up the frozen package she had taken from the freezer and poured herself a glass of wine, gradually beginning to unwind. She glanced through the local free paper that was lying on the hall table. There were several auction sales being held the next day. She wondered if she dared to go or whether Simon would be there. That was where it had all begun. No, it wasn't. Not really. It had all begun with a dig. That world-famous, earth-shattering dig. She really must look out the old photographs some time, when she was feeling less emotional . . .

Despite her long afternoon sleep, she managed to have good night and woke feeling refreshed and very much more in control.

'I'm really getting over him, Bonza,' she said to the cat as she sat on the back doorstep. 'All I have to do now is decide what to do today and where to go.' She glanced round the garden, noticing there were several chores that needed doing. Mr Kernow came in once a week to mow lawns and generally tidy, but he never had the time to do everything. A day in the fresh air and some hard, physical work was just what she needed.

She collected tools and a wheelbarrow and began work. She pulled out weeds and clipped off the dead rose heads, working relentlessly and not allowing herself to stop or to think. It was late into the afternoon before she allowed herself to rest. She stretched, feeling stiff after the unaccustomed work. She went to lie in a hot bath, soaking her aching joints and muscles. She heard the phone ringing downstairs but couldn't be bothered to climb out of the warm water. They'd have to leave a message – so long as she had remembered to turn on the machine.

The evening was glorious, warm and sunny. A sudden impulse drove her to go for a walk, despite her earlier weariness. She set off for the site of what she had christened the 'fateful dig' and wandered around the woodland where Simon had once camped. Strangely, she felt none of her usual regrets, and began to see the place only as gently nostalgic. Surely further proof that she was getting over that wretched man, she thought.

The site itself looked very different now, with the chain-link fence and neat little office filled with guidebooks and ticket machines. There was a rack of hard helmets for the visitors to wear inside the tunnels and give that extra frisson of excitement, a sense of danger even where it did not exist. The tiny exhibition was designed to whet the appetites of tourists and send them on a visit to the local museum. The old press picture of her wearing the bangle, standing close to Simon was reprinted in the guidebooks, together with an account of the discovery. It was her own moment of fame. But the site was locked up and closed for the night, so she turned away, walking back through the nearest village.

Another impulse took her into the pub, where she bought a shandy, downing it quickly to quench her thirst. She saw the people at the next table being served with huge plates of home-made pie, and as she hadn't stopped for any lunch rashly ordered some for herself. She quickly checked in her pocket, to make sure there was enough money in her purse to pay for it. It would have been highly embarrassing if she had ordered it and been unable to pay. She had just about enough cash. There was a good atmosphere in the pub, and she sat listening to locals and tourists sharing stories and jokes. This was how ordinary people lived, she thought. Not dashing round the world, working all hours. She could actually quite enjoy it, she decided.

The cottage was in darkness when she returned. She made a coffee and sat down to watch some television. She remembered the old box of photographs in the loft and, bored with what was on offer on television, climbed the ladder to see if she could find it. This would be something of a test, to see if her new-found confidence that she was over Simon really was true.

While she was delving around she thought she heard the phone ringing, but as she couldn't possibly have reached it in time to answer it she ignored it. She also remembered that she had never got round to switching the answering machine on. It was probably Sarah, fussing as usual, she thought fondly, then became totally occupied with her search through the loft.

There was stuff going back years – much of it belonging to her. She found a box of dolls, several books and games, remembering the pleasures of childhood. Trust Sarah to have kept it all. There were several boxes of materials from the many digs that her aunt had made over the years. Old rocks and bits of pottery, all neatly labelled with a brief history of where they had been found.

The phone rang again, but Jenna was totally engrossed in her foraging. Another good thing about not working was that she could organize her days as she wanted to, with no one else to be considered. If she chose to stay up half the night and sleep during the day, so what? Finally she found the box of photographs that had been the object of her search and, clutching it tightly, began to descend the ladder.

She could never remember whether the box slipped out of her grasp and she tried to retrieve it or whether she slipped first and dropped the box. Whichever it was, Jenna ended up with her leg trapped in the folding ladder and her head down on the ground. She fought to free her arms. Dazed, and with a painfully throbbing foot still trapped in the ladder, she came to her senses. Once she had regained her breath, she tried unsuccessfully to dislodge her foot. She glanced at her watch, which had luckily survived the fall. It was well after midnight. She heard the phone ringing yet again, but was powerless to answer it.

This was ridiculous; she couldn't lie here all night, trapped by one foot. On the other hand, she couldn't move either. There were no near neighbours, so shouting was out of the question, nor did they even have a milk delivery due the next morning. It had been cancelled since Sarah was away from home. It looked as if Jenna would be staying where she was indefinitely, trapped by the foot and helpless to do anything by herself. The loft light spilled down on her, like a spotlight on some macabre stage set.

She pulled one of Sarah's rag rugs over her; rough it may have been, but at least it would stop her getting any colder. She would rest for a while, and when she had recovered her strength she could try again to free her twisted foot. Her head began to throb, and various other parts of her body were rippling with aches and pains. Her stomach hurt; she felt rather sick, and her headache had really developed now. It was quite ridiculous to think she was lying here in this predicament, totally helpless. Another ring of the phone. Sarah would probably be getting really worried by now. But she knew she was quite incapable of doing a thing.

One o'clock. Two o'clock. She lay half-asleep, powerless to move, undiscovered and unlikely to *be* discovered until heaven knew when. Every now and again the silence was punctuated by the strident ringing of the telephone and she was forced to lie, resignedly listening, until Sarah or whoever it was gave up the attempt.

Jenna heard a new noise downstairs. There was definitely someone there. Should she shout for help or stay quiet in case it was a burglar? But even a burglar would surely have the decency to help her. She wriggled her foot again, desperately trying to free it. Every movement was agonizing and she winced with pain. She had begun to think it must be broken. Miraculously, she heard a voice calling. She heard footsteps coming up the stairs. She heard her name being called. It couldn't be . . . no, she must be hallucinating.

'Well, now, what have we here?' said the miracle, as he turned into Simon. 'My poor love. Thank heavens Sarah had the sense to call me. Now let's see what you've been doing to yourself.' His hands gently tried to disengage the trapped foot, and she cried out with pain as he finally gave a tug and it came free, leaving her trainer stuck in the ladder.

'You don't believe in giving yourself an easy time, do you?' he said gently, while Jenna was weeping tears of sheer relief. He lifted her gently and carried her into her room. She rested against his comforting warmth and strength, nestling her head into his shoulder and basking in the security of his arms around her. He'd called her 'my poor love', she thought irrationally. He laid her on the bed. 'How ever long had you been lying there?'

'I've no idea. I went up around eleven, but I suppose it was some time before I tried to get down. Simon, whatever are you doing here?'

'Sarah phoned me earlier today. She was worried about you when you didn't answer the phone, nor did

213

you have the machine on. She said you'd sounded funny when she last spoke to you – whatever she meant by "funny". Anyhow, I told her to let me know when you returned home. She called me again tonight and said she still hadn't heard from you. I offered to come over to see if you were all right. We assumed you were probably out somewhere for the day and had stayed on for the evening. It was only when it got past midnight that she began to get really worried. She seemed to think I should come over to see for myself and I agreed. I set out as soon as I could. Everyone at the hotel seemed to want to stay up late tonight. If I'd thought you might be trapped like this, I'd have sent them all packing much earlier.'

His glorious eyes bathed her in their light and she felt instantly comforted by his presence. His tender concern made her feel even weaker and more tearful than ever.

'Thank you so much for coming. I don't deserve it. If I hadn't been trapped like that, I'd probably have given you a mouthful of abuse for daring to come near me, ungrateful beast that I am.'

'I did wonder,' he laughed. 'We hardly parted on the best of terms, did we?'

Jenna grimaced, but she couldn't apologize as she did not truly believe an apology was due – from her at least.

'Do we ever? What on earth did Paula think of you disappearing like this? She must have thought it very odd.'

'What's anything got to do with Paula? I keep telling you, Paula is nothing to me.' He looked impatient.

'I shall never understand how you can say that.'

'She is a . . . a distant cousin and that's all. Look, I don't want to start all that again. I've really had enough. We must decide what to do with *you*. We ought to get you to the hospital, in case that foot is broken.'

'Can't it wait till morning? Or do you have to be back at Tregarth before then?'

'I'm sure as hell not leaving you here alone,' he announced. 'But maybe it would be easier to wait for daylight. I'll make a hot drink for us both and then you might try to get some rest.' He went down the narrow stairs and she heard the comforting sounds of the fridge door being opened and the clatter of mugs. Moments later Simon climbed the stairs again, carrying two mugs of cocoa. She pulled a face at the sweetness, but he insisted that the sugar was necessary for shock. She shivered slightly and he tucked the duvet round her.

'I feel as if I should be providing you with a teddy bear,' he joked. He sat on the edge of the bed, next to her pillow, and put a comforting arm round her. She snuggled up to him, sharing his warmth until she dropped off to sleep. She felt safe, with the same comfortable feelings she could barely remember from her childhood, when her father had cuddled her.

Simon sat in a semi-doze. Some time later he tried to ease his arm out from under her as it was beginning to cramp, but she pressed herself even closer. He looked down at her, sleeping like a child. Her hair was spread over his arm and the pillow. The long dark lashes rested on smooth, clear cheeks. He touched their softness with his free hand. She moaned slightly in her sleep and the faintest glimmer of a smile touched her rosy lips. His heart constricted with love. How ever had they managed to make such a mess of something that should have been so good? Somehow he had to find a way, to find the words to explain. If she had been guilty of sleeping around, as it seemed from all the innuendos, then she must have had good reason. Could he possibly forgive her all of that? Whatever she had done in the past had made her the woman she was today. Wasn't he always saying that? He was not all innocence himself, but surely there must be some way to build on this love he felt for her?

It was six o'clock when he felt Jenna stirring. He was instantly awakened from his doze. His arm felt quite dead and his fingers began to tingle with pins and needles. He eased his arm from beneath Jenna and smiled at her.

'How's the foot feeling?'

'Stiff and sore. Ouch,' she said as she tried to move it. There were aches and pains in several other places and she still felt very slightly sick. She kept quiet about this, however, thinking she had complained quite enough already about her injuries.

'I'll make us some coffee and then we'd better see about getting you to hospital for an X-ray. Will you cope with sitting in the back of my car, do you think?'

'I'll call for a taxi or an ambulance. I couldn't put you to all the trouble of taking me.'

'Nonsense. I'll call Tregarth later on. They'll

just have to manage without me for once. We're not too busy at present. The next lot of guests aren't due for a few days. We weren't too sure how long your film lot would be staying, so it's fairly quiet.' He went downstairs again and she could soon smell fragrant coffee filtering through the machine. She could also smell toast, and felt ridiculously hungry. She heard the phone ring and Simon answered it. A few minutes later he came up the stairs, carrying a loaded tray. He balanced it on the chest beside her bed and poured the coffee.

'Please, no sugar this time,' she begged. 'I hate sweet coffee, and you don't want to add sickness to my other discomforts.'

He grinned and said he would allow her to miss the sugar if she ate some toast and marmalade. 'That was Sarah on the phone. She was worried, of course. I got thoroughly reprimanded for not phoning her back last night. I did say that under the circumstances that particular chore had been far from my mind. She sends her love, by the way.'

'I suppose she's hot-footing it down immediately to fuss over me?'

'Actually, no. She's going to leave that pleasure to me.'

'You? Don't be stupid.'

'I have my boy-scouts' first-aid badge, I'll have you know. It's no problem. I'm going to stay and boss *you* about for once.'

Jenna stared at the man she had known as a scruffy youth, a cultured, rich businessman, hotel owner, and now he was proposing to act as nursemaid. She giggled, despite the pain she was suffering.

'Somehow I never imagined you in the Florence Nightingale role. But, feeling about me the way you do, having such a low opinion of me, why would you want to do anything for me at all?'

He looked at her, gave a slight shrug and said in a low voice, 'I owe a lot to Sarah. She's been very good to me in the past, and perhaps I see this as a small way to show some gratitude.'

'I see,' whispered Jenna quietly, her heart sinking. He was helping her for Sarah's sake rather than out of his concern for her. She should have known. Even so, it was a very generous thing for him to be considering at all.

The small, local hospital had only a limited accident unit, but they did look at her foot and take an X-ray. Miraculously there was nothing broken, and Jenna breathed a sigh of relief. At least she was saved the much longer discomfort of a drive to Truro. The doctor asked if she was in any pain elsewhere, and she admitted to the slight discomfort in her lower abdomen. The sickness had passed since she had eaten the toast earlier, and she had put it all down to indigestion following her large pub meal the previous evening. That, together with all the tension she had been suffering in the past few days, must have affected her in some way.

The doctor, however, insisted on a full examination. He looked gravely at her after examining her flat stomach.

'Is there any chance you could be pregnant?' he asked casually.

'No. Of course not,' she said quickly. Then she paused. When had she last had a period? She tried to calculate. She was late. Why on earth hadn't she thought of it before? 'Actually, I suppose . . . I am rather late. I hadn't given it a thought, but . . .' Her voice tailed off. Simon had not used any protection that magical night, before everything went wrong. It had been so spontaneous that neither of them had given it a thought at the time. She hadn't been using anything either, having seen no need when she had no intention of starting a relationship. But she had never even considered she might be pregnant, not after just the one single occasion that they had made love. 'Why do you want to know?' she asked the doctor.

'You have some bruising at base of your abdomen, and you do seem a little tender.'

'Perhaps it's my period starting.'

'No, I don't think so. I'll organize a simple test. And we'll keep you in for a day or so, just to keep you under observation.'

'But you can't. I can't,' she burbled, panicking.

'I can and I will,' he insisted, smiling.

Jenna lay back on the trolley, her mind buzzing with so many diverse thoughts. If she really was pregnant, she was obviously miscarrying. She felt suddenly horrified at the thought of losing this fragile little life that had barely begun. How much she had wanted Simon's baby once . . .

Practically, though, the thought was quite impossible. She would be a single mother. She would become just another statistic. She would have to face all the problems of bringing up a fatherless child. Luckily, her own parents had left her well provided for, so money wouldn't be a one of those problems. But where would she live? Her flat in London wasn't remotely suitable for a baby.

She would have to live at Sarah's cottage . . .

Her brain scurried on, quite out of control, as each new image presented itself. What a mess. But a baby was unlikely to survive after that awful fall. She would never have the chance to know the joy of Simon's baby in any case, so what did anything matter?

'I'll tell your husband to come and sit with you for a moment. I think I'd better fill him in first, though. We won't know for a while which way things are going.'

'No. You mustn't say anything to him. He isn't my husband. He's just a friend. Promise me you won't say anything.' She tried to sit up in her anxiety to stop him. Simon mustn't know. Not ever.

The doctor pushed her back down again.

'Relax, will you? If you're sure, if that's the way you want it, I won't say anything. You are my patient and you have the right to confidentiality. I was trying to make it easier for you, that's all.'

'You must say nothing to Simon. He doesn't even suspect about the baby. I never dreamt of such a thing myself. Simply say you don't want me to walk on the foot. Say that's why you want me to stay in hospital. Anything, but don't mention babies, please.'

The doctor nodded and left her to fetch Simon. She was to be taken to a ward later when a bed was ready, and meantime she had to wait to have her foot bandaged.

'Are you all right, Jenna? Really, I mean?' Simon asked. He was looking quite white himself. 'Damn it, I hate these places,' he said softly. 'It must be the smell of disinfectant or something.'

'I'm fine. Really. They're keeping me in the rest of the day and overnight for observation. I really don't know why they think it's necessary. They're just making a fuss.' She was holding firmly on to her emotions. She needed time to adjust to this new scenario. 'You might as well go back to the hotel. I shall be fine. You've already done quite enough. Besides, you freely admitted that you hate hospitals. Perhaps you could phone Sarah for me? Let her know what's happened. I expect she'll come down to look after me when I get out of here. Or at least until I can travel back to London, that is.'

'Shut up, Jenna,' Simon said, almost conversationally. 'I'm going to look after you for a few days. If you really do have to stay in overnight, I shall go back to Tregarth and get things organized for a few days away. I'll tell Sarah everything is under control and I'll be back here tomorrow to collect you. I'll come and visit tonight, if I can get things sorted. Don't worry about anything. I'm well overdue a few days off.'

'Simon, I –'

'I said, shut up for once! I'm not listening to any more of your protests. Now, be a good girl and lie back and do as you're told for once in your stubborn life. Enjoy being waited on.' He kissed her on the nose and gave her a highly comforting, totally unsexy cuddle. 'I'll see you later.' He turned and left the room, winking at the nurse who was coming in at the same moment.

'What a dish,' she remarked to Jenna, nodding at Simon's retreating figure. 'You married or just living together?'

'Neither, he's just a friend,' she replied miserably.

'You want to snap him up before someone else does,' she laughed.

'Too late. He's taken.'

'I'm not at all surprised. Now then, dear, we have to do a few tests. Take a few samples.' She began the first test in a long morning of being pushed and prodded, stuck with needles and asked endless questions.

The pregnancy was confirmed.

She lay back, trying to come to terms with the news. About lunchtime, she was assaulted with a series of ghastly pains and felt very sick. A few short hours later, it was all over. She no longer carried any vestige of Simon's baby. Now he need never know anything about it.

She slept for several hours and awoke to see the largest basket of flowers she had ever seen. The card said, *'With Love, Simon.'* She felt tears burning her eyes, and silently she wept for the loss of the child she hadn't known about until it was too late. She felt she should allow herself this short period of grief, promising herself that this would be the only time she cried. She would then push it out of the way for ever and look only positively at the loss of something that would have changed her whole life. She had been spared the problems of deciding how to face the future. And she was spared from telling Simon, with all the turbulence that would have brought.

Simon arrived at nine o'clock the next morning to collect her. She had a thick bandage on her leg, a collection of pills and a walking stick. She had changed back into the skirt she had been wearing when she came in, discarding the hospital robes before he had arrived.

'You look better this morning.' He grinned, taking her arm in support as she limped her way to the door.

'I managed to get a decent night's sleep,' she replied, 'despite what everyone says about hospitals. Look, it's very kind of you to help me like this, but I don't want to cause you any trouble.' Her face was pale but her expression showed no indication of the deep heartache she was suffering.

'Don't be silly. I wouldn't have offered if I minded.'

Simon seemed to have noticed nothing amiss, and she knew that somehow she would cope with the next few days. He thought she was simply suffering from the shock and trauma of her injured foot after the fall. 'How are things back at Tregarth?' she asked, hoping she sounded sufficiently casual. 'Will Paula cope for the day?'

'For the next few days,' he said with a smile. 'I've taken some time off, so I can look after you for as long as it takes. Don't worry. I haven't taken any sort of holiday in years.'

'Some holiday,' she whispered. 'But, Simon . . . you can't . . .' she began.

'It's all sorted. I've told Sarah what's going on and she's perfectly happy with the arrangements. Now, if you will allow me to help you get into the car, I can drive you home. All right?'

She settled back in the comfortable seat and tried to relax. Would she ever manage to keep her new heartache from him? If only he knew how she felt about him, he would probably run a mile rather than offer to stay in the same house for a few days.

CHAPTER 13

There had been a time, even in the relatively near past, when Jenna would have believed herself in seventh heaven at the very prospect of just one day, let alone several, in the exclusive company of Simon Andrews. But she had barely survived the past few weeks, knowing she might bump into him at any moment, round any corner at Tregarth. She had also had loads of work to do then, hadn't been just sitting around, waiting for her stupid foot to heal.

'Simon . . . we must talk. I can't allow you to give up your work simply to take care of me. I don't need a nursemaid. I'm sure Mrs Kernow would come in to help me. I only need some help with cooking and shopping. In fact, cancel the cooking. I can manage with the microwave for a few days. I should be able to go back to London quite soon, and then it will cease to be a problem.'

Simon listened carefully.

'Have you quite finished? Don't you think I might quite like the opportunity to look after you? It isn't the first time I've stayed in this area, remember. I might easily have chosen to spend a little holiday here, in one of my favourite places in the world.'

Jenna said nothing. For all she knew, he had been to very few places in the world other than Cornwall. But then, as she had to admit, she knew very little of Simon and his activities over the past few years. Presumably he must have travelled around on business. She couldn't really believe that the hotel alone was making enough money to cover the cost of the many luxuries he was obviously accustomed to. Basically, she was scared. Every time they had been alone together, things had quickly got out of hand. They always seemed to end up arguing. Besides, he had said some unforgivable things about her before she had left Tregarth. If he so hated what she was supposed to have done, what on earth was he doing here? And another thing concerned her deeply . . . she didn't know whether she would be able to resist this powerful, sexy man if she was living in such close proximity to him for several days. At this moment she didn't actually believe that she would ever allow herself to sleep with anyone ever again! It had all become too painful, both physically and mentally.

They drove home to Sarah's cottage in relative silence. It was barely twenty-four hours since Jenna had left it, but it seemed an absolute lifetime ago. It *was* almost the lifetime of her lost baby, she remembered ruefully.

'Garden or inside?' Simon demanded when they arrived.

She was feeling rather shaky now . . . emotion, she

assumed. She chose inside. He made coffee for her and set it out prettily on a tray, complete with a cloth.

'My, my. We have come on from the days of chipped mugs and no milk,' she commented, as light-heartedly as she could manage.

'Did you find the photos you were looking for?' asked Simon a little later. 'We ought at least to take a look at the cause of all the trouble.'

'I dropped the box when I fell. It must be somewhere around the bottom of the ladder.'

He went up the stairs and picked up the rather battered box and its scattered contents. The pile of old pictures covered several years and many expeditions. They spent a couple of hours reminiscing and talking through experiences, shared and otherwise. Several times Simon touched her arm, or caught her hand, smiling that knockout smile of his. Jenna laughed softly, almost forgetting her problems and traumas for moments at a time.

'You've lost that haunted look. It suits you when you laugh,' he remarked. 'I've been missing that spontaneity lately.'

'I haven't been feeling much like laughing. I expect I've become a drag.'

'You've had your moments, but let's forget all that now, shall we?

'Don't remind me of what I can never have, Simon.'

'Please don't start that again. How do I make you believe me? I do have obligations, yes, of course. But that needn't stop us from being together. Come on Jenna. Get real. This is nearly the end of the twentieth century. I can't live like a monk. Look. No strings. Let's try to forget the unpleasant past and spend the next few days really getting to know each other. Let's make this a real holiday and let's both of us try hard to enjoy it. Look, I've even switched my phone off, so we won't be pestered.'

'But you have too low an opinion of my morals, surely?' she remarked bitterly.

'I am also guilty of letting my mouth free-wheel a bit too often. Now, relax, will you, woman? Accept that I'm going to look after you, however difficult you try to make it for me.'

Jenna lay back on Sarah's comfortable sofa. She closed her eyes and contemplated the paradise she had just been offered. Could she really spend this time with him? Do the thing she most wanted to do? Could she forget about Tregarth, Paula, Tom, the baby and everything else? She knew that she might regret her decision later, but she also knew that she would regret it more if she didn't seize this chance.

'OK, Simon. Thank you. But there have to be a few ground rules. I can't cope with sex. Not at present. Not that I'm suggesting that's what you meant, but, believe me, now is not the right time. Do you understand?' A vestige of dismay crossed his face for a moment, but a flicker of understanding quickly followed.

'Fine, but I can't be expected never to touch you at all, not when you're looking so very desirable. Let this be our own private world for a while. Let this few days belong only to us.'

'I'll have to give Sarah a call sometimes, just to let her know I'm all right.'

'Fair enough. This is her house after all.'

Apart from her limp, Jenna was quickly recovering from her ordeal. By the next day she was already wanting to do more, but Simon rationed the amount of time she was allowed to spend on her foot.

'You're really quite a bully, do you know that? It's a shame we haven't got a pool here,' Jenna sighed. A spot of swimming would help her foot, and she could certainly use the exercise. All she seemed to do was sit around, eat and drink.

Simon's immediate response was to help her into the car and drive to the nearest indoor pool. They went at lunchtime, when most other people were doing things other than swimming. It was glorious to feel the freedom, and Jenna was soon able to swim at something approaching her usual pace. She could never have kept up with Simon normally, but on this occasion he matched his speed to hers and they swam companionably around the huge pool. After the swim they both felt ravenous, and took packets of fish and chips down to the beach. They sat on the sea wall and behaved like perfectly ordinary holidaymakers.

'I've never been to the seal sanctuary,' Simon announced, having seen a poster advertising the attraction.

'It might be a long walk for someone with a damaged foot,' she protested.

'Nonsense. I can always carry you, or borrow a pushchair from some unsuspecting mum. Come on.

No excuses.' She laughed and allowed herself to be manhandled into the car. All the time he was keeping his word about not making any demands on her and she loved him all the more for his self-control.

Each day seemed endlessly pleasure-filled. He kept finding different things for them to do and places to visit. He was attentive, kind and always full of fun – everything and more that she remembered from the past, that student she had fallen in love with. Only now he was different. The self-assurance of a successful businessman had added so many more qualities to him. He was powerful and charismatic, and he had a particular charm, tinged with mysticism, that these past few days had peeled away to reveal the man inside. She found herself staring at him at odd moments, as if she were trying to freeze a special moment in time, as if she might revisit it in the future, when she no longer had him around. She tried not to think about the day that must be drawing ever closer.

'I'm not getting heavy or anything, Jenna, but I have to tell you how very much I've enjoyed these past few days. Somehow I'm only just beginning to realize what I missed out on during my youth. When we met all those years ago, I was a relatively carefree student. When circumstances began to change for me, I had to grow up – virtually overnight. I had to take charge of things and take responsibilities I hadn't bargained for. Not only did I lose one of the greatest passions in my life when I gave up archaeology, but I lost my youth as well. That included you. However untouchable you were, I think I was falling in love with you even then. You do realize that I love you, Jenna?'

She gulped. He loved her? Her dream of having him love her might have come true, but basically nothing had changed. Despite the injured foot, she too had known more fun in the last few days than she could ever remember. That she loved him had never been in doubt, but this mock honeymoon period must be nearing its ending. He would have to return to his normal life, and to his wife and child.

'I'm sorry. Perhaps I shouldn't have said that. You obviously don't feel the same way about me. But you have enjoyed yourself, haven't you? I know you have.'

'I have loved it,' she admitted. 'And I do feel the same way about you. But . . . there always seems to be a *but*.'

He stared at her until she felt his eyes would burn right through her.

'I'm going to ask you something. I don't want an answer until this evening. I want to you to give it your full consideration. Sleep with me tonight? Let us have one last night to remember for ever. Obviously, whatever you're saying about loving me, you seem to think there is some reason we can't be together always. No one else need know anything about it, if that's the way you want it.'

She stared at him. The reason they couldn't be together was perfectly obvious, wasn't it? Nothing to do with her at all. That apart, she wasn't entirely sure whether she could cope with sex yet. Admittedly, an early miscarriage like hers didn't seem to have caused too much of a problem, but one thing was certain: she would insist that he took precautions on this occasion. She realized she had already made up her mind. There had never been a doubt. She had no choice.

'Yes, please,' she said flatly.

'You must think about it seriously, Jenna.'

'I have. Yes.'

He flung his arms round her waist, moving his hands to touch the sensitive places which he had been longing to touch for ever, it seemed to him. He kissed her lovely soft mouth with a tenderness that made her almost want to weep. He fondled her full breasts, sending shivers of delight coursing through her entire body. She touched him, feeling his erect nipples and smooth, firm muscles. She stroked his smooth back, feeling the flesh warm through his fine cotton shirt. She moved her hands, hands that had suddenly become expert, down his back until she enclosed his buttocks. She laughed softly.

'And what is so amusing?' he demanded.

'Just that I've been longing to do that for days. You have such a sexy bum, did you know?'

'Hussy. Ladies don't say things like that.'

'Then I mustn't be a lady. But don't you believe it. Every girlfriend of mine talks about men's bums. In fact, one friend of mine awards points out of ten.'

'And how many would I score, do you reckon?' he asked, grinning happily.

'Oh, at least twelve, I'd say.'

'I think you should introduce me to this friend of yours,' he teased.

'No way. I'm keeping this discovery of mine all to myself, at least for the moment.'

'If you don't stop doing that right now, I shall spoil any chances of us spending the night together. You are all right, aren't you? I mean, you have finished your period, I take it?'

He was nothing if not practical, she thought. He might not have understood what had really happened but her explanation had satisfied him. She nodded. Everything was fine and she seemed to have recovered completely. After all, many women had early miscarriages without ever knowing they were pregnant.

'Let's go out somewhere for the day,' she suggested. 'Then we can tease each other all day long.'

'You're quite wicked, do you know that? I was planning a picnic lunch and a lazy day on the beach anyway.'

'Along with a thousand holidaymakers? Great!'

'So what would you rather do?' he asked.

'How about a boat trip somewhere? We could find a quiet little beach somewhere instead of driving there along with the rest of the holiday hordes.'

He rose and picked up the local paper to look through the small ads. He made a short phone call.

'Right. All fixed. Now, go and change into something suitable for boating. It looks like being a hot day. Cover yourself with something so you don't burn. The sun's always hotter on the water, because of the reflection.'

Jenna went upstairs to change. She was feeling very fit and walking almost normally now, though the strapping on her foot still restricted completely normal movement.

They drove to a marina nearby and stood looking at the array of moored boats. There were all shapes and sizes.

'Stay there and look around,' Simon commanded. 'I'll be back in a minute.' She leaned over the rails and speculated about who might own the various boats. They varied from tiny two-man dinghies to huge power boats. She saw Simon emerge from the office, accompanied by a man.

'Seems we have a choice. You can come and see which one you'd prefer.' They walked along the boards between dozens of moored boats. Some of the larger boats had people sitting on the decks, most of whom nodded their good mornings as they passed by. At the end of one line there were two launches, both with small day cabins and open decks to sit in the sun.

'They do have a cover to pull over in bad weather,' said the yard-owner in his broad Cornish accent. ''Andsome craft, they are. Both of 'em.'

'Which do you like the look of, darling?' asked Simon, looking his usual immaculate self in well cut olive-green shorts and cream shirt. Even when he was dressed quite casually, Simon managed to look stunningly perfect.

'Sorry,' she stammered. 'What did you say?'

'Which do you fancy? Either of these two? Or perhaps you'd prefer another?'

'Any. Whatever you like,' she said. He seemed to be making rather of meal of a day's boat-hire. He pointed at one of the boats and the two men agreed.

'If you don't like it, you can always try another,' the man suggested.

'Fine. Done. I'll give you a cheque for the deposit.'

'Right you are, sir. Pleasure doing business.'

The two men went back to the office, leaving Jenna sitting on the deck of their chosen craft. It smelled faintly of diesel, of hot sun on fibreglass, of sea and sand. She leaned back, relaxing totally by forgetting about the difficulties of life and giving herself to the warm sun. Simon seemed to be taking ages, she thought. She got up from the comfortable seat and went into the cabin to look around. There was a tiny galley and even a small gas fridge, run on bottled gas. It was empty, of course. Pity they hadn't got round to making the picnic, she thought. They could have stored things in the fridge. She smiled. It was a bit like playing house. There were two bunks, doubling as seats, and a table which unfolded from the side of the boat. There was even a rather too tiny closet, housing a loo and shower. She went back up on deck and looked around for Simon, but there was still no sign of him as yet. What on earth could he be doing? It surely didn't take all that time to hire a boat for the day.

'You've been a long time. I missed you. We've got all mod cons,' she called out to Simon, as she saw him returning at last. He was carrying a box of groceries – the basics for a picnic, she assumed. The box also had a bottle of champagne sticking out of the top.

'Wow. What's the celebration?' asked Jenna.

'Anything you like.' He gave a grin. 'We could

always celebrate the renaissance of our love. Sorry,' he added, putting up his hands in mock surrender. 'OK. It will simply have to be in celebration of our new boat.'

'If only for a day.'

'No. It's ours. I've bought it.' He gave a boyish grin of delight and started up the motor. 'I've always meant to get a boat but never quite got round to it. Well, are you going to put that champagne in the fridge to chill or do we have to drink it warm?'

'You've bought this boat? It must have cost thousands!' she burst out. 'I only suggested a little trip on a hired craft. A rowing boat would have done.'

'I could change it if you prefer.'

This man was totally outrageous, she decided, with a shake of her head. This was impulse-buying gone completely mad. She hadn't realized he could be so utterly reckless and impulsive. He always seemed to be in such control.

She put the champagne in the fridge, as requested and unpacked the picnic things. He'd done very well, considering it was only a little shop at a marina. Obviously the sort of people who shopped at marina stores had expensive tastes. In addition to the champagne there was a delicious-looking tub of pâté, cheeses, smoked salmon and several pots of ready-made salads. There was also a granary loaf that looked delicious enough to break pieces off it right this moment. Obeying her instinct, she pulled a chunk of the warm crust and put it in her mouth. It was quite

heavenly, and she broke a piece for Simon, taking it
to him on the deck. She pushed it into his mouth
and he nodded appreciatively. He was busy negotiating through the channel out towards the sea. It
was a perfect day, calm, scarcely any breeze, and
brilliant sunshine.

'You are crazy,' she said to him once they were
properly underway. 'Quite crazy and utterly mad.'

He grinned down at her. 'I haven't been this crazy
in ages. It does me good.'

'But to spend that much money, just like that. How
on earth can you justify it?'

'Some of my shares rocketed yesterday. I sold half
of them and this is the profit. Easy, really.'

'Just like that, eh? But how did you . . . when did
you do that? Sell shares and things?'

'Ah, confession time. You may have noticed I'm an
early riser? I have a very clever little phone and fax.
It's very new, very compact, and it also gives me
access to the Internet. I did my dealings hours before
you were even stirring.'

'I suppose you've been using it to keep in touch
with Tregarth as well, and probably with Sarah.
Has she been getting daily reports on my progress?'

'You can bet your sweet life, honey,' he said, with
an awful pseudo-American accent. Jenna stared at
him. She really didn't know him at all. She'd known
nothing of all these investments, the Internet or
anything else. She gave a shrug and settled down
again to her sunbathing.

'You have used some sun-block, haven't you?'

'Don't keep fussing. Of course I have,' she murmured sleepily. It was all too much for a so-called convalescent. She suggests a boat trip and he promptly buys a launch.

'Remind me not to suggest we go to look at a zoo,' she said. 'You'll probably buy a safari park, complete with a set of lions or something.'

'Funny you should say that,' he began with a perfectly serious expression. 'I was thinking we needed something to liven up Tregarth. Do you think . . .?'

'No,' she shrieked. 'I didn't say a thing.'

It was as near perfect as a day could be, Jenna thought, leaning against Simon as he held the wheel and they skimmed over the blue waters. It seemed a million miles from reality, from her job, London, even Tregarth Manor. Thoughts of Paula and Tom had not intruded once on this magical day. Whenever she and Simon were close, they touched each other. Hands, bodies and occasionally lips. Whenever things looked as if they might get out of hand, they pushed each other away, laughing.

'Save it till later,' one of them always said.

They ate lunch, anchored a little way off the shore. They had sailed a short distance along the coast, carefully following the chart they had been given and keeping well away from the many treacherous rocks. They lay back on the comfortable sunbeds and finished the champagne.

'What are you going to do with this boat?' she asked him. 'I mean, where are you going to keep it?

What's it called, by the way?'

'Something crass, like *Spraylady* or *Sprayday* or whatever. Sounds like hair lacquer. I could be equally corny and call it something like *Jenna-rate*.' They both grimaced at the pun. 'And I don't know where I shall keep it. Probably move it further up the coast, nearer Tregarth. I'll leave it here for now. I shall have to sort out the insurance and everything, but the guy at marina will deal with all that.'

'He was very trusting, letting you take it just like that. I mean to say, we could have absconded with it and sold it for a fortune, if you only paid a deposit.'

'I have an interest in one of the yards down here. They gave me a reference. One of the reasons for my taking so long. We phoned them and had to wait for a while.'

'You mean you own part of a boatyard?' Was there no end to the surprises this man could produce?

'It's more a commercial venture rather than pleasure craft. I have a fishing boat. Part of the deal is to keep me supplied with fresh fish. The ex-owner now works for me, and it gives him a decent living. There's also a repair yard, which he manages in the winter. I believe in supporting local industry and enterprise and that seemed like a sensible way to do it. Diversification. That's the name of the game. Now, let's head back towards the river. It's still a long way back to the marina.' They hauled the anchor up on its well-oiled chains and started the powerful motor. Soon they reached the mouth of the river and motored in.

'Let's have something to eat and drink. I'm starving,' he announced when they were almost in sight of the marina. She was leaning against him once more, together they shared the wheel within the circle of his arms.

'You are totally amazing.'

'I know, but forget that and get me something to eat, woman!'

'I mean your capacity for food. I'm sure I'd end up like a barrel if I ate even half of what you put away.' She relinquished the wheel and went into the cabin. After the enormous lunch they'd eaten, she could scarcely believe he was hungry again. However did he manage to stay so slim? There was still some bread left, so she made a cheese sandwich for this man who claimed to be starving. She also made some tea and took it out to him.

'Ah, proper job,' he said cheerfully. 'See, I'm really Cornish after all, my 'andsome.'

'Yes. Typical Cornishman, I'd say. Luxury cruiser; large hotel complex; shares in places and companies I've probably never even heard of – oh, and a fishing boat, complete with boatyard. Just your average, ordinary guy. Anything else I don't know about?'

'This and that, you know. Come on, Jenna. What do *things* matter? It's life itself that is for living. I've worked bloody hard for what I've got, and for a very long time. I may not have wanted to take this route but I did, and I've been successful. Now it's time I started to enjoy life a bit. I can afford to pay staff to look after everything for me. Right now, the more important things come first. What are we doing about dinner this evening?'

'That's right! We *must* get the important things sorted out,' she laughed.

'I know what I want for dessert,' he said softly, his voice filled with innuendo. She felt a thrill of expectancy, of desire, rushing through her body, and she knew she was blushing. She glanced at him, suddenly, inexplicably shy. She noticed the tell-tale bulge in his closely fitting shorts and grinned. He followed her eyes and it was his turn to blush, just very slightly.

They arrived back at the marina and moored the boat in its place. Simon went in search of the owner, to sort out his business, and Jenna cleared the remainder of the picnic. She tidied the little cabin and wiped out the sink, putting the rubbish in the box. It might be fun to take a longer cruise some day, and stay in the cabin overnight. She giggled at the thought of Simon's long body curled up in one of the bunks. It would be a tight squeeze, especially for two of them. She shivered in delighted anticipation of the coming night as she sat on the deck, listening to the gentle lapping of the water round the boat. Life was good, even if these wonderful few days were rapidly coming to an end. But hopefully they were not quite there yet.

They drove back to Sarah's cottage, relaxed and happily chatting. They had found an ease with each other, a companionship that allowed them to talk or to be silent, always feeling togetherness. The tight lines of worry had melted from Simon's face, and he smiled much more often now than when she had first met him again.

'We didn't decide about dinner,' Simon commented when they got back. 'I think we've used up most of what was in the freezer. Any ideas?'

'Do you want to go out again?'

'Not really. How about a takeaway?' he suggested.

'If you like. I'm not madly hungry so it's up to you.' Jenna felt she could well benefit from doing without a few meals. All the sitting around she'd been doing for the past few days was quite alien to her nature. 'You know something? You're worse than Sarah for wanting to fatten me up. She's always complaining that I don't eat enough!'

'Well, if you think I can exist on half a lettuce leaf, you're wrong. I suppose they don't do home delivery out here?' he asked.

' 'Fraid not. They'd get lost even trying. I could probably do you an omelette,' she offered.

'I'm more in a pizza mood. Something substantial to keep me going.'

'You're just a hopeless glutton,' she laughed. 'Fetch whatever you like. I'm going to take a shower.'

'Oh, no, you're not. I propose to share a long bath with you later.'

She gave a shiver of anticipation.

'But we don't have a long bath – not in this cottage.'

'You're hopeless,' he said, kissing the tip of her nose. 'And I adore you. I'll go and find something to eat, even if it means driving to Penzance again.'

'If I'm not allowed to take a shower, I might as well

come too. Means I can keep a check on you – just in case you meet my friend who might give you twelve out of ten for a having sexy bum.'

He took her hand and squeezed it as they walked up the path to the car.

CHAPTER 14

The first place they reached that was open was a Chinese takeaway. Simon ordered a massive meal, choosing all of their favourite dishes. Jenna quailed at the thought of so much food, but it was pointless trying to tell Simon anything.

'I'm going to wait outside. I could do with some air,' she said, suddenly realizing that she still hadn't broached to the subject of contraception. It wasn't likely he would have any condoms, but then who could tell with a man like Simon? She felt weak at the knees at the thought of his body loving hers, in just a few short hours. She hoped he would follow her outside, as she didn't want to talk in front of the man taking orders inside. Seconds later, Simon did come out.

'Are you all right? You look a bit pale.'

'I'm fine. Just a bit hot. The thought of dessert, I guess.'

Simon put his arm round her and drew her close. He kissed her gently and grinned.

'Go to it, mate,' called a gang of youths walking past.

Simon smiled, waving them away with a flick of his wrist. He looked at Jenna again.

'Are you sure there's nothing wrong? You haven't changed your mind, have you? About tonight, I mean?'

'Of course not. Only, well, there is something. I think we should take precautions. You know, use condoms. I assume you haven't got any?'

'I'm not in the habit of carrying them around with me, if that's what you mean. I'm particularly fussy about whom I sleep with. But if that's what you want, I'll make sure I'm equipped.' His face had taken on a grim look, and weren't those the old tension lines back at the corners of his eyes?

Jenna bit her lip. She had always felt it was going to be a difficult topic to talk about, but his reaction was not quite what she would have expected. He had, after all, made various comments about taking precautions just a few weeks ago at Tregarth. Admittedly he had been saying it for quite different reasons at that time, but another pregnancy for her at this time would be a disaster.

He went back into the shop and she saw him speak to the man inside. He gave a grin and indicated the men's toilet. Still grim-faced, Simon disappeared, and came back a few moments later. Obviously he had found what he needed. He waited inside the shop for a few moments more. A large carrier bag was brought through, filled with the ubiquitous aluminium foil boxes. Simon nodded and the man spoke again, with another leer. Jenna could only imagine what he had said.

She took the bag from Simon when they reached the car and she sat hugging the warmth close to her. He had spoken scarcely a word since he came out of the shop, and she was beginning to experience a desperate feeling of panic inside. Something she had said had totally ruined the evening. He surely couldn't object to using condoms? It was for both their sakes, after all. Though he didn't know it, they had only just escaped from one catastrophe – that was how he would surely view an unwanted pregnancy. Tempting though it was, the prospect of bearing Simon's child was fraught with too many difficulties.

'I put a bottle of white wine in the fridge before we left,' she said, trying to break the silence. This was not what could be described as one of their 'companionable' silences.

'Fine,' he replied, with no flicker of emotion.

'Simon –' she began.

'Hush. We'll talk later. Let's get back before the food gets cold.' She obeyed and leaned back unhappily against her seat. She sensed it might be best to remain silent.

Back at the cottage, Jenna took chopsticks from the drawer and put plates out.

'We don't need plates,' he said, making a huge effort to smile. 'We can feed each other from the boxes.'

Jenna put the plates back. She felt momentarily relieved. Perhaps everything was going to be all right after all. She got a heated food tray and plugged it in, then unpacked the boxes and set them out on top. At least the food would stay hot that way. Simon collected wine glasses and put them on the kitchen table. He opened the bottle and poured them each a glass, then raised his to propose a toast.

'Here's to a successful nursing mission. I think we can assume that you are sufficiently recovered for me to leave you now.'

Jenna felt the blood draining down her body. So it really was all coming to an end, just as she had suspected. After the day they had shared on the boat, she had wondered for a while if this affair might possibly go on. She had deliberately pushed all thoughts of Paula and Tom from her mind for several days. Simon had asked her to forget everything that seemed to come between them and she had done that – all too successfully, it appeared.

'I'm very grateful to you,' she said with a sense of formality. 'It was good of you to spare so much time for me.'

His deep golden eyes stared into her icy blue ones. He looked away.

'Simon, what's wrong? Have I done something to upset you?' He remained silent. 'If I have, surely you can tell me what it is? I can't do anything about it if I don't know what I've done.' His mouth remained a grim, tight line. 'You've been stony silent ever since I mentioned using contraceptives. Is it something to do with that? Have I spoilt it for you?'

'I just wondered why it had become important all of a sudden.'

'I should have thought even you would realize that,' she snapped.

'You didn't seem to be bothered last time. Surely it's a bit late now.'

'Simon, I don't know what you think I am. But whatever you might think, I do *not* sleep around.'

'I thought it didn't matter to me. But now I find that it does.'

'I simply don't want to get pregnant,' she said softly, emotion constricting her throat.

'There's no chance of that. Not with me. I can't have children.'

Once more she felt the blood drain from her face.

'I don't know what you mean.'

'I should have thought it was obvious. I should be glad, I suppose, that children don't figure in your plans. If we ever *had* managed to overcome all these difficulties that you've placed between us, I believe I might have had a problem with telling you that I'm infertile. I cannot father a child.'

She sat silent, frowning, totally baffled by his words. She had recently had a miscarriage, and that had certainly been his child. What on earth did he mean? Besides, what of Tom? He was the absolute image of his father. Even if he had had a vasectomy after Tom, the baby she had so recently lost could not possibly have been anyone else's. Her short affair with David had been over many months ago, and there had never been any chance of a baby then.

'What on earth are you trying to tell me? You *can* father a child! You have living proof.' And I have dead proof, she thought sadly.

'I suppose you mean Tom. You think he is my son. You're wrong, so very wrong, Jenna. There's obviously no trust between us. I've had enough of it all. I think it would be better if I left straight away.'

He ran up the stairs and into the tiny room he had been using during his stay. Jenna heard the sounds of cupboard doors opening, of clothes being bundled into bags. She heard drawers slam shut, and finally he thundered down the stairs again. He picked up his car keys and glared at her.

'Get back to London, where you so obviously belong. You might as well have these. I won't be needing them.' He flung down the tiny packet of condoms onto the table and turned to the door. 'If I've left anything behind, perhaps Sarah can return it – if she ever decides to contact me again. Doubtless you'll have plenty to tell her. If I don't see her again, perhaps you can sell it the way you obviously sell yourself. I'd hate you to be at all out of pocket.' He slammed the door behind him, and for the second time in a few short weeks she heard the mad screeching of tyres as he revved his powerful car and drove out of her life for what must be the final time. It would be for ever this time; she just knew it.

Jenna threw the untouched boxes of food into the bin and unplugged the heater. She was too sick inside even to look at them. She stared at the tiny foil packet Simon had thrown down onto the table. How could so small an object ruin everything like this? Why was he lying about his ability to father a child? It was so ridiculous as to be laughable. But she could perhaps understand his reservations about her. He must still believe there was been some truth in what Alistair had said. The whole world knew of Mr Dodds' supposed reputation, whether or not it was deserved, and the silly, vain man had dropped enough of his insinuations all over the place. But she had felt certain she had convinced Simon that nothing at all had been going on with him – or anyone else.

Anger began to burn inside her. To think she had almost fallen into his trap. At this very moment she could so easily have been lying in his arms, making the most wonderful love ever. All those special moments during the day flooded back. He had teased her, taunted her, brought every nerve end to excited life a dozen or more times. She had excited him too, she knew it. However inexperienced she was, she had known without a doubt that he had wanted her. It seemed so sadly ironic now that they had saved everything for this one night. If they had made love impetuously, floating on the ocean, she would probably not be in this situation now. What a rat Simon was, she tried to convince herself. He obviously didn't like the idea of a condom coming between him and his pleasure. It must be that. All that garbage about being infertile must be his usual line with the women he slept with. 'Men. Who'd have them?' she shouted angrily at the four walls. 'And Simon flaming Andrews is the worst of them all.'

'Miaow', said Bonza, coming in through the open door.

There was only one thing to do. She would return to London first thing tomorrow. She smiled ruefully. The last time Simon had flung himself out of that door, she had made exactly the same decision. On that occasion she had found herself returning to Tregarth Manor, of all places, just a couple of days later. But there was no way she would ever go there again.

She stamped upstairs, as much as the still weak foot allowed, and hauled the sheets off Simon's bed. This time she would not overload the washer and cause a flood. The first train tomorrow, she was out of here. She glanced round the room to see if anything had been forgotten. All she saw was a small square box. She pulled the lid off it. The paperweight. There was a card inside, written in Simon's handwriting.

I hope this time you will accept this with all my love. You were right, it is valuable, and so is my love for you. You really are the best ever.

Three kisses followed.

Jenna gazed at the beautiful object. Perhaps this was what he'd meant by selling anything he'd left behind. This was probably worth hundreds, if not thousands of pounds. He sure as hell hadn't written that card just before he'd left, though. He hadn't had the time and certainly would never have composed a note like that in his current mood. Thoughtfully, she slid it back into its box and pushed it to the back of a drawer in her own room.

The rest of the ruined evening she spent packing. Most of her stuff she would leave here to save having to carry it. She could always buy new things if she needed them, when she got back to London. A day's shopping with Sarah would certainly go a long way towards cheering her up. And work. Kurt had told her to ring him as soon as she was better. She was physically recovered, perhaps, but as far as men were concerned she didn't want to know. Probably *never* would be too soon, the way she felt at present.

There was a total sense of *déjà vu* about the next day. She travelled to London by train, took a taxi back to her flat and opened up the door, pushing the pile of letters to one side. The answering machine was flashing its signal of stored calls. She went into the kitchen to put the kettle on for coffee and played back the messages. Several were from Sarah, that dreadful night of her accident, and others were from various people she would deal with later. The last one was from Sarah, asking her to call back as soon as she arrived. It was timed at four o'clock today. If she knew Jenna's return was imminent, it must mean that Simon had called her. There was no other way she could have known. Damn him, she thought. Goodness knows what tales he had told her. She quickly dialled the number.

'Jenna, darling. Are you all right? I've been out of my mind with worry. How's the foot? Are you quite recovered? Are you well enough to be there on your own?'

'Oh, Sarah. You'll never change,' Jenna said almost happily. 'Will you come round to the flat?'

'On my way, love. See you soon. Keep smiling.'

Jenna wondered what the comment meant. There were no worries about her being cheerful. She fully intended to *stay* cheerful, if that was what it took. She

252

was no longer tearful about what might have been, simply mad with herself for falling into such a stupid trap for a second time. She had always known that Simon would have to leave her at the end of those enchanted few days and return to his wife and family. His hotel took up his working time, plus the rest of his own particular empire. Whatever he said about living life to the full, he had chosen his path and he would have to follow it. He had obviously made some mistakes – mistakes he would have to live with. But whatever he did, it was no longer any concern of hers. She was still young, fit and healthy; she had a good job and she was quite capable of making her own way in the world. Nevertheless, she was looking forward to a good heart-to-heart with Sarah. It had been far too long since they had spent time together.

She flicked through the rest of her mail while she waited for Sarah to arrive. Another letter from Kurt – this was getting to be a habit – and he had also left a message on the answering machine. She ignored his request to call back urgently. There was no way she was admitting to being back in circulation, not for a day or two at least. In his letter, he also asked her to call him as soon as she could. Obviously he was missing her, for whatever reason, but she assumed it had to be work. She pushed the rest of her mail to one side. There was nothing that needed her urgent attention.

She poked around her tiny freezer to see if she had any food in. It was virtually empty. Obviously a shopping trip was needed. She went to the local newsagent's and bought some milk and a jar of coffee. At least it was a start. She also picked up a packet of chocolate biscuits. She never ate chocolate, or biscuits, but then, this was a new start, and if it included chocolate biscuits, so what? Simon had a passion for them and he had bought several packets during his stay. It was still a matter of amazement to her that he ate so much and stayed so slim. *Now then*, she chided herself. *You're allowing yourself to think of him again, and we all know he isn't worth the time it takes.*

The doorbell rang and she rushed through to greet her visitor.

'Sarah! I can't tell you how good it is to see you. I've been missing you so much. Come in. Coffee? I've even got some chocolate biscuits.'

'Hello, darling. Chocolate biscuits, did you say? Now who's trying to fatten up who? And where did you get such bad habits? As if I couldn't guess. But are you really all right now? How's the foot?'

Jenna filled in the details, missing out the bit about her miscarriage. Simon, it seemed, had kept her aunt well informed about the injury and her niece's progress.

'He must have done a good job in convincing you. I was actually quite surprised that you managed to stay away,' Jenna said. 'I thought the chance of a captive audience who you could stuff with food non-stop would have been just too much to resist. What *has* been keeping you so busy?'

'I told you. My book.' Sarah talked at length about her work, and gradually she got around to talking about her mysterious friend, Michael. He too was an archaeologist, it seemed, and they were co-authoring a book at the request of a major publisher.

'Wow, I'm impressed,' Jenna remarked. 'Most writers would give their eye-teeth to get a publisher to even look, let alone have one demanding their work. Congratulations. I hope it's an enormous success.'

'It's largely Michael's contacts. It's a coffee table extravaganza. Loads of pictures – you know the sort of thing. He's also hoping to get a TV company interested in some film rights.'

'And when do I get to meet this Michael? I need to see if I approve of him for my favourite aunt. Is he an A or B?'

Sarah chuckled. It was total role-reversal. The number of boyfriends she had been forced to approve when Jenna was young had led eventually to a grading system.

'Definitely A. You'll get to meet him soon enough, but he's away at present. I'm flat-minding,' she said with slight hesitancy.

Jenna stared, and waited for her aunt to continue. But she would say no more on the subject.

The two chatted until almost eight o'clock, when they decided to go and have dinner somewhere. There was a little Italian place nearby, and they ate bowls of steaming pasta, drank cheap red wine and chatted like the two old friends they truly were. They planned a day's shopping, and Jenna was invited to visit Michael's flat. He would still be away for some days, but they would meet as soon as possible.

The one subject that Sarah did not broach was Simon. Jenna was truly amazed. Her aunt's usual curiosity was obviously under strict control, and she felt relieved to be given a breathing space. One day, perhaps, she might be able to talk about it, but this was not the time. Granted, Jenna thought she felt in complete control, and kept telling herself that she had done the right thing. It was only when thoughts crept in unbidden that she realized how much she was missing the man she still loved, despite all that had happened. She just had to stay angry with him and she would survive. Anger was a positive reaction; feeling weepy was totally negative.

Michael's flat was wonderful. It was situated near Regent's Park and was the ground floor of one of the typical, huge old houses in the area. It had an old, well-established garden, with masses of roses tumbling over every possible wall. No wonder Sarah could manage to live so happily in London . . . the garden was almost as good as her own in Cornwall. Almost shyly, her aunt showed Jenna round the flat. The rooms had high ceilings, giving the impression of spaciousness despite a great many pieces of furniture. The lounge had French windows, opening into the garden, and was furnished in various shades of cream and white, broken only with splashes of colour from bright cushions. It was cool and elegant but very comfortable. The kitchen was a dream – very homely and welcoming, but with masses of time-saving gadgets and equipment. There was a large pine table in the middle and chunky brown pottery on a dresser. There was also a delicious smell coming from the oven.

'Haven't lost your touch, I see,' Jenna remarked, sniffing appreciatively.

'Come and look at the rest of the flat,' Sarah invited. The separate dining room had been turned into a study, with two computers on opposite desks. The large dining table was covered in books and piles of photographs.

'This is the workplace,' Sarah announced. 'See? I've even managed to get myself modernized,' she laughed, indicating one of the computers. 'That's mine.' Jenna was impressed. Previously her aunt had always waved away such things as beyond her. Whoever he was, this Michael had worked a miracle on the normally almost reclusive woman.

'This is the bedroom,' Sarah announced, pushing open yet another door. The room was delightfully furnished in shades of green, cool but bright. Apricot and misty green curtains hung at the window, seeming to sweep the colours from the garden right into the room. The huge double bed made Jenna stop dead in her tracks. She glanced at Sarah, who coloured slightly.

'I didn't know how to tell you. I know it seems ridiculous at my age – our ages – but, well, I do really love him.'

Jenna gave a gulp. She was thoroughly shocked to the core – not at Sarah's revelation, but because she had never even considered it as a possibility. Sarah, dear Sarah, had always been around for her. She had never known Sarah go out with any man, let alone move in with someone. No wonder she had been so content to leave Simon to care for her niece when she was injured.

'You're looking really good, you know, Sarah. I begin to see why. You've kept this one a secret,' she laughed.

'You're sure you don't mind?'

'Mind? Why should I? It's got nothing to do with me. Besides, it's about time you did a spot of living in the present instead of always poking round in the past. Come on, spill the beans. I want to know everything. How long have you known him? Where did you meet? What's he like?'

'Slow down. I thought you always accused *me* of asking too many questions.' Happily, Sarah filled in the details. She and Michael had known each other for years; had met at a conference; he was still unmarried, having spent too long working when young. He claimed he had missed all chances of meeting anyone he could love.

'I can't wait to meet him. I'll give you my grading after that. But I must say I give him full marks for good taste. Not only has he managed to snaffle the highest prize in females, he's also got a delightful home. He can't fail to impress, can he?'

'Oh, Jenna, darling. I can't tell you how relieved I am. I've been dreading what you might say. And it was all at such a difficult time, with you and Simon. I am *so* sorry about that. You can talk about it whenever you're ready, you know. I don't want to pry, but it is important that you don't bottle things up.

'Thanks, Sarah, but I haven't got anything to say.

Not really. He's just a liar and a cheat and I shall have nothing more to do with him.'

Sarah bit her lip and looked worried.

'You're sure we mean the same Simon? The one with the heavenly eyes? Hotel-owner extraordinaire? Delightful, tall and handsome Simon Andrews?'

'Sounds like the same one. Sleaze international and rival to any politician in his ability to avoid telling the truth. Honestly, Sarah, if you knew half the lies he's told me . . . I assure you, I desperately wanted to believe what he was saying, but I don't think he understands the first thing about honesty. Now, I thought I was invited here for dinner? I'm starving.' Sarah shrugged and asked no more. Jenna would talk when she was good and ready.

London was stifling. The heat wave had gone on and on since Jenna's return. She had gone back to work and, although they had a few commissions, it was reasonably relaxed. The training film for Hudson's was ready for distribution, and there was to be a small gathering for its very low-profile, internal première. Then it was to be sent round to all Hudson's companies and subsidiaries before being released for general circulation. It was hoped that many other companies would use the ideas for staff training sessions, bringing in royalties to Hudson's. It would serve as good publicity for Kurt's product, and hopefully lead to more work from other companies for Reality Plus. Expansion into different areas was always Kurt's ambition.

Kurt insisted on escorting her to the evening's

function, and collected her from her flat. He seemed remarkably subdued, for him. He had instructed her to 'put on her glad rags' and she was wearing a stunning white linen sheath dress that she had bought on her shopping spree with Sarah. The top swathed over her shoulders, dipping almost down to her waist at the back. The skirt was full-length, with a slit extending above one knee. It had cost a fortune, but she'd felt it was worth splashing out for once, if only as a morale-booster. She wore her hair piled up high on top of her head and looked very sophisticated. Most unusually, Kurt didn't make a single comment about her appearance. Jenna even asked him if everything was all right, but he only grunted some response that she took as meaning he didn't want to talk about it.

'Jenna, darling. Wow! You look sensational, doesn't she, Kurt? Lovely to see you again,' called Greg, as he spotted her coming in. He pressed a damp mouth against her cheek and she drew away as quickly as possible before she was forced into any further contact with him. Alistair Dodds was holding court in another corner, with various members of Hudsons' staff flocking to rub shoulders with the great man.

'We did invite the young man who runs the hotel, but he wasn't able to get here. You knew him rather well, didn't you?' Greg was asking.

'We're old friends,' she said, thanking some guardian angel for sparing her that meeting. It would have been unbearable to have to meet Simon again so soon – especially on a difficult social occasion like this one. Just imagine if he had brought Paula too, she thought. But then, with all these men flocking round her, she might have made them both stop and look twice. Though that would probably have achieved nothing more than to confirm his low opinion of her, however unjustified it might be. She gave a tiny sigh. If everyone thought she had some sort of a reputation, she might as well live up to it in a mild way and enjoy flirting. Perhaps if she was consistently friendly with everyone, no one would make any more false accusations about her. She made up her mind to be thoroughly charming to everyone and set about the evening with renewed enthusiasm, as if it was another work assignment.

'Hallo, Jenna,' said a female voice behind her. She turned to see Sylvia, looking pretty in a simple deep blue dress. She looked rather tired, and Jenna assumed she was still having problems at home.

'How's your mother?' she asked.

'Mum died a couple of weeks ago,' Sylvia replied casting her eyes down.

'Oh, I'm so sorry,' Jenna said, biting her lip. How tactless she was. 'How did it happen?'

'She went wandering outside in the middle of the might and managed to fall onto the railway line near our house. It was terrible. I'd gone out for an evening. The neighbour who was supposed to have looked in on her missed her, but by then it was too late. I should never have let myself be talked into it. Going out, I mean. It was so selfish of me.' Sylvia turned away, but not before Jenna had seen the glint of tears in the girl's eyes.

'I'm so sorry. But you shouldn't blame yourself. You couldn't be expected to stay with her all the time. You do have to work, and that naturally involves occasional evenings too. You mustn't be so hard on yourself.'

'But it wasn't work. Not really. It was . . . well, Kurt asked me out. I'm sorry. I know he's supposed to be with you, but, well, you were away. We thought you may not be coming back, or at least that's what Kurt said. He was even suggesting that I might like to take over your job. Not that he'd really want that, but when you didn't come back from Cornwall he was as mad as anything.'

'He knew I'd had an accident. He knew I was coming back as soon as I could.' Jenna was puzzled, and felt slightly hurt.

'He said he'd written to you and telephoned you. Left messages. He said if you didn't get back to him in the next day or so the job would be mine. But then Mum died and there was the funeral and everything. I didn't hear from him again. And now you've come back anyway. I've been even more stupid than usual.'

Sylvia's voice died away as she left Jenna's side. Poor, silly girl. She wasn't the first woman to be promised the earth by Kurt. He always liked to have some devoted, admiring female hanging around. But Jenna hadn't been willing to play his games; she should have expected him to retaliate, however much it hurt.

'Hi, there, Jenna.' Another voice broke in her reverie. 'I didn't think it possible, but you look even

more ravishing than usual. Have you been somewhere exotic on holiday? I've missed you.'

'Hallo, Alistair? How are you?'

'Fine. And yourself? How's the love life? The
dashing Simon been around lately?'

'The "dashing Simon" as you call him, is history.
It was nearly something but it turned into a big fat
nothing.'

'Shame. You two seemed so well suited. Made a
very handsome couple. I suppose I couldn't offer
myself as a substitute? I can forget about the age
difference if you can.'

She laughed.

'Thanks, Alistair, but I'm having nothing to do
with men any more – apart from the occasional light-
hearted fling. Nothing heavy ever again. No one can
love a person who tells lies all the time. Lovers don't
lie to each other.'

'Ah, well. Who can blame me for trying? Play your
cards right, and you could probably get the managing
director. He's been staring in your direction for the
past five minutes, but then, you're easily the most
stunning woman in the room.'

Jenna blushed rosily. She felt embarrassed by the
flattery, but it certainly helped to boost her confidence. The small talk went on and on, interminably.
Jenna did her duty, as she saw it, working her way
from group to group and trying to be charming to
everyone. At least Kurt couldn't criticize her for
failing to circulate on this occasion.

The film was shown and everyone applauded
enthusiastically. Alistair was congratulated on a

first-class performance and the managing director of the whole Hudson International Corporation came over to have a personal word with Kurt and Jenna. He was delighted with the result and promised he'd be promoting the company to his friends and colleagues. A man with his contacts could only do them good. But this even lavish praise failed to shake Kurt from his miserable mood, and Jenna questioned him as they drove home.

'I've missed you, Jenna. I tried going out with the little secretary woman. Sylvia. But that didn't work at all. Never heard another thing from her. When I saw you tonight – so at ease with everyone, so much in charge – I realized how much I need you. Can't we forget the past? Start again? Please, Jenna. Try to love me.'

He looked so miserable that she almost felt sorry for him. But he was so entirely self-centred. Never did he think of others, only of how *he* was feeling. But he was an old friend, though she hadn't really known him as anything other than a boss. Whenever they were away on location together, there was always work to be talked about during the many shared dinners. Everything had always remained on a professional level, except for that one awful night he had got totally drunk and collapsed onto her bed at Tregarth Manor. Funny how every single thing seemed to go back to Tregarth Manor.

'Can we have dinner together tomorrow night? Please say yes.'

'I'm already doing something tomorrow,' she said hesitantly. Tomorrow she was invited to have dinner with Sarah and Michael. She was going to meet her aunt's lover and wild horses wouldn't keep her away from that date.

'I see,' Kurt said shortly. 'And the next night, and the next, I suppose? I'm wasting my time, aren't I?'

'I could go out with you on Saturday night, if you like,' she offered.

He smiled. 'If you're sure? I don't expect charity.'

'I'm not offering charity,' she replied.

CHAPTER 15

'Thank heavens for ordinary people,' Jenna whispered to Sarah after dinner the following evening. She had immediately taken to Michael. He was a very good-looking man, in his late forties, she guessed. He wasn't at all the dusty old professor of her earlier imaginings. He actually reminded her of her father, though her memories of him were rather hazy. When she mentioned this to Sarah, as they were filling the dishwasher together, her aunt smiled.

'He is a bit, I suppose. I hadn't thought of it, but you're probably right. You do like him though, don't you, love?'

'Would it make any difference if I said no?'

'Of course it would. I couldn't settle down with someone you didn't like.'

'Oh, you are thinking of settling down, are you?'

'I . . . well, I might be. You haven't answered me, though. Does that mean you're only being polite? You do have doubts?' Sarah looked very anxious.

'He's wonderful, Sarah. I love him already and I hope you'll be very happy. You deserve it after all the years you've worked for everyone else . . . all the time you've given to me.'

'Oh, darling, you were always my greatest pleasure,' Sarah said, rushing to fling her arms round her niece. 'But I'm so relieved. Michael? You can come through now. You have the official seal of approval.'

'Does that mean I can make an honest woman of you at last?'

'Yes, please,' whispered Sarah, and her eyes filled with tears of joy as she drew him into the circle. The three of them stood with arms wrapped round each other, each filled with their own particular emotions.

'Time to break out the champagne,' Michael announced, and collected a bottle of Bollinger from the fridge, where it had been waiting for the appropriate moment. Three beautiful cut-glass champagne flutes were set on a tray and they all went through to the lounge. Michael popped the cork with a flourish, and poured the wine. He handed the glasses round and paused at Sarah's side.

'I hope you like this, darling. I had it made for you by a friend of mine who knows about such things.' He fished in his pocket and handed her a ring box. She was obviously startled by the unexpected gift and her cheeks coloured with excitement. She opened it with trembling fingers.

'Oh, Michael. It's quite exquisite. Look, darling. Isn't it the most beautiful ring you've ever seen?' The single blue-white diamond set in fine platinum flashed its icy fire in the tiny box. It was a truly beautiful stone, and perfect for Sarah.

'It matches your eyes, Jenna. I shall have to get my

friend to look out for another stone like this. Or similar, should I say? Can't have my future wife and niece wearing identical diamonds, can we now?'

'When are you planning to get married?' Jenna asked.

'We haven't decided yet. We shall have to see how the book goes. We think we might have to take a trip to South America to do some more photos for it. We might be able to combine the trip with a bit of a honeymoon,' Michael replied impassively. 'Oh, dear, I don't suppose that sounds very romantic, does it?'

'It actually sounds very *Sarah*,' smiled Jenna. 'Here's to many happy years, and books and trips, and everything else you wish for.' They clinked glasses and drank their toast. The only momentary pang came when Jenna thought of the last occasion she had drunk champagne. It had been off the Cornish coast on a boat named after something like a hair lacquer. She pushed the thought away, where it belonged, deep in the past, while she concentrated on the present, sipping the wine.

Jenna slept late on Saturday morning. It had been well into the early hours before she had finally taken a taxi back to her own flat. The three of them had talked late into the night about all manner of plans for the future. She lay in bed, thinking about the surprises that had continued to pour out during the conversation. Sarah was intending to live most of her time in London and keep the cottage in Cornwall for times when any of them wanted to go there. Bonza would be brought to the London flat after the wedding, and they hoped he would enjoy his retirement as a city cat. They had all laughed at the thought of him ruling the local roost. Left to him, the whole neighbourhood would be terrorized by the huge animal.

'So you'll still be able to stay at the cottage whenever you like. Your room will always be your room. And when you've got dozens of kids, you can all share the same room together,' laughed Michael. He hadn't noticed the flicker of pain that flashed across her face, but Sarah had missed nothing. One day, Jenna realized, her aunt intended to find out the whole truth about Jenna and Simon.

Jenna's phone rang. Doubtless it would be Sarah, checking up on her, making sure she had returned home safely. Dearest Sarah. The answering machine cut in and she could hear her voice. She smiled fondly. Happiness for her aunt was almost as rewarding as her own happiness would be. With little enthusiasm, she thought of the evening ahead with Kurt. She wondered again what could have possessed her to agree to go out with him. Pity for him? Pity for herself? But for whatever reason she had agreed to go, and that was it. It might be nice, she tried to convince herself. After all, they had shared very many evenings together when they were working. But she knew inside that this was different. This wasn't work. This was supposed to provide an opportunity for them to get to know each other away from work.

Kurt had made it clear that he still hoped their relationship would develop into much more than just working together. She knew it was hopeless. Perhaps it was unfair of her to give him any grounds for encouragement; perhaps the whole evening was wrong and unfair of her. She could never feel for Kurt anything like the love she felt for Simon, even though that was now in the past. Simon, whom she could never have, whom she should never meet again. In truth, she should not even allow herself to spend time thinking about him, but she wasn't yet ready to attempt the impossible. At last she dragged herself out of bed to start a new day.

Once she had finished her household chores, she should give some thought to what they might be doing that evening, she mused, and, consequently, to what to wear. Kurt had mentioned dinner, but that could mean anything from the Savoy to a wine bar. Perhaps she should give him a call and see what he was planning. Just so long as he didn't drink too much and become impossible . . .

Jenna did some shopping, cleaned the flat and put her washing in the machine. What a glamorous life she was leading, she thought cynically! She was becoming a truly sad person. But then, everyone had to do washing and cleaning at some stage, she thought. Unless one kept an army of servants, or lived in a hotel. No, hotels were banned from her thoughts. No hotels, no Cornwall, no launches, white and gleaming in the sun, and most definitely no Simon. Lovers – for that was what they had almost been – lovers didn't lie to each other.

Kurt arrived to collect her at six-thirty. He had called during the afternoon and suggested she should wear something smart but casual. He'd asked her to be ready early but wouldn't say what he was planning. She was relieved. The Savoy was not what she felt like this evening. He suggested she might need something warm. A wrap or jacket. She was curious. It was still very warm, and a wrap was the last thing she would have thought she might need.

'So where are we going?' she demanded as she climbed into his car.

'Wait and see. It's a surprise.' He looked better tonight, she thought. He was smartly dressed in a white open-necked shirt and grey trousers, all neatly pressed. It made a change from his usual uniform of jeans and polo shirts. But it still felt strange being with him purely socially, without the motivation of work behind the evening.

They drove through the bustling London streets, crowded with people seeking their Saturday night entertainment. They reached the river and he found somewhere to park. He opened her door and helped her out. She gazed around for a restaurant, but there was nowhere immediately obvious.

'So, where are we going?' she asked.

'A cruise. You said once that you missed the sea when you were in London, so I've booked dinner for us one of the boats. We go along the river while we eat. It may not be the sea, but it's the best I can do. There's music and dancing if you like, or we can sit on deck and sip endless cocktails.'

'Not too many cocktails, I hope. I want to stay awake long enough to enjoy it,' she added hurriedly. She hadn't intended to nag him about his drinking, but she couldn't help the odd dig. Oh, dear, poor Kurt. He was trying so hard, and yet he'd chosen the one venue she would rather have done without. Boats and cruises were not top of her list of things to do, not so soon after . . . But then, a night cruise up the Thames was hardly comparable to a day spent sailing round the Cornish coast.

It was a large boat, with two decks filled with dining tables. The band was on the top deck, in the open air. The food was good, largely prepared before sailing and heated on board as it was ordered, so the service was not too slow. Kurt was attentive, and tried hard to talk intimately, though the noise of the live band made this particular endeavour rather difficult.

'You see, Jenna,' he was almost shouting, 'I've been out with dozens of women but they never understand me, not like you do. They take umbrage if I'm not gazing into their eyes all the time, or sulk if I talk to anyone else. You always know me so well.'

The band finished their number just before the last sentence and he practically shouted it, allowing everyone to hear. There were a few knowing smirks from the other diners and Jenna smiled, giving the faintest hint of a shrug. She certainly did know him well, but not the way the other diners would have assumed! The music started again.

'Dance?' asked Kurt.

'I'll try, but don't expect too much. My foot is still giving the occasional twinge.'

Kurt moved surprisingly well for a large man. He had a natural grace and sense of rhythm and Jenna was surprised at how much she enjoyed their dance on the open deck of the boat, bobbing along the river in the heart of London. She was in a little pain by the end, however, and suggested they spend some time sitting on one of the other decks. The lights on the shore were beginning to shine down on the water, each one reflected in thousands of tiny ripples.

'Amazing how pretty even traffic lights look when they're reflected in water,' she mused.

When they came back to their landing place, Kurt slipped an arm round her waist to help her off the boat. He didn't remove it once they were safely back on dry land, and she wondered what she could do to escape without hurting his feelings yet again. She didn't want his arm there. She didn't want him there. She tensed as they walked uncomfortably back to the car.

'Do you fancy a nightclub?' he asked.

'I'm really rather tired,' she said. 'I had a late night last night. My aunt got herself engaged and we stayed up rather late celebrating. It's been a lovely evening, Kurt. Thank you, but I'd prefer to go home now.'

'Why is it that all the women I know want to go home as soon as possible, except those I'm married to, and then they want to be out all night.'

'Perhaps you push them too hard, Kurt. You need to be a little more patient. Could you have been referring to Sylvia, by any chance, when you mentioned women needing to be home early?'

'What do you know about her?'

She told him briefly about their conversation during the film presentation. She also suggested that the girl might like to be asked out again.

'Don't you try to organize my love life, woman,' he

growled. 'You're bad enough at work. I want us to get right away from work. No wonder we can't get it together. It's always work, work, work with you.'

'Look, Kurt, you and I – well, it wouldn't ever work out. I like you, love working with you, but I can't fall in love with you. I can't give you what you truly want. Not what you need from a woman. Go out with Sylvia. She likes you a lot. She's bright and attractive, when she stops trying to be the perfect secretary.'

'What's this? Are you setting up as the village matchmaker?'

'I'm trying to help, Kurt.'

They sat in the car and managed to develop the casual chat into a full-blown row. He told her she was a cold, calculating woman. He said he was sick of her tantrums and that if she was going to continue to behave this way she should seriously think about getting another job. She told him he was behaving like a spoilt brat who couldn't have what he wanted and so started kicking everything in sight in retaliation.

'I think I'd better get a taxi home now,' Jenna said, heartily sick of the whole conversation. Kurt had deliberately kept away from taking excessive alcohol, so she couldn't put the blame on that for his present state.

'I'll drive you back,' Kurt insisted. 'I'm sorry, Jenna. My life's a mess and I thought you seemed as if you might be the one to sort it out. I blew it with Sylvia. Completely. One date which I thought went really well and then zilch. She wouldn't even speak to me again. Never returned my calls when I left messages. Nothing.'

'But surely that was because of her mother?'

'Didn't approve of her dear little girl going out with a man? Don't give me that. Or perhaps she'd heard something about me? Was it me she disapproved of? Because I've been married before or because I drink too much?'

Jenna carefully repeated what Sylvia had told her of the night of their date. He hadn't even known about her mother's death, and the resulting guilt Sylvia felt.

'Good heavens. Poor girl. But what can I do now? No wonder she avoided me at the Hudson's bash.'

'Try sending her some flowers. It might work wonders.'

'Did she tell you everything? That I offered her a job?'

'*My* job, you mean?'

'I think I was within my rights. If you really find me so unattractive, I'm surprised you want to work for me.'

'Oh, Kurt. You just don't understand anything, do you? Stick to films. You're good at them. With people, you're hopeless.'

His jaw tightened and he started the car. In total silence he drove her home. He was obviously considering what she had said. When he pulled up outside her flat, he spoke again.

'Are you going to invite me in for coffee?'

'If you like. But that's all it will be. Coffee.'

'Don't put yourself out. And I don't want any

coffee, come to think of it. I need something stronger than coffee. If I did come in, I might be tempted to touch the mighty Miss Brown, and that would never do. Saving yourself for your millionaire hotel-owner, are you? Will he get a divorce for you, do you imagine? Perhaps we could make a video for him.'

'Not that it's any of your business, but Simon and me – well, it was over before we'd really begun. We never really had any chance at all.'

'Says you. Goodnight, Jenna.' He leaned over her, opening the door and almost pushing her out. 'I think perhaps I'll go to that night club now. See if there's anyone there with a bit of spirit. Someone who hasn't forgotten how to enjoy themselves. I need some fun.' She got out of the car and he drove away almost before she had shut the door.

'Thank you for a nice evening . . .' she murmured politely, but it was to the retreating car.

She lay in bed, going over and over the evening. She bit her lip. Kurt was quite capable of taking his revenge simply because she had rejected him. He might well dismiss her from her job, even though he knew he would be lost without her. The week ahead looked like being a little fraught, to say the least.

Kurt came into work with a hangover on Monday morning, and was in one of his foulest moods. He demanded coffee, and rejected it as too strong. He asked for tea, and sent that back too. He grumbled at the delay when he rang someone and their phone was engaged.

'Why am I surrounded with incompetents?' he yelled at Jenna. 'Do I have to do everything in this place? Pass me the stamps, why don't you? I'll lick them myself.'

'I'm going out for lunch,' Jenna announced at noon. It was almost an hour earlier than usual, but she didn't trust herself to stay her normally calm self. She would shout back if Kurt continued to behave this way, and that would do no good at all.

She wondered if Kurt had taken her advice about sending flowers to Sylvia. Perhaps it hadn't been the right thing to do after all, and he'd been sent away with the proverbial flea in his ear. She might even give the girl a ring herself and see if all was well.

When she returned to her desk, there was a note from Kurt:

> *Time you decided, Jenna. Do you want to continue in your job or have you had enough? I can't do with any more of your moods and lack of interest or professionalism. You have to make your choice. Me plus your job, or you might as well clear your desk.*

The note was signed with his untidy scrawl. Jenna stared at the words with mounting dismay. *Lack of interest? Lack of professionalism?* Her? Whatever had she done wrong? Kurt was intolerable to work for at present, but this was outrageous. Totally over the top. Basically, he was trying to find excuses. He was really saying that if she didn't agree to 'go out with him', to put it euphemistically, she could say good-bye to her job. Thoughts of industrial tribunals, sexual harassment and the like, swarmed round her head. But even if she was successful and was awarded damages she wouldn't want to continue working for him. OK. If that was how he wanted to play it, she would call his bluff. He'd never survive without her.

She asked one of the secretaries to find an empty box. She began to clear out her desk.

She spent most of the afternoon turning out drawers that held papers and mementoes from dozens of previous projects. She had signed photos of pop stars going back over several years, and programmes of concerts, even odd flight ticket stubs from particularly memorable trips. Everything was dumped in the box. She could always throw it out later if she decided not to keep it. Of Kurt there was no sign, even when it was time for her to leave at the end of the day. She hung around, waiting for him to come back, but he was obviously choosing to stay away. It was nearly seven when she finally decided to go home. Extravagantly, she phoned for a taxi. No way could she fight her way onto the tube with her box of worldly goods.

She scribbled a quick note to Kurt, saying she had taken him at his word and cleared her desk. She shut the office door, wondering if she was closing yet another phase in her life. He would surely ask her to reconsider. He couldn't have *wanted* her to leave, not really.

She was in a very different situation now. When she had first been given this job, she'd been inexperienced, young, and very lucky to get the chance. She had worked hard, taken on considerable responsibility and now had experience beyond her years. She had a very creditable portfolio of successes behind her. She should have no trouble finding a job in another studio, if it really came to that.

It was a restless evening. Jenna phoned Sarah but she was out. She was expecting to hear from Kurt, but the phone remained silent. She shrugged. It was too bad. She watched a bit of television and ate some scrambled eggs. She even considered phoning Sylvia, but wasn't sure of the number. Kurt would doubtless offer her the job that Jenna had so recently vacated, if only to get back at Jenna. Sylvia had ability, of that there was no doubt, but what was needed was a very specialized set of talents that she wasn't certain the girl did have. She worried that she had made a rather rash move. Perhaps Kurt hadn't meant her to leave, but he was virtually blackmailing her into doing what he wanted. How could she ever have loved Kurt when she had known Simon?

They would be finished serving dinners at Tregarth by now. It was odd to think of everything still going on as normal, without her being there. Simon would probably be in his office, sorting out the takings . . . doing whatever it was he did with a shares portfolio . . . dealing with his boatyard. Boats. Launches.

'Damn, damn, damn,' she said out loud. 'Get out of my head, will you, Simon Andrews?' She knew she had to stop thinking about him. Stop completely. Push him out.

She made herself start doing something new, moving to the carton of papers and souvenirs from her desk and shuffling through, wondering what to keep and what to throw out. She picked up a file of personal letters from all sorts of people she had met over the years, and, seeing that she had a large collection of addresses and contacts, began to formulate a plan of action. She would write to everyone she could think of, let them know that she was in the market for a new position. Using such very personal contacts, she was confident that one of them would bring her some offer of employment.

She began to feel a sense of being on the brink of something new, that she might even look forward to a whole new way of life. She might begin to feel more settled in London if she didn't have to travel around so much. She could spend more time with Sarah. See more plays and concerts. Yes, being positive was good. She would start to carry out her ideas the very next day. She must start by getting her own laptop computer and a printer. It was important to produce professional letters and a decent CV. She had plenty of money in the bank, as she had earned a good salary and often went for weeks without spending very much. Even food was provided when she was working away, and her father's legacy had paid for the flat outright and still left savings. Even if she didn't get another job for a few weeks, she would have no immediate money worries.

Jenna was up early the next day, eager to make her purchases. A small computer would be much more use than a larger system, even though the prices were similar. She went to one of the larger stores and made her choice. She was used to her software package at work, so bought a machine with the same one. The whole thing was very compact, and she could carry everything, printer and all, in a bag the size of a small briefcase. Whatever job she got, having her own portable computer would be most helpful. Why hadn't she thought of it before? She bought some disks, paper and envelopes, and went home to begin her methodical search for work.

She looked at her phone, still expecting to receive some reaction from Kurt, but there were no messages flashing. She even picked it up to see if was working and got the dial tone. Strange. He must still be having one of his sulks. She shrugged her shoulders, made a pot of coffee and began her writing. Perhaps it was a case of good riddance on both sides.

First she produced a CV, then went on to write a letter which she could personalize for each person she was going to contact. It took her most of the day. By evening, she had a neat pile of envelopes waiting to be posted. If she hurried, she could just catch the evening post. Then all she had to do was sit back and wait for the offers to come in.

It was a tense few days. Each morning she rushed to her letterbox to see if she had any replies. She scarcely went out, hoping that someone would telephone. But there was nothing. No calls, no letters. It seemed strange, she thought. Surely at least one of the companies would have replied, even if it was only to say no. It would only be common courtesy. She had even enclosed stamped, self-addressed envelopes.

The week seemed to drag, and the weekend took a

very long time to arrive. She called Sarah. She, too, was surprised that Jenna had heard absolutely nothing from any of the companies she had written to. Jenna had poured out all the details of Kurt's actions over the phone one evening early in the week, and Sarah had praised her niece for her swift and confident actions to find a new job, she felt disappointed on her behalf that she had not been successful.

By the end of the second week, when Jenna had still not received a single response, even from people who had once offered her many incentives to leave Reality Plus, she began to suspect that something was wrong. She decided to telephone someone she knew, to ask if they had received her letter. Feeling slightly nervous, she dialled the number.

'Cosmos Films, how can I help you?' the voice of the receptionist replied.

'May I speak to Tony Blackmore?'

'Who shall I say is calling?'

She gave her name.

'One moment, I'll see if Mr Blackmore's in.' She was put on hold to listen to irritating jangly music for several seconds. At last there was a series of clicks.

'I'm afraid Mr Blackmore is not available.'

Jenna talked for a few more moments, trying to get information from the receptionist. Was he in or out? In, but unavailable, or was it that he simply refused to talk to her? By the time she had finished she was fairly certain it was the latter. She tried a couple more of her contacts, but on each occasion it was the same response. People who had been trying desperately to tempt her away from Kurt just months before were now refusing to speak to her. Finally, she found one young secretary, whom she had once met, who admitted that they had been specifically ordered not to speak to her, let alone employ her.

Kurt had systematically blacklisted her. He had ruined her chances of getting another job out of sheer malice. She could scarcely believe that he was so petty-minded as to try and ruin her. What on earth could he have said? And all this from a man who, only days before, had been begging her to marry him. Thank goodness she had never really given it serious thought. The man was sick, she tried to comfort herself.

She felt totally despondent and let down. What could she do now? She had no experience of anything other than films and video-making, and even that experience was not on the technical side. Hating to interrupt what she knew was working time, she phoned Sarah and begged to go over and talk.

'So what can I do now?' Jenna asked, after telling the whole story to her aunt.

'You could probably sue for defamation of character,' she said practically.

'That's not the point, though. I want a decent job on my own merits, because of what I can do. Not following some great legal wrangle that could cost a fortune in time and money, not to mention emotions.'

Aunt and niece chatted throughout the morning over several cups of coffee. They sat in Michael's comfortable kitchen while he worked in the study. Jenna apologized for keeping Sarah away from her work, but they both pooh-poohed the idea. She was far more important to them than a missed morning's work.

'You could always do some work for me,' suggested Sarah. 'Your typing is far better than mine. And you have the great advantage that you're about the only other person in the world who can read my writing.'

Jenna thanked her aunt for the offer, but it wasn't what she wanted to do. She would, of course, do anything she could to help, but that was only providing a temporary solution to her problem. Besides, typing was the sort of thing she hated doing, and she only used those particular skills when there was absolutely no one else to do urgent secretarial work.

'I just can't decide what's the best thing to do. If I can't find a job doing something I'm good at, I might as well give up living in London. If Kurt has blacklisted me with every possible film company, there seems little or no point trying.'

Jenna looked so miserable that Sarah felt herself growing worried.

'If you wanted to go and live at the cottage for a while, you'd be quite welcome to. We could still come down whenever we wanted to, and I'd be happy for you to make any alterations, do whatever you liked with the place. I dare say you'd get a good price for your flat. You could probably live on the money if you invested wisely. Easily enough anyway, if you weren't too extravagant. I'm sure Simon would advise you . . .'

'Do you mean to say you're still in touch with

Simon?' Her heart did a somersault, beginning to pound at the very mention of his name.

'Only casually. I was speaking to him about one or two matters recently. That's all. Sorry, I shouldn't have mentioned him.'

'Did he ask about me?' Jenna wanted to know. It was a stupid thing to ask, she knew. If the answer was no, she would feel sad that she was not in his thoughts; if the answer was yes, then she would begin to feel anxious all over again.

'I thought you didn't want to talk about him?' Sarah replied, knowing her niece well enough to understand what she was feeling.

'You brought the subject up in the first place.'

'Slip of the tongue. That's all it was. Sorry. But you do know you can tell me anything you want to, don't you, darling? I'm always ready to listen, and I did mean what I said about the cottage. Think about it. It might do you good to make a complete change.'

'I couldn't spend my time lazing around. It would drive me potty, doing nothing.'

'Maybe you'll hear something from one of those companies you've applied to soon. You never know.'

Jenna stared curiously at her aunt. She almost sounded as if she had something up her sleeve, and that always made Jenna feel suspicious.

'I don't want you interfering, Sarah,' she said gently. 'I know you mean it for the best, but you can't organize my life for me. It was a disaster when you tried to push Simon and me together. I know you meant well but it all turned sour, and I can't cope with any more of it.'

Sarah stared at her. She drew breath as if she was going to say something, but thought better of it and smiled and shrugged her shoulders.

'Have it your own way,' she said resignedly.

CHAPTER 16

A few days later, Jenna received a telephone call. She was invited to an 'informal discussion' at the offices of a new company being set up to make video commercials for the tourist industry. It sounded exactly the opening she had been looking for. If she could have designed the job herself, it couldn't have been closer to her blueprint. She arranged to be there the following morning. Excitedly, she called Sarah with the news.

The offices of the company, Solo Films, were small but impressive. The room where she was interviewed was beautifully furnished, light and airy. The company was managed on behalf of the owners by two men and a woman, all of whom had some long-standing connections with the film industry. They seemed to know all about Jenna's background and experience, and it was clear that they were impressed with her as a person and with her expertise in such a wide variety of subjects.

'Well, Miss Brown, I think you are exactly the person we're looking for. Is there anything you'd like to know about us?' the chairman of the small committee asked.

'There's just one thing. How on earth did you get my details? How did you know I was looking for a job?' The man smiled and turned to his female companion.

'Mrs Jenkins? You can answer that one, I believe?'

'I have a friend who works for Hudson's International. You did some work for them recently and they were impressed, especially with you. I happened to mention that we were looking for someone and they suggested you for the job. Your CV had been sent to another company I used to work for and I managed to get it from them.'

'I'm flattered that you went to so much trouble,' Jenna said, truly amazed at this saga. 'But didn't the company also mention that I was considered unsuitable for pretty well anything, after my "dismissal" from Reality Plus?'

'Well, we did hear the odd rumour. But we also heard that poor Kurt Smedley is not in the best of health, or so we understand. We felt that we should ignore the bad reports about you. It didn't sound terribly professional to us that he should act in that way. But, if his health is precarious, such reports are hardly relevant. As long as you are honest with us, we don't have a problem.'

'Seems like we have a deal,' Jenna said happily. 'When do I start?'

As she almost skipped out of the building and along to Oxford Street, Jenna realized she had completely failed to mention money. Who cares?

she thought. It was the job she wanted most of all. She could always negotiate a salary later.

When Jenna called at the house with the news of her success, Michael and Sarah were delighted. They insisted on opening a bottle of wine to celebrate, even though it was only three o'clock in the afternoon. They exchanged delighted glances and drank a toast to the new job. Jenna burbled happily about the opportunities that awaited her and possible places she would be visiting.

'It's so good to see you happy again,' Sarah said, after about an hour of her niece's excited chatter. 'Why don't we go out for a celebratory dinner?'

'Good idea. Where do you fancy?' Michael asked.

'I'm certainly lucky to have been head-hunted like that,' Jenna said cheerfully. 'Well, virtually head-hunted.' She was still on a high with success, especially after the long weeks when nothing seemed to be happening.

During those weeks, almost every time she had been alone in her flat she had wondered if Sarah could have been right. She should have gone back to live in Cornwall. But whatever would she have done? She had even considered starting in antique dealing for a brief moment, as it was a subject she already knew a little about. She could quickly learn more . . . But one major trouble with this idea was that she would probably keep meeting up with Simon, and she could not, must not, allow that to happen. She tried to imagine a scene, some time in the future, when she was an old spinster and might meet the old man Simon would have become. They would talk unemotionally about antiques and neither would feel anything for the other. Wishful thinking, she thought. She would always see him as a sexy, desirable man, probably even when they were both in their eighties.

'Wake up, day-dreamer. Where do you want to go and eat?' Michael was saying.

Jenna's first day at the new office seemed very strange. After the years spent working with Kurt, knowing just about every one of his foibles, it was a whole new world to begin with a totally new director and crew. They had a small, state-of-the-art studio and editing suite, and several other rooms which were not yet in use. One of them was to be her very own office. Besides being a little scary, it was very exciting to be in at the birth of a new company. She tried to probe around and discover who was behind it, but it seemed there was some anonymous consortium of investors, who had little interest beyond profit and expansion.

She spent much of the time in discussion with her three interviewers, who were all interested in her ideas and eager to set her to work. Their first project was to be a short information film about a Norfolk seaside town, sponsored by and featuring one of the larger hotels there. A broad plan was outlined, and the message the clients wanted to put across, and they were away. Ideas were flung from person to person, notes made, ideas discounted, and finally they had put together a dossier of points to be researched immediately.

'I suggest Jenna and I drive up to Norfolk tomorrow and scout round a bit. OK with you, Jenna? I can pick you up around seven-thirty then we shall get onto the M11 before the rush hour.' Bill, the director, seemed very straightforward and nice, and much less emotional than Kurt. But she would be able assess his true abilities when she saw him at work on location. It might be rather less exciting than Kurt's pop extravaganzas, but it looked like being a much less demanding life. And who could tell at this stage what it might grow into?

'Sounds good to me. I'll be ready and waiting.' She reminded him of her address and gave brief directions.

'Oh, there's a mobile phone for you out at the front desk. We thought you'd better have a car as well, and we'll get that organized as soon as possible. Do you have any preference? Make? Model? Colour? I'll get Joan to give you some brochures and you can let her know the details.'

Jenna stared at her new boss. A mobile phone? A car? She was basically only a dogsbody at present, yet she was being treated almost as royalty. And she still hadn't quite got over the size of the salary they had offered. If Kurt came back on bended knee, he couldn't begin to approach her new earning capacity.

'Th-thank you very much,' she managed to stammer. 'I wasn't expecting any of this.'

'You'll have to work for it all,' Bill laughed. 'Believe me, it's in our own interests to have you mobile, and the phone means we can always contact you whenever we need to. I don't mean you can't ever switch it off, of course, but there's a message service. Right, I think that's about it for today. Seeing that we have an early start, you'd better get home early. See you in the morning.'

Jenna left the building, almost hopping with joy as she went along the road. She had a couple of glossy car brochures in her briefcase and her very own mobile phone in her pocket. She stopped in a shop doorway, seeing the inevitable group of mobile phone users, all concentrating on chatting as if what they had to say was so important it couldn't wait. Their hands were clasped to their ears as if they had found some bizarre new way to pray. Being a new mobile phone owner, she joined them, punching in Sarah's number.

'Just calling on my mobile,' she said, as casually as her excitement allowed. 'And you'll never guess what! They're giving me a car. Can you believe it? Well, I can't believe it. It feels like all my birthdays have come at once.'

'We're delighted for you, darling,' Sarah said when Jenna had finally run out of breath. 'All we have to do is sort out your social life and we're well away. Any possibilities at your new place?'

'Sarah, you are incorrigible. You never change, not even now you're practically a married woman. It took you long enough, so don't try hurrying *me*!'

If she could have heard her aunt's comment to Michael, after she had rung off, she might have been slightly concerned.

'Well, it all seems to be working out very nicely so

far,' she said to her husband-to-be, with a satisfied smile.

Bill seemed very pleasant, and Jenna believed he would prove to be a good, solid director. He lacked Kurt's flair and imagination, but for the particular style they were currently looking for he would do a good job, she believed. They had chatted comfortably on their journey, visited the hotel and then set out to gain an impression of the town.

'It's so different from Cornwall,' Jenna remarked, after they had walked along the sea-front. 'I suppose it's a bit like Newquay, as a holiday town, but this isn't quite what I think of when people talk about the seaside.'

'I adore Cornwall. Went there for years for holidays when I was a kid. My own children are more into Disney World and the like. Modern kids, eh?'

On their return journey, Jenna discovered that Bill had three children and a wife who was something in advertising. She thought he must be around forty, and he was comfortable rather than good-looking. She tried to question him, discreetly, about Solo Films, but he didn't seem to know much more than she did, and next to nothing at all about about the backers. As far as he knew the other members of the board had accountancy and advertising backgrounds, with plenty of ideas for potential customers.

'Actually, we mentioned Kurt Smedley the other day – your old boss . . . Were you close? I wondered if you'd heard. He's gone into some sort of special clinic. Drink problem, I understand. Poor sod.'

Jenna blanched. 'Oh, no. I hadn't heard. I've always known he drank too much, but I didn't know he was that bad. What's happening to the company? Do you know?'

'Well, not exactly, but I have heard rumours. Something about temporary management? It's all a bit, . . . well, you know – hush, hush. Sufficient to set the rumours flying. It's a close-knit community, ours. Everyone always tries to keep this sort of problem under wraps because of outstanding contracts.' Bill was, perhaps, guilty of being a little too free with his information, Jenna thought. But maybe it was merely that he sensed he could trust her.

'I suppose your source didn't also tell you where Kurt is? I should really like to go and see him.' After she had spoken, she wondered if she had been quite wise. She was now working for one of Kurt's rivals, but she was just thinking of him as a friend, and also, she admitted to herself, she did feel slightly guilty. If she hadn't been forced to walk out, she might have been able to help him. She might even have managed to help prevent things reaching this particular bad state of affairs.

'I'm not certain. Perhaps there's someone you could ask among your own contacts. I did hear some rumour that he was getting married. Some connection with a business he did some work for.'

Well, well, Jenna thought. It had to be Sylvia. Shy, lonely Sylvia. She had certainly been quick off the mark.

'Yes. I think I might have a friend who would be able to fill me in. I'll have to give her a call.'

'Well, see what you can find out about any outstanding work they have while you're at it. There might be something we can pick up on.'

Jenna gave him a sideways glance. That had sounded a little contrived. Was this the whole point of his conversation?

Bill continued, 'Meantime, one other useful thing you can do is to think of any hotels in Cornwall you think we might try. Places you know personally. That's always a good start. We want to target hotels who would consider making videos to send out for promotion. Other companies often advise that anyone interested can send for a free video. We're not quite into that league yet, but who knows where it can lead? Start with British hotels and see what happens.'

Jenna gave a little shiver. She scarcely knew any hotels in Cornwall. She never used them as she had a home there. There was only one place she knew which might benefit from this sort of video targeting, and that was the one place she would certainly not be mentioning.

It was a week later that Jenna took delivery of her car, a deep blue Astra. She had rented a lock-up garage round the corner from her flat and treated her new toy as if it were made of gold. She even had a special polishing cloth she used on the windscreen each day before setting off on any journey. When she drove over to Sarah's house, she parked it proudly outside the door, insisting Michael and her aunt both came out to admire it straight away.

'I know it isn't anything like as posh as yours, Michael, but you have to admit it does look nice, doesn't it?'

Sarah gave her a hug and shared her joy to the full.

'Just think, darling, you can't accept any more of our spontaneous invitations to share bottles of wine at any odd times we choose. Would you like a coffee instead?'

Jenna had called Sylvia a number of times but had never managed to speak to her. She had even tried dialling Kurt's home, in case she had moved in there while he was away. Finally she plucked up the courage to phone Reality Plus and spoke to the secretary. The girl had obviously been told not to give out any information to any enquirers, but once Jenna got her chatting she did admit that things had changed somewhat since her departure. Kurt was indeed away from work, but she thought he was on holiday somewhere. Sylvia was not working there at all.

The girl obviously knew so little that the call was pretty much a waste of time. It was rapidly becoming an intriguing mystery, one that Jenna was determined to get to the bottom of. She would make some excuse to go round to the offices and see what was going on for herself. Official termination forms had never been completed, so she was still owed the balance of her salary. She planned to make her visit at the first opportunity.

'I've put a list of hotels on your desk,' Bill said one morning. 'There may the odd one or two you recognize. We've been through various directories and selected the sort of place that's keen to market itself for business. You know – conferences, seminars, that sort of thing. It's the new way to go for these large places out of season. We could also encourage them to develop all-round entertainment packages, so that the conference participant can bring his or her partner. The spouse can be kept happy while the other half confers, or whatever it is they do.'

'Right. I'll take a look as soon as possible.' She felt it was almost a one hundred per cent certainty that the dreaded name of Tregarth would be there. Bill might have been describing the place exactly, even though he didn't know it. She picked up the list and unclipped the attached pages with photocopies of the directory entries. Surprisingly, there were quite a number of places she had actually stayed in. When she'd been dashing around with Kurt, they'd always stayed in the larger hotels, and she was able to write her comments on a surprisingly large number of them.

Inevitably, Tregarth Manor was featured, and she stared long and hard at the thumbnail sketch that accompanied the text. She closed her eyes and remembered the wonderful swimming pool and glorious antiques everywhere. The sea views. The beautifully appointed rooms. The owner. The owner's wife. The owner's son. When the burning began at the back of her eyes, she knew it would probably take for ever for her to be able to forget what the place meant to her . . . or rather what the owner meant to her.

'Nice place, that,' Bill said, looking over her shoulder. 'I thought that one looked a dead cert. Very go-ahead management – but you'd know that, of course.'

'Yes, I know it,' she replied softly, to hide the crack in her voice. 'We made the Hudson's training film there.'

'And you know Simon personally, I believe? Simon Andrews?'

Jenna stared at him, her mouth opening and refusing to close again naturally.

'How on earth did you know that?'

'Oh, I don't know,' he blustered. 'You must have mentioned it sometime.'

Jenna knew full well she had *never* mentioned his name. She would never have done anything like that . . . even under normal circumstances.

'I don't think so, Bill,' she said with an icy calm. 'I want to know why you made that comment.'

'I have no idea,' he said firmly. 'It was no more *than* a comment. Now, if you will excuse me, we both have work to do.' He turned and walked out of the room, looking distinctly guilty, she thought.

Jenna tried hard all day to concentrate, but her mind was ploughing through a mire of different thoughts. She finally abandoned the task she was working on. It was nothing urgent and, given a few minutes of sensible, concentrated time, she would finish it off tomorrow. No, she decided she would make her visit to Reality Plus, – ostensibly to collect her forms and cheque, but mainly to see what was going on. She left her office, left details of her

destination with Reception and drove herself the
short distance between the two companies. The
traffic actually made it a slower trip by car than by
tube, but she was so in love with her new toy she
didn't want to miss any chance to drive.

It felt very strange to be a visitor going into a
building that was so familiar to her. One or two of the
technical staff were in the reception area and greeted
her with hugs and calls of, 'Come back, all is
forgiven!' It seemed that things had very rapidly
deteriorated since her departure, and there were
even the faintest hints that she herself had contrib-
uted to the cause.

'Hang on guys,' she protested. 'You can hardly
blame me for Kurt's "little problems". He's been
hitting the bottle as long as I've known him.'

The men looked at each other uncomfortably.

'Actually, you obviously haven't heard that he got
married. The new Mrs Smedley insisted he went for
help almost before they went on honeymoon. Right
little tyrant he got himself.'

'Not Sylvia?' she asked, her body beginning to
shake with laughter.

'I believe that is the name of the lady in question,'
one of the lighting chaps confirmed. 'They met on
location somewhere, and it was *lurve* at first bite' he
quipped. 'There was a time we were laying odds on
you snaffling the major prize,' he went on, 'but then
you suddenly disappeared without trace. Rumour
has it that you were so heartbroken when the news
of his marriage broke that you could no longer stand
seeing him every day.' His voice took on such a mock

melodramatic tone as he spoke that everyone burst out laughing.

'You mean you *haven't* gone into a deep decline at losing your man? The tales are unfounded? I'm surprised,' one of the men said facetiously.

'I must say, I'm surprised at the speed of Kurt's decline. And what about this wedding? If I didn't know him so well, I might think there was almost an indecent haste about the whole thing. Heavens, it must have been practically the week after I left.'

'Oh, so you're suggesting rebound, are you? Can I interest you in a kiss-and-tell story, Miss Brown? My paper will pay you well.'

'You lot are dreadful,' laughed Jenna. 'And I really miss you all. They're all a bit intense at my new place, but I'm working on them.'

'Don't forget your old mates when you're handing out new contracts,' another of the group said. 'There could be a number of talented – sorry, I should say, *very* talented technicians looking for work soon. Life in this establishment has become distinctly dodgy, to say the least.'

Jenna bit her lip. It looked as if the rumours could just be true.

'Keep in touch. You've got my address. If you let me know what's happening, I'll see if there are any opportunities with the new firm. We haven't really got going yet, and the plans are still modest, by comparison with how this place used to operate. But you never know.'

She collected her documents and left without any further discussion. So Kurt and Sylvia *had* got married? That was very quick work indeed. She sensed that Sylvia must have been a little desperate to marry a man she hardly knew, but then, the girl *had* spent quite a lot of time with Kurt at Tregarth. She had a flash of memory of the noises she had heard from the next room on one of those dreadful sleepless nights she had spent there. Sylvia had obviously spent that night with Kurt. Everything always went back to Tregarth, it seemed.

She drove straight home as it was too late to return to work now. Her mind was racing. It looked very much as if Kurt's company was going under. It could be the perfect opportunity for a takeover. If only there was someone she could talk to, someone who knew about such things. It was a great opportunity for Solo Films to expand. Hadn't Bill said something about the owners, who were only interested in profit and expansion? But it would cost many hundreds of thousands of pounds – millions, even. She didn't know enough about that side of the business to begin to know where to start.

If only she could talk to Simon. He'd know exactly what to do. Sarah had said something about keeping in touch with Simon. Maybe Sarah could call him and talk to him on her behalf? Get the advice she needed? Impulsively, she turned off her route and diverted to Michael and Sarah's home.

'Me again, come to plague you,' she announced as the door was opened. 'Am I being an awful nuisance to you lovebirds?'

''Course not. You're just about the only family we've got between us,' laughed Sarah. 'Come in.

How's the new toy? Still wonderful?'

Jenna explained about the purpose of her visit, Kurt and his marriage, his enforced stay in some clinic or other and the comments made by her old friends, the technicians.

'I need to know whether I should say anything to my directors about the possibility of taking over Kurt's business. It's a great opportunity, but I know so little about the money side of it. I'm sort of fond of Kurt, in a way, and I don't want to knock him when he's down. It seems disloyal, but he treated me pretty badly. On the other hand, there's still a lot to salvage, if we could move quickly. I'd really like some advice and I simply don't know who to ask.'

'Michael and I don't know anything about business either. You could put what we know on a pinhead.'

'You said you were still in touch with Simon? Do you think that you might ask him?'

Sarah's face went a shade paler than normal. She clamped her mouth tight shut as she contemplated what Jenna was asking. She sat down. She looked rather uncomfortable, twisting her fingers in a totally uncharacteristic gesture.

'If you'd rather not, . . .' Jenna began, disconcerted by her aunt's strange reticence.

'No, it isn't that. Oh, it's all a bit complicated. I've been trying not to upset you by talking about Simon. I do know what he means to you, and how hard you've been working to get him out of your system.' Jenna drew breath to speak, but Sarah stopped her.

'No, I don't want to force you to tell me anything

302

you'd rather not talk about. As I said, I do realize
what you meant to each other, and I don't know why
you decided it wasn't going to work, but it was your
decision. I respect that, even if I do think you've
made a mistake. You had obviously discussed everything with each other before you suddenly came back
to London. It's your life, and that has to be good
enough for me. I'll think over what you said. I
assume that if I *do* think I should call him, you'd
rather I had this talk with Simon when you are out of
the way? I think that would be best. For all concerned. I'll talk it through with Michael, and if we
think it will help I'll call Simon and let you know if he
has any suggestions.'

'Thanks, Sarah,' Jenna said gratefully. 'Now I'll
get out of your hair and leave you to a peaceful
dinner.' She kissed her aunt and went out to her
car. She waved as she drove away, suddenly feeling
rather lonely. She was delighted by Sarah's new-
found happiness, but there were moments when she
felt just the tiniest bit left out.

'Don't be selfish,' she told herself as she stopped
outside her rented garage. After all Sarah had done
for her, all her life. And had she been making an
excuse to have this indirect contact with Simon?
Surely – sensibly – she could simply have chatted
things through with Bill and the others? It was too
late now. Sarah would probably be phoning Simon at
this very moment. She had probably been waiting for
an excuse to push her niece and Simon together
again.

The moment she got inside the flat, Jenna dialled

her aunt's number. She wanted to say that she had changed her mind. But the number was engaged. She kept trying, but the engaged tone was persistent. It was obviously too late. She pottered around restlessly. She started to cook some supper, but changed her mind and put the food back in the fridge. She kept trying Sarah's number but it was always engaged. Perhaps Sarah hadn't replaced the receiver properly. She couldn't possibly be still talking to Simon. She dialled her aunt again. At last, it was ringing. After a few rings, the answering machine cut in. She left a brief, moody message, asking Sarah to call back. Life was ridiculous! Here she was, after years of complaining that she was never in the same place for five minutes, settled into a routine, and she was totally, mindlessly *bored*. She must do something about it in the very near future.

Something that had not yet been decided was the details of Sarah and Michael's wedding. Why shouldn't she get involved in arranging *that*? She could take over much of the work from Sarah, even organize most of the event. It would be part of her wedding present to the couple. Cakes to organize; invitations; flowers; clothes; food; venue. Oh, yes, it would be great fun – and she would be so involved that she wouldn't have time to feel sorry for herself . . . at least not until it was all over. As soon as she could speak to Sarah again, she would suggest it.

CHAPTER 17

Sarah's answering machine fielded all her calls for the rest of the evening. Jenna took herself off to the cinema, if only to get herself out of the flat, to try and seek escape from her teeming thoughts. Simon must have been out when her aunt had phoned. Or perhaps she and Michael had decided it wouldn't be a good idea to call him. The long time the phone had been engaged could easily have been Michael making calls. But it wasn't like to Sarah to leave her niece hanging in limbo like this.

The cinema had seemed like a good idea at the time but she simply could not concentrate on the film . . .

When she finally returned to the flat, she rushed to see if there had been any messages. The light was flashing on her answering machine and she quickly stabbed the replay button.

'It's Sarah. Sorry, love. Nothing to report. Afraid we're going to be busy for the next few days. The book, you know. Reaching a critical stage. I'll phone as soon as we're free again. 'Night.'

Jenna frowned. It was so unlike Sarah to leave that

sort of message – even to make that sort of comment. Being busy had never been a problem for Sarah before Michael came on the scene. Sarah had always had time for Jenna. She pulled herself together. She was behaving like a spoilt child again. She realized that she was actually showing every sign of jealousy over her dearest aunt, and that was quite outrageous. She thought about her actions of late. Maybe she had *always* been selfish – expecting people to run to her aid when any little thing went wrong. Recently she had thought of no one but herself, and how much *she* was hurting. It was high time she stood on her own two feet. She might have thought she was an independent woman of the nineties, but it was quite obvious from her own behaviour that she was far from being that. She wanted all the perks but none of the emotional responsibilities.

After a couple of days of deep thinking and self-criticism, she decided to confront her boss with the scanty pieces of information she had gained. She went into Bill's office and told him what little she knew.

'I think there may be some opportunity to pick up work and even take on some of the technical guys. They are the very best. I thought you might like to know and pass it on to the others, if you think it's worth pursuing.'

'You're a bit late, Jenna. It's already in hand. One of our consortium has been in town and he's busily negotiating at this very moment. Seems like he isn't quite the sleeping partner we thought he was. Anyway, if you'll excuse me, I have to arrange our

Norfolk filming. We're starting it in a couple of days.'

'Oh, I thought it would be a few weeks yet?'

'We're bringing it forward. I did send you a memo. There isn't any problem, is there?'

'No. Of course not. I must have missed your memo. Sorry. I'm really looking forward to getting back into the field – doing something on the practical side.'

'It shouldn't take more than a day or so. We'll travel up the night before and see where we go from there. The hotel's booked. Obviously we're staying at the Seacliff.'

They talked through the coming project and Jenna felt the familiar rush of pleasure at doing the part of the work she liked best. She had been away from it for too long.

Packing a holdall for the trip, she realized she had been nowhere since her hasty retreat from Cornwall. What a lot had happened since then. She could never forget how angry she had been about Simon's seemingly irrational behaviour, but she had been so busy pushing all thoughts of that time into the back of her mind that the anger had subsided a little. Her mind had somehow managed to blot out the unpleasant memories of the loss of the baby, and her deep, deep hurt when Simon had left her.

She hugged her arms around herself, feeling very much alone. With the dissipation of the anger, she recognized that she still felt deeply unhappy. Somehow, she needed to get the anger back, so that she didn't start moping again. She must drive herself forward and get a new life. Starting with the very next day. There would be dozens of men around – men who would be delighted to take her out. And surely, among them, there must be someone she could grow to love?

Her short trip to Norfolk proved lively and interesting. Late one evening the technical crew insisted on her accompanying them on a coach and horses ride round the town. It was well after Bill had retired to bed, and was great fun. Afterwards, they went along the promenade and stopped at a couple of amusement arcades, stuffing coins into machines that whirred and clicked and gave out useless plastic toys or tokens to be spent on yet more machines. It was all so different from the sort of thing she had done over the past few years, and she thoroughly enjoyed the novelty. She also realized that she hadn't needed to push away thoughts of Simon for at least two hours.

The filming was also most enjoyable. They took many feet of video film, made recordings for sound, did interviews and generally obtained a very broad flavour of the town and, more importantly, the hotel. Skilful editing would produce a snappy, short film which, once approved by the clients, would be duplicated and distributed. The systems were all in place. The product would be set at an affordable price, and once they had made a few films they would be able to expand, become more automated, thus keeping costs down. It might not be particularly glamorous work, but there was opportunity for expansion in the future. Every major hotel in the country, in Europe – the world, even – would eventually have to have a Solo Films video of their enterprise if they were to be seen as successful. The team would become more professional, and as they developed together they hoped to get contracts from major advertising companies, just as Reality Plus had. If Jenna Brown had anything to do with it, Solo Films would soon be up amongst the big boys.

Jenna flung her energies into the job, working late at the office and often taking work home to complete on her own computer. Sarah had maintained her silence, and Jenna was determined not to contact her again but to wait to be contacted. If her aunt wanted to be left alone, then she would not be the one to intrude on her. When thoughts of Simon paid their hourly visits to her mind, she rapidly sent them out again. It was hard work but she was winning, slowly and surely.

She was summoned to the large office rather pretentiously known as the boardroom early one morning. The three directors were already seated at the large table, looking rather pleased with themselves, she thought.

'We thought you should be the first of the staff to know. Solo have acquired Reality Plus Videos,' the woman who was only ever called as 'Mrs Jenkins', announced.

'Brilliant,' Jenna said with enthusiasm. 'At least, I suppose it's brilliant. Poor Kurt, though.'

'I don't think you need worry about him. He – or rather his wife – has negotiated a very generous settlement. She's a tough lady, but I expect you know that already. We have a proposal to put to you. We should like to put you in charge of that company, if you agree.'

Jenna sat gaping with shock. First she was hearing that the quiet little mouse, Sylvia, had turned into a 'tough lady'. And that was followed by the totally mind-blowing suggestion that she was to be in charge of Kurt's old company. No longer the assistant but the actual boss. She experienced a moment of sheer panic.

'Me? If you really think I can do it then yes-yes, please! Good grief! I can hardly believe it.' It was like some crazy dream, and she expected to wake at any moment. 'I hope I won't let you down, and I appreciate the opportunity and the trust you're placing in me.'

'Nonsense, Jenna. You're a talented woman and we have every confidence in you. If the consortium are happy with you, that's good enough for us. Congratulations.'

'Have the consortium actually approved this appointment?' Jenna enquired. 'Or is this just a temporary post?'

'It was a condition imposed by the consortium itself when we made the takeover. It seems your reputation is well known,' replied Mrs Jenkins.

'I don't understand. Just who are these people, exactly? It seems unfair that everyone seems to know except me.' Jenna was becoming more than a little curious about her benefactors, which was how she was beginning to see them.

'I'm afraid that's also one of the conditions of the job. They refuse to have their identities revealed. It doesn't make any difference to your taking the position, does it?'

'No, of course not,' she replied, but nonetheless a slight twinge of apprehension crept into her mind. Something just didn't seem quite right, and she couldn't help but wonder who was behind ridiculously rapid promotion.

Everyone relaxed and began to question Jenna on the many aspects of the company she knew so well. They worked through the morning, sending out for sandwiches and coffee so that they could also work through lunch. They considered all the similarities and all the differences between the two companies. There were savings to be made where things were duplicated, and opportunities for expansion in other areas.

'I think we should spend tomorrow at *Reality*'s offices and decide on some of the more practical aspects of the amalgamation. We'll meet there at nine-thirty, if that's agreeable?' Bill suggested. Everyone nodded, and the meeting began to break up. Bill called Jenna back, asking her to spare him a couple of minutes.

'I just wanted a few words with you. I know you were instrumental in bringing this about – this takeover, I mean.'

'I really don't know what you mean! I had little or nothing to do with it. I did visit the offices, but there was nothing significant in that. I just collected my income tax forms. I did think I might seek some advice, but that came to nothing. The person I intended to ask was unavailable.'

'As you like,' Bill said, but a quiet smirk on his face suggested that he knew better.

'If there's something you want to say, go ahead and say it,' she demanded. 'You look as if you know something I don't.'

He gave a shrug and would say no more.

All that evening her mind was going over and over the peculiar situation. Her sudden promotion somehow didn't ring true. There were too many unanswered questions. No one with more than a grain of intelligence could believe that she, a mere assistant to the director only weeks ago, could possibly be so well known that an anonymous consortium would insist that she be put in charge. So well known that she was suddenly raised to the dizzy heights of director of a well-established company.

A possibility occurred to her. Sarah herself was quite well-off; and Michael obviously had wealth behind him, and contacts. No! They couldn't possibly be responsible for so huge an enterprise. But there *was* one other possibility . . . Simon. He was an astute businessman. He seemed to have unlimited wealth behind him. And he was in contact with Sarah. Jenna remembered Bill once assuming that she knew Simon Andrews. Why would he have picked that name out of the blue?

She was growing more and more convinced, the more she thought about it. Dear Sarah, probably worried out of her mind about her niece, must have set this whole chain of events into all too rapid motion. It was nepotism that had got her to this exalted position. The good old-fashioned 'who you know' – or 'who you're related to'. It was nothing to do with her own 'brilliant' talents and expertise. What an absolute fool she had been! What a gullible idiot.

Furiously, she ran down the stairs and out of her flat. She went to the lock-up garage to retrieve her car and drove straight to her aunt's house. She was seething with a mixture of anger, indignation, hurt pride and the desperate need to discover the truth immediately.

Outside Michael's house there were two cars already parked. Damn. They must be entertaining. Well, it was too bad! She would have to drag her aunt away from her guests, if necessary, in order to have a straight talk. She pressed the doorbell and kept her finger there for an excessively long time.

'Jenna! What on earth are you doing here?' Sarah's expression was one of mingled shock and discomfort. 'I'm afraid it isn't very convenient. We're in the middle of a . . . a business dinner.'

'Well, I apologize, but this can't wait! I have to talk to you immediately. I need answers to some questions.'

'Could we possibly do this tomorrow?' Sarah asked feebly.

'I'm sorry. It won't wait. You have some explaining to do!'

'Oh dear. I said you'd never buy it! You'd better come in. I hope you're ready for this!'

Jenna suddenly realized that she recognized the other car parked outside. It was a familiar silver blue sports model, one that she had been driven in on a number of occasions. She walked into the dining room.

'Hallo, Jenna,' said Simon, rising from his seat.

She thought her heart would stop. She felt her face pale and she was decidedly dizzy at the sight of this man. He was even more handsome than her tortured mind had remembered. He put out a hand to steady her and pulled out a chair for her, next to him. His light touch on her arm set it on fire. She felt a glow of heat spreading throughout her body. This man, of all people, having dinner with her own aunt. She turned to look at Sarah, whose expression was one of deep distress.

'How could you, Sarah?' she whispered. 'How could you, of all people do this to me?'

'It has nothing to do with Sarah. I'm afraid I am the guilty party,' said Michael unexpectedly. 'You see, I was trying to think of some way to help you, Jenna. Sarah had been driving me mad; she was so worried about you. I have several friends in the film world – I've been involved in a number of documentaries, purely as a consultant, you understand – and I do know a lot of people. I think you know my sister quite well. Harriet Jenkins?'

Jenna gave a gasp of total surprise.

'No wonder she knew so much about me. Your sister? Amazing!'

'I'd been looking for a new investment and it seemed the perfect opportunity. Harriet and her friends had been trying to interest me in this idea and suddenly everything gelled.'

'And where do you fit in, Simon?' she asked, her

voice sounding like a squeaking gate, or so she thought.

'I only came into things when Sarah phoned to ask advice about the proposed takeover. It seemed like a good business proposition – especially as you already knew the company inside out. Poor Jenna. I gather you lost your devoted swain to another woman?'

'If you're referring to Kurt, I was partly responsible, I suppose. I encouraged the match. I suggested he take Sylvia out when I refused his proposal for the umpteenth time. I guess he took on a little more than he bargained for.'

'I shouldn't worry about him,' Sarah put in. 'He's got a whole lot of money out of this deal. His wife has organized a new life for him, a huge place in the country, and I believe she intends to start breeding – what was it dear, horses?'

'Just breeding, probably,' laughed Michael. 'So, it seems all the ends are neatly tied up.'

'Oh, no,' Jenna began, 'We've hardly started on this business of tying up of ends. I want to know more. Why have I been promoted like the proverbial rocket? The car, the mobile phone, whose idea were they?'

'Guilty,' Michael confessed. 'But you do have the talent for the job. I wouldn't have hesitated to fire you on the spot if you weren't up to it. Now, I believe we still have dessert waiting for us, don't we, Sarah? You will join us, won't you, Jenna?'

'I need time to think. You go and finish your meal. I'll go and put some coffee on, if you don't mind.'

She went into the kitchen. For once Michael and

her aunt were eating in the dining room, the table cleared of the piles of manuscripts and photographs. Jenna paced up and down the room, her brain working overtime. One thought dominated everything. Simon was here. Simon was right here, in this house. Was he actually staying with Michael and Sarah? Was he the reason for Sarah's silence for the past week? She felt a flood of jealousy rage through her body. Simon, who already had everything, might be staying in her own aunt's house. Was he taking over *here* as well? She had spent a miserable week or more, waiting for news, wondering if she could have done something wrong. And all the time he'd been busy taking over more of her own special people and places.

A little later, Sarah came into the kitchen with some dirty dishes from the dining room. She put them on the table and crossed to put an arm round her niece.

'Don't touch me, Sarah,' she hissed. 'How could you? How could you patronize me like that? Compromise me. How ever can I have a proper working relationship with my new colleagues once they know I'm related to the backers? When they discover the circumstances of my appointment? They wouldn't dare to criticize or say anything was wrong. It's a totally impossible situation. And as for Simon's involvement – well, really! You *know* how I feel about him.'

'I know you love him. And I know he loves you.'

Jenna stared. Surely Sarah couldn't condone Simon's behaviour? Simon had a wife and child. He wasn't free to love her, Jenna. Besides, he had the very lowest opinion of her. He believed she was little more than a whore, if their last conversation was anything to go by.

'Loves me? He has a funny way of showing it. No, Sarah, you're living in cloud cuckoo land if you think we can ever have any sort of relationship.'

'Give him a chance. He truly wanted to help you.'

'That's as may be, but you have your opinion and I have mine. I think I'd better leave now and let you get back to your guest. Goodbye, Sarah. Say goodbye to Michael for me.'

Stifling her sobs, Jenna rushed to the door and, fumbling to open the heavy catch, went out into the night. She leaned against her once precious car. Now it was a symbol of something almost immoral. She had really believed that her meteoric success had all taken place because of her own talents. But if she had been anyone else she would never even have been invited for an interview, let alone have got the job. She decided to leave the precious car where it was and walk to the nearest tube. It had become a representation of her personal failure. How could they all have been so naïve as to think they would get away it?

She walked slowly along the pavement. A car slowed down beside her and stopped. She quickened her pace. She was in no mood for a kerb-crawler. The streetlights were bright, even if the road was relatively deserted. The car moved to catch her up and stopped again. She turned to look at it, ready to shout for help. The words died on her lips as she recognized the silver-blue car.

'Go away, Simon. I don't need this.'

'We have to talk, Jenna. You're being ridiculous. Please. Get into the car.'

'There is nothing left to say. Nothing between us. I can't take the risk of seeing you alone.'

'I'm sorry, Jenna. I've behaved badly to you and I apologize.' His voice sounded as if he was forcing out every single syllable between clenched teeth.

'So you should be. You *have* behaved quite unforgivably to me – not to mention to your wife and son.' She struggled to keep her voice steady. Between her emotion at seeing him again so unexpectedly and her anger at what she saw as his interference in her professional life, she felt as if she was being torn in two.

'Jenna, once and for all, I am not married and I have no son. If you can't believe me, can't accept that, then there's no future for us.'

'If I could possibly believe you, I would. But the evidence of my own eyes tells me differently. You demand too much from me whenever we meet. And each time we part . . . well, let's just say it has taken me a long time to get over it. You've told too many lies for me to be able to trust you now.'

'I have never lied to you. Oh, what's the use? I give up. Have a good life, Jenna.' He slammed the car into gear and drove away with the all too familiar screech of car tyres.

There was a high wall behind the spot where Jenna had been standing. Gratefully, she leaned back against it. Everything was happening too quickly. What a day! She had gained a huge promotion, discovered that it wasn't genuinely earned and she had unexpectedly seen again the man she adored – would always adore. She had probably also seen him for the last time ever. She had ruined everything. Blown all her chances in one fell swoop. And she had exploded with temper against the very people who were trying to be so kind to her.

She appreciated now that they had all been trying to do what they had seen as their best for her. It had been done out of love for her as well, at least in Sarah and Michael's cases. For Simon there could be no reason other than to have power over her, to get back at her. And money. He would surely never have made such an investment for love or charity. He must hate her to take such drastic steps to control her life.

She pulled herself away from the wall and began to walk towards the main road. She could pick up a taxi or travel by Underground to reach home. There were always people wandering around the city at all hours of the day or night. Thoughts of her own safety did not occur to her. At this particular time, personal safety meant nothing to her.

It was almost midnight by the time she finally returned to her flat, having walked for much of the way, her mind occupied trying to make some sense of recent events. The inevitable flashing light on her answering machine told her a message had been recorded. She played it back.

'Give me a call to let me know you're safe,' came Sarah's voice. Then came another bleep, followed by, 'Jenna, please let us know you're back.' There was a

319

third and a fourth call. At the end of the fourth there was an additional message.

'I hope you and Simon are together and making it up, but, please, just take a moment to calm my fears. Why did you leave your car here? It seems such a futile gesture.'

Sarah probably thought that she and Simon were wrapped in each other's arms, too busy making love to have time to answer the phone. If only! She felt tempted to call back, but she still felt too angry at Sarah's and Michael's well-intentioned interference.

As she saw it, there were a number of options ahead. She could take the job they had contrived for her and do it so well that she would satisfy even her own high standards, or she could turn it down. She could retreat to the cottage and lick her wounds. She could try for another job – abroad if necessary. She had received offers in the past from America, but had put them down to the fact that Americans liked an English accent. She could possibly join millions of others trying to get that mythical *break*.

She most needed what she didn't have at present: time to think everything through.

The hammering at her door finally roused her. She glanced at the clock beside the bed and wondered who on earth could be there, at gone three in the morning.

'Who is it?' she shouted through the door.

'It's Michael. Sarah was worried about you. I came to see if you were all right.'

She pulled the safety chain away and opened the door.

'There was no need. Really.' She let him in and immediately he picked up the phone and called Sarah.

'She's OK. She's on her own.' He raised quizzical eyebrows as he spoke and she nodded. 'At least we've located one of the missing sheep.' He listened for a moment and then nodded. 'OK, if that's what you think is best. I'll wait here, then. Bye.' He replaced the receiver. 'She's driving your car over now. No, it's no use protesting. She's determined to come and see for herself that you really are all in one piece. I suppose you don't know where Simon is?'

'He's gone to hell as far as I'm concerned. I'm still very angry with you. Sarah has interfered in my life for as long as I've known her, but you're a whole new ball game. She did it for love. What's your motivation?'

'Would you believe love as well? I may not know you very well yet, but I do love Sarah – very much. And she loves *you* very much. If she is unhappy, then I shall do everything in my power to make her happy again. If that's a problem for you, then I'm sorry. But I would do the same thing again if the situation arose.'

'I'm sorry too. I *do* understand, but I guess I'm still in total shock. Not only at your admission of involvement but at seeing Simon again so unexpectedly.'

Michael stared at her shrewdly, and she waited for him to make some comment about the other man. Wisely, he decided to say nothing.

'I'd better put some coffee on,' she said, going into the kitchen.

321

CHAPTER 18

Two weeks had passed since the fateful discovery of the identity of the so-called consortium behind Solo Films and their takeover of Kurt's company. Jenna had worked hard every single moment of the day and through most evenings. Weekends had become just more working days and her social life had ceased to exist. She had contacted just about every company Kurt had ever done work for to let them know they were in business once again. Single-handedly she had lined up several possible commissions, and even taken on a secretary-cum-personal assistant, to help with the workload. Everyone from Solo had been very supportive – coming to help where necessary but leaving her the responsibility of organizing things. She was determined to prove to the world that she could succeed in the job, even if she had been given it under rather dubious circumstances.

'I'll show Mr Simon Andrews,' she muttered, with an almost alarming regularity.

Her private life was non-existent too. She had given no more thought at all to her aunt's wedding. Her intention to take charge of the planning and organizing had all gone by the board because of the new job and everything associated with it. In fact, the subject of the wedding had never cropped up again since the evening she called her own 'particular nightmare'. She had seen little of either Sarah or Michael, since that night, when they had talked until morning, all trying to come to terms with the situation.

That evening, when she had crawled home from work practically exhausted and fallen straight into bed, Sarah rang.

'Have you made any plans for your birthday, darling?' she asked.

'What birthday? Oh, yes. I suppose it is approaching again. No. Haven't had time to plan anything. Think I'll just give it a miss for this year. Slows down the ageing process, if nothing else!'

'You'll do no such thing. We'll have dinner. Come over here and either I'll cook or we'll go out. We've hardly seen a thing of you for ages.'

'I've been working hard.'

They chatted almost normally for a few minutes, and by the time the conversation ended, Jenna had agreed to go out for dinner with them on her birthday. She had also extracted a promise that there would be no surprises – especially no surprise guests. She could hardly believe she was almost twenty-six. Some of her schoolfriends were already married and had a couple of kids. She had always expected she would have children and she'd wanted to have them early, while she was young enough to have fun with them. If she hadn't suffered that miscarriage, she would be nearing the fourth month of her pregnancy by now.

She glanced at herself in the mirror and tried to imagine what she would look like with a huge 'baby bulge'. Her flat stomach remained flat. She stared critically at the reflection. She was actually looking thin. Gaunt, almost. If Sarah had been there at that moment, she would have scolded her niece for not eating properly. Perhaps she had been skipping a few meals, but there was never enough time. She was always too tired to cook for herself by the time she got home in the evenings. Some days she was forced to miss lunch as well, when she was either travelling to a meeting or in the throes of some crucial negotiations. Doubtless Sarah would be urging her to eat vast quantities of food next week. But she knew enough to see that she must take her diet in hand, in addition to making time to do some real exercise. She felt unfit, and her usual healthy glow had faded into pallor. It was all too easy to say she didn't have the time and allow herself to sink into bad habits.

'Happy birthday darling,' Sarah said enthusiastically the following week when Jenna arrived on her door-step. 'We're eating at home. Hope you don't mind. It's easier to talk here and there are a few things we'd like to discuss with you. Anyhow, come on in.' She took Jenna's jacket from her and looked critically at her niece.

'You've lost weight.'

'You always say that,' she teased.

324

'No, Jenna,' Sarah said without her usual teasing smile. 'You have lost serious weight. You aren't taking proper care of yourself. In fact, you don't look at all well. What's wrong with you?'

'You always did fuss over me, and bless you for it, but I'm fine. I've been working a bit too hard, that's all. It's all about to change, don't worry.'

Sarah still didn't smile but ushered her into the lounge, where Michael was waiting with a bottle of champagne at the ready. Jenna kissed him on the cheek, as she usually did, and put on a bright smile.

'Champagne, how lovely.'

'You can stay the night, so enjoy yourself and don't worry about driving. Sarah's got the spare room all ready. We insist, don't we, dear?' Michael said as he gave her a glass. They toasted her and sat down in the comfortable chairs, nibbling the assortment of cock-tail savouries Sarah had provided.

'Oh, I was forgetting your present.' She leaned over and picked up a beautifully wrapped, tiny package. 'With our love, darling,' said her aunt.

Jenna unwrapped the box and discarded the gold bow and paper. It was obviously jewellery of some sort; she could tell from the size of the box. Inside was a pair of perfectly matched ice-blue diamond earrings.

'Oh, how perfect,' she whispered, quite overcome with the generosity of the gift. 'But they must have cost a fortune,' she added, before she had thought what she was saying. 'I'm sorry. That must have sounded rude, but I am quite overcome.'

'I said I'd find a stone the colour of your eyes. Now

you have two, one to match each eye,' Michael joked.

'Thank you both. Very much,' she said shyly.

'Drink up. We have to finish this before we eat. Champagne simply won't go with duck,' Michael urged. 'Sarah is quite set on feeding you up.'

'Some things never change,' Jenna laughed, delighted to be back among people she loved once again.

After dinner, they sat sipping coffee and generous brandies, in outsize glasses.

'I hope you don't mind, it being your birthday, but we wanted to talk about the wedding,' Sarah began. 'I know it seems silly to make a fuss at our age but – well – we want it to be a special day.'

'Of course it must be *very* special. I had intended to take on lot of the organizing for you, but everything's got a bit out of hand now. I'd hoped to do the cake and everything.'

'It isn't necessary. The manuscript is safely with the publisher, and apart from the extra photos we have to do, we're both relatively free of work for the next few weeks. We're definitely going to South America and we want to get married before then. Mid-October and we're off!'

'Heavens, that's only about four weeks away – no, three,' she corrected. 'Are you seriously going to arrange everything in just three weeks?'

'I don't see why not. We've got the licence arranged already, and we know someone who can organize a fairly professional video for us.' Sarah sounded even more laid-back than usual, Jenna thought.

'But what about the ceremony? The reception,

guests, invitations, everything. There are millions of things to do! It's not just a case of a licence and a video. And clothes. What's everyone going to wear?'

'For a well-organized lady, you sound in a complete panic,' observed Michael lazily.

'Neither of you has any idea of the complexities of planning a wedding. That much is obvious.' Jenna brain began to race. She sifted bits of information and filed details in her mind, just as she did when planning her work.

'I know that look, darling,' Sarah said. 'Stop organizing and listen. It's all taken care of.'

'But the invitations?'

'Done.'

'How can they be if you haven't fixed the day or venue?' Really, these two were totally out of it, she thought.

'We have booked the venue, and the marriage official. Invitations went in the post today and the ring is being made, even as we speak. Oh, and the cake is also already in hand too, before you mention it again.'

'I see. It looks as though everything's settled. Am I to be told when and where, or aren't I invited?' Jenna said a little huffily.

'This is what we wanted to tell you personally. We're going to be married at Tregarth Manor. They are licensed for weddings and our guests can all stay there as well. So you see, everything's planned and organized.'

Jenna stared at both of them. They looked so

happy together, so excited by their plans. She felt as if a lead weight had dumped itself on her head and spread itself round her heart.

'It had to be there, didn't it?' she said at last. 'I should have guessed.'

'You won't disappoint us by refusing to come or anything, will you?' Sarah asked anxiously.

'Of course not,' she tried to reply lightly.

'I simply had to be married in my beloved Cornwall, and Tregarth is the obvious place.'

'As if I could miss the wedding of the year, wherever it takes place.' She felt her voice quaver. Was she ever going to be free of that man? Whatever the occasion, Simon came bursting in to destroy her peace.

'That was partly why Simon was here that night. We were discussing the wedding plans, as well as the business deal, of course.'

'What happened to him after he drove away from me in a blinding rage?' asked Jenna, trying to sound uninterested.

'Mad idiot drove all the way back to Cornwall. I must say, you two certainly have the ability to put long distances between you at the drop of a hat. Such intensity of feeling. Makes me glad to be old,' Michael added wryly. 'Isn't anyone going to tell me I'm not old?' he wailed in mock self-pity.

'The only thing I have done absolutely nothing about, Jenna, is what to wear. Do you think you could find time to come with me to choose something?'

'If you're certain Simon hasn't organized that as well!'

'He's only sorting out the men's things. Hiring the suits and so on,' said Michael seriously. 'I could ask him about something for you, ladies, if you like.'

They managed to laugh, breaking the growing tension.

'Of course I'll help you to choose something. Can we go at the weekend? Saturday?'

'You'll need something too. You will be my bridesmaid, of course? Do people of my age have bridesmaids? Oh, dear. It all sounds a bit silly. Well, you might have to settle for guest of honour or matron of honour or something.'

'I could give you away. Can a woman give an aunt away?'

'Well, actually, Simon is performing that duty. He's as qualified as anyone I know; I think. I wanted you to be more special, and sort of standing with me. Do you understand?'

'Of course,' Jenna replied, hoping she sounded much braver than she was feeling.

It was extremely late when they went to bed. The alcohol had helped Jenna to relax, and her own exhaustion allowed her to fall into a deep sleep. She awoke late the next morning and sat up in the unfamiliar room wondering where she was. Memory flooded back and she frowned. An unexpected frisson of excitement ran through her body at the thought of her aunt's wedding. She would at least *see* Simon again . . . however disturbing that might be. She was totally haunted by that particular pair of honey-gold eyes.

It might be difficult, but she would not allow her

own personal feelings to intrude on Sarah's big day. She would buy something stunning to wear – not to rival Sarah, of course, but to let the world see that she was someone in her own right, a capable woman who intended to get what she wanted from life. If her greatest desire remained out of bounds, no one would see her suffering, at least not on Sarah's wedding day. She would show them all. A knock on her door interrupted her thoughts.

'Are you awake?' Sarah called.

'Come in.'

'I've brought you some breakfast. I also took the liberty of calling your office, to say you'd be in later on this morning. Boss's perks, I think,' Sarah said cheerfully. 'Looks as if you slept quite well, anyway.'

'Must have been the booze. Wow, this looks good.' She smiled, looking at the loaded tray Sarah was carrying. 'Good grief. There's more food on this plate than I've eaten in a month.'

'That much is obvious from the state of you. I don't want any stick insects at my wedding. I'm going to take you in hand, my girl. Get you looking a little more healthy before the big day.'

'If you persist in keeping me away from the office, your investment could suffer,' Jenna said, tongue in cheek. 'Oh, but it's so good to be here. I've missed you.'

'How about we spend a couple of days at the cottage before the wedding? Just you and me?' Sarah suggested.

'That sounds blissful, but I don't think I should take the time away from work.'

'Leave that to me, and Michael of course. I'm sure

Harriet will organize something.'

'She's a nice woman, but then she is Michael's sister, so what can you expect?'

Jenna ate the delicious scrambled eggs and crispy bacon with great relish, something she had not done at breakfast-time for many months.

'You will cope with seeing Simon at the wedding, won't you?' asked Sarah anxiously. She sat down on the bed, sipping a cup of coffee.

'Don't worry about it. I'll be fine.'

'There is such chemistry between you,' Sarah continued. 'You seem to have an energy, so that sparks are visible when you are close.' Jenna stared at her aunt. She knew it was true. Any contact between Simon and her was like a flash of lightning finding its mark.

'I didn't realize it showed,' muttered Jenna. 'Now. About this shopping trip . . .' she asked, successfully changing the subject.

The two talked for almost half an hour, planning their day out to buy wedding outfits. Jenna glanced at the time and squeaked in alarm.

'Good heavens. I must rush! I'm *horribly* late for work.'

'But you're the boss, darling,' Sarah told her. 'You call the shots. Late is only late if you decide it is. Enjoy your position and make the most of it.'

'Well, maybe I am, but if the boss sets a bad example, how will the rest know what's expected?'

It was fun shopping for such special outfits. They went to all the larger West End stores and giggled like a pair of schoolgirls as they tried on outrageous hats. Exhausted by midday, they stopped for lunch then resumed the battle, fortified by good food and wine. Sarah finally decided on an elegant suit in palest blue silk and an extremely feminine silk top hat trimmed with streamers of palest blue and cream ribbon and a neat half veil at the front. The shoes were blue, to match the suit, and she added a soft kid clutch bag.

'You look sensational,' Jenna told her when she finally emerged from the changing room. 'Michael will totally flip when he sees you.'

'I think the hat may be a bit too much, seeing as it's an indoor ceremony. I'll think about it. We must sort you out now. Have you seen anything you like? This is, of course, on me. I want you to have the most sensational garments we can find – next to mine, of course.'

Sarah would not listen to Jenna's protests and insisted on buying her niece everything, top to toe. As Jenna was taking a major role in the wedding party, she wanted to complement the bride without detracting in any way from Sarah's impact. They found a delightful corded silk dress, also in pale blue, whose designer price tag made Jenna gasp in horror. The dress was short, showing off Jenna's well-shaped legs, and the close fitting waist made the most of her slender figure. Long sleeves and a prettily shaped neckline made the whole effect perfect.

'You will be a sensation, darling,' Sarah said fondly, hugging her niece in excitement. 'In fact, we shall make an astounding couple in every way.'

'Can we go home now?' Jenna asked, when they had bought shoes, bag and a complete set of matching silk undies. 'I'm totally shattered. I think a whole two days at the office would be more restful any time!'

The next two weeks flew by. Everyone was full of plans, both at Sarah's home and at Jenna's workplace, though the purposes might have been differently motivated. Jenna simply didn't have the time to be nervous about the coming visit to Cornwall, or, more importantly, to Tregarth. She was quite determined that nothing, but nothing, would be allowed to intrude on Sarah's happiness, or the wedding itself. If she attempted to erase all thoughts of Simon, she was able to see the whole event almost as an assignment, to be completed without glitches of any sort.

At last, the Tuesday before the wedding arrived, and Sarah and her niece set off together for the long drive to the cottage. It would be late when they arrived but Mrs Kernow had promised to buy a few basic necessities and she would have aired the house. Sarah had not visited the place for many months and Jenna's last stay had ended in her dramatic retreat, after Simon had left for a second time. She felt relieved that she was not alone on this visit. The cottage held a few too many ghosts. Briefly, she allowed her thoughts to stray back to those few days. She honestly thought it had probably been the happiest time of her life, despite the traumas that had followed.

'It's lovely to be home,' Sarah said excitedly rushing from room to room. 'I'd forgotten what wonderfully peaceful, beautiful place this is. And

Bonza, my darling. Have you forgotten me completely? I wouldn't blame you.' The huge cat, who had been living with Mrs Kernow, miaowed his welcome and left immediately to do the things cats have to do.

They had stopped to eat *en route*, so a last coffee before bed was all they needed. Their wedding outfits had been taken in Michael's larger car, carefully wrapped in tissue paper and packed in large boxes. Instructions had been given that they were to be unpacked by one of the staff and definitely not to be seen by the groom.

The two women were planning to spend a completely relaxed couple of days, doing nothing but enjoying a break before the big day on Friday. Their only fixed appointment was a dinner party on Thursday evening for a few of the special guests who would be staying at the hotel. Sarah and Jenna were also booked to stay at the hotel for that night.

All day Wednesday, they pottered in the garden, enjoying the October sunshine, chatting and playing games of 'Do you remember when . . .? They sat down to their evening meal – the last one they would eat alone before the marriage. They had a bottle of Pouilly Fumé, one of Sarah's favourites, and some local fresh fish. Jenna set the table formally, even using candles to create her own special atmosphere in the tiny room. It was the end of an era and it threatened to be an emotional evening.

They took turns to propose toasts and they clinked glasses. They were each filled with many memories of happy years shared together. Jenna's final toast was simply, 'To Happiness.' With tears in their eyes, the two clutched each other's hands.

'Thank heavens we could do this here, tonight. What a pair we'd have looked with everyone around us tomorrow night,' Sarah said with a tremor in her voice. 'You'll find someone special too, darling, one day.'

'I found someone special all right. It was just too late, that's all.'

'Simon?'

'Yes. He is everything I could ever want. Oh, but you must never tell him all this. Promise you won't?'

Sarah shook her head. 'Trust me, darling. I have only ever had your best interests at heart. But please tell me, why is there such a barrier that stops you two getting together?'

'Isn't it obvious? Paula. Tom. They present a rather unscaleable barrier.'

'Is that all? There's nothing else?

'Isn't that enough?'

'But why are you so certain Paula is Simon's wife and Tom is his child?'

'She told me as much. Not in so many words, but it was the way she said it. She called me a marriage-wrecker. I knew she was telling the truth.' Jenna paused and looked into her glass, knowing that this was the occasion to tell Sarah everything.

'And it didn't occur to you that she could be lying and that Simon was telling the truth?'

'Simon is a man. All men say they're not married when there's someone else they want. Or that their wives don't understand them – not like *you* do. Then, when they've had what they want, it's goodbye and back to the wife and children.'

'I'm sad that you're so cynical, for one so young – as the saying goes.' Sarah paused, looking hard into Jenna's eyes. 'I can't tell what you're thinking any more. You have a sort of shield that covers your eyes these days.'

'Defence mechanism.'

'Jenna. Why have you assumed that Tom is Simon's son . . .?'

'It's patently obvious by looking at him. You have met him, I suppose?'

'Let me finish. Yes, I agree. He *is* the image of Simon. I haven't met him, but I have seen a recent photograph. How much do you know about genes, heredity and all that? Well, have you never considered that Simon must have got his looks from somewhere – his own parents, perhaps? His father in particular? His father could have produced a second child who looked like Simon.'

'Don't be ridiculous, Sarah. Simon's father died. Years ago.

'Seven years and a few weeks. Tom is almost eight.'

Jenna went pale. This couldn't be possible, could it?

'But surely Simon's mother must be too old to have an eight-year-old son. She's nearly seventy, according to Simon. Even today's miracles of science couldn't achieve that one.'

'Oh no, of course not. Paula is undoubtedly Tom's mother.'

Jenna stared, the possibilities tumbling round her mind. Simon's father and Paula? It couldn't be? Almost in whisper, she asked how Simon's father had died.

'Too much alcohol. He finally went on a binge and ended up having a dreadful accident. Fell over the cliffs, I believe. It was a terrible time for the family. The mother went back to Scotland and what was left of the family money scarcely paid the death taxes. Simon gave up his beloved archaeology and set to work to rebuild the family home; he also took on a variety of business ventures. Practically the only bit of luck he had was when Paula's father, Simon's father's former partner, died and left her a few thousand. In return for a guaranteed home, she gave it to Simon to invest in the hotel, or whatever else he decided. He invested in the stock market and managed to hit the jackpot. Since then, he's discovered he has a real flair for the markets, and he's built himself a tidy fortune. Nowadays, his only connection with archaeology is his interest in antiques. And even that has turned into a small goldmine. He undoubtedly has the golden touch in many areas. It's not really much compensation for something he loved as much as archaeology, but that's life, or so it seems.'

Jenna listened to her aunt's speech with a growing sense of discomfort. If Simon had really been telling the truth, she'd badly misjudged him. All her own fears, suppositions and anguish had been self-imposed. The responsibilities he'd talked about weren't Paula and Tom after all. He must have been talking about the hotel, and presumably providing a home for the woman to fulfil the promise made to his dying father. It all fell into place but it was too late. She had ruined everything.

'I'm very ashamed,' she finally managed to whisper. 'Why couldn't I have listened to what he was saying? I simply closed my mind to any possibility that he was telling the truth.'

'You must have been let down badly at some stage. I didn't realize.'

'I had an affair with someone who turned out to have a wife back home. I swear I didn't know at the time. It was so awful I vowed I'd never do it again. When Paula whispered her own brand of malicious words, I was more than ready to believe her.'

'Wishful thinking on her part. She desperately wants to marry Simon. I expect the "marriage-wrecker" title she flung at you was because she saw you as a rival to her own plans. If she and Simon were to marry, he would become the father she needs for her son and give her a stable, secure home. And money, of course. Though her own original little stake in the hotel has risen beyond all measure. If she would agree to it, Simon would buy her out and acquire her shares. That would give her plenty of capital to set up a home and provide a modest income. But she's hardly likely to do that – not when she sees Simon still free and as a potential husband.'

Jenna sat quietly absorbing all this new information. She could well understand Paula's motivation for trying to get rid of her. She must have looked like one huge impediment, standing in Paula's way. A young, attractive female, actually staying in the hotel, whom Simon knew and liked, was the last thing she wanted. If she could manage to direct her lies straight at the person concerned, hopefully she could remove the possibility of any potential threat. Doubtless Paula had played the same game with Simon, and had told him all sorts of lies about *her*.

Jenna's mind churned on. That must have been why Simon was ready to think the worst of her, pairing her both with Kurt and Alistair within a few days. Then Alistair's cheap comments had exacerbated the situation and naturally Simon had believed what he saw, putting two and two together with the help of Paula's lies.

'There's just one more thing. One lie no one can explain. Simon told me most assuredly that he couldn't father a child. I didn't believe him because of Tom. I was certain that he was Simon's child, but anyhow I know for a fact that he *can* have a child.'

'What do you mean?' Sarah looked puzzled for a moment, and then the truth hit her. 'Oh, no – you couldn't . . . Jenna, you didn't have an abortion?'

'Of course not. As if I could ever have considered such an action! I had a miscarriage, and it couldn't possibly have been anyone else's child.'

Sarah stared hard at her niece.

'So, my little Miss Morality, even though you believed he was married, you did sleep with him after all? And when exactly was that?'

'The night you set us up. Remember your urgent call back to London?'

'But I never meant . . . oh, dear. So it's all my fault after all, isn't it?'

'Of course not. I knew I was doing wrong but, well, I loved him so much, and it was just too tempting. I nearly did it again, when he was staying at the cottage to look after me. We'd had such a wonderful day. Did you know he actually bought a boat? We were going out for a day trip and the crazy guy actually bought a boat. I couldn't believe it.'

'It doesn't sound much like the man I've come to know. Very rash of him. You must have *some* effect on him, you know. Poor man. He hasn't had much pleasure in life up till now. You must have been good for him. But go on. You were telling me that you nearly slept with him again.'

Jenna recounted the whole sordid business of the contraceptives and his consequent reaction. Sarah was sympathetic and very understanding, just as Jenna had known she would be. But she knew nothing of Simon's apparent problems and could offer no explanation for his subsequent actions.

'Does Simon know anything about the baby?'

Jenna shook her head. 'No. And he isn't to know. I don't want him even suspecting I've told you this much.'

'So what now, Jenna?' Sarah asked.

'I think we should get some coffee and finish our meal. We've got a wedding to get ready for. The celebrations begin tomorrow!'

CHAPTER 19

Sarah was rather quiet and thoughtful the next day. They drove together to Tregarth during the late afternoon. It was a cloudy day and there were only occasional, brief glimpses of the sun.

'Hope it stays fine tomorrow,' Jenna commented. There were such beautiful gardens at the manor, it would be a pity to have to stay indoors the whole time. She felt surprisingly calm about everything today. She had been anticipating a sense of dread, waiting for it to descend on her, but now she knew that Simon had mostly been telling her the truth she felt only her own shame and embarrassment. At least those particular emotions could affect no other person. It was something she would have to cope with. She also felt sad. Sad that she had destroyed all her chances of happiness with Simon. There could surely be no way they would ever be able to forgive each other for all the mistakes, misunderstandings and the lack of trust that lay between them.

'Here we are again,' Jenna said, as cheerfully as she could. She would be on her very best behaviour for

341

the next two days. Nothing, but nothing was going to spoil Sarah's wedding.

'This is it, then,' Sarah whispered back, gently, nervously squeezing her niece's fingers.

'Hallo, darling,' Michael called out, the moment they entered the reception area. He had obviously been waiting anxiously for their arrival. He kissed his bride and turned to kiss Jenna. 'Gosh, I've missed you.' Sarah laughed and, completely oblivious to their surroundings or any other people, Michael and Sarah talked together with an intensity that made Jenna smile with pleasure. They were going be the happiest of couples, of that she was certain.

'Hallo, Jenna,' said Simon, crossing Reception to greet her. He kissed her lightly on the cheek and she smiled back at him, for once managing not to blush or shake. She was holding a very tight rein on her emotions. Perhaps her self-consciousness had finally been exorcised. She looked at him, and found him as devastatingly good-looking as ever, though there were a few faint lines of strain at the sides of his eyes, and he looked slightly tense and, for him, unusually ill at ease. Only someone who knew him as well as she did would have noticed anything amiss.

'So,' she began, 'is everything on schedule? Cake sorted, flowers and all?'

'I think so. Several guests are here already, and more are arriving later. Perhaps you'd like to come and give the ballroom the once-over? See if everything is as you would like it?'

'I'm sure you've got it all organized beautifully, Simon,' she said, her heart beginning to react in the way it usually did when she was close to this man. But things were different now. She could stop feeling guilty, stop looking round in case Paula came unexpectedly into the room.

'Fine. Well, please ask for anything you require. I'll leave you to settle in.' He turned and went back into the office. She was just another guest arriving and he had done his duty.

The large table in the middle of the dining room was set for the twenty or so guests who were invited to the pre-wedding dinner party. Harriet Jenkins and her charming husband were there, several unknown relations from the groom's side, and one or two old friends whom Jenna remembered from her early days of digs with Sarah, when she'd been on school holidays. There remained an empty place next to her, and she wondered who was missing. Each place had a name card except for this one. She looked questioningly at Sarah, who merely shrugged her shoulders in reply.

They were well into the first course before Simon arrived, apologizing profusely for being late. He was wearing a dinner jacket and black tie, as were most of the men. Jenna caught her breath. She hadn't seen him in formal dress before and she was suitably impressed. Several of the other women also gazed in frank admiration at the newcomer.

'I'll forego the soup,' he said to the waiter who arrived at his elbow to spread a napkin over his boss's knees. The waiter melted away. 'Everything all right?' Simon asked Jenna.

343

'Wonderful,' she replied, almost happily. It was so typical of Sarah to invite Simon to join them for this evening, she thought. She was glad she had taken her aunt's advice and was wearing her newest evening dress: midnight-blue silk with a full skirt and close-fitting top.

Simon behaved perfectly, charming all the women but attending to Jenna's every need before she even realized she needed anything.

'You've lost weight,' he whispered. 'Have some more vegetables?' he offered in a louder voice. 'You need building up,' he whispered again. She glared at him, but it quickly turned to a grin.

'How are you, Jenna?' he asked later, when everyone had split up into groups to drink their coffee. 'Really, I mean.'

'Just fine, thanks,' she replied. No way was she going to get herself involved in any heavy discussions. Not this weekend of all weekends.

'And how's the job going?'

'You'll get an official report by the end of the month! Things are looking promising and I'm sure you'll be pleased with your returns.' Keep cool, she told herself. Keep at a distance.

'I'm not talking about business details. The last time we met . . . well, it was unexpected and difficult. We hardly parted on the best of terms, did we?'

'Tell me about it! It's the story of our lives, isn't it? When did we ever really part on good terms? I reckon there are just some people who will always manage to get in each other's hair.'

'And I presume you consider us to be those sort of people?' he said, his face grim.

Jenna raised her eyebrows and gave a slight shrug. 'Maybe.'

Further conversation was prevented by the arrival of one of the discreet waiters who almost seemed to glide around without making a sound. He whispered something into Simon's ear.

'Will you excuse me for a moment, Jenna? Something's come up.' He left her, smiling reassuringly at Sarah.

Jenna rose and went over to her aunt.

'It's a lovely party. Are you enjoying it?' she asked.

'It's good to see everyone again. People are so kind. I feel like royalty, all the attention I'm getting. And how is Simon? You look as if you're getting on well. I hope this isn't all proving too awkward for you.'

'Not at all. It's fine. I'm determined not to let anything get too heavy. This is far too special an occasion to spoil. It's your day – well, tomorrow is, and I count this as the start of it. Now tell me, how's your dress? Is it hanging up properly and everything?'

'Of course. Michael and I are having separate rooms tonight.' Sarah giggled in embarrassment. 'It's silly, I know, but it makes the ceremony seem sort of more special, if you can understand that.'

'Silly, old romantic thing,' Jenna laughed. 'I quite understand and I think it's lovely. Now, get back to your guests. I've had you all to myself for the past two days. Thank you, Sarah. Thank you for everything you've ever done for me.' She kissed her aunt and gave her a hug.

She still hadn't found quite the right time to give her and Michael the wedding gift she had chosen for them. She wanted a quiet moment, but she was beginning to think there would never be that moment, not among this crowd. She went over to Harriet and was introduced to her husband. By the time Simon returned to the gathering she was deep in conversation, and there was no further opportunity to continue their earlier talk. He spent the remainder of the evening circulating, chatting dutifully to the rest of the party.

Most of the guests started to drift away around eleven-thirty. Sarah was beginning to look weary and Jenna, firmly into her role as matron of honour, or whatever was the latest title she had been given, went quietly to her aunt's side and suggested maybe it was time to call it a day.

'I'll just say goodnight to Michael first.'

'All right, but no nonsense,' Jenna joked. 'I want my charge in bed before midnight.'

'Takes her duties seriously, doesn't she?' Michael said.

'I don't want the star of my video with bags under her eyes,' replied Jenna smartly.

The two went upstairs to Michael's room to say goodnight and Jenna realized this was probably the only chance she would have to present her gift. She collected it from her room, went along the corridor and tapped on Michael's door.

'My word, she doesn't trust us at all, does she?' Michael complained. 'Two and a half minutes we're allowed. And I've been parted from my bride for three whole days.'

'I wanted to give you this,' Jenna said gently, almost shyly. She was reasonably confident that they would like the gift, but inevitably, with people she knew so well, there was a worry that they might think it rather trivial. It would be embarrassing for them all if Michael and Sarah were unable to hide their dislike, or to had enthuse falsely over something they hated!

'Thank you, darling,' whispered Sarah, her voice thick with emotion. She put the beautifully wrapped box on the table and pulled at the ribbons. Michael helped and, painfully slowly, it seemed to Jenna, standing watching, they peeled the paper off and opened the blue box inside. The pair of matched brandy goblets, engraved with their names and the occasion, lay in a bed of white satin.

'Darling, they are exquisite,' Sarah said, smiling her thanks.

'Quite beautiful. We shall always treasure these, won't we, Sarah?' Michael added. 'Thank you so much.'

Jenna was relieved. She had worried long and hard over what to give them. They already had everything they could need in their homes, and they had money enough to buy anything they wanted. She had been searching for inspiration for weeks. A friend had suggested the glasses and knew someone who could engrave then. It seemed it had been a good choice.

The hotel staff had worked wonders on the ballroom. Banks of flowers were set round the area where the ceremony was to take place. White seats were set in rows, with pedestals of blue and white flowers arranged at the end of each row. Jenna processed slowly, behind Sarah, whose arm was being held by Simon. They all smiled at the many friends who were assembled for the occasion. Jenna grinned at her own friends, the two cameramen, who were discreetly hidden among the flowers. Few of the guests could have been aware that they were even there.

When the party arrived at the front of the room, next to the officiator, Michael stepped forward and squeezed Sarah's hand. She smiled back, her gaze one of pure love. Once the ceremony had begun, Jenna stepped back and found Simon close at her side. Discreetly he passed her a handkerchief, and took it back when she had used it to mop her streaming eyes. He took her hand and, squeezing her fingers, smiled at her. He sensed exactly how she was feeling and she was immensely grateful for his support.

'You look quite astoundingly beautiful,' he whispered to her as she stood waiting for the ceremony to conclude.

She stared at him. Moments later, when the movement of the bride and groom could cover her words, she whispered back with a smile, 'You don't scrub up badly yourself.'

The silver-grey morning coats of the principals gave an air of elegance to the whole occasion, and Simon himself, tall enough to carry the outfit off to perfection, was quite heart-stopping. *No complications*, she kept telling herself. *Keep it light*.

The music, provided by a small orchestra, heralded the end of the ceremony. Everyone clapped.

'You know, it all feels a bit like one of those opulent American soaps that I now realize I miss,' Jenna announced later. It was a dream of day, with wonderful food, perfect service and possibly the happiest two people in the world in at the centre of it all. The whole affair was simple, yet dignified, and exactly the right sort of wedding for Sarah and Michael.

As they had been together for so long already, the idea of escaping on honeymoon had lost its urgency. They were staying on for another night at the Manor and leaving for London, and eventually, South America, after lunch the next day. As most of the guests were also staying over, the party went on late into the night. The orchestra were replaced by a group who played dance music, during the early evening, and almost everyone joined in the variety of different dances they provided. Jenna had danced with everyone imaginable, except the one person she would most have liked to be with. He had been occupied with various tasks of hotel administration for much of the evening. But at last he sought her out, and together they waltzed across the floor, their steps perfectly matched.

'Now there's a sight,' Michael whispered to his new wife. 'Don't they move beautifully together?'

'Certainly do,' she agreed. 'And how! If only you knew the whole story.' Her husband looked at her curiously but said nothing. She would tell him when the time was right.

Jenna felt as if she were floating on air, and it was not just because of the champagne.

'I didn't realize you could dance so well,' she whispered to Simon.

'Nor I, you.'

As they were whirling round to the music, Jenna caught a glimpse of Paula, standing watching them, inside one of the doorways. The woman had been strangely absent during the day, which had been a source great relief to Jenna. Thoughts of the 'spectre at the feast' occurred to her, and she laughed softly. When the dance came to an end, Simon returned her to a seat, bowing in an old-fashioned, gallant style.

'I'll see you later. I have a few things to do. Did you realize those diamonds match your eyes perfectly?' he observed as he left.

Why was he being so nice to her after all that had happened? She left the room to go to the cloakroom. Someone followed her in, and as she left the cubicle she wondered why she wasn't surprised to see Paula, standing scowling at her.

'We never seem to be rid of you,' she said unpleasantly. 'Why do you have to keep coming here and spoiling everything for me and Tom? We were all right until you came. Simon doesn't love you. You should hear the things he says about you. Give him up once and for all. He's no good for you. He can't have kids, for one thing, and I'm sure you wouldn't like that. I saw how you looked at my Tom.'

'Oh, Simon's little brother, you mean?' Jenna said innocently. 'I'm sorry, Paula, but I know the whole story. I nearly ruined everything because of my conscience, due entirely to the thoughts you had planted in my head. I was never a marriage-wrecker, as you seemed to suggest, because there was no marriage to wreck. But that's all over now. If Simon still wants us to be friends or hopefully even more, that's our business. And don't you believe he can't have children. I really don't know what gave you that idea.'

'What do you mean?' But Jenna was almost out of the room. She had nothing else to say to the woman.

It was almost one o'clock in the morning. The band had gone some time earlier and now soft recorded music was playing over the hotel's sound system. A few stragglers were left, sipping last drinks. The weary waiters were collecting glasses, doubtless wishing everyone would disappear so they could get to their own beds. Jenna stood by the window, looking out at the floodlit garden and reflecting on the day's events. Simon came to stand behind her, resting one hand on her shoulder. She didn't turn, knowing instinctively that it was him.

'I gather from Paula that you now believe me, when I say that we aren't married.'

'Simon, I'm so sorry. Sorry not to have believed in you. Not to have trusted you. But the evidence, Paula's comments and Tom. What was I to think?'

'Does this mean we can give it – *us* – another chance? Are we going to try again?'

Jenna's heart began to pound in her chest. Could she afford to allow this man near her again?

'I don't know. I want to, but I'm scared. Can *you* give us another chance? You have this belief that I'm some sort of *femme fatale*. If we try and it doesn't work, how can I possibly pick myself up again?'

He bent forward to her soft lips and kissed them, tenderly. She kissed him back, and slowly, their bodies drew towards each other. He stopped and drew back.

'No further, Jenna. I just wanted to be sure you felt the way I thought you did.'

She gasped in disbelief. What was he trying to do to her?

'If we don't move away from this room,' he continued, 'I shall ravish you on the spot. And I'm not certain your hidden cameramen have taken themselves to bed yet.'

'So what exactly are you suggesting, Mr Andrews?' she asked just a little coyly, her relief evident on her lovely face.

'Come to bed with me, Jenna. I can't wait any longer.'

'Your room or mine?'

'I take it that means yes. My room has the disadvantage of a built-in small brother, likely to bounce in at some unearthly hour of the morning.'

'Sounds strange. You with a little brother.'

'Yes. I can't really think of him as a brother. In fact, I'm not sure how I *do* think of him – except as a very nice little child who looks uncannily like me. I gather Sarah filled in all the gory details? But we're wasting time. I have to get up early in the morning and it also looks as though I might be having a restless night.' His grin, tinged with a leer of pure lust, made Jenna laugh.

'You will if I have anything to do with it.'

'Isn't that what wedding nights are all about?'

352

Simon asked innocently

'Only when it's your own wedding.'

'Now are we going to let a little thing like that stand in our way? Besides, it's traditional. Best man and bridesmaid.'

'But you weren't the best man and I wasn't exactly a bridesmaid.'

'Why do you always have to be so picky? It's near enough for me.' Hand in hand, they climbed the stairs.

'I expect it's a bit of mess. I haven't been back since we got dressed this morning.' Jenna opened the door to find that everything had been tidied away in the tissue paper, shoe boxes, everything.

'Wow! I could get used to having people to clear up after me,' she muttered.

'Come here, woman,' Simon said, pulling her over to him. He tugged at her zipper with one hand, not daring to release the other hand from holding her close to him. His breath was coming in rapid bursts as his excitement mounted. 'Damn these fasteners. How are they supposed to work anyway?'

'Careful,' Jenna laughed. 'This dress cost a fortune.'

'I'll get you another,' he promised. The dress slid to the floor at last and he gasped with pleasure as her body was revealed. Her pale blue lacy bra showed the aroused nubs of her nipples, and the dark triangle of hair was barely covered by the matching panties. Sarah's expensive extra gift was obviously worth the money, if his expression was anything to go by. He gazed admiringly at her.

'You're even more beautiful than I remembered,' he said, his voice thick with emotion.

'I thought I was too skinny for you?'

'You are perfect, Jenna, in every way. I love you and want you. For always. Life is too painful, too empty without you.'

'I know what you mean,' she agreed, and leaned forward to pull his zip down.

'Careful, these trousers cost a fortune,' he teased. 'And they're not even mine. Hired for the day.'

'You'll have to buy some more, then, won't you?'

When they were both finally naked, he gently pulled her onto the bed. For several minutes they rediscovered each other, stroking and caressing bare flesh until they were both breathing heavily with their increasing desire, each wanting the other so badly it was almost painful.

'Oh, Simon. Come into me, quickly . . . I want you so very much.'

He hesitated. 'I'd better get some protection. I remember how you feel about it.' He rolled off the bed and went to his trouser pocket and pulled out a foil packet.

'You were sure of yourself, weren't you?' Jenna teased.

'Just say I had very high hopes, and, remembering the last time, I didn't want to face any new problems. But I did tell you the truth, you know. I can't have children.'

'Oh, but you can, Simon. I know for a fact that you can.'

He stopped dead in his tracks, the moment of passion temporarily lost.

'What are you talking about?'

'Remember the dreaded loft ladder? It wasn't only my foot that was hurt. I had a miscarriage as well. That's why I didn't want us to make love during that week. It wasn't the period you assumed I was having.'

He stared at her in silence, sitting down heavily on the bed. The pause was so long that she began to feel uncomfortable. Surely, surely she couldn't have blown it again?

'I don't understand. We had only made love once. Surely you couldn't have . . . But I was told . . . Are you absolutely certain it would have been mine?'

'Of course I am! I've always told you the truth. I don't sleep around. There was only ever one brief relationship before you came bursting into my life again. David – the man I told you about. But that was all over and done with many months before you and I made love. It was definitely your child I lost.'

'Well, what do you know?' His look of pride turned to one of tender concern. 'My darling are you sure you're completely recovered?'

'Yes, I'm fine now. Though I would have loved to be still expecting your child.'

For a moment they were silent, thinking of what might have been, then Jenna asked softly, 'Why were you so sure you couldn't have kids?'

'It's a long story. I'll tell you some other time.

There are other more important things on my mind. Now, where were we?'

Gently, they rekindled the passion that had been temporarily postponed. As he fumbled for the condom, Jenna gently pushed his hand aside.

'I don't really think that's necessary now, do you? Not now I know you're not married.' He kissed her again, and together they were soon riding the heights of passion they both remembered so well from that first magical occasion. He was a passionate lover, wild and thrilling. Together, they could be adventurous, imaginative, and above all deeply sensuous. It just got better and better, they both realized, as wave after wave of love swept over them. Finally they were both sated with passion, and, totally exhausted, they slept, entwined in each other's arms.

After barely a couple of hours' sleep, Simon woke and gently eased himself out of Jenna's arms. She stirred sleepily and he pulled the cover over her. He dressed quickly in his wedding suit from the previous day and slipped out of the room. He had work to do, and as soon he had finished he intended to get back to this woman he had finally been able to love so completely. They had things to discuss, plans to make.

If he was any judge of character, he knew that Jenna would insist that Sarah should attend *their* wedding. Tomorrow, Sarah and Michael would be leaving for South America, and their trip was likely to last for the best part of three months. There was no way he could possibly wait for such a long time – not after all they had been through. Urgent action must be taken. After all the time he had spent loving, wanting, longing for Jenna, he wanted them to be together now and for always. He was certain she wanted it too.

CHAPTER 20

Simon rushed through his morning chores, ensuring the smooth running of his hotel and attending to all the aspects of his many other business interests that needed his urgent attention. By eight o'clock he had finished, and he ordered a lavish breakfast for two to be sent up to Miss Brown's room. He leapt up the curved oak staircase, taking the steps two at a time. He used his master key card to open the door and rushed over to the bed. He stopped dead. The duvet had been flung back and there was no sign of Jenna. He peered into the bathroom, but she was not there either. He felt a sudden growing sense of panic. Surely, she couldn't have left? He had planned to return to her side before she was awake, hoping that she might not even have missed him.

He pulled the wardrobe doors open and all her clothes were hanging in their place. Even the hastily discarded dress from yesterday was hanging neatly amongst the rest. He felt relief sweep through him. He would be glad when they were finally married and there would be no more absences from each other –

even if this one had only been for an hour or two.

Suddenly he knew where she would be. He phoned down to the kitchen to postpone the breakfast, and almost ran across to the barn where the swimming pool was situated. He could hear the splashing before he opened the door. He shed his clothes and plunged in naked. He quickly caught Jenna and put his arms round her, pulling her close. She pressed herself against him and grinned.

'I wondered if you might find me. But really Mr Andrews, you're hardly wearing appropriate dress for the occasion.'

'For the occasion I'm thinking of, this would seem totally appropriate,' he argued, closing his own mouth deeply over her own. 'You taste of chlorine,' he laughed.

'I think perhaps we should move back to my room, don't you?' Jenna suggested. 'A stray guest might come in at any moment, and I sense you have something that needs my urgent attention.' Her hand touched his arousal and he kissed her again.

He laughed, delighted with her openness, and scooped her up in his strong arms, setting her down gently on the side of the pool. With a light bound, he joined her, pulling her robe around them both.

'We can hardly walk across the gardens like this,' she protested.

'Then you'll have to give the robe to me. You have at least got a bikini on,' he argued.

'Get dressed, then. You must have been wearing something when you came over.'

'Can't ruin an expensive hire suit with chlorine.

Besides, it will take so much longer to undress when we get back to your room.' He bundled his clothes under his arm and pulled the inadequate robe over both of them as they walked back into the hotel. They met only one other couple, who were going in to breakfast. He nodded to them, polite as always, and totally ignored the slightly shocked expression that crossed their faces. Jenna burst out laughing and they scampered up the stairs like two children.

Over the breakfast that Simon finally re-ordered an hour later, he looked seriously at Jenna.

'We have some sorting out to do – and quickly. By this time tomorrow Sarah and Michael will be on their way to somewhere in the depths of South America for three whole months. I can't possibly wait for that long to marry you, so I have a proposition to make.'

'Excuse me! Did I mis-hear, or did you say "marry you?" – "marry me." . . . oh, I don't know. You know what I mean!'

'Yes, of course. We are going to get married, aren't we? I can't have you running away from me all the time, and on the other hand me rushing away from you has also got to stop. My mechanic tells me I'm much too hard on the tyres of my car!'

She laughed happily.

'If that was a proposal, then, yes, we *are* getting married.'

'Right. Thank heavens that's out of the way! Now, what I was thinking, was this . . .' He outlined a plan which caused her jaw to drop in amazement, she finally grinned with delight.

'Oh, yes, please, Simon! Yes, *please!*'

'Now, eat your breakfast. You're looking a bit skinny these days.'

'Why do I get the feeling that you're taking over where Sarah left off? And you've got no room to talk. You're hardly overweight yourself.'

'But I,' Simon said carefully, 'am almost solid muscle, and I'll prove it to you one day.'

Later that morning, and for probably the first time since they had met, Paula sat drinking coffee with Jenna. Simon had left the room for a moment and the two women sized each other up.

'Simon's told me you're getting married,' said Paula awkwardly. 'Congratulations.'

'Thank you' Jenna replied, feeling equally awkward.

'I suppose you'll be coming here to live?'

'We haven't really had time to discuss it yet. But probably, yes, we will.'

'I expect I'll have to move out, then.'

'Let's wait for Simon to come back. We can talk about it together.' There was a moment of silence before Jenna continued. 'Tom's a wonderful little boy. You must be so proud of him.' Jenna was trying so hard to be nice, but this woman was making it very hard work. To her great relief, Simon came back into the room.

Together, they discussed the future. He suggested they should build a bungalow in the grounds for Paula and her son. That way, she could still work at Tregarth and they would all be able to have their privacy. The owner's accommodation would be refurbished for himself and Jenna to return to after their marriage, and they would continue to live at the hotel, when work allowed. Jenna had no intention of giving up her career entirely – at least not before it became necessary for other reasons. With an air of resignation, Paula nodded her agreement. She still looked unhappy, but at least she was being offered a home and some work for as long as she wanted it.

'So when's the big day?' she asked sullenly.

'We're waiting to discuss plans with Sarah and Michael, but in true honeymoon style they haven't emerged yet.' Simon smiled.

'Shame you couldn't have made your minds up earlier. You could have shared the expenses with them and made it a double wedding,' Paula said.

'If it hadn't been for you we might well have done just that,' Simon complained.

'No. I'd never have taken anything away from Sarah's day,' Jenna said quickly.

Over a quiet lunch with her aunt and new uncle, Jenna and Simon talked over their plans.

'So, if you didn't mind too much, we wondered if we could join you in South America in say, a couple of weeks' time, and get married out there. We'll spend a few nights somewhere and then, if you agree, we can all go on a dig somewhere, for old times' sake.' Jenna watched carefully to see their reaction, but she needed have no worries.

Sarah got up from her place and flung her arms round her niece's neck.

'I can think of no nicer wedding present than this.

It all sounds quite perfect, doesn't it, darling?'

'Excellent. Now, I suggest that hotel at Iguassu Falls,' Michael began. 'It's a lovely place, and they'll certainly be able to arrange the ceremony there. You can stay on for a few days and then fly to join us in Peru. We will have completed the Brazilian stuff by then, and in Peru you can help us with some research. There are one or two places we're thinking of pursuing. Machu Pichu might only be the beginning, or so we think –'

'Hang on,' Jenna interrupted. 'You're getting a bit carried away here. What was the first place you mentioned?'

'Iguassu Falls. It's on the border between Brazil, Argentina and Paraguay. Quite spectacular and . . .'

He continued to talk excitedly for several minutes. Simon was listening intently, and with growing enthusiasm. Sarah winked at Jenna and nodded towards the cloakroom.

'They'll never miss us for a minute or two. I foresee we might have problems with those two men of ours. I'm not sure we'll either of us get much of a honeymoon if we let them take us over this way. We shall have to make our stand. Are you absolutely certain it's what you want?' Sarah asked.

'Unless you have any objections? We don't want to spoil your trip, but we can't think of two nicer people to share a honeymoon with. Besides, we all have the rest of our lives together. A couple of months of travelling round one of the world's most exciting places? Honeymoon? You've got to be kidding. I've only been to the glitzy bit of Rio on an assignment with Kurt. That doesn't count as seeing a country the way you do . . . Oh, Sarah, I'm *so* happy!'

Sarah and Michael postponed their flight and stayed on for another night at Tregarth, to allow the younger couple some extra time to sort out their plans. Jenna still felt slightly concerned, worrying that they might be spoiling her aunt's honeymoon, but everyone seemed so happy with the arrangements that she soon forgot her anxiety. The newly weds finally left on the Sunday afternoon, along with the remaining few guests who had stayed on for the weekend. When the last couple had gone, Jenna sank back exhausted in the little office behind the reception area. Simon came in with a tray of tea and the pair relaxed. Their plans were made and the excitement of the past days was beginning to subside a little.

'Just think,' Jenna remarked, 'if we'd carried on the way we were, I'd have been back at my little flat in London, feeling the greatest sense of anticlimax anyone ever knew. Thank heavens Sarah talked to me that night. If she hadn't set things straight, I'd probably have gone on thinking that you and Paula were married, even if not happily.'

'And I might have gone on thinking that you were an easy lay,' he teased. She leaned forward to slap him and he caught her arm. 'You are one very sexy lady,' he said. 'I couldn't blame anyone for trying, but just let anyone try anything now and I shall prove how good I am at martial arts.'

'Really?' Jenna asked, her eyes widening.

'No. But they're not to know that!'

He took her in his arms and they kissed, at first gently, but as their passion increased the kiss grew more intense, until once more they were heading upstairs towards the bedroom.

'At least we won't feel we're missing out on a honeymoon if we keep up this pace,' Jenna said. Each time they made love, it seemed that they were able to find some new delight, some new aspect which made it a new experience.

'I hope you don't get tired of making love with me,' Simon said, his eyes for once solemn.

'I expect I shall,' Jenna said. 'In about two hundred years' time.'

'Fickle woman. You'll have to change your attitude when we're married. Chained to the kitchen sink all day, minding babies, cleaning the house.'

'Simon,' she said, sitting up suddenly. 'There's still something you haven't told me. What *is* all this business about you not being able to father babies? I don't understand.' With the rush of all the recent excitement, she had pushed the question to the back of her mind.

'I had mumps a few years back. Caught it from Tom, I suppose. It affected me badly, and afterwards old Dr Humphries nodded sadly and said that was the end of children for me. It's a well-known side effect of mumps, isn't it? I believed him anyway. Perhaps I shouldn't have?'

'I believe it *is* a suspected contributor to infertility ... though I don't think it's that common. And obviously not in your case! Let's hope there aren't dozens of little Simons running around somewhere as a result of your beliefs!'

'Impossible! I'm not denying there have been other women in my life – you surely wouldn't have expected anything different at my age . . . particularly as I never dreamed you'd come back into my life again . . . But don't worry about the "little Simons". Before you, even though I didn't think I could get anyone pregnant, I always took precautions – can't be too careful these days!' He paused and smiled at Jenna tenderly. 'I have truly never loved anyone else. At least, not now that I know what love really means. I may have *thought* I was in love a couple of times in the dim and distant past, but now I know differently!'

'But didn't you have tests to prove you couldn't have children? Or did you just automatically take what the doctor said as being true?'

'I had no reason to check upon what he'd said. I didn't have any plans to marry or start a family, so I suppose I didn't feel too bothered. I was so sickened by my own family's behaviour – especially my father.' Simon's expression grew bleak. 'I hated him, you know. I never could do anything right in his book.'

'I'm sure he would have been very proud of you now,' she said softly. 'And as for having children, let's just wait and see what happens. If we do, it will be marvellous. If not – well, that means we shall have even more time for each other.'

'You're quite a lady,' Simon said, his eyes fixing intently on hers.

366

'I'm a starving lady! Shall we have some dinner?'

'Is there no romance in your soul, woman?' he asked in mock anger.

'Nope. Nor food in my stomach. You said I needed feeding up. Well, get on with feeding me.'

They ordered dinner from room service, and Simon was not in the least embarrassed by the knowing looks he received from the waiter who served the food in Jenna's room.

'You'll have not a single shred of reputation left,' Jenna said when he had left.

'On the contrary. Every one of them will see this as *enhancing* my reputation. I bet they think we've only just met and that I persuaded you to let me share your room.'

'Unless you've changed the entire staff since we stayed here for the film, I don't think so! I don't think I've ever been so happy in my life, but, Simon, I will have to get back to London very soon. There's so much to do, and if we're flying out to South America in three weeks, there's masses of stuff that needs to be arranged.'

'At least there won't be any wedding preparations. Michael's booking the hotel when he gets out there, and as those two are the only guests all we need is accommodation at the hotel and dinner for four. You are certain you don't want a repeat performance of the wedding here? We do a nice line in wedding receptions, ma'am.'

'That's exactly what it would be, isn't it? A repeat performance. It would be a copy of Sarah's day and I'd hate that. Besides, there wouldn't be any decent men for me to chat up. Except the bridegroom, of course and we can all admit that would be very boring. Ouch,' she yelled as he began to tickle her.

Jenna travelled back to London two days later, driving herself in her blue car. She went into her flat, following her usual routine. Press the answering machine. Fill the kettle while listening to the messages. Flick through the mail. How many times in her life had she done just that? This time, though, it felt different. This time it was probably the last time she would ever do it. They had decided to keep her flat as a useful base in Town, but she would be finding a new director for the company, to replace her. Most of the time she planned to live with Simon in their beloved Cornwall. She thrilled at the thought, then realized she was daydreaming and hadn't heard a single one of the messages. Two of them were from Kurt, surprisingly enough. His voice sounded clear, no more slurring of the words that everyone had begun to accept as part of his normal speech.

'Can we have dinner some time?' he requested.

Jenna was shocked. The last she had heard was that he was in a clinic, recovering, and that he was married. She wondered if that could possibly have gone wrong – surely not so soon?

She dialled his old number and a female voice answered.

'Sylvia?' Jenna said, thinking she recognized the voice.

'Yes. Who is this, please?'

'Sylvia, it's Jenna. Jenna Brown. How are you?'

'Hi! Good of you to call back,' she said, most politely. 'Kurt would like a word.'

Jenna waited, curious to know what they wanted and why there was this constraint between them all.

'Jenna? Good to hear you. Look, I wonder if we could meet some time? Have a bite of dinner somewhere and talk? What do you say?'

'I suppose so. But what's the mystery? Why are you talking to me like a stranger?'

'I wasn't sure what you'd heard about me – us – since we last met. I mean – well, I know about the company, the takeover, of course, and that you are the main man, as it were. But I wasn't sure if you've forgiven me for dumping you the way I did? Quite unforgivable. I behaved very badly.' This did not sound like the Kurt she knew. If she hadn't known better, she would have said he was on the verge of grovelling.

'I'm pretty busy, but we could maybe have a drink one evening after work?'

'Not a good idea.'

She bit her lip. How tactless could she get? The man had only just left a clinic – only just dried out!

'Come to the office tomorrow. We'll have some sandwiches at lunchtime. Best I can offer, I'm afraid.'

'My, my, how mighty you've become, Miss Jenna Brown.' There was a silence, then distant, muffled mutterings. Obviously Sylvia was giving him one of her reputed scoldings. 'I'm sorry,' he continued. 'That would be great. Tomorrow around midday? Er, I wonder if I might bring Sylvia with me? Would you mind? Only we sort of work together these days.'

'Fine. I'll look forward to seeing you then.' She put the phone down. He was obviously after a job. But would it work out? He was definitely a talented director, much better than she herself could ever be, but was he sufficiently reliable? With Sylvia in tow, maybe, just maybe, they could provide the solution she needed.

The flat seemed empty, and provided exactly the anticlimax she had been dreading. She had only been away from it for a week but it seemed like a lifetime ago after all the wonderful things that had happened so quickly. With the rather dramatic changes she was planning in her life, this would probably be the last peaceful moment she would know, possibly for ever.

She unpacked her few things and looked in the freezer for something to eat. She had promised Simon that she would eat properly and take care of herself until he came up to join her. He had a few things to finish off, and the building of the bungalow for Paula to be set underway. He wanted the planning sorted and building work to be started before they were back from their honeymoon. No way could Paula occupy a part of their personal space when they were married. In fact, the woman had taken it badly that she was not to be invited to the wedding, and was appeased only when Simon had promised her a free hand in the design of the bungalow. He had an excellent architect friend who would handle Paula well and quash any totally unrealistic ideas she might have.

Jenna gave a small sigh. There was nothing more to

eat than a piece of rather dry cheese and a sliced loaf in the freezer. With all the rush before the wedding, the last thing she'd had time for was shopping. It looked like a gourmet meal of cheese on toast. She could always sprinkle some herbs on top. That had to make it haute cuisine, she thought. She made coffee and put the meagre meal on a tray, preparing to sit in front of the television. She had barely sat down when her doorbell rang.

'Damn,' she muttered. 'Who on earth is that?' She put the tray down and went to open the door. 'Who's there?' she called out.

'Delivery, ma'am.'

Simon must have sent her some flowers or something. Bless him. How typical and how very nice. She released the safety chain and opened the door. The huge bouquet of daisies and carnations seemed to fill the entire doorway.

'How lovely,' she said, and a smiling Simon peeped out from behind the flowers.

'I missed you,' he said, taking her into his arms.

'You idiot! You must have left almost straight after I did.'

'Couldn't last a moment longer without you. I just had to come. Am I in time for dinner?'

Jenna looked guilty. He walked into the flat and looked around.

'Compact, isn't it? But perfectly charming – like its owner.'

'It may be a bit on the small side, but it's good enough for what I want,' she defended.

'No criticism intended. I think we might need a bit

371

more space, though, don't you? I'll get on to some estate agents in the morning, while you're at work. I shall be a man of leisure while you go out to earn our honest crust. Then I shall come and take you out for a slap-up lunch. How does that sound, Miss Brown?'

'I already have a lunch engagement, I'm afraid,' she replied.

'That was fast work. You haven't been back for more than two minutes and already you have a lunch lined up. Who is it?' he demanded.

She told him about Kurt, and her idea to appoint him as acting director while she was away. If he could cope, the appointment might become permanent. After all, she didn't want to spend all her time stuck in London when her life, Simon, had moved back to Cornwall.

'If you think he can do the job, go for it. But what about the alcohol problem?'

'Seems husband and wife work as a team these days. The redoubtable Sylvia comes with the deal. I think it will work, and "the problem" will continue to be a thing of the past.'

'Why don't I join you for lunch? I do own part of the company, after all.'

'If you don't mind, Simon, I'd prefer to handle this myself. If I'm to make any sort of success of this company, I need to organize my replacement myself.'

A slight flicker of annoyance flitted across his face but he soon smiled again. 'You're quite right, Jenna. I know nothing about this business and should leave it to the experts. Am I allowed to dine with you, then? Good grief. Is this what you call dinner?' He had spotted the congealing plate of cheese on toast and the cold coffee.

'There wasn't anything else in the house and I couldn't be bothered to shop. Not tonight.'

'Hat and coat on then, miss. We're eating out yet again. I don't know anywhere in this part of London, so you'll have to suggest somewhere convenient.'

They went to the local bistro and ate freshly made pasta and drank cheap Italian wine and enjoyed it as if it were Tregarth Manor itself.

When she returned home from work the next evening, she could smell cooking as soon as she opened the door.

'I'm home,' she called.

Simon, clad in one of her oldest aprons, came through, waving a wooden spoon.

'Sit down, darling. Put your feet up. I'll get you a drink. Had a good day at the office?'

She burst out laughing. Talk about role reversal!

'Is this how it's to be from now on? So, how was your day?'

'Awful,' he parodied. 'First it was the washing machine, then I had trouble at the supermarket – that awful woman down the street, she hit me with her trolley. Can you imagine? She actually hit me . . .' Jenna was helpless with laughter and begged him to stop.

'OK. Shall we make love straight away or would you like a drink first? Or perhaps you'd like to eat first? I have a delicious little chicken dish, with a cheeky white to accompany it.'

'Just kiss me, darling. I do love you so, Simon.

Let's eat, and then we can go to bed and stay there until tomorrow.'

'Such lust. She's only interested in my body. Ah, me. How I have to suffer.' He disappeared into the tiny kitchen and began to serve the meal.

'I could get used to this,' Jenna said, wiping French bread around her plate to catch the last of the sauce. 'If I'd realized you could cook like that, I'd have snapped you up sooner. Wife or no wife. Seriously, apart from cooking, and obviously shopping for all this lot, what have you been doing today?'

'Thought you'd never ask.' He produced a folder and, opening it, she saw two tickets – first-class, of course – to Rio. The date on them was just over two weeks' time. He also produced a form for her to fill in. 'It's a notification of intent to marry, so that your passport remains valid. Can't have my wife barred from the country.' She liked the sound of 'my wife'. Finally, he produced a small box. 'I hope you like it,' he said, unusually shy for him.

She took it and opened it carefully and slowly, as if she was trying to prolong the moment The solitaire diamond was quite perfect. It glinted in the light, reflecting every colour of the rainbow, simple and understated.

'It's beautiful,' she gasped. 'Thank you, Simon. It's quite perfect. Put it on my finger, please. What a wonderful surprise, I didn't even think of having an engagement ring. Not when the wedding is so close.'

Tenderly, he reached over and placed the ring carefully on her left hand.

'I wasn't going to be done out of an engagement

just because we're having such a short one. We've already wasted too much time. You're sure you like it?' he asked. 'I can always change it. I did wonder whether you'd have preferred to choose it for yourself.'

'Don't even think of it. I love it . . . and I love you. Now, if that's everything for tonight, can we retire, Mr Andrews? I have an early start tomorrow and it is nearly half-past eight.'

'Is it always going to be like this? No social life at all?'

'Not until after we're married. Then we can start to develop a social life. I've had to wait a long time for you and I intend to make the most of it now that I've got you here. You'll be dashing back to Cornwall any minute.'

'But let's go back to this lack of social life. I thought you liked to exercise regularly? How do we fit that in?'

'I've got an excellent substitute for time spent at any gym or pool. Now, stop raising objections and come to bed.'

'Did I mention I've got to work tomorrow as well? You'll have to organize dinner, I'm afraid. Woman's role in life, and all that. Oh, unless of course, you can curb your sexual demands for a little and then we can go out to eat somewhere.'

She answered by flinging a pillow at him, before they relaxed into what had rapidly become their favourite activity.

CHAPTER 21

Life rushed by at a frantic pace for the next two weeks. Each evening after work they worked on the plans together, trying to decide exactly what they wanted in their shared home. For so many years, Simon had settled for a large bed-sitting room at the hotel where he had few of the comforts one would expect for so wealthy a man. He had left Paula to use the living quarters provided for the owners of the hotel.

'I really can't make my mind up, Simon,' Jenna had said wearily, one night. 'I've got too many other things on my mind. Why don't we just settle for redecorating the apartment for now and decide on major changes later, when we're living there?' She had only looked around the hotel suite briefly, and was beginning to forget exactly what it was like.

Now, it was just two days before Jenna and Simon were due to fly out to join her aunt and uncle in South America. After a week spent in London, Simon had returned to Cornwall to finalize the details of the plans for Paula's bungalow and to give instructions for the changes to his own apartment at Tregarth.

Two days to go before they flew out. Jenna still had so much to finish off, but at least it seemed that Kurt's appointment as caretaker/director was going to work. The redoubtable Sylvia came with him, and together they made a surprisingly effective team. What was even better was that they were obviously in love with each other. What might perhaps have begun as a marriage of convenience had already blossomed into a real and loving partnership.

'I think we're going to be OK,' Sylvia had confided to Jenna one day. 'As long as Kurt lets me off the leash just occasionally. I think I must have been born as one of nature's carers. After all my years with a dependent mother, I end up married to a totally dependent man.'

Now, Jenna opened her briefcase with a sigh. Simon was returning tomorrow, and she had a million things outstanding. She was hoping to finish work at lunchtime the next day, leaving her just the one afternoon to finish any shopping and pack. She hadn't even bought her wedding outfit yet, and, remembering how long it had taken her and Sarah to find anything suitable for her aunt's wedding, she was beginning to panic. The phone rang. She left the answering machine to take the call while she poured herself a glass of wine and settled to her work.

'Darling? Where are you?' Simon's voice echoed through the flat. She rushed to the phone and snatched it up.

'Here I am. I wasn't going to answer anyone else. I've got far too much to do.'

'That's a pity. I wanted you to do me a favour. Still, if you haven't got time. Not to worry.'

'What is it? Of course I'll do anything for you – whatever else I have to do.'

'Could you open the door and look outside?'

Jenna raised her eyebrows. What was he talking about now? Frowning, she went over to the door, carrying the phone with her. She opened it and saw a small box lying on the floor outside. She picked it up and spoke into the phone again.

'Is this box something to do with you?' She came back inside and shut the door.

'Open it.' She did as she was told. Inside was a spray of the most beautiful tiny purple orchids.

'Oh, Simon, they're lovely. But why orchids tonight, particularly?'

'They're the national emblem of Singapore. Lovely, aren't they? Open the door again.'

'Simon, what are you playing at? I don't have time for silly games. I told you, I have too much to do.' But, despite her words, amused by his slightly crazy ideas, she opened the door again. She looked out into the corridor but could see no one. This time there was a larger box on her doorstep. Where had it come from? It was a dress box, stamped with the name of one of her favourite boutiques. She took it inside and opened it, gasping as she pulled out a long, slim-fitting lilac silk dress from among the layers of tissue paper.

'Are you still there?' Simon called down the phone.

'Yes, of course. Simon, it's lovely – quite beautiful. But why? I mean, what's it for?'

'Open the door again.'

'Simon, what is going on?'

This time outside the door stood Simon himself, his mobile phone clutched to his ear. She rushed to put her arms round him.

'Oh, darling, what a lovely surprise! But I thought you weren't coming back till tomorrow?'

He flung his arms round her and carried her inside. They kissed, but he drew away rather more quickly than she would have liked.

'We haven't got time to start any of that. We're dining out tonight and you have to change. Thus the new dress, the orchids and my own particular brand of sartorial elegance.'

'You're wearing a dinner jacket.' She noticed for the first time. 'Whatever is going on?' He picked up the dress box and pushed Jenna through to the bedroom, handing her the box and urging her to hurry. She gave a shrug, her work forgotten, took a quick shower and slipped the dress on. It was a delicate silk and draped itself perfectly over her soft curves, the tiny bootlace straps holding it over her graceful shoulders. It was such a simple, straight line that she recognized it must have been extremely expensive. The flowers were a perfect complement, she thought, as she tucked them into her hair, which she had quickly swept up high on her head.

Simon smiled his approval, flung a coat round her shoulders and rushed her outside, to where a taxi was waiting.

'You are one crazy guy, you know,' she said, almost breathless from her enforced dash. 'I was planning a quiet evening doing some notes for tomorrow and a hundred and one lists of the other things I have to. Then you land on my doorstep. Where are we going anyway?' But he silenced her by placing a kiss firmly on her mouth. 'And now he spoils my carefully applied make-up. What am I to do with this man?'

'Just make certain you love him for ever,' he said quickly. 'Come on. We're here.' The taxi stopped and a uniformed doorman opened the cab door and helped her out. She looked up, realizing they had stopped at one of the more exclusive restaurants, renowned for its food and fashionable clientele. Simon took her arm and steered her inside. The bright, glittering lights of the foyer dazzled her, and she was relieved when they went into the much darker dining room. Suddenly the lights went up, and she saw the room was crowded with dozens of people she knew. Everyone from her days at Reality Plus, Solo Films and many guests from the films she had helped with. Everyone was clapping and cheering and she stood silently, quite overwhelmed, clutching the arm of her fiancé.

'We couldn't let you slink off to South America without a decent send-off,' Sylvia laughed, kissing her on the cheek.

Kurt put his arm round Jenna and grinned. 'Now I know why you didn't want to marry me. I don't blame you one little bit. Besides, my wife would never have forgiven me.'

'I don't know what to say. How on earth did you arrange all of this? Without my knowing a thing about it?' she demanded to know. But she was too busy greeting all the guests to hear the reply. Alistair was there, as were various people from Hudson's, including the man she called Greg the Grope. His pretty little wife was with him for once, so he was very well-behaved.

They ate, drank and danced for several hours. When she finally managed to dance with Simon it was very late and they were both exhausted.

'Thank you for a wonderful evening. It's all been perfect – once I got over the shock! I still don't know – whose idea was all this?' she asked him. 'And how did you organize it?'

'Kurt and Sylvia, of course. We've been plotting for days. They knew of our plans to have a quiet wedding and decided we weren't getting away with it entirely. They contacted everyone and booked this place. The dress was my idea . . . just a little bonus. Besides, I didn't want any complaints that you had nothing to wear. You look sensational, by the way. Did I tell you?'

'Just the nineteen or so times,' she laughed. 'I begin to think the man I'm marrying has got some fetish about silk. He keeps stroking it and telling me how sensuous it is.' They kissed gently, their passion for once kept under strict control. At two o'clock they finally returned home, to an empty flat and the pile of unfinished paperwork still sitting in Jenna's brief-case.

'They'll just have to manage everything without me, won't they?' she murmured, as they slipped into each other's arms in the big soft bed.

★ ★ ★

It was the second week in December. Simon and Jenna, Sarah and Michael had reached Cuzco, the little town at the heart of Peru, known to travellers as the gateway to Inca Country. They had visited the world-renowned Inca City of Machu Pichu and the Valley of the Kings, marvelling at the sheer size and grandeur of the sights. They had found some of the tiny, remote settlements where other ancient relics had been recovered, and had bought masses of souvenirs in true tourist fashion. They had been travelling for several weeks, spending some days with Sarah and Michael and some on their own. Most nights they had tumbled into each other's arms, longing for the joy of each other's bodies and the fulfilment of their love. Some nights, exhausted by the day's activities, they had fallen asleep quickly, always wrapped in each other's arms.

'I shall never forget our wedding day,' Jenna said so often that all three of them teased her unmercifully about it. 'Well, I mean it. That funny little man with his peculiar accent. I hope we really did get properly married. None of us speak Portuguese, so we've only got his word for it – unless you count the bit of paper none of us can read either.'

'Of course we're married properly,' Simon bantered. 'We must be. We drank a bottle of the single most expensive champagne I've ever drunk just to prove it.'

'Cheapskate. I told you we should have had something local,' Jenna said, falling for the teasing for the hundredth time. 'But that waterfall. It was quite unbelievable. Better than Niagara, even.' The others smiled indulgently at Jenna's continuing enthusiasm.

The four of them had shared their first view of the magnificent falls from a helicopter, flying over the tumbling waters in a most spectacular way. They had followed this with a delicious meal, specially prepared by the hotel chef, who had even made his own version of a wedding cake – a sort of pastry case filled with tropical fruits and his own ice-cream. It had been a simple day. Even their wedding clothes had been almost casual, suited to the rather humid weather of the area.

'Sure you don't regret the full white gown and flowers bit?' Sarah had once asked. One look at her radiant niece provided the answer. Never had Jenna looked more beautiful nor her groom more handsome. Sarah had never herself felt happier. She had the man she loved beside her, and her beloved niece had married the only other man she had ever really cared deeply about since her own brother had died so tragically. He would have been so proud of his daughter, Sarah often thought, tears burning at the back of her eyes.

Though she had loved every experience this remarkable journey had provided, Jenna was beginning to feel wearied by the long trip. Each place they visited had added to the amount of luggage they seemed to be carrying, and, though she didn't really want it to come to an end, she was beginning to feel the occasional twinge of homesickness.

'You've gone very quiet,' Simon said, watching his wife staring absent-mindedly through the window of their hotel. 'Is something wrong?'

'I was just thinking. It will soon be Christmas. I wonder where we'll be?'

'Where would you most like to be?' he asked.

'I was just wondering if it will snow at home this year. Whether it will be a white Christmas,' she said wistfully.

'And exactly how many white Christmases have you actually experienced?' her husband enquired.

'What do you mean? Plenty. Well, I'm sure there must have been one. It's more an idea – even an ideal, isn't it? Christmas cards always have snow on them.'

'You're an old romantic, do you know that? Do you really mean you'd like to go home for Christmas?'

'I don't know. Does it sound ungrateful? Yes. No. I don't know. Am I being silly? I just felt sort of nostalgic for the whole English Christmas – right from the crowds desperately filling every shop to the tree and turkey and pudding . . . oh, just everything.'

Simon didn't mention the subject again, not even when they were discussing the next day's activities over dinner that evening. He just disappeared for an hour or so early the next morning, while Sarah and Jenna wandered round the shops picking up odd items of jewellery and clothing. Everywhere children tried to sell tiny souvenirs – cheap trinkets that cost so little that one wondered if there could really be any profit at all. They all met back at the hotel for an early lunch.

'Did you buy anything nice?' Simon asked over lunch.

'Not much. What did you do?'

He handed over an envelope. Jenna pulled at the flap and looked inside curiously.

'Oh, darling. Are you sure?'

Simon nodded his agreement.

'What is it?' Sarah asked.

'Tickets for a white Christmas. Your sentimental niece thinks we might stand a chance of getting one in Cornwall this year, so we're going back. It's been a fabulous trip, and we've both loved it, but I think it's time we got on with the rest of our lives now. I hope you don't mind?'

Sarah and Michael began to laugh. They held hands as Michael reached into his inner pocket.

'Great minds think alike, obviously,' he said. 'Sarah has been making noises about returning home for Christmas for the past few days. We were wondering how to break it to you.'

'Do you want to be at your place or ours?' Sarah asked, with a happy grin on her face.

'We really ought to be at Tregarth, if we're going to be in England. It's usually frantic, and I was a bit concerned at leaving Paula alone for the whole of the holiday,' Simon said anxiously. 'Well, *I* should go to Tregarth, at least. Jenna? Where will you be?'

'I think I'll have to be there too. My husband is a very jealous man. Quite irrational. If I don't do as he says, he can strip the rubber off four tyres in two seconds flat.'

'So it looks as though it's settled. Can you book us a room at Tregarth at such short notice?'

'A service only available for very special clients,' Simon replied.

Jenna looked at the extremely handsome man sitting in the seat next to her. He smiled at her, sending her heart soaring with pure joy. The deep, honey-gold eyes lit up with his love for her. However many times she looked at him, she always felt the same thrill of delight, the rush of love.

'I'm so lucky to be married to you,' she whispered.

He grinned. 'I know you are. When I think of the number of times we nearly messed up . . . I could never understand why you were so convinced I was married to Paula, of all people. Is she really my type, do you think?'

'Certainly not. But she was very clever. I realize now she never once said you were actually married. She called me a marriage-wrecker, and I suppose that hit home. She said Tom was "the image of his father". He was so like you, I fell for it. I never met your father, so how was I to know that you were the spitting image of him as well as Tom? You even mentioned the responsibilities you'd been forced to face up to, and the promise you made that had tied you down. What was I supposed to think? It all fitted in rather too neatly.'

'And you couldn't believe me, could you?'

'We shall be arriving shortly at London Heathrow. Please resume your seats and fasten your seat belts ready for our descent,' came the anonymous voice over the aircraft loudspeaker system.

'Well, Mrs Andrews, are you quite ready for the joys of an English Christmas? White or not, we're about to land.'

'This will be our first Christmas together,' Jenna said happily. 'What do you like to do on Christmas Day?'

'I think we're about to start our own customs. We're a new family, you and I. Whatever we do is the beginning of our life together.'

'Until there are loads of little Simons running rampant around the place.'

'You don't mean . . .?'

'No, of course not. You can't have children, remember?'

His face took on a serious expression and he said gravely, 'I think it's very important that we keep practising. If we could manage it once, I'm sure we could manage it again. And next time you will not be climbing any ladders of any sort.'

'I love you, Simon,' said his wife, laughing. 'I'll love you always.'

As the plane landed with a gentle bump, he leaned over and kissed her. 'And me,' he whispered.